W9-CEA-348

*Love Over Gold*

# SUSANNAH JAMES
# LOVE OVER GOLD

## BANTAM PRESS

LONDON · NEW YORK · TORONTO · SYDNEY · AUCKLAND

TRANSWORLD PUBLISHERS LTD
61-63 Uxbridge Road, London W5 5SA

TRANSWORLD PUBLISHERS (AUSTRALIA) PTY LTD
15-23 Helles Avenue, Moorebank, NSW 2170

TRANSWORLD PUBLISHERS (NZ) LTD
3 Pickering Drive, Albany, Auckland

Published 1993 by Bantam Press
a division of Transworld Publishers Ltd
Text copyright © Transworld Publishers Ltd 1993
Published in association with Nestlé UK Ltd

'Nescafé' and 'Gold Blend' are registered trade marks
to designate Nestlé's coffee products

The right of Susannah James to be identified
as the author of this work has been asserted in accordance
with sections 77 and 78 of the Copyright Designs and Patents
Act 1988.

All of the characters in this book
are fictitious, and any resemblance
to actual persons, living or dead
is purely coincidental.

A catalogue record for this book is available from the British Library

ISBN 0593 034457

This book is sold subject to the Standard Conditions of Sale of Net Books and may not be
resold in the UK below the net price fixed by the publishers for the book.

All rights reserved. No part of this publication may
be reproduced, stored in a retrieval system, or
transmitted in any form or by any means,
electronic, mechanical, photocopying, recording,
or otherwise, without the prior permission of
the publishers.

Set in 11/12pt Linotype Plantin by
County Typesetters, Margate, Kent

Printed and bound in Great Britain by
Mackays of Chatham PLC, Chatham, Kent

*Love Over Gold*

# 1

April in Venice. A pale golden day with one of those blue skies which made you remember the last time you fell in love. A hint of summer's heat already in the air.

Matthew Prescott sat at a small marble-topped table in the Piazzetta San Marco, smiling at nothing in particular. The waiter brought him a second *espresso* and he drank the tiny cup of strong black coffee slowly, staring across the Grand Canal past the magnificent façades of Santa Maria della Salute to where the sun danced and sparkled on the waters of the lagoon. Although the first summery frocks were in evidence, the tourists had still not begun their seasonal descent on the city: it would be June before the gannet migration of camera-clutching seekers after culture took place, ruining the city for those who lived and worked there, clogging the ancient squares, filling the restaurants and cafés, disturbing the air with a thousand alien tongues.

But, for the moment, Venice was at its best. It was the perfect day, in the perfect city, and there he was, drinking a coffee in perhaps the most perfect square in Europe. What more could a man ask for?

He stretched out his long legs and frowned. As a matter of fact, a man could ask for a whole lot more than this. Quite apart from anything else, a man could reasonably ask for the perfect companion to be

1

added to the list of other perfections. And two weeks ago he would have had no hesitation, if asked, in nominating Gabriella for the role. Beautiful Gabriella. But then two weeks ago he wouldn't have had to nominate: she'd have been here with him as a matter of course. He shook his head gloomily. Fourteen days is a long time in a love affair. Especially a love affair which, let's face it, was dying on its feet. If not already dead.

He had been slow on the uptake, no doubt about that. It had been a while before he realized what was happening, though at the age of thirty-four he ought to have been able to recognize a brush-off when he got one. Because even if at first he had assumed it was just another of Gaby's temperamental flounces, brush-off, he now saw, was indubitably what it was. What else could you call it when a woman refused to return your phone calls, didn't answer the door when you called round, sent back your letters unread – or so she would have you believe?

Despite himself, he smiled. Gaby was probably the nosiest woman he'd ever met: he knew perfectly well that she would have been unable to resist holding the envelopes over a hot kettle and steaming them open before she sent them back to him. She was always saying that she liked a good read – and those letters must certainly have provided her with one. Especially since he had written most of them after a session alone in his Rome apartment with only a wine bottle for company.

Yeah. Well . . .

He'd got the message now, thanks. It was over. He and Gaby were washed-up. Finished. Finito.

He kicked at the pedestal of the little round table and wished he could be more heartbroken about it.

The trouble was, he had been able to see the split coming for quite a while. The two of them were, basically, completely incompatible. He, a phlegmatic Englishman, and she, a volatile American-Italian: the thing was doomed from the start. At first he'd found their spectacular rows – always *her* fault, of course – rather stimulating. It wasn't what he was used to. Then they began to irritate, to exhaust. And finally, to bore.

And this last one, when he'd told her that he was being transferred back to London . . .

'London?' she had said incredulously, her voice rising. 'No way. You seriously think I'm going to live in London, Filth Capital of the world?'

'Rome's not exactly renowned for its squeaky-clean image,' he retorted, stung by this criticism. 'And what about New York, if it comes to that, your own home town?'

'*What* about it?'

'Last time I was there, the garbage was piled higher than the Empire State Building.'

She ignored that, as she ignored anything she found inconvenient. 'But *why* are you going to London?' she demanded, standing in the blue-tiled kitchen of the apartment he had been renting for the past year and a half. Behind her, steam rose from the pan in which she was boiling spaghetti.

'I don't have much choice,' he tried to explain. 'If the firm wants me to go back to England, then that's what I have to do.'

She banged a saucepan full of bolognese sauce down on the stove, forcefully enough for some of it to slop out on to the gas ring. He tried very hard to keep the Guess-Who's-Going-To-Have-To-Clear-That-Up-Later kind of expression off his face.

3

'Aren't we good together, huh?' she demanded. 'Is that it? Don't you enjoy it with me any more?' She opened the door of the refrigerator then kicked it shut again.

'I love it, you know that,' he said, wincing as she dropped a pan lid on the floor and it skittered noisily into silence.

'Then why the hell are you going, Matt?' She switched on the Mixmaster, then adjusted the knob of the radio to compensate for the sound of the whirring machine.

He had grabbed her by the elbows, turned down the radio, switched off the mixer. 'Listen,' he had said, his face an inch from her huge black eyes. 'I don't have a choice in the matter, OK? I've got a job – a good job – and as an art-investment counsellor, I have to go where there's counselling to be done.'

'What's wrong with Rome?'

It was hard to believe that this was a girl with a good degree in art history from Berkeley. 'Nothing at all is wrong with Rome,' he said patiently. 'But I've done my stint here and the firm want to give me a different field to cover.'

'Why can't you cover it from here? There's plenty of rich guys in Rome need someone to tell them what kind of paintings they ought to be buying, what they ought to off-load. I mean, basically, that *is* what you do, isn't it, Matt?'

'Basically, I suppose it is. But—'

'So why can't you stay in Rome?'

He shook her hard. 'Have you got shares in the city, or what?' he said, angered by her obstinacy. 'I go where I'm sent, OK? Besides, I *want* to go back, do you understand that? I've been here for eighteen months now and I want to go back home. To England. To London.'

She had stood with one hand on her hip. Even with her black hair coming loose from its combs and a smudge of tomato sauce on her chin, she was unbearably pretty. 'And I'm supposed to come with you?' she asked.

He had made the fatal mistake of hesitating.

That was *it*.

With a dramatic gesture borrowed from the Italian grandmother who, the way Gabriella told it, had terrorized three and a half city blocks in Brooklyn for over thirty years, she dumped the half-cooked spaghetti into the kitchen sink. The bolognese sauce she'd spent most of the day preparing followed. Tearing off her apron, she had stomped out. He hadn't seen her since.

Sitting now in Venice, with the sun glinting off the golden archangel on top of the Campanile, and a salty breeze blowing in from the lagoon, he shrugged. Why the hell had he hesitated? Why had he been unable to say wholeheartedly: 'Yes, Gabriella, I want you to come to England with me.'

She would have come if he'd asked, he knew that, even though both of them shied away from any commitment, even though they avoided using the word 'love'. But faced with the possibility, standing there in the steamy kitchen with the bolognese sauce blurping like a mud-hole, he had realized all at once that he couldn't cope with the noise level. He'd tried to tell her once.

'Noise?' she had said, slamming a drawer shut, dropping a bunch of knives and forks on to the table, banging some glasses about. 'What damn noise?'

And when he'd explained that she moved in a

permanent jet stream of the stuff, whirring, grinding, singing, shouting, running baths or marathons or seminars on primal therapy for other expat American girls right there in his living room, she had uttered the first in what had seemed like an endless series of screams, each one of a higher decibel count than the last.

It exhausted him just to think about it.

He gestured to the waiter for another *espresso*. Outside one of the cafés across the square an orchestra was playing an old jazz tune. Fat pigeons waddled, red beaks pecking at the corn which children were throwing for them. It was impossible to avoid feeling guilty about Gabriella. However much he pointed out to himself that he had promised her nothing, that she'd *asked* for nothing, that it was understood between them that it was just one of those nights – well, one of those eight months, to be exact – he still felt like a major heel.

Was he a male chauvinist because he found that if peace was what you were looking for, you might as well bed down on the M25 as let a woman move in with you? Was he an unreconstructed male simply because he longed to find a girl who didn't need several paragraphs to say what could be said in a single sentence? A girl who didn't bang and crash and shout. A girl with – he let the fancy wash over him, knowing it was no more than an unrealizable dream – one of those deep rich quiet voices which sounded like melted chocolate being poured over honey and left a man feeling weak at the knees.

A gondola slipped past the end of the piazza, heading out towards Murano. Recognizing the man in it, Matt raised his hand in a half-salute. Ricardo San Lorenzo, the client he had driven up here at the beginning of the week to see. His last assignment before he went back to London on Monday. Ricardo San Lorenzo, who had made a great deal of money out of reproduction furniture, was a man stuck firmly on the horns of a dilemma almost as tough as Hamlet's, a man unable to make up his mind which he wanted more: to be recognized as a patron of the arts, or to spit in the eye of Carlo, his nephew and heir.

Since by working towards the first aim, he also achieved the second, Ricardo ought to have been a happy man. The amounts of money he had recently spent on buying modern art – ably advised and assisted by Matthew Prescott, it went without saying – ensured that by the time Carlo came into his inheritance, there'd be damn little inheritance left for him to come into. Unfortunately, as well as Carlo, Ricardo also had a demanding mistress – he was probably on his way to see her now – and what she demanded more than anything else was diamonds and real estate. No-one could blame *her* if Carlo ended up a rich man. The way Ricardo told it, she was doing her level best to reduce the amount of Ricardo's fortune available for the purchase of anything at all, let alone for works of art.

Again Matt smiled. He had not met Carlo San Lorenzo, who worked as a public relations consultant in Milan. Carlo seldom came to Venice. Carlo had apparently stated several times that as far as he was concerned, his uncle's art collection could be dumped in the nearest sewer.

'What can you do with a philistine like this?' Ricardo said frequently, turning his mouth down at the corners, spreading his shoulders wide, shrugging hugely.

'Disinherit him,' Matthew suggested, the first time this – admittedly rhetorical – question was put to him.

Ricardo had been shocked. 'He is the *heir*,' he explained. 'The eldest male, my poor sister's son. Of course I cannot disinherit him.'

'See to it then, that he can't sell off your collection,' Matthew said, and that, duly, was what Ricardo was in the process of doing.

He and Matthew had spent the best part of the past week together, walking through the high half-empty rooms of Ricardo's *palazzo* on the Grand Canal, discussing business, discussing paintings. And all the time, the light reflecting off the canal sent a panorama of watery images across the ceilings and the dusty marble floors, so that the whole place seemed constantly to shimmer.

They had become friends, he and Ricardo. Once their business was done each day, they spent hours on the roof terrace, companionably watching the *va et vient*, the busy bustle of the canal, the swarming tourists in the narrow streets below, the birds wheeling at sunset above the intricate Venetian roofscapes. Their discussions were punctuated by long elaborate meals during which Ricardo would complain incessantly, either about Carlo, or his importunate mistress, or even, when the second bottle of wine was almost empty, about the intricacies of his digestive tract, which frankly, he assured Matt, with another engaging Italian shrug, was giving him unmitigated gyp . . .

Down in the square, Matt called for the bill. Nothing, not Gabriella, nor Ricardo, nor the total lack in his life of women with beautiful voices, could ruin the day for him. Tomorrow he would drive back

8

to Rome, pack up his apartment – most of his stuff had already been sent ahead to his London flat – attend a last farewell party at the firm's grand headquarters off the Via Veneto, and on Monday he would take the first flight out. Now he had a couple of hours before his final meeting with Ricardo, time to stroll one last time through this most beautiful city, to look at some of the finest art treasures in the world, and forget that he was here alone.

If I ever find her, he told himself, pushing back his chair and standing up, I'll bring her here, this woman with the soft voice.

He stood for a moment on the Molo, the waterfront of the Piazzetta San Marco, and watched the gondolas and excursion boats bobbing and rocking on the water. I shall fall instantly in love with her, he told himself, and wished he believed it. Falling in love implied commitment, and Matthew Prescott was definitely not into commitment. Not after giving his heart to Laura all those years ago, only to have it returned in a thousand tiny pieces. He had been trying to put it together again ever since. And one way of doing that was to avoid falling in love ever again.

Love . . . he turned and walked past the Doge's Palace towards the Ponte della Paglia, and leaned on the stone balustrade to look at the Bridge of Sighs. Love – in spite of Gabriella – was a commodity distinctly missing from his life at the moment.

He had plenty of friends; he had a loving family. But *love* . . . Hmm. Five years ago, perhaps even two, he would have laughed at himself for giving it a thought, let alone worrying about it. But increasingly he was beginning to wonder if the determinedly single lifestyle he had made for himself was really what he wanted. Was it old age creeping up on him? Or a deeper dissatisfaction with the way things were turning out?

He turned to gaze as the *vaporetto* crept up to the landing stage and a group of girls disembarked, laughing and chattering, pretty as a cageful of finches. Idly he watched them. Once his pulses might have quickened, but at thirty-four he had lost any taste he had ever had for twenty-year-olds. He wanted someone more mature, someone with a mind of her own, a career of her own. Someone who was looking – as he himself was – for something more out of life than the mortgage-and-marriage trap, the two-point-four kids and the Volvo estate in the double garage. She was out there somewhere, he was certain. It was just a question of finding her.

But as the breezes ruffled his hair, he knew that even if he did, he would probably pull back. Matthew Prescott, the King of No Commitments: was he really likely to change his ways now?

The Rome offices of Cadogan's, Dealers in Fine Art, were situated just off the Via Condotti. Standing in the wood-panelled boardroom, Matthew sipped champagne and thought wryly that if his colleagues were devastated by the fact that he was leaving the next day, they were doing a good job of concealing it, even though, over the past eighteen months, he had come to know most of them pretty well, and to like them. They appeared to like him too, always a bonus in a working environment.

Cadogan's occupied a small but prestigious place in the world's art markets, which were still, thanks to the big auction houses of Sotheby's, Christie's and Phillips, dominated by London. Matthew had been taken on by the Fine Art department a couple of years after leaving university. Since then he had built up a particular field of expertise in work by younger painters, and seemed to have developed an uncanny feel for which artists would become stars, and which would merely burn for a brief space of time before fizzling out. It was this aptitude which had placed him so firmly in the fast lane at Cadogan's, and ensured his phenomenally swift rise through the ranks. Thanks to his fluency in both French and Italian, he had been promoted two years ago to head the foreign art department. The posting to Italy had merely been one more step in his route to the top. An early directorship was already being hinted at.

He enjoyed his work. He liked jet-setting about the globe. He relished the lifestyles of the rich and famous which he briefly shared each time he was called in to advise on some collection, or suggest a new acquisition, a change in direction. Collectors, he had found, were often unsure of their own tastes and liked to have the reassurance of an expert opinion before they actually opened their chequebooks and began signing on the dotted line.

He glanced round the room, surely one of the most luxuriously furnished business environments in Europe. It was crammed with sculptures and paintings. Display cabinets housed porcelain and silver; among the pieces of furniture were two or three examples of the finest seventeenth-century Italian craftsmanship outside a museum. Ironic, considering that Cadogan's had built their reputation on specializing in modern art.

Rather like the kind of architect, he mused, who designs ultra-futuristic dwelling modules for other people, but prefers himself to live in a thatched cottage full of oak beams and inglenooks. Not that he had anything against inglenooks, for heaven's sake. In fact, the bonuses he had gained over the past eighteen months might go a long way towards the purchase of one when he got back. Plus the cottage to go round it. It was something he had been considering for a long time. London living, according to his friends back home, was growing ever more stressful and a place in the country – as well as sounding good – might be considered almost a necessity for the up-and-coming art investment man.

If he closed his eyes, he could almost see it: roses round the door, twisted apple trees in the rough grass at the back, whitewashed plaster, raspberry canes and—

'You all right, Matthew?' It was Charlie Tempest, who had joined the firm at the same time as himself, and whose career had followed an almost identical path. Except that Charlie was permanently based in Rome, after he married the daughter of a steel manufacturer from Turin, and, unlike Matt, had found his career more or less happily on hold.

'Absolutely fine.' Matthew cheerfully abandoned the phantom cottage.

'How did you get on with the San Lorenzos?'

'Liked Ricardo, haven't yet met Carlo.' Matthew laughed. 'From the way his uncle speaks of him, I should think I'd loathe him.'

'A common enough impulse among those who come into contact with him,' sighed Charlie. He was a tall thin man with a permanently melancholy expression.

'According to his uncle, if ever a man was asking for a boot up the backside, it's Carlo,' Matthew said.

'I gather that among other faults, he not only loathes modern art but also thinks he's God's gift to woman-kind.'

Charlie nodded gloomily. 'Trouble is, enough women share his opinion for him to have no cause to revise it.'

'I hate to think what will happen to Ricardo's collection if Carlo ever gets his hands on it.'

'Which is why, dear boy, I presume you have spent the past week doing your best to see that the whole deal is closed up tighter than a Scotsman's purse.'

'Something like that.' Matthew laughed again. 'Carlo's in for some nasty surprises.'

'Good. There's probably no-one who deserves them more.'

'You know him, do you?'

'Not personally, dear boy. Not as such. But my wife has a friend who has a cousin . . .'

'A female cousin?'

'Precisely.' Charlie snatched a bottle from a passing waiter and filled both their glasses. 'To love,' he said.

'To work,' said Matthew. They clinked glasses together.

'So it's off to dear old Blighty in the morning, is it?'

'Yes.'

'Looking forward to it?'

'Very much.' Matthew spoke with conviction, even though, over the past eighteen months, Rome had come to seem more familiar than London. And that was despite the fact that he had worked for the London branch of Cadogan's for nearly ten years before being sent to Italy. Nonetheless, Matthew

13

knew it would be good to get back to work in the environment where he had cut his teeth.

'They say that London has deteriorated a lot recently,' Charlie said sadly.

'Practically a hardship post, if you believe everything you hear,' Matthew said. 'But where isn't, these days?'

'True,' Charlie murmured. 'Very true. But if you've got to live behind the barricades, you might as well do it with panache.'

'By panache, you mean booze.'

'Precisely, dear boy. A country that doesn't produce a passable wine is scarcely worth bothering with. And besides, the Italians have such style, such elegance.' He waved a hand at the room around them. 'Take a look at the women here: where would you see that kind of chic in London?'

'I don't really—'

'The thing is, Matthew, Italian women take fashion seriously, just as Italian men take wine seriously. Whereas the English – and I'm one myself, so I know what I'm talking about – are incurably flippant about almost everything. Especially important things.'

'I never heard such a load of drivel,' Matthew said amiably. 'Have another glass of champagne and shut up.'

'No, it's true,' insisted Charlie. 'I read a report in the paper recently which claimed that Englishmen prefer their cars to sex. I ask you . . .'

The Italian head of the branch joined them. 'I am sorry to see you go, Matthew,' he said. 'You've done some good work while you were here. Naturally, I've reported back to London.'

'Thank you.'

'Some of the deals you pulled off here have been pretty prestigious. I've made sure they realize how much of that has been due to your enthusiasm and expertise.'

'Let's hope there are a lot more deals waiting,' Matthew said lightly. Excitement, anticipation, energy churned together in his mind. As far as his career was concerned, he was on the crest of a wave, he knew, riding high. It was only a question of deciding where he wanted to go, and then going there.

The flight from Rome was almost empty. He found himself sitting next to a window and hoped no-one would be allocated to either of the two empty seats beside him. He was out of luck. Or not, depending on your point of view. The girl who was shown to the aisle seat was very attractive. At first he kept himself occupied with papers from his briefcase, not wanting to get embroiled in conversation, but when the flight attendant came round with drinks, the two of them started talking.

The girl ordered wine in a strong determined sort of way, ignoring the soft drinks and fruit juices. Matt liked a woman with robust appetites. Quite apart from anything else, fizzy drinks during lunch often meant burps after it.

'I'll have the same,' he said, and smiled at his neighbour as the flight attendant moved further up the narrow aisle.

'Helps wash down the "snack", doesn't it?' the girl said. Like Laura, like Gabriella, like all the women he had ever fallen for, she had dark hair, a brown which was almost black, despite chestnut high-lights which glinted when she moved her head.

15

'Are you going back to London, or do you live in Italy?' he asked.

'I'm living there at the moment,' she said. 'In Milan. I work for a publisher there.'

He leaned across the gap and held out his hand. 'I'm Matthew Prescott.'

'Annie Carter.'

They smiled at each other. Their conversation became animated. By the time they were circling Heathrow, prior to landing, Matthew was beginning to feel that it would be a good thing if they could meet again. 'Next time you're in London, will you call me?' he said.

'I don't think so.' Annie stared soberly into his eyes. Her own were hazel, flecked with green.

'Why not?'

'Because I won't be back for at least a month,' she said. 'By then, you'll have completely forgotten who on earth I am.'

He displayed astonishment – and meant it. 'Here's my card. How could I possibly forget someone like you?'

'Oh, sure,' she said, but she laughed as she said it.

Victoria was waiting for him at Heathrow. 'Darling, it's been such ages. And you look wonderful!' she exclaimed, throwing her arms around his neck. She smelled, as she always did, of some flowery perfume, which perfectly suited her everyday persona.

'So do you.' What he always found so intriguing about her was the way she became transformed after dark, how she could change so effortlessly from a working wife and mother – she was a successful barrister – into a glamorous entertainer, witty hostess, superb cook. In all the years he had known her,

16

she still remained something of an enigma to him.

'Welcome home!' she said. 'We're all so pleased to have you back. The children can't wait to see you.'

'Nor me to see them,' he said. 'I take my duties as an uncle very seriously indeed.' He patted his bags in a meaningful way.

'I know that, Matt.' His sister put a hand on his sleeve. 'And I'm not just talking about the fabulous presents you bring them.'

Behind her back he rolled his eyes as he followed her to the short-stay car park and dumped his bags in the back of her car. He knew what was coming next: with two sisters and a mother who had never bought the theory that mothers should sit back and let their children get on with their own lives, he had heard it all before.

As they drove out of the airport and on to the M4 into London, Victoria said, as he had known she would, 'Going back to children, when are you going to have some of your own, Matthew?'

'I refuse to answer that question,' he said lightly, 'on the grounds that I've answered it at least five million times already.'

'And the answer's still that you don't know?' Victoria slowed down and peered closely at him, ignoring the blaring honk of a lorry right behind her.

'Exactly,' Matt said. He closed his eyes, pretending a fatigue that he did not feel. He loved his sisters, but they could be royal pains in the backsides once they got on to the It's-Time-Matt-Was-Married kick. Over the years, how many terrible women had he found himself sitting next to at dinner? How many times had he been tricked into making up a four for the theatre, or a concert? It wasn't that he didn't

17

appreciate their efforts on his behalf, recognizing that they sprang from the purest of motives, i.e. the happiness of their little brother. It was just that they didn't have the foggiest idea what kind of woman suited him.

Trouble was, neither did he.

'We'd kind of hoped you might have met someone in Rome,' Victoria said.

'Well, I didn't. And I can make my own marital arrangements, thank you very much indeed. And when I've made them, I'll be sure to let you know, OK?'

'OK.'

Victoria drove in silence for a while. Then she said, 'I've checked the flat out for you. Mr Hassan was a pretty good tenant, all things considered—'

'What things considered?' Matt sat up. 'What do you mean?'

'It wasn't so much the livestock . . .' murmured Victoria.

'What livestock?'

'. . . as the belly dancers.'

'*Belly* dancers?'

'Troupes of them, night after night. All those drumming feet did terrible things to your beautiful parquet flooring.'

'You *are* joking, aren't you?'

'Yes, Matthew. Of course I'm joking. Everything's fine. I've stocked up the fridge with all the basics.'

'Smoked salmon, fresh asparagus, caviar?'

'Milk, bread, eggs and fruit,' she said firmly. 'If you want caviar you can buy your own.' Changing gear, she added, 'Remember that flat which was up for sale?'

'On the floor below mine?'

'Yes. It's finally been sold. They had the decorators in when I went to your place to put the groceries away.'

'Any idea who bought it?'

'None. I don't think anyone's moved in yet. I peeked in but the rooms were completely empty except for paintpots and dust sheets.'

'Mmm.' Matt was not particularly interested. His block of flats was large and impersonal. People came and went all the time, most of them only meeting each other occasionally in the lift or the car park. This was exactly the way he liked it. The job he did was demanding enough: when he got home he didn't want to be forced by proximity into making conversation with a bunch of almost-strangers.

He stared out of the window of the car. London seemed dingier than usual, the sky greyer, the buildings dirtier. He put his mood of depression down to post-flight reaction. What he wanted most of all was to get home, switch on the CD player and relax with a drink to something cool and soothing: the winding sophistications of Kenny Barron's jazz piano, perhaps, or the silvery brass notes of the altoist, Lee Konitz.

Between them, he and Victoria humped his bags upstairs in the lift to his apartment. Opening the door, taking the first step back into the environment he had created for himself, Matthew braced himself for changes. For a moment he stood still, taking it all in, the pictures on the wall, collected over the years, the carefully chosen objects, the family mementoes, the furniture, modern, the best of its kind that he could afford.

In the early days of furnishing his own place, he had preferred to sit on cushions rather than make do with something he found aesthetically displeasing. His mother had not shared his view.

'Sorry, darling,' she had said once, pulling on her gloves and adjusting what she called her Town Hat in the mirror in the hall. 'I'm not going to come and visit you again until you get something reasonable to sit on.'

Matt had fallen to his knees, grovelling, his tongue lolling disgustingly. 'Mother, please,' he said. 'Say you don't mean it. Not come and visit me? How can I stand it?'

His mother had ignored him. 'I don't ask for anything much,' she said. 'A simple kitchen chair will do. But you really can't ask a woman of my advanced age to squat down on cushions like a witch doctor.'

'Witch doctors squat on the ground,' he had said, laughing, 'they don't bother with cushions.'

'Well, I do,' she said. 'Preferably ones with a chair attached. I suppose it's expecting too much to hope that you'll get round to acquiring a sofa before I'm in my grave.'

'Much much too much.'

He'd gone out the following week and bought his first Italian-design chair.

Remembering, he said, 'How's mother?'

'Fine,' Victoria said. 'Terribly excited about you coming back. I expect she'll be on the phone any minute now.'

'If she mentions marriage, or women, or babies, or anything remotely resembling any of the above, I shall burst into tears.'

'Don't do that,' Victoria said vaguely. 'By the way, Geoff and I are having a dinner party three weeks from now. You will come, won't you?'

'Love to. Should I bring someone?'

'It's all right. I've got the right numbers for once.'

'Uh-oh.'

'What's that supposed to mean?'

'You've asked some unspeakable woman, haven't you?'

'I don't know what—'

'Some hideous earnest female with a voice like a corncrake—'

'What exactly *is* a corncrake? I've never known.'

'– and a face like a prune, who you want me to ask out afterwards. Some one-legged single mother I'm supposed to be sorry for or a—'

'I have *never* invited a one-legged mother, either single or double, to meet you.'

'What about that dotty woman from Dawlish?'

'Delia?'

'That's right: dotty Delia from Dawlish.'

'Oh, Matt. Honestly. She had two perfectly good legs.'

'She did not. I distinctly remember—'

'She was on crutches, as you very well know, beause she'd broken an ankle skiing.'

'Which proves my point exactly.'

'It proves nothing of the sort.' Victoria hugged him, her mind already on picking the two children up from school. 'We'll talk on the telephone, all right?'

'Soon,' he promised.

'And again, it's lovely to have you home.'

'It's lovely to *be* home.'

At least, he thought it was. He poured a stiff whisky from the duty-free bottle in his bag and added ice-cubes, sipping it slowly, savouring the feel as it went down his throat, anticipating the pleasurable burn as it hit his nerve ends. Tomorrow he would be back in the office. It was always difficult to pick up threads, take the reins up from where they had been dropped. There would be people working there who would have joined since he was seconded to Rome, to whom he would be a complete unknown. There would have been inter-department rows and changes of which he knew nothing. To some extent, he would be a stranger.

He riffled through his CD collection, found some Charlie Parker, put it on softly and lay back on the long low sofa. Tomorrow could wait; for the moment he would simply enjoy this moment of being back home.

# 2

The room was crowded. *Over*crowded, actually. But then any room in New York where a party was happening was going to be overcrowded. After living here for a year, Alex knew how the system worked. The party organizer – the hostess or social secretary or whatever – made up two lists, invited everybody on the A list and then, when the first refusal came in, panicked and proceeded to invite the entire B list as well. Result? No more turn-downs, everyone who had been invited showed up, often with an extra in tow, the venue began to split apart at the seams, and the food and drink invariably gave out just as people were beginning to enjoy themselves.

New York was like that. Frenetic. Hysterical. Constantly on the edge of terminal partying. Nobody dared to turn down an invitation in case this was *the* party which they couldn't afford not to have been at. For a lot of the people she came into contact with, partying was the single most important activity in their lives. After seeing their analyst, of course. And working out at the health club. And picking up their dry-cleaning. New Yorkers were very hot on dry-cleaning. But even she, Alexandra Maitland, a visitor who had arrived here twelve months earlier knowing only one person in the entire city, could have gone out seven nights a week if she had wanted to.

She stood at the big picture window, thirty storeys

up, and looked out at the pearly light descending over the smog above Manhattan. *On a clear day, you can see across the road* . . . She wished the window was the kind which opened. But that was out of the question. After all, suppose some nut decided to freak out and jump. And New York was full of nuts. Not to mention weirdoes, flakes and screwballs. So the window stayed shut. If it opened, she would at least be able to breathe some air which had not been recycled three hundred times already. And she would also be able – maybe – to get away from the smoke.

Out on the West Coast, the anti-smoking lobby was so powerful that you had to do your smoking after midnight, in disguise, behind closed doors with the blinds pulled and the air-conditioning on full blast to disguise the smell. Here in the Big Apple, or at least in the bit she occupied, a kind of anti-anti-smokers' lobby seemed to have sprung up. People defiantly puffed carcinogens in the most unsuitable places, just to show they didn't give a damn for public opinion, heedless of their responsibilities to their fellow-humans . . . Alexandra looked down at her Oscar de la Renta suit: not only was she likely to die of passive smoking, but she would also have to have her clothes cleaned tomorrow, to get rid of the smell. Just what she needed, with tomorrow being her last day at the office, and a thousand things still to do before she flew back to London the day after that.

Starting in on the shallow-breathing to minimize the threat to her lungs, she turned and surveyed the room packed with wall-to-wall people, the caterers' men circulating – or trying to – with calorie-conscious titbits, the animated faces as everyone networked everyone else, at the anxious eyes. She was sorry to say goodbye, but London might be a little more relaxing.

'How's the Ice Maiden?'

She raised her eyebrows in what Donna liked to call her Virgin Queen look. 'I missed that,' she said coolly. 'Did you say something?'

Donna Fratelli, her closest colleague on the paper – her *friend* – burst into the raucous squawk of a laugh for which she was famous. 'Don't give me that stuff: you heard perfectly well.'

'If you're asking how I am, I'm fine, thanks.'

'Gonna miss us?'

'Some of you,' Alexandra said pointedly.

'Gonna miss *me*?'

'Why would I miss you?' said Alexandra, then smiled suddenly. 'Of *course* I am. You most of all.'

'Likewise, I'm sure. Especially that cute British accent.' Donna sighed. 'You know what?'

'What?'

'It's going to be kind of lonesome around here, when you've gone.'

'We'll see each other again.'

'You bet we will,' Donna promised. 'Just let me know when you've beaten the new guys into shape and ordered in the champagne, and I'll be on the very next flight.'

Alex leaned a little closer. 'Donna, I don't have to say how much I appreciate—'

'You're darn right, you don't have to say it,' Donna replied brusquely.

'If it hadn't been for you, I'd have been completely lost.'

'Yeah, yeah.' Donna looked around. 'Hey, where's Cameron? I can't see him anywhere.'

Alex too surveyed the room. 'You're right – I hadn't realized he wasn't here yet,' she lied.

'What happened – he get delayed in a meeting or something?'

Alex gave her unconcerned expression full play. 'Something, I suppose.'

Someone from Layout came up and dragged Donna off to meet someone from Publicity. Alex stayed where she was. The truth was, something *had* happened to Cameron. More specifically, something had happened to the relationship – if that was the right word – between the two of them. It had been about a month ago, and so far she had not been able even to think about it, let alone tell Donna.

She looked out again at the Manhattan skyline, dominated by the twin towers of the World Trade Center. She had read somewhere that its observation deck was a quarter of a mile above the ground – it seemed an unimaginable height for a building to be. Just as the gulf between her and Cameron was so unimaginably wide that nothing could ever bridge it, however much she wished it were possible.

Tears came unexpectedly into her eyes. She blinked them furiously away. If there was one thing she had learned long ago that you did not do, it was to show emotion. How many times had the Colonel, her father, drummed that into her? 'Stiff upper lip, old girl. Spine straight. Where's your pride? Don't want to let the side down, do we?'

And however many times the answer – only spoken inside her head – was 'Yes, as a matter of fact I *do* want to let the side down!' she never had. Never would. Even if the starch had long since washed out of her upper lip, and sometimes she felt she was suffering from fatal curvature of the spine . . .

She had known Cameron for years, ever since her first job on the *Mail* when she was new in London. He'd been working over in England at the time, they had met at some press thing, he'd asked her out. There had been an obvious attraction between them, but they had remained just good friends – until that summer night when he had asked her out to dinner. The sky had been a mysterious blue, no longer daylight but not quite dark, as they drove out of London and found a small pub restaurant with a terrace overlooking the Thames. Afterwards she was unable to say what they had eaten, what colour the wine was, whether they had been alone in the restaurant's dining room, or just two people among many others.

All she remembered was Cameron's eyes looking into hers, the feel of their entwined fingers, the way his touch had made her skin jump, his voice caressing her. There had been candles on the table; his handsome face had hung between them, lit like a painting by one of the Italian Masters.

They had taken brandy out on to the terrace. He put his arm around her and they had listened together to the river chuckling past beneath their feet, the harsh cry of some restless water-bird, the sound of a night breeze among the reeds.

'It's late,' he had whispered, after a while.

'I know.'

'Too late to drive back to London, don't you think?'

'What do *you* think?' she had murmured, turning in his arms.

'Far too late. Besides . . .'

'Besides?'

'To everything there is a season,' he said, kissing

her hair, her closed eyes, her waiting mouth. Then he had gone to find the pub owner to see if there were any rooms available. They had been shown into a cottagey bedroom under the eaves, with tiny diamond-paned windows overlooking the river. There had been a brass bedstead, old-fashioned print curtains, the scent of summer drifting in through the windows from the hayfields on the other bank.

It had been one of the most perfect evenings of her life.

He had had to go back to New York almost immediately. For a while they had stopped communicating. A year ago, when the chance came, she had followed him.

The second night after her arrival, he had telephoned. 'Got your number from your father,' he said. 'Why didn't you let me know when you were arriving?'

'I didn't know if you'd want to see me,' she said, suddenly shy.

'I could have picked you up from the airport. Brought you back here . . .' The implications of what he said were obvious, delightful.

'I didn't want to bother you.'

'Bother me? Don't be so dumb. I've been living for this moment, you know that.'

'I would have called you.'

'I called you instead.'

'Yes.'

'Dinner tonight?' he said. 'I'll pick you up at eight.'

And she had fallen in love with him all over again. Head over heels. Hearts and flowers, roses-are-red kind of stuff. I love you till the seas run dry, the sun grows cold, the moon is made of green cheese . . . It was the first time since her teenage years that she had allowed herself to be so unrestrained. And for a while, six or seven months, it had been wonderful. Fantastic. Celestial.

Then all of a sudden the sun grew cold, the seas had turned into deserts. She didn't know why, whether he had met someone else, whether he just wanted more space, whether she had been too intense about the whole thing. The fact was he simply drifted away, leaving her with an aching hole where her heart used to be, and the determination never, *ever* to let a man do this to her again.

*Straight spine, old girl. Where's your pride?* Perhaps there was something in her father's injunctions. Because after Cameron, although there hadn't been much pride left, there was enough to prevent her from letting on even for a second that all was not well with her.

Donna came bouncing back to her. 'Come on, Alex. You can't stand mooning by the window all evening. This party's for *you*, you know.'

'Right.' Alex smiled at her. 'Who shall we go and talk to?'

'See the guy standing by the bar?'

'Just about,' Alex said. 'An inch shorter and he'd be *under* it, not standing *by* it.'

'Don't mock,' said Donna. 'He may be vertically challenged—'

'*May?* No question: he *is*.'

'– but he's also one of the most powerful men in the fashion trade. When I introduce you, be sweet.'

'Aren't I always?'

'No, Alex. You are *not*.'

'What's his name?'

'Jarrett Keach.'

29

'Oh, my God. *That's* Jarrett Keach? I never realized he was only two feet high.'

'Depends which bit of him you're measuring,' said Donna. 'Anyway, these days you're not allowed to be sizeist. What happened to your Political Correctness rating?'

'Guess it just slipped to zero,' Alex said. She stared across at the slight young man ordering a drink from the barman. Although Jarrett Keach had only come on to the fashion scene in the past couple of years, he was already making a mark for himself, dressing some of New York's most prominent hostesses and social X-rays, regularly getting spread features in the top glossies. She would have to go and chat him up: it might be something of a coup if she could do a feature on him once she was back in Engand.

'I wonder if everybody at home is into all this PC stuff,' she mused.

'Sure they are. If they got it in New York, they got it in London,' said Donna. 'You know what copycats you Limeys are.'

She fished in her purse and pulled out a gift-wrapped box. 'By the way, in case I miss you later. This is for you.'

'What is it?'

'Open it, you clunk, and see,' Donna said. 'But not here, for God's sakes. Wait till you get home.'

'Thanks, Donna. You really are—'

'Don't be embarrassed; it only cost me an arm and a leg.'

'You're sweet,' Alex said. 'I left something for you on your desk.'

'Didn't want me to find it till you'd gone, huh? What is it – a thigh reducer?' Donna slapped at her ample figure. 'God,' she said without much conviction. 'Madame Arbuckle, that's me. How I wish I was thin and gorgeous like you.'

'You'd hate it,' Alex said. 'No more double chocolate chip cookie ice-cream. No more pizzas and a milk shake to go. No more of your mother's linguine.'

'True,' sighed Donna. 'And what's so darned unfair is that all the time I'm stuffing my face with Momma's pasta so she doesn't think I'm rejecting her, she's bitching at me to find a nice man.'

'A nice Catholic man?'

'A nice *Italian* man.'

'Isn't that a contradiction in terms?'

'A nice *man*,' Donna said. '*Any* man. Just so she gets to be a grandmother before she dies.'

'*Any* man?'

'Except one who's already married to someone else. Fat chance.' Donna grinned. 'Talking of fat chances, how come you eat exactly the same things I do and never put on an ounce?'

'It's in the genes,' Alex said.

'Which I very definitely am *not*. I long ago accepted I wasn't cut out for jeans. Or jeans weren't cut out for the bigger women like me.'

Alex smiled, her brain industriously picking over the conversation. While not as insatiably voracious as television, the women's magazines had pretty healthy appetites, and she was always on the lookout for possible features. And what Donna said generated an idea.

*Bigger women* . . . It was a description which covered approximately three-quarters of the Western world's female population. Where did it come from, this idea the fashion pundits had that anyone over a size ten was not only one of nature's freaks and ought

31

to be making a living in a sideshow, but was also in some way sinning against the whole notion of Womanhood?

It would make a good feature, especially since, though there were some marvellous clothes available for Bigger Women, they were not always easy to find. And because it was one which the readers never tired of, it was a theme which could be followed through to produce spin-off articles. Thinking of the new job in London, the new desk she would be sitting behind very soon, she realized that in spirit she had already left New York, that she was already thinking like the new features editor of *Athene*, a glossy London monthly magazine. Launched eighteen months ago, to cater to the woman who liked to dress well but didn't have a fortune to spend nor time to spend it in, who liked to read good fiction, who liked to hear about new design, trends in art, politics, music and theatre, but wasn't above reading articles about the rich and the famous, its readership figures had climbed consistently. Having served an apprenticeship first on a daily paper and then on the women's pages of one of the quality Sundays before coming to work in New York, Alex had been absolutely thrilled to land the job with a magazine which had *Athene*'s potential.

Quite apart from being a smart career move, going back to England meant she would be able to see more of her father. He had recently fallen and broken his hip, which was taking longer to recover than it should, according to her brother.

Which reminded her: the new flat. Had she been merely optimistic in trusting David to find her a place to live? Or had she been just plain dumb? Despite the fact that he held down a fairly senior job with a merchant bank, her younger brother was not exactly renowned for his responsible attitude to life. Particularly when the life belonged to someone else. Particularly when the life belonged to *her*.

It would probably be his idea of a good joke to find her some rat-ridden, cockroach-infested den in the most run-down part of London and then tell her that all the best people were moving south of the river these days and that anyway, this was the *fun* place to be.

She smiled to herself. Over the telephone he had assured her that the place he'd found was absolutely the sort of thing she liked, and she had had to believe him because she had no other choice. She had even given him power of attorney – though she would make absolutely certain to cancel it the minute she got back – because there hadn't been a single minute in the past three frantic months since her appointment to *Athene* when she could have found time to fly across the Atlantic and look for herself.

It could all have waited until she got back, but she had decided it would be much easier to have everything ready for her to move into. She wanted to be able to concentrate on the new job. Working at the magazine would be challenging. It would take a hundred per cent of her time and energy if she was to do it well, if she was to overcome the opposition which she knew from experience is always built-in when someone from outside comes in and takes over a senior job. And there were bound to be hiccups, innuendoes she didn't understand, internal hierarchies to be dealt with, prejudices to pander to and egos to be placated. All part of the job.

And she was more than ready for it.

Meanwhile, there were a couple more days to get

through, a few more hours in which it was quite possible she might bump into Cameron – handsome, faithless Cameron to whom she had given her heart and to whom, if he were to appear suddenly and beckon her over, she would go without a second's thought. Whistle and I'll come . . .

She heard her father's voice again: *Where's your pride?* and realized that where Cameron was concerned, she didn't have any. It was as simple as that.

She braced her shoulders, walked across the room to Jarrett Keach, held out her hand. 'Hello,' she said. 'I'm Alexandra Maitland.'

Looking up at her, his eyes widened. 'Are you indeed?' he said. He took her hand in his own tiny one and pressed her fingers.

What did you say to a question like that? 'Yes,' sounded too schoolgirlish for words, especially since she'd just *told* him who she was. Wondering whether he'd ever eaten a square meal in his life, she said nothing, which left the ball in his court.

'Alexandra Maitland, huh?' He nodded a couple of times. 'From England – am I right?'

'Certainly are.' God, she hated herself when she got cute. 'How in the world could you tell?'

'That accent,' he said. 'I just love it.'

'It's a real pleasure to meet you, Mr Keach—'

'Jarrett, please.'

'– because I start work next week as the features editor of one of the newer English glossies and I'd simply love to do a spread on your work sometime,' Alex said, seizing the opportunity.

'Tell me more.'

She gave it the pitch. 'Lots of pics, nice write-up. It could be terrific for you, boost your transatlantic sales.'

'Sounds good,' he said. 'Why don't you give me a call about it sometime?'

'I'll do that.'

He stared at her, his knowledgeable eyes taking in the de la Renta suit, the quality body underneath, the designer earrings, the thick brown-blonde hair swept up on to the top of her head. 'Better still,' he said, winking, 'I'll give you one. Maybe we could do lunch sometime.'

'Why don't we swap business cards?' she said coolly. 'Then we'll be able to call each other.'

'Great idea.' He fished around in the pocket of his jacket. 'What was the name of this magazine again?'

'*Athene*. If you haven't already, you'll be hearing a lot about it in the future.'

'And you too, honey, I'll bet. Have you ever modelled? You really got the figure for it.'

She opened her mouth to say something sharp. *Honey*, indeed. Hadn't he heard of verbal harassment? Didn't the name Judge Clarence Thomas mean *any*thing? Any minute now he would start trying to pinch her backside or peer down her cleavage – though he'd need a stepladder for that. And if she *was* going to be patronized, she would rather it wasn't by a munchkin in a jacket made out of what looked like dishcloths. Was that one of his own designs? She hoped not.

'So I've been told,' she said pleasantly.

'Good luck with the new job, anyway.'

'Thanks.' She fumbled in her bag for an *Athene* card and handed it to him with her best smile.

Could anyone see that behind it, somewhere inside, she was crying? She had already wept enough tears over Cameron, she didn't want to waste time on him any more. Particularly not tonight, in front of her sharp-eyed colleagues. She bit her lip. Why did she always fall for men like Cameron? And why did they always do this to her?

On the other side of the room, Donna was watching her. Spreading a smile insecurely across her face, Alexandra crossed the room towards her.

On her desk the next day, lying on top of the piles of magazines, the trial-size lipsticks and new shampoos, the files on new trends from Paris and Rome, the press cuttings, the sample swatches of Thai silk and Irish linen, was a long box of see-through Cellophane. Inside lay a single perfect rose.

She opened it, her fingers trembling slightly. Even before she saw the familiar black writing, the bold capitals and heavy downward strokes, she knew it was from Cameron.

*Corny, I know,* he had written, *but you know what it means. We'll see each other again soon, I promise. Meanwhile, my love, go for it – knock 'em for six.*

Her palms were sweating. She glanced around the room but nobody seemed to be staring at her. Picking up the rose, she sniffed it, but it was scentless, a hothouse rose grown for its perfect beauty and not for the perfume.

Is that what was the matter with me and Cameron? she wondered, and hated the way her heart was thumping with the longing to see him again. Were we too much the beautiful couple, all perfection but with no scent? Is that why it failed?

'Back in time for the cricket season,' David said, with satisfaction. He slung Alexandra's cases into the back seat of his Aston Martin. 'I can't say I enjoyed going to matches alone last year.'

36

'I'm enormously flattered,' said Alexandra. 'But you must have hundreds of girlfriends who'd like to go with you.'

'Hundreds of girlfriends, yes,' David said complacently. 'Who like to watch cricket, no.' He swung on to the motorway and headed for London at a pace which Alexandra found toe-curlingly alarming, especially after the modest speed limits imposed in the USA. 'The thing is, Alex, you're a girl in a million. Not only are you reasonably decorative—'

'Gee, thanks, David.'

'— but you like cricket too. I mean, what a fantastic combination!'

'Any chance of you slowing down to under a hundred?' Alex said.

'What I don't understand is why you and Cameron—'

'I mean, seventy's the speed limit, and you're doing at least—'

'— a good bloke, I really liked him—'

'And I come out in spots if I travel faster than the sound barrier,' Alex said loudly. 'I might even throw up.'

'Not in my car, you won't,' David said, glancing sideways at her. 'Are you serious?'

'Absolutely. I'm well-known for it.'

Grudgingly, David put his foot on the brake, reducing their rocketing pace to something more likely to win police approval. 'It'll take all day at this rate,' he complained.

'At least we'll arrive alive.'

'What I don't understand,' said David again, and she realized she had not managed to deflect him from the subject, 'is why you and Cameron haven't got it together yet.'

She was silent.

'Is it because you come on as someone who's got it made?'

'What do you mean?'

'You know,' said David, cutting in front of a gigantic truck ferrying frozen chickens from Norfolk. 'You seem so capable, so independent. What men want—'

'You think you're qualified to say?' she asked, feigning surprise.

'– what men want,' he said loftily, 'is someone more—'

'If you say vulnerable, I'll smack you.'

He shrugged. 'We want to feel protective. We rather like it when women weep on our shoulders. When men look at you – and they do so all the time because you're beautiful, even if you are my sister – they see someone perfectly armoured against life, someone who doesn't need looking after.'

Recognizing the truth of his words, she was nonetheless hurt. Her voice a little shaky, she said 'Listen, kid. If you want insecurities, I've got them. If you want someone to weep on your shoulder, try me.'

'Have you talked to someone about this?' he said innocently, opening his eyes wide. 'I mean, I'm your *brother*.'

They laughed together. But while he concentrated on overtaking as much traffic as possible, she thought: I want to be protected as much as anyone else. Just because I'm good at my job doesn't mean I'm some kind of battleship, impregnable.

'Talking of cricket, as we were a while back, I've already booked us tickets for some of the matches,' David said, having satisfactorily endangered life and limb to gain about three minutes. 'There's a one-day international on 12th July you'll simply—'

'David, I'm a working girl,' Alex said. 'I can't just take time off whenever there's a test match. For that matter, neither can you.'

David groaned. 'Don't tell me you've defected to baseball,' he said. 'Or, even worse, to American football. All those shoulder pads and black patches under the eyes.'

'Better under than over them,' said Alex. 'Anyway, have you ever looked at an American footballer?'

'Of course I have. But probably not in the way you mean.'

'Then you probably won't have noticed how cute their backsides look in those tight trousers.'

'Dear me,' David said, pretending outrage. 'A man dedicates himself to his sport and all you can think of is the fit of his gear.'

For a while they were silent. Then Alex, fiddling with her silver earring, said, 'How's the Colonel?'

'Fine.' David stared through the windscreen.

'The truth, David.'

He was silent for a moment. Then he said, 'Not too good.'

'Still hobbling about?'

'And roaring a lot. The damn hip's taking for ever to mend.'

'Poor Pa.'

'Now that you're home, he'll probably perk up. You know how he misses you.'

'Yes.' And how he would never in a million years admit it, Alex thought.

'I hope you're going to like this flat I found for you,' David said.

'Not as much as I do. Tell me about it.'

'It's fairly central. Nice high ceilings, the sort you're always raving about. Some – and I quote – "original features" like an open fireplace and ceiling roses.'

'A picture rail?'

'Rails everywhere. And a real Edwardian chain in the loo with a porcelain handle which says PULL on it. In case you weren't sure of the procedure.'

'Those Edwardians didn't miss a trick, did they?'

'Not one.'

'So what's wrong with it?'

'Nothing.'

'Honestly?'

'Honestly.' He hesitated. 'Did I say it had two bedrooms?'

'Two? Why? I told you I only needed one.'

'Yes, but I thought you probably wanted a place for guests.'

'I've got a perfectly good sofa-bed which—'

'Or even brothers, if they should want to—'

'Forget it, David. You are not moving in with—'

'A bed for the odd night, that sort of thing.'

'How much extra am I paying for the privilege of putting you up from time to time?' she said suspiciously.

'It was still well within the price range you gave me.'

She thought about it. A second bedroom was obviously a plus. 'Come across any of the neighbours?' she asked, changing the subject.

'Not yet, except for one. A Lady somebody or other.'

'Very grand.'

'She's quite a young Lady. Not a dowager or anything. She's a portrait painter.'

'She's a pretty Lady, is she, as well as a young one?'

'She is quite, as it happens.'

'Aha!'

'What's that supposed to mean?'

'That I get the message.'

'Do you really?'

'Loud and clear.'

'She said I ought to bring you down for coffee some time. Or dinner.'

'I *see*,' Alex said meaningfully. 'And were you aware how young and pretty she was *before* you found this flat for your sister, or after?'

He grinned at her. 'Guess.'

# 3

'Matthew Prescott?'

'Yes?' he said cautiously. He had learned through experience that if the voice was eager and female, cautious was the best way to be. Act too friendly, and you found yourself stuck having dinner with some woman you would never in a million years have had dinner with, if the choice had been yours. Some woman picked out of the mass of social misfits and weirdos with which the world teemed, and sicked on to you by either your mother or your sisters. Dammit, the three of them handed out his telephone number with the eagerness of someone trying to flog last season's stock through the Small Ads.

Last season's stock: perhaps that was exactly how they saw him.

'It's Annie. Annie Carter.'

He had never worked out the best way to handle total blankness. Was it easier to say '*Annie*,' in a deep and hearty voice, and hope that memory returned during the ensuing conversation? Or ought he to opt for honesty, admit he hadn't a clue who Annie was, and risk having his ear chewed off or the phone flung down or both?

Hmmm. Tricky one.

'I said you wouldn't remember me,' she went on, before he could come to a decision.

'Uh . . .' Nice voice, faintly familiar, where the

hell had it been – that business meeting in Kensington last week? Or the—

He was saved when Annie Carter volunteered the information herself. 'We met on the plane four weeks ago.' There was a pause which Matthew found himself quite unable to fill. 'On the plane from Rome?'

Her voice took on a rising inflection which heralded embarrassment and a wish to be anywhere but on the end of a telephone line talking to an idiot who was obviously suffering either from premature senility or regret at having asked her to call.

But he *did* remember. 'Annie!' he said, and the warmth in his voice was genuine. 'How nice. I'm so glad you rang.'

'Really?'

'Absolutely delighted. Are we going to meet?'

She laughed relievedly. 'I'm here for a couple more days. I wondered if we could do lunch or something.'

'Make it something,' he said. 'Come to my place and I'll cook you dinner.'

'Your place?'

'Why not?'

'It sounds like the kind of invitation my mother used to warn me about.'

'She must be a sensible woman.'

'Would *I* be, if I accepted?'

'I gave away my etchings only last week, if that's what you mean,' he said.

'I guess it's safe then.'

'Besides, I'm a terrific cook,' Matthew said. 'My sisters saw to that.'

Because he was busy that night, they arranged to meet the following day in a wine bar, after which he would bring her back to his flat. He found himself cheered by the thought of seeing Annie Carter again. Part of her appeal lay in the fact that neither his mother nor his sisters – none of whom had the slightest idea about the kind of woman who attracted him – were involved in the meeting. That gave it a halfway decent chance of being a pleasant one.

Which reminded him. He dialled his mother's number.

'I'm just going out to buy you a lavender-coloured fedora and a pink Cadillac,' he said sternly.

'What's a fedora?'

'A wide-brimmed hat.'

'Why do you want to buy me a wide-brimmed hat? Or any kind of hat? Or a new car, for that matter?' His mother sounded astonished. 'I've got a perfectly good BMW in the garage, and anyway, lavender really isn't my colour.'

'I have it on the best authority that all pimps wear lavender fedoras,' he said coldly.

'Pimps? What *are* you talking about, Matthew?' She swallowed something. 'I'm sitting here reading the newspaper and having a quiet cup of coffee and you suddenly ring up and start babbling complete nonsense at me. Have you taken your temperature recently?'

'A woman showed up at my front door last night,' said Matt. 'She had a bottle of wine in one hand and a cello in the other—'

'That must have been Tessa's daughter. I know she plays with the Philharmonic Orch—'

'She looked more like Godzilla's daughter to me,' Matt said brutally. 'And she seemed to think I was expecting her. She said you'd given her my address. I had the most embarrassing time getting rid of her.'

'She's very nice,' his mother said. 'Not perhaps the prettiest girl I've ever—'

'Mother, I've seen better-looking *wart*-hogs.'

'I thought the two of you would get on very well.'

'I'm sure we will – as long as she stays on her side of town and I stay on mine.'

His mother sighed. 'I only want you to be happy, darling.'

'I *am* happy, thank you. Extremely happy. Absolutely ecstatic. Except when I open my front door at night and find a cello-playing wart-hog standing outside.'

'Well, I don't know what gives you the right to call your own mother a pimp,' his mother said vigorously, rallying her defences.

'It's the way you always try to take over my—'

'And if I were, with the success rate I've had so far, I'd have started a new career years ago.'

'I just wish you'd stop trying to find Miss Right, that's all,' he said, signing off. 'I can find her perfectly well for myself.'

'Then hurry up and do it,' said his mother.

'All right, I *will*.'

Banging down the phone, he reflected that there was one thing you could say about Annie Carter: she was definitely not a wart-hog.

Already, in the short time he had been back, London had overlaid the long months Matthew had spent in Italy. Rome was distancing itself from him, his life there assuming something of the quality of a dream. Though he sometimes still thought in Italian, he had reaccustomed himself to his own language, to English headlines in the newspapers and English voices on the television. It no longer seemed strange to take the Jubilee or the Victoria Line, rather than Line A or Line B. He had stopped automatically looking for yellow cars when he wanted a taxi.

Driving through the rush-hour traffic into central London, he found himself smiling at the thought of seeing Annie Carter again. Perhaps there was life after Laura, after Gabriella.

And his fears about difficulties at work had proved unfounded. Despite the recession, Cadogan's was still doing business as usual. Although the fantastic prices of the eighties had vanished into some limbo from which Matt privately thought they would not return, global interest in modern art had not diminished, particularly as a business investment. Art was prestigious, the acceptable face of capitalism.

Art, he thought with a certain cynicism, implied that the conglomerate which could hang a Franz Kline or an Allan McCollum in its board room – or even in its well-protected lobby – was showing the world another side of itself, a gentler, kinder persona. No matter how sharp the knives were when they came out, if the big deals were taking place in the same room as a Picasso or a Lichtenstein, it gave the cut-and-thrusters an intangible advantage which was quite separate from any aesthetic the painting might hold in itself.

Waiting in a throbbing stream of traffic crawling down Baker Street, Matthew shook his head. Aesthetics were often the last thing his clients were interested in when they came to him for advice on what to buy. Sometimes he wondered if he should chuck the whole thing in, as a matter of principle. Take up market gardening or boat-building, get to grips with the elemental verities, something closer to the source of life itself.

He'd had these doubts before, of course, but usually only after dealing with a particularly obnoxious client, or when he had been daydreaming about his thatched cottage, and then not for very long. He generally had the sense to realize that digging in turnips or glueing bits of wood together was really not his kind of thing. On the other hand, given the often hectic pace of his life, somewhere turnip-free where he could spend rural weekends wouldn't come amiss. Next time he went down to see his mother in Somerset, he might take the opportunity to look at some estate agents' advertisements, see what prices down there were like . . .

Hanging up his raincoat in his office, he reflected that he was luckier than some. He enjoyed his job and the hustle and flurry that went with it. He liked – without in any way envying – the super-rich he came into contact with. He was still thrilled by the travelling his work entailed. He liked the spurious glamour of airports, the encounters with people during flights, the stepping-out of aeroplanes on to alien tarmac, the meeting of strangers with different outlooks but a shared interest in art. Because that, above all, was why he loved what he did, what it was all about: art itself, in general, and specifically, the particular works about which he advised his clients.

While they sucked in their cheeks and consulted with their financial consultants, he got to see the paintings, handle the sculptures, meet the artists, spend time in studios. He knew he had an eye for recognizing that touch of genius which would sooner or later make the painter a Name. And nothing compared with the excitement of looking at a new canvas or a just-completed bronze, taking a deep breath and thinking, 'Yes!'

47

'You've been summoned,' Ruth, his assistant, said, as he walked into the office.

'You mean that parking ticket finally caught up with me?' he said.

'Summoned, not summonsed.'

'Who wants me?'

'If we're talking purely in the physical sense, I do,' Ruth said archly. She was a capable woman in her early forties, long married to a merchant seaman, and the mother of three daughters. 'But as we're talking business here, the answer is Anthony Cashman.'

'Should I know him?'

'He's that youngish billionaire chappie who's always in the news,' said Ruth. 'Made his first million in property speculation before he was thirty. Diversified into airlines and shipping, made another million in each before he was forty. He's just finished building himself a mansion in Hampshire.'

'I don't do interior design – are you sure he asked for me?'

'He's decided that money can't buy happiness,' Ruth said.

'How I'd love the chance to find that out for myself,' murmured Matt.

'Says he wants more out of life than fifteen yachts and seven luxury residences scattered round the globe,' said Ruth.

'What is he, crazy?'

'I offered to go down myself, see what I could do to add meaning to his existence, but he turned me down flat. Said it was you he wanted.'

'Obviously a man of taste and refinement.'

'You might change your mind when you see the mansion,' Ruth said. 'I've been down to the file room and dug out what I could on the guy. Refined he is *not*.'

Matthew lounged back in his chair, smiling. 'As long as there isn't a swimming pool in the shape of Concorde . . .'

'Not Concorde, no,' Ruth said, throwing a copy of some architectural magazine down in front of him.

Matthew picked it up. 'Break it to me gently,' he said.

'Would you believe a saxophone?'

'A swimming pool in the shape of a sax? You cannot be serious . . .'

'Never more so. Look through the pics and you'll see for yourself.'

The article she had picked out was about the latest in designer swimming pools. The excellent aerial photographs accompanying it made it clear that Ruth was not exaggerating: the blue-tiled Cashman swimming pool was definitely in the shape of a saxophone. 'But why?' Matt asked.

'He took the saxophone up five years ago. Says it's better than a therapist for releasing tension.'

'I can think of several responses to that,' Matthew said.

'Well, keep them to yourself – I'm a married woman.'

'And he told you all this stuff about saxophones and wanting more meaning in his life on the telephone?' asked Matthew, incredulously.

'Of course not. I got it from the cutting files. He's been interviewed over the years by practically all the newspapers and magazines in the country.'

'Run the official story by me, then.'

'His father was a butcher in Croydon. His mum used to clean council offices – the media love rags-to-riches stories like that.'

'Quite right. It gives us all hope.'

'After that, he bought his first derelict property with the help of his dad's life savings – and the rest is history. There's these, too . . .' Ruth handed him a back issue of *Hello!* magazine. Inside were pages of pretty pictures featuring Anthony Cashman in front of, inside, leaning out of or looking up at a vast modern house, built of ugly red brick. The interior appeared to be mostly empty, except in a few rooms where it was furnished entirely with the kind of white wicker furniture Matthew's mother kept for the garden. There was also an office full of Tudor beams. 'What a ghastly mishmash,' said Matthew.

'I know. Look at that fireplace . . .'

'I'd rather not.' Matthew turned another page. 'Who's the bimbo?' he asked, stopping at a photograph which showed a gorgeous blonde posing beside the pool. She wore a bikini which looked as if it had just been painted on by someone who was worried that the supply of eggshell gloss was going to run out before he had completed the job.

'That's his wife.'

'I'm sure I've seen her somewhere.'

'I'm sure you have too. On just about every fashion cover you've ever drooled over.'

'I do not drool.'

'That's Cindy Hill, the model. She's really something, isn't she?' Ruth picked up the magazine. 'I'll take this away so you don't get distracted.'

'What from?'

'Mr Cashman wants you to go down and look at the house with him, then advise him what to do.'

'I'd say instant demolition was the only answer, frankly,' Matt said, looking with distaste at the house in the photographs.

'Mr Cashman has got pots of money and a desire to

spend it on Art with a capital A. And you're the one he wants to tell him what to buy. So you'd better get on with your homework.'

'And when am I supposed to see this chap?'

'Tomorrow morning.'

'Right. Leave the stuff on my desk and I'll go through it before then,' Matt said.

The phone on his desk began to bleep. Picking it up, he was soon immersed in a big-bucks discussion with a Japanese bank, one of whose clients was looking for some expert advice before a sale due to be held in San Francisco next month.

He spent the evening with Stephen Wellcome, a client who wanted to show his appreciation for the fact that a couple of paintings bought three years ago under Matt's guidance were now worth approximately double what he had paid for them. From dinner at Wellcome's club in St James – staid food, superb wines – they had moved on to Annabel's, where Wellcome had begun drinking whisky. Everyone who ever featured in the newspaper gossip columns or on the glossy pages of *Tatler* or *Harpers & Queen* seemed to be there, raving the night away. Looking round and stifling a yawn, Matthew felt old and dull. Didn't these people have jobs to go to in the morning? How could they keep up the raving and still show up at the office the next day – or were they all so well-off they didn't need to work?

His host leaned across the table. 'See that chap over there?'

'Where?' Matthew was beginning to flag. He focused somewhat bleary eyes in the direction Wellcome indicated, a noisy party of young people who seemed to be having an extremely good time.

'The one in the middle, with the red hair.'

'Oh yes.' Another yawn rose. He was getting a bit past this kind of caper. He took in the rakish young man with a headful of copper-coloured curls, who was languidly sipping champagne in an open-necked St Jermyn Street striped shirt under a navy blazer. 'What about him?'

'He's the one who was photographed skinny-dipping with the Earl of Hamlyn's wife.'

'Really?'

'In the secret hideaway.'

Matthew's first thought was: so what? He kept it to himself; to the super-rich, these things obviously mattered.

'Caused that scandalous divorce case,' Wellcome continued. 'You must have read about it.'

'Probably.' Looking at the whisky sitting in the bottom of his glass, Matthew wondered whether to drink it or leave it there.

'And the chap on the other side, that's Chow Lee, the hairdresser, or hair artiste or whatever they call themselves these days.' Chow Lee was an attenuated oriental wearing black leathers ornamented with a large number of gold chains. From his expression of extreme hauteur, Matthew didn't mind betting that the gold was twelve-carat, minimum.

'Gosh,' he said.

'And the girl in between – that's Cindy Hill.'

'Cindy Hill?' The name was familiar somehow. Through a haze of alcohol, Matthew struggled to recall the circumstances in which he had previously heard it.

'You know. The model.'

'Oh yes.' He remembered now. Cindy Hill was the wife of the man he was going to see tomorrow. Wife

52

of the property speculator turned shipping magnate turned saxophonist, with an unfortunate propensity for Doric columns where Doric columns had no business to be, and a seemingly unquenchable passion for mosaic flooring, judging by the photographs of the house – sorry, *mansion* – he had built for himself.

Matthew stared across at the model. He had never even heard of her until this morning and now he had not only seen photographs of her which stopped just short of soft porn, he was also looking at her in the flesh. And very succulent flesh it was. He blinked. Cindy Hill was astonishingly pretty, living up fully to the promise of her poolside snaps. But there was something about her which intrigued him. Was it his imagination – or perhaps some piece of masculine wish-fulfilment – which made her seem, at that moment, seated between a rakish skinny-dipper and an oriental hair artiste, much less a nubile siren having a whale of a good time, and much more a girl longing to be tucked up alone in bed with a cup of hot cocoa?

Imagination, almost certainly. Nightclubs and the clientele which patronized them were what super-models liked best, weren't they? As he asked himself the question, Cindy Hill turned her beautiful head in his direction and caught his eye. Her slightly wistful I-wish-I-was-anywhere-but-here expression changed immediately. She raised both her eyebrows and gave him the fish-eye, then turned to the leather-clad hair artiste and broke into peals of artificial laughter at something he had just said.

Serve him right for gawping.

'Listen, Stephen,' Matthew said. 'It's been great but I think I'd better get home. I've got work to do in the morning, even if no-one else here has.'

Stephen looked at his watch. 'Lord. Is that the time? I'll come with you. Can I drop you off?'

Matthew thought about it. His car was still in the underground car park of Cadogan's. And he was, in any case, in no fit state to drive. 'Thanks,' he said.

When Stephen had delivered him to the apartment building and driven away, his Rolls making no more noise than a time-bomb as it purred down the street, Matthew walked into the foyer and rang for the lift. He leaned against the cool marble walls, eyes closed, and felt the booze swill around inside his skull. He was almost asleep when it occurred to him that the lift was taking a long time to come down. Stuck on the top floor, no doubt, because the last person to use it had forgotten to close the doors. He supposed he'd better start walking the four flights to his flat.

Cursing, he reached the third floor, and saw immediately why the lift had not descended at his summons. Someone had propped it open and was moving what looked like the entire contents of Heal's into one of the flats. Vaguely he registered that this must be the one which had been empty for some time and had recently been sold. Were these the new tenants: that woman with her tawny hair tied up in a knot on the back of her head and the man whose back view he could just glimpse inside the flat's hallway? Whether they were or not, they were damned inconsiderate, commandeering the lift like that, forcing exhausted modern-art consultants to drag themselves up eight sets of stairs at the back end of the night.

For a moment he thought about walking towards them and having a word – and not a particularly friendly word – but decided against it. He was tired, it was late, he doubted if they would take any notice anyway.

But just don't come to my place asking for the loan of a cup of sugar or telling me you're having a dinner party and you've run out of coffee, he thought sourly, turning to the next flight of stairs and starting to pull himself up by holding on to the banister. Because short shrift is what you'll get if you do.

It suddenly seemed important to let them know. He leaned over the banister rail. 'Short shrift,' he mumbled, finding it difficult to get his tongue round the words. The woman paused halfway between the lift and the open door of her flat and looked up at him enquiringly. He wagged his finger at her. 'Short bloody shrift,' he said, and saw her laugh and then turn away.

He had never been in a charnel house but knew instinctively that the experience would very much resemble the way the inside of his mouth felt. He groaned. He hardly ever had hangovers these days. Drinking too much was something he left to the younger men. Life was too short to be wasted on splitting heads and feeling on the verge of throwing up all day.

From the experience of the past – the *distant* past – he knew that one of the best ways to handle a hangover was to eat a good breakfast, however much the stomach rebelled. He grilled bacon, cut slices of wholemeal bread and put them into the toaster, spooned coffee out of a jar and made himself a proper cup. He scrambled two eggs, then opened the fridge. He stared at the carton of fresh orange juice for a moment, then quietly closed the door again. Eggs and bacon yes, he could handle that.

But pouring more acid down his throat definitely did not make sense, even if it was chockfull of vitamin C.

He felt much better as he emerged from the Tube at Bond Street and joined the crowds making their way down the road. The sun was shining, casting a buttery-yellow light which glanced off the shop fronts. High above the complicated roof lines of Oxford Street was blue sky, with occasional puffy white clouds drifting about in it. He felt unaccountably cheerful.

Ruth had prepared a folder for him. He had already done some preliminary work, putting together a portfolio of the artists he intended to offer for Anthony Cashman's consideration. He had borne in mind the kind of house the millionaire chose to live in and the size of his holdings, information which the capacious files stashed away in Cadogan's basement had yielded without too much difficulty.

A piece of Jeff Koons's erotic sculpture, he thought. Perfect for those vast spaces waiting down in Hampshire. Especially since this Cashman has Cindy Hill for a wife. It would mean a trip to New York, but that wouldn't be too much hassle. And some huge canvases to fill those empty mosaic-floored rooms. Some modern bronzes – maybe a South American mural. Given the right things, even the Cashman mansion could be turned around, made to look like some kind of – he raised his eyebrows at the thought – Temple to the Arts, rather than a hideous hodge-podge of trendy eclecticism.

He took the lift down to Cadogan's underground car park – the best perk of the job – and picked up his car for the drive to Hampshire.

★　　★　　★

The entrance to Cashman's place was guarded by tall wrought-iron gates. There was a box attached to one gatepost. He climbed out and spoke into it, giving his name, explaining that he was expected. After a pause, presumably while his credentials were checked out, the gates swung silently open and he was motoring up a long sandy drive towards the red-brick monstrosity – there was no other word for it – which waited at the end.

At the sight of it, acid bit at the delicate tissues of his stomach lining, reminding him that only a few hours ago he had been feeling distinctly unwell. As, indeed, he felt now.

Dear me.

He blinked. It had been bad enough in the pages of *Hello!* The full frontal effect of the building was even more daunting. Acres of newly seeded grass spread away on either side, with not a tree in sight. A wide expanse of black tarmac sat rawly in front of the red-brick façade. South Fork, Caesar's Palace and a Third-World airport rolled into one, he thought. All it needed was a sixty-foot-high neon shark on the roof or a pair of plastic golden arches.

Was there such a thing as good or bad taste? And was bad taste always invariably what everyone else had, or was there, in fact, some perceived norm of what was and was not deemed aesthetically desirable? He had learned long ago that in his job it did not pay to be judgemental about what other people con-sidered to be beautiful. But surely only someone on hallucinogens could have found the building in front of him to be pleasing.

A stone fountain featuring four sea-horses support-ing a basin was set into the middle of the area in front of the mansion. He circled it and parked discreetly to one side. When he reached the bottom of the flight of shallow steps which led up to a massive oak door, he found Anthony Cashman himself waiting for him.

'Hi.' Cashman had the brisk over-firm handshake and manner of the international businessman. 'You must be Matthew Prescott.'

'That's right.'

'Got your name from one of my mates.'

'Who was that?'

'Johnny Dawson.'

'The former jockey?'

'That's the one. He said you were the top man in your field.' Cashman had the chunky body of a weight-lifter and one of those brutal slash-and-burn type haircuts which always made Matthew wish he was wearing a cricket box, in case the haircut's owner should suddenly decide to kick him in the groin.

'Let's hope you agree with him,' he said.

'We'll soon find out, won't we?' Cashman was in his early forties, wearing a shell-suit chevroned in vivid colours, and pump-up Reeboks. 'Come on in.'

He led the way into a vast marble-tiled atrium, the far side of which was walled entirely in glass and gave on to an enclosed garden bounded on the other three sides by monastic-looking cloisters. These, however, were built of some shiny white material like bricks from a child's construction set, rather than from medieval stone. Hardly conducive to quiet contemplation, Matt thought.

A comment was clearly called for.

'Very striking,' he said. It was one of those multi-purpose expressions which committed the user to nothing. Over the past ten years he had had occasion to use the phrase a considerable number of times.

'Isn't that something?' Cashman said with pride. 'I

got the idea from looking at pictures of villas in ancient Rome.'

'Very nice.'

'My architect wasn't too keen. Said we'd freeze in winter and boil in summer.'

Matthew thought the architect was probably spot-on. He nodded wisely.

'I said, "Look here, matey. Who's paying for this place, you or me?"'

'I bet I can guess what his reply was,' Matthew said.

'Right. I told him not to forget it, either.'

No wonder Cashman had made such a success of business, Matthew reflected, following him into a room which was evidently used as an office. In just two short sentences, Cashman had managed to convey three important facts.

One, that money was no object. Two, that though he employed professionals, he didn't take too kindly to advice. Three, that he was definitely the boss. Matthew had no intention of forgetting any of them.

Despite the Roman influence in the hall, the office – as he knew from *Hello!* – had clearly been inspired by a later age, one which featured heavily in Cashman's large collection of videos, extensively displayed along one wall. Without even moving his eyes, Matthew could see at least a dozen costume dramas of the I'faith-m'lady-let-us-hie-us-hence variety. The fireplace, built of dressed stone, was big enough to house one of the larger mammals plus several of its offspring, and contained a variety of instruments designed to roast, boil, or stew all or any of the above. A number of blackened beams hung precariously from the ceiling. An escutcheon had been carved on the chimney breast. Oak settles sat against the wall, marvellously at odds with the computer terminals which glowed eerily in the mock-Tudor gloom and the filing cabinets, the forty-two-inch video screen and the tableful of telephones in different shapes and colours.

'Remind you of anything?' Cashman asked.

'Uh – not offhand,' Matthew said. What could it possibly remind him of? Surely such a combination of the Olde and the new was unique.

'Remember that scene in *Man For All Seasons*, where King Henry comes into the Great Hall looking for Anne Boleyn?'

Sure I do, thought Matthew. And the Great Hall had been crammed with computers, just like this . . . 'Vaguely,' he said.

'I used the same—'

A green light began to wink on a telephone shaped like a pair of crimson lips. Cashman picked it up. 'She's not here,' he said, after listening to whoever was on the other end. 'I'll get her to give you a bell, minute she gets back, all right?'

Whether it was all right or not the caller had no chance to say, since Cashman replaced the receiver as soon as he had finished the sentence.

Clearly through the Elizabethan windows came the sound of a car, travelling up the drive at high speed and coming to a screeching halt inches from the door.

'That'll be the wife,' Cashman said. 'Before we get down to anything let's just say hello, all right?'

'Fine by me,' said Matthew. He followed Cashman back into the huge hall and out on to the steps as Cindy Hill came running up them.

'Darling!' she cried. She flung herself into her husband's arms and looked up at him.

''Ullo, love.' Cashman had come over all gruff. 'Had a good trip?'

'All right.' Cindy Hill wore immaculate jeans which covered her long legs like clingfilm, and a denim jacket over a white T-shirt. She looked tired but nonetheless fabulous. She leaned back in the circle of Cashman's arms. 'You know what those roads are like. That's why I'm so late.'

'And how's your mum?'

'Fine,' Cindy said. 'Just fine.'

One arm around her, Cashman turned and brought her into the hall. 'Want you to meet someone,' he said. 'Cindy, this is Matthew Prescott. He's going to tell us what kind of pretty pictures we ought to be hanging on our walls. And we may or may not take his advice, depending on how we feel about it. Isn't that right, Matthew?'

'Absolutely,' said Matthew. If that was the way Cashman wanted to play it, so be it. Nobody said you had to like the clients.

'Cindy's just driven up from Ebbw Vale,' Cashman said. 'Been down to visit her mum in Wales. The old girl's been under the weather a bit lately.'

'Really?' murmured Matthew. He held out his hand. 'How do you do, Mrs Cashman?'

Cindy Hill's eyes took him in and then widened. He knew she must have recognized him from last night, just as she knew he recognized her.

'Nice to meet you,' she said. She held his fingers a fraction longer than necessary and there was no mistaking the message she wanted him to take in. She still managed to convey the same impression as the night before, that, figuratively speaking, she was good homebaked bread masquerading as patisserie.

She was obviously worried. It was unfortunate

61

that Matt was not in a position to reassure her. On that point at least, their interests coincided. No way was he going to jeopardize what promised to be a lucrative commission by letting Cashman know that his beautiful wife had been in Annabel's last night, two hundred miles or so away from the bedside of her sick mother.

He met Annie Carter in the wine bar, as arranged. After a glass of wine, they moved on to Le Caprice.

'I thought you were going to run up some nifty little steak au poivre, or something,' Annie said.

'I was. But I decided I could concentrate better on you if someone else did the cooking,' Matt said.

She raised her eyebrows. 'Oh, yes?'

She was good company. Funny. Warm. Tuned into the same things as himself. When she said she loved jazz, he took her on to Ronnie Scott's. They sat very close, the music coiling about them, binding them together. In the taxi going back to her hotel he put an arm around her shoulders and was glad that she did not move away.

'It's really been fun,' she said, standing up against him in the hotel's lobby.

'Hasn't it, though?' He looked down at her. 'How about inviting me up for a nightcap?'

'I'd like to, Matt,' she said. 'But I've just got this thing . . .'

'What *thing*?'

'You know . . .'

'I don't. Do you mean like a pet boa-constrictor? Or something more personal, like a wooden leg or an iron lung?'

She laughed. 'I know it's old-fashioned and all that, but I was brought up to believe that . . .' her voice dropped almost to a whisper, '. . . Nice Girls don't, not on the first date.'

'Don't what?'

'You know very well what I mean. And if I invite you up for a slug of duty-free whisky – which I would *love* to do, no question – you know what will happen. So it's better if you don't come up.'

'What do Nice Girls do on the second date?' he asked.

'You'll have to ask me for one and find out.'

'Tomorrow?'

She shook her head. 'I'm having dinner with the managing director of my company, plus a couple of other colleagues. And I fly back to Rome the day after that.'

'When are you here again?'

'In four weeks.'

'That's a long time to wait.'

'Isn't it, though?' She grinned up at him.

Matt took both her hands in his. 'Swear you'll have dinner with me the first night you're back.'

'I swear.'

'I can hardly wait.'

'Nor me.'

He kissed the tip of her nose and watched her walk away from him across the lobby to the lifts.

# 4

'I want you to remember, Alex,' said Nina Burden, Editor of *Athene*, 'that I have my own regime.'

'Naturally—'

'It may look to you like a relaxed, almost lackadaisical way of getting things done—'

'On the contrary, it seems—'

'– but in fact it's all very tightly controlled.' Nina tilted a nose which could only be described as retroussé and bared her teeth in the ferocious grin which had made her one of the most feared magazine editors on Fleet Street.

Not that it *was* Fleet Street any more, Alexandra thought, desperately wondering whether she was supposed to make any meaningful comment. 'Right,' she said. Keep her sentences to one word, and she might stand a chance of finishing them.

She was in Nina's office for a preliminary briefing before she started work the following week and to meet her new colleagues. So far, so good. She wasn't too keen on the open-plan office – she liked to control her own field of operations – but the people she would be working with had all seemed both positive and friendly.

'I like to think of the way we work here as an enlightened despotism, masquerading as a democracy,' Nina said, frowning at her own highly-lacquered nails.

Would you mind running that one by me again? Alexandra thought. Enlightened *what*? She nodded sagely. 'That's very good.'

'We run *Athene* on a shoestring, with a skeletal staff,' Nina said. 'But we get things done.'

'That's why I was so glad when you—'

'Skeletal, Alex. Remember that.'

Surely she meant 'skeleton', not 'skeletal', thought Alex, though now was hardly the time to start correcting her new boss's grammar. Or was this some subtle way of hinting that she herself needed to lose weight? Was this a piece of discreet telegraphing that she would be wise to take note of? Nina herself was bordering on the anorexic – as soon as the interview was over, Alex decided she'd dash into the rest room and take a careful look at herself in the full-length mirror hanging on the wall.

Last time she had done that, she'd been with Donna Fratelli in New York, the two of them slightly high after a giggly lunch helped down by a bottle of Stag's Leap Chardonnay.

'Gee, Alex,' Donna had said.

'What?'

'What are you doing in an office, for God's sake?'

'Trying to earn an honest penny. How about you?'

'With those legs, that terrific figure, those huge brown eyes, that to-*die*-for hair, you really shoulda been a model,' said Donna.

'Thanks, Don.' Alex surveyed herself. Seen through an alcoholic fuzz, she *did* look rather stunning. 'But I'd find it horribly boring.'

'Think of the money, honey. Think of that cottage with roses round the door you're always mouthing off about. Boy, if I looked like you, I'd own *ten* cottages by now.'

'All that dieting,' said Alexandra. 'All that angst about spots or hangovers or bags under the eyes. You've met the models, Donna, just as often as I have. They're not exactly happy people, are they?'

'How happy does a person have to be, for God's sake? Didn't one of them say something about not even getting out of bed in the morning for less than ten thousand dollars? I sure wouldn't mind being that happy.'

'That's exactly it.' Alex had wrinkled her nose in the mirror. 'Whose bed? If it's her own, why not? But suppose you felt you'd never get anywhere unless you slept with people like Jarrett Keach?'

'First *find* your Keach,' Donna said, slurring the words a little.

'Is that Keach as in cheese and onion keach?'

'Real Men Don't Eat Quiche,' Donna said. She hiccuped. 'Keach, I mean.'

Blinking at her reflection, Alex said, 'Anyway, I *like* what I do.'

'I know that,' said Donna. 'Which is why you're so darn good at it.'

'. . . and I'm sure I can count on you to be one hundred per cent with me on this one,' Nina was saying.

Alex nodded vigorously. 'Of course.' What the hell *had* she been saying?

'So go for it, Alex.' Another of the alligator smiles, a further lift of the retroussé nose. 'We'll see you on Monday, all right?'

'I'm really looking forward to—'

'And remember, I'll be keeping my eye on you.'

A remark calculated to put a new recruit completely at ease . . .

*       *       *

66

She loved the flat. Walking into it, that first night, she had moved through the empty rooms, admiring it, and then turned and flung her arms around David. 'It's terrific,' she said.

'The boy done good, did he?'

'The boy done *wonderful*.'

David had been right about the original features. The sitting room had a marble fireplace, and so did the main bedroom. The ceilings were unfashionably high, lending themselves to dramatic drapes over the windows. There was elaborate plasterwork, wide skirting boards, an arched hallway, brass light fittings. Even the kitchen was terrific, modernized by the previous owner and left intact with all the appliances she could have wished for.

'It'll be fantastic for entertaining in,' she said happily. 'And my pictures are going to look *marvellous* on these walls.'

He grinned at her with his head on one side. 'Would you say you owe me one, then?'

'Why?' she said guardedly.

'I'd just like you to remember that spare bedroom.'

'Don't worry,' she said. 'It's yours whenever you want it.'

Skeletal or skeleton, what Nina really meant, Alex realized after her first fortnight, was that *Athene* was run on the lines of a commune. Although Alexandra, for instance, held the title of Features Editor, in practical terms this meant nothing. Regardless of job description, everyone chipped in to get each month's issue out on time.

Thus, although the Health and Beauty Editor might just have turned in a long article on the advantages and disadvantages of liposuction as a slimming aid, she could also be asked to contribute a piece on 'The New Europe' or 'The Case for Aphrodisiacs'. So too, might the Literary Editor be expected to produce a thousand thoughtful and provocative words ('by lunchtime, darling, if you possibly can, clever you, I *know* you can do it,' with the implied threat that if she couldn't, she might just find herself out on her ear) on new fashion trends, provisionally entitled 'The Shape of Things to Come?' even though she had also handed in something on 'The Books That Everyone's Reading and Why'.

In the same way, the Cookery Editor was just as likely to find herself producing copy on the latest thing in leg-wear as slaving over a hot studio stove to produce non-alcoholic *crêpes Suzettes* (though, as David remarked when Alex told him about it, why would anyone in their right mind *want* to?).

Similarly, Alex was writing an article on 'Stress-management for the 30-something Woman' one day, and discussing millinery with the Queen's hatmaker the next, while on the third she might be asked to come up with a serious in-depth article on English xenophobia, with comments from those celebrities known to be against all foreigners in whatever size or shape they came.

'Old Kingers is always good for a curmudgeonly quote,' Nina said airily, giving her this assignment. 'I'll let you have his phone number, as long as you promise not to pass it on to anyone else. And Bron can usually be relied on to say something appalling.'

Alex thrived on it all. In her previous jobs, the parameters of her work had always been strictly defined; after the first few weeks on *Athene* she found herself exhilarated by the constant challenge, the hectic pace, the sense of things being thrown at you from all directions.

And it worked. There was a freshness and lack of predictability about *Athene* articles which came partly from the fact that the journalist producing them was not always completely *au fait* with what she was writing about, and partly from the magazine's keyword: outrageousness.

Outrageous was the name of the game at *Athene*.

'As we're all aware, readers these days want to know about something more than just hemlines or Princess Di or orgasms,' Nina said at the first of her regular Monday morning brainstormers that Alexandra attended.

'If I'd known *anything* about orgasms I wouldn't be in the middle of divorcing Barry, believe me,' muttered Carol, the Cookery Editor, a large girl who had the luscious beauty of a cream bun and the analytical brain of a Henry Kissinger.

'Or if Barry had,' said Petronella, the Problem Page person, a committed feminist with unshaven armpits.

Nina frowned at the Cookery Editor and the Problem Page person over the rimless half-moon specs she wore when she wished to emphasize her professionalism. Fingering the delicate ski jump of her nose, she addressed Alex. 'The team here at *Athene* likes to see itself as way ahead of that kind of outdated thinking, isn't that right, people?'

'Yo!' said the Health and Beauty Editor, who had spent some time working in California.

'We all know what we're trying to do here, so let's go for it as hard as we can.'

'Talking of which,' Alex said. 'I've got several ideas I'd like to ask about. Is now the time?'

'Could be. What sort of ideas?'

Alex outlined three or four features she had in mind – it didn't hurt to demonstrate your keenness, show them how right they were to choose you instead of someone else – and listened as they were tossed around by the others. 'I particularly like the jewellery idea,' said Felicity, the Fashion Editor. 'It would tie in with something I had in mind.'

'OK, Alex,' Nina said approvingly. 'Go ahead on that one.'

'Fashion for Fatties,' Carol said. 'I like that idea, too.'

'Not, of course, that we call them Fatties,' Alex said hastily.

'Or even *think* of them as such,' said Felicity.

'And even if we did, what's wrong with that?' Petronella said belligerently, swelling out her not insubstantial bosom.

'Nothing. Nothing at all. No way,' they said, remembering what kind of an issue fat was.

'I mean, we're normal young women, and proud of it, right?'

'Right!' exclaimed the Health and Beauty Editor, who habitually wore a Lycra leotard to work, under a man's shirt, and cycled in to the office every day from her home in Putney.

'What we like to do here at *Athene*,' Nina said, looking at Alex again, 'is think outrageous.'

'Mmm, yes. What exactly does that entail?' Alex asked.

Nina frowned. 'Isn't it obvious?'

'Thinking outrageous,' said Alex carefully. 'How exactly do you—'

'People?' Nina raised her eyebrows at her team.

'If you're profiling a restaurateur,' Carol said, 'you

don't just mention his food, but also his smelly feet.'

'If you're interviewing a Royal, don't be reverent,' said Felicity.

'And if you're talking to an actress, mention her halitosis as well as the way she played Desdemona,' remarked Lydia, the Literary Editor.

'Talking of bad breath,' said the Cookery Editor, 'I was wondering whether—'

Nina was not too keen on interruptions when she was giving them her pep talk.

'Outrageous, people,' she said, raising her voice a little. 'Keep thinking outrageous. The proof of the pudding is in the eating, and so far we're obviously providing exactly the kind of pudding our readers want. Circulation figures were up again last month, and we're increasing the print run for the next issue.'

'Way to go!' said the Health and Beauty Editor.

'So let's go on making 'em think, shall we?' Nina exhorted, sitting with one minimal buttock perched chirpily on the edge of the desk which had been allocated to Alex.

'Make 'em laugh, make 'em cry,' said Petronella. The advice she offered to her readers on the problem page was often so outrageous that she had become something of a fixture on Radio 4 comedy quiz programmes.

'Show 'em something a bit bigger than their own back garden, something more stimulating than the loss-leaders in their nearest shopping centre,' Nina said, as the phone beside her cheeped and the meeting began to break up.

Nina took her work very seriously, as indeed did all her staff. It was the real reason behind the magazine's success. This did not stop the chorus of complaints about the long hours, the poor pay, the open-plan office space, even the coffee in the machine.

'You'd think,' Felicity, the Fashion Editor, said in disgust, staring down at the melancholy brew she was drinking from a mug marked I ♥ DJAKARTA, 'you'd think that with all the modern advances in technology available to us today, they'd be able to produce something better than this, wouldn't you?'

'They're obviously using the wrong brand,' Alexandra said. After the first two days she had brought in her own jar of Gold Blend, but kept it hidden, knowing from experience it would have vanished by the end of the first week if she wasn't mean about it.

Rather than spend Saturday nights brooding about Cameron and what had gone wrong between them, Alexandra decided to give a dinner party. Despite the promise of his note before she left New York, she had not heard from him since her return to England. If she was to ward off melancholia, some sort of action was necessary.

Eight people, she decided. Sitting at an immaculately laid table. She didn't want one of those evenings where people stood around with plates of food in one hand, wondering where to put their wet wine glass while they ate and eventually opting to set it down on her most precious piece of furniture, the bureau which had belonged to her grandmother.

Just eight people, with elegance and sophistication being the note to go for. 'Which obviously rules *you* out for starters,' she said to David, detailing her plans over the telephone.

'You're so sweet,' he said.

'I know.'

'On the other hand, as you were doubtless going to add, I'm witty, charming and urbane.'

'A must at any elegant and sophisticated dinner party?'

'Exactly. And in addition, as your little brother, one who can be relied on to help with pouring drinks and carting away the dirty dishes when needed.'

'Precisely.'

'Not to mention giving the bum's rush to those of your guests who start chucking bread rolls around or trying to swing from the chandeliers.'

'Read my lips,' Alex said. 'Elegance. Sophistication. I don't know anyone who chucks bread rolls around, I'm happy to say.'

'Don't you?' David said disingenuously. 'Gosh. So who are you going to invite?'

'I thought Nina Burden and her husband – she's my editor at *Athene*, and he's some weighty political journalist with one of the quality dailies.'

'Who else?'

'Lucy and Hugo.'

'Lucy's always good for a laugh.'

'And Toby Dawson and his wife – you don't know them, but I worked with him on the *Mail*.'

'Sounds like a nice mix,' David said. 'I'll come early, shall I?'

'What for?'

'You'll need some help with opening the wine bottles.'

'You're so amazingly thoughtful.'

'It's vital to get them open in advance,' he said. 'Give them a chance to chambrer. And someone really ought to sample them, check that they're OK, not corked or anything.'

'Heavens. Just think, if you hadn't mentioned it,

I'd have forgotten and the dinner party would have been ruined.'

'What are brothers for?' he said modestly.

'And remember, David. We're talking a suit and tie here, not jeans and a torn T-shirt, all right?'

'A suit and tie?' he breathed. 'Do you want me to wear a shirt as well?'

'Yes please,' she said briskly.

'Oh my. That's *real* sophistication. I take it you don't want me to bring anyone.'

'Not this time, David.'

There was a silence. What both of them were thinking was: why is Alexandra inviting her brother to this dinner party as a single male? Why doesn't she have a man of her own? More specifically, they were both thinking: where is Cameron? And if not Cameron, a Cameron substitute. Or some other gorgeous hunk? *Any* gorgeous hunk. Even a hunk who *wasn't* gorgeous would have done. There were plenty of them around, after all. Where Alexandra was concerned, hunks were fairly thick on the ground. This was part of the trouble. Nearly all of them were exactly that: thick.

Alex liked men with a considerable degree of *savoir faire*. Men who could talk to her, men who had been around. Almost by definition, the hunks who rang her up and asked her out to dinner were too busy flexing their gym-developed muscles and gazing at their own reflections to spend much time on things of the mind. It was perhaps stretching a point to talk of minds, their biceps invariably being bigger than their IQs.

There were others, of course. Men who wanted to take her to the opera. Men who suggested visits to National Trust houses. Men who bought tickets for concerts at the Festival Hall. Kind, sensitive men. Intelligent caring men, who shared her tastes in art and music but who did not turn her on.

She longed for Cameron, who combined brains with brawn in a most satisfying . . . but it was pointless dreaming about him, especially with eight people to dinner in a couple of days' time, and a crisis at the office because the Cookery Editor had come down with chicken-pox.

'At least it's not typhoid,' Petronella said. She was used to looking on the bright side.

'God,' said Felicity, giving vent to some ugly gagging sounds. 'I should hope not. Especially after we all made *pigs* of ourselves on that chicken and pistachio galantine or whatever it was she produced last month.'

'I bet she breathed all over it,' Helena, the Health and Beauty Editor, said. 'Yuk.'

'What are the symptoms of typhoid, anyway?' Alex asked. 'I mean, how would we know if we had it?'

'Yes,' said Felicity. 'For all we know, we could be infecting half of London.'

'Think of Typhoid Mary,' said Alex.

'But she hasn't *got* typhoid,' Petronella said. 'She's got *chicken*-pox.'

'Same thing,' said Helena.

'Of *course* it's not.'

'Infectious-wise, I mean.'

Alex hoped it wasn't. It would be rather embarrassing if her guests all broke out in spots the week after her dinner party. She had carefully timed it for the week-end following the appearance of the next issue of *Athene* on the news stands. Although the pace in the

75

office was unrelenting, there was nonetheless something of a respite for the first few days after each monthly issue came out. She spent what free time she had planning the food, shopping, getting as much done in advance as she could manage, wondering how to seat her guests, especially Nina and her husband.

Lying in a bath laced with coconut-scented foaming oil, soaking out the day's tensions, she thought about Nina and then about herself. The image was marginally worrying.

She rang Lucy, who had been her best friend since their university days. 'Be honest,' she said. 'Do you see me as devious and manipulative?'

'I need notice of that question,' said Lucy. 'Darling Hugo's just poured me a second martini and my brain seems to have slipped out of gear. Devious and *what*?'

'I mean, I like Nina, my new boss at the office, but I don't *know* her, not yet. So why am I asking her to my place for dinner?'

'Because you want to confirm for her just what an excellent choice – suave, capable and talented – she made in choosing you as the agony aunt for her magazine.'

'Do you mind? I'm the Features Editor.'

'What's the difference?' Lucy said vaguely.

'On *Athene*, not a lot, actually.'

'Anyway, you're giving this woman a subtle message to the effect that if anything should – God forbid – happen to her, like agoraphobia or a severe attack of beriberi, then she need not worry,' said Lucy.

'How do you mean?' Alex heard the clink of the Gordon's bottle against the side of a glass.

'Because, darling Alexandra, she will realize that

the right person is standing there ready to step into her shoes at a second's notice, poised to take over the editorship of *Athene*. Take over, if necessary, the editorship of the *world*.'

'What's that, the latest unisex multi-interest magazine?'

'Very droll.'

'But what does that say about me? You make me sound so hard-headed. So calculating.'

'Let's face it, Alex,' Lucy said. 'Let's be brutally frank here. You're a career girl. You're not interested in the things we lesser morsels – I mean mortals – go for. Things like husbands, and children, and Volvo estates.'

'Aren't I?'

''Course not.'

'How can you be sure?' There was a pain in Alexandra's heart which was beginning to feel seriously life-threatening. Tears pricked at her eyelids. If only Lucy *knew* . . .

'Because if you wanted them, you'd have them by now. You're one of those people who always gets what they want. Unlike me, who ended up with terrible Hugo and have been miserable ever since,' Lucy said happily.

When she had switched off the telephone, Alexandra ran more hot water into the bath. Were those tears, or was it simply heat-induced sweat rolling down her face? Lucy had got it all wrong – hadn't she? If Cameron were to burst in through the door at that moment – she should be so lucky – with a dozen red roses and a proposal that the two of them rush out to the nearest registry office and get married without delay, she would . . .

*What* would she do? Would she really rise from the

77

bath covered in coconut-scented foam and say shyly, 'Yes, Cameron. Of course, Cameron. Just let me put some clothes on, Cameron, and I'll be right with you'?

Or would she hesitate?

And if she did, would it be because she knew instinctively that though she longed for Cameron, the feel of him, the smell of him, the easy way they were together, she nonetheless knew in her heart of hearts that he was not the right man for her?

On the ledge round the bath, next to the natural sponge David had brought her back from Greece last year, the telephone bleeped. She picked it up.

'Hi,' Cameron said. 'How're you doing?'

The dinner party was a success. Nina seemed to be fascinated by David; her husband took an immediate and obvious liking to Lucy, who threw herself into her Suburban-Housewife mode without so much as a flicker of an eyelid. Listening to her regale him with a highly-coloured account of her daily problems with washing-machine repair men, dog hairs in the refrigerator, soufflés which failed to souff, the perils of conjugal couplings when there were small children in the house, no-one would have believed she held a first-class degree in physics from Oxford.

David behaved impeccably, giving Nina the Why-Are-All-The-Best-Women-Married? treatment, and at the same time, as Alexandra had known he would, subtly talking up his sister.

Alex herself moved graciously between kitchen and dining area, cleared plates, smiled. But Cameron filled her thoughts.

'I'll be in London next week,' he had said.

'Oh.'

'You want to see me, don't you?'

I want to see you so much I'm almost fainting with it, she thought. 'Of course I do.'

'I'll make my own way in from Heathrow,' he said. 'Shall I come by the office? Pick you up? We could have dinner.'

'Jet lag,' she murmured. 'Won't you be spaced-out?'

'It never hits me until the next day,' he said cheerfully.

She wanted to ask what he planned to do *after* dinner. Was he going to come home with her? She wished she did not feel so unsure of him. Of herself.

'I can't wait to be with you again, Alexandra,' he said, his mouth very close to the telephone.

She wanted to ask why, in that case, he had waited for so long before getting in touch with her again. She remembered the red rose on her desk in New York, that scentless red rose. She thought of husbands, and children, and Volvo estates.

'Me too,' she said quietly.

'Coffee?' David was saying from the other end of the table, raising his eyebrows at her, and she realized she had been miles away.

'Of course.' She smiled at her guests. 'I'll get it. David, there are liqueurs in the sideboard . . .'

She was glad of a few minutes alone. She splashed water on her flushed face and wished it was as easy to cool her bruised heart. Cameron would be here in just a few days . . .

She opened the kitchen cupboard and frowned. Where was the coffee? Surely she had . . . she had a distinct recollection of picking it up at the super-market . . . *hadn't* she?

She opened another cupboard door and saw what

she was looking for – except that the jar was nearly empty. If you liked weak coffee, there was enough for one cup . . . and she couldn't, running over her trip round the supermarket, actually remember buying any more.

The neighbours. She'd have to slip out and borrow some. But Nina mustn't know. The image she was trying to project wouldn't exactly be enhanced by having forgotten such a basic dinner-party requirement as coffee.

She went back to her guests, smiled vaguely without stopping, and carried on into the hall. Quietly she opened her front door and pulled it behind her. Which way should she go: upstairs or down? The people who shared her floor were away, she knew that, having bumped into them as she came out of the lift two days ago. Up or down? For no special reason, she opted for up.

Pressing the old-fashioned brass doorbell, she automatically smoothed her black Jean Muir dress over her hips, checked her earrings, patted her hair. The door opened on a waft of Mozart; there was a warm smell of freshly-made coffee.

My God, she thought, it's that drunk, the one who was mouthing imprecations at David and me when we were moving my stuff into the flat. He had come weaving up the stairs, leaned over the banisters, wagged a finger at them and mumbled something incomprehensible. She remembered laughing, he had looked so comic, so incapable.

'Look, I'm sorry to bother you,' she said. 'But I'm having a dinner party and I've – well, I've run out of coffee.'

He gave a little laugh.

Rather dishy, she thought. Pity he's got a drink

problem, but we can't all be perfect. 'Come in,' he said.

His flat was built to the same plan as her own. Almost automatically she walked towards his kitchen, conscious of his gaze on her back, her somewhat naked back, glad, without knowing quite why, that she was looking particularly glamorous that evening. He opened a cupboard, took out her favourite brand of coffee, and said, 'I hope this isn't too sophisticated for your guests.'

What a nerve, she thought. I don't have to take this sort of thing from a man who staggers home after midnight tanked to the eyeballs and starts hurling ruderies at complete strangers.

She remembered her father warning her: 'You can always tell a true gentleman by the way he behaves in his cups.'

'They have very sophisticated tastes,' she said coolly.

'Do they?' he said. He arched his eyebrows in what she assumed he thought was a sophisticated way.

Honestly.

Since he did not seem to want to let go of his coffee, she took it from him. 'Yes,' she said.

He was staring at her, at her face, her jewellery, her dress. She fingered her earring, a habit she had when not quite sure of herself. Though why she should be nervous in front of someone who was probably a founder member of Alcoholics Anonymous, she couldn't imagine.

'Well, I must be getting back,' she said composedly. She gave him a deep look and flashed a hint of her Cleopatra smile – provocative, promising – at him. His – not exactly handsome but more than acceptable – face flushed a little. One eyebrow lifted slightly.

She turned and felt his eyes on her back all the way to the door.

In her own flat, no-one seemed to have noticed her departure, nor her return. The talk had become animated. With large gestures of his hands, Toby Dawson was telling Nina about some of his newspaper assignments in the days when he was a foreign correspondent on the *Mail*. His wife was discussing the latest exhibition at the Royal Academy with Nina's husband. David and Lucy were giggling with Hugo.

She brought coffee in, served it, sat down. Lucy leaned forward. 'By the way,' she said. 'I've been meaning to ask. Met your new neighbours yet?'

'Oh,' Alex said airily. 'I've dropped in for coffee.'

And wondered why she should be smiling to herself, why she felt an altogether unexpected lift of the heart.


Invitations to the end-of-term shows at the Royal College of Art and Goldsmith's College had landed on her desk and she took the afternoon off to view them. The art colleges were turning out some marvellously talented young workers with refreshing new ideas about exactly what constituted jewellery, and exciting views on the materials which could be used for personal adornment.

Strolling around, Alex reflected that once it would have been gold and silver, possibly pewter or steel. Now the fashionable collector pieces were being exquisitely crafted from every conceivable material: ceramics, brass, titanium, glass, wood, even some of the newer synthetic fibres.

From the receptionist she collected information about some of the recent diploma students so that later she was able to contact them, interview them, give them room to express their views, have their work photographed. At the same time, as a counterbalance, she arranged an interview with a young Parisian jewellery agent and socialite, and also set up meetings with a couple of the more established female jewellery-makers, who were still using traditional material.

There was one in particular whose work she had long admired. When she telephoned, Emma Chisholm agreed to see her the following morning, as long as she didn't mind coming up to Hampstead. Alex had no objections at all.

On the day, she was able to park right outside the house, a typical four-storey terrace which she knew instinctively would be full of stripped pine and flowers and good pieces of furniture. A French au pair girl let her in and led her down to a basement studio where a slim woman in black velvet jeans and a black fisherman's smock was working at a table in the middle of the room.

'I'm Alexandra Maitland, from *Athene*,' Alex said.

'Hi.' The woman at the work-table removed a pair of goggles and put down the blowlamp she was working with. She held out her hand. 'Emma Chisholm.'

'I've got several of your pieces,' said Alex. 'I practically never go out without a pair of your earrings.'

'So I notice.' Emma Chisholm smiled. 'Did you say you were the fashion editor of this magazine?'

'Features, actually. But we all chip in with ideas and articles.'

'So it's still quite a compliment that you choose to wear my work.' Emma looked at the watch on her wrist. 'Eleven thirty: it's easily late enough for a glass of wine. What do you think?'

'That it sounds like a great idea.'

'Drink before eleven in the morning and you've definitely got a problem,' Emma said. 'But after that, it becomes a pre-lunch drink, don't you agree?' The two women laughed. Emma found glasses and hoicked a bottle of white wine from a small refrigerator on a counter.

'I always feel so decadent, drinking before six o'clock,' Alex said, sipping from the glass Emma handed her. 'It must be a throwback to my father. He's always going on about suns over yard-arms.'

'What exactly *is* a yard-arm?' Emma said. 'I've never known.'

'Nor me. I always think of it as some kind of gibbet.'

'Gruesome sort of thing to want the sun over, isn't it?'

The wine turned into lunch, and then into tea. Alexandra and Emma found themselves in complete agreement on almost everything, ready-made friends. It was the kind of easy instant relationship Alex had not experienced since she was a child at school.

As she was leaving, her notes safely in her bag and the photographer booked for the following week, Emma said impulsively, 'I know we've only just met, but I'm having some people round next week and I'd really love it if you'd come.'

'That's very—'

'I'm not trying to push my friends at you or anything, but some of them work in other disciplines – there's a ceramicist coming. And a needlework designer. You might find them worth writing up for your magazine some time.'

Alex laughed. 'That'd be really great. I'll look forward to it.'

'It's perfectly simple, Pa,' David said. 'And you'd be so much more mobile if you learned to operate it.'

'I'm not going to be stuck in the bloody thing long enough for it to matter,' said Colonel Maitland. He leaned out over one arm of the wheelchair in which he sat and stared irritably down at the various handles. 'One of these things has to be the brake lever, but I'm damned if I know which.'

'David's already told you,' Alexandra said. 'The one on the *left*.'

The French windows out on to the lawn were wide open; she could see roses blooming in the well-tended beds and smell lilac on the air. It was so different from London. From New York. Even after all these years, she still thought of this long low house as home. This was where she had grown up and she loved the familiarity of it all, the security, everything as it always had been, her brother and her father gently teasing each other, the garden outside the windows, the furniture which had been there since her childhood. And whenever she came back to it, the smell of the house was always the same: polish, flowers, something cooking in the kitchen from where Mrs Hope ran things in her cheerfully imperturbable manner, as she had done for the past twenty years.

'Is it too much to ask that damned woman to leave the paper within reach?' grumbled the Colonel. He sat glaring forlornly at the small table on the other side of the room, a handsome man in a white open-necked shirt and meticulously creased flannels.

'Mrs Hope's got far too much to do looking after

85

the house,' Alexandra responded unsympatheti-
cally. 'And you *asked* to be moved over to the
windows.'

'If you'd only learn to operate it,' repeated David,
fetching the paper for his father, 'you could get the
paper for yourself. Or anything else you need.'

'All I ever wanted out of life was a case or two of
decent port and a chance to read the cricket scores,'
the Colonel said pathetically, turning to the back
page. 'God knows it's not much. No-one could say I
was a demanding chap, could they?'

'Demanding? Good Lord, no,' said David, winking at his sister.

'Imperious, maybe,' Alex said. 'What do you
think, David?'

'Dictatorial?'

'Authoritarian,' said Alex. 'No question about
it.'

'But definitely not demanding.'

'Not,' said the Colonel, ignoring this banter, 'that
the cricket's worth reading about these days. No
sense of discipline any more, no pride in representing
their country, let alone their county. Stands to
reason, really, when half of them have set themselves
up on the side as journalists or TV stars with poncey
hairdos.'

'Any minute now,' Alexandra said to David, 'he's
going to start quoting Housman.'

'And who wouldn't?' said her father. 'Chap might
have been a bloody old poofter, but he knew what
was what, all right.' He banged at the arm of the
wheelchair. 'Have you got any idea what it's like,
being treated as though you were a damned invalid?'

'"See the son of grief at cricket, trying to be
glad,"' David said.

'I get the distinct impression that you two are making fun of me.' The Colonel turned his handsome head first towards his son, then his daughter, trying to maintain his expression of severity.

'Whatever gives you that idea?' asked Alex.

'And why aren't you married yet? That's what I want to know. Good-looking girl like you, image of your mother.'

'Because I haven't found the right man yet,' said Alex.

'Why not? Must be blind, the lot of them.'

'It's not that there aren't men around, Pa,' David explained patiently. 'Simply that Alex isn't interested in marrying any of them.'

'Besides,' added Alex. 'I don't want to spend the rest of my life washing underpants?'

'Underpants? Bloody funny way to look at marriage, isn't it?'

'When you *do* find Mr Right,' David said, 'don't make the mistake of bringing him down here, will you?'

'No fear,' said Alex.

'Why ever not?' demanded the Colonel. 'Always made your friends welcome, haven't I?'

'Remember that French chap you were so keen on?' said David.

'Jean-Pierre?' Alex smiled. 'Oh yes. He came down once.'

'And only once.'

'Your fault, Pa.'

'I suppose you're going to accuse me of being rude to him.'

'You *were*,' Alexandra said, laughing.

'Bloody rude,' said David.

'Garlic or no garlic, I was perfectly civil to the

87

fellow. Not my fault he wore that ridiculous beard, looked like a ponce.'

'You didn't have to tell him so, Pa,' Alex said.

'Before he'd even had his morning coffee,' added David.

'Well, anyway,' the Colonel said, looking down at the controls of his wheelchair again. 'You two can mock, but it's pretty ghastly being here with only that woman for company. Never answers when I ring the bell. Might as well be living in a morgue. Don't know what I'm supposed to do if there's a fire or something.'

'Mrs Hope would rescue you,' said David.

'Probably,' said Alex.

'I'd be burned to a bloody crisp, like as not, before *she* stirred her stumps.'

'Who can blame her? You're always so horrible to her.'

In fact, the relationship between Mrs Hope and the Colonel was, as it always had been, long-standingly amicable, even though both of them pretended otherwise. Alex took hold of her father's hand. 'Cheer up, Pa. You'll be out of there soon.'

'I just hope it's before the cricket season's over.'

'What you need,' said David, 'is the love of a good woman.'

'Or even a bad one,' Alex said.

'You two talk a lot of nonsense,' said the Colonel. He looked hopefully at his watch. 'I say, the sun's well over the yard-arm. How about a noggin?'

It was the following evening, just after she had got back to her flat after another hectic day at the coal-face of *Athene*, that the doorbell rang. Answering it, Alex found a very short blonde girl standing outside.

88

'Hi,' the girl said. 'You're David's sister, aren't you?'

'That's right.'

'I'm Charlotte,' the girl said. 'I don't know if David mentioned me. I'm a painter and I live in one of the flats upstairs.'

'You must be the Lady,' Alex said.

Charlotte blushed. 'Well, yes, I suppose I am. But I prefer to stick to my professional name – Charlotte Hanover – if you don't mind. I don't approve of titles.'

'Would you like a coffee or something?' Alex stood back.

The girl stepped into the hall. 'That would be great. Thanks.'

While the kettle boiled, Alex said, 'And do you see a lot of my brother?'

The girl blushed again. 'A fair bit.'

Alex made coffee, trying to remember when *she* had last blushed, trying to remember what it was like to be as young as Charlotte seemed. 'You're a portrait painter, aren't you?'

'That's right.'

'A good one?'

Charlotte looked away. 'I've won a prize or two, yes. But how would you decide whether a portraitist was good or not?'

'I don't know. If the sitter likes it?'

'That's not really the point, is it?'

'If you're painting portraits, I'd have thought it was at least a factor.'

The girl put her elbows on the table and cupped her chin in her hands. 'It's something I'm still trying to work out. Is it more important to maintain the sitter's integrity, or the artist's? As far as I'm concerned, perhaps the most essential thing is to succeed in saying something significant about the subject. Especially if it's something they themselves are trying to hide.'

'Do you get a lot of work?'

'A fair bit.'

'Even in a recession?'

'It's amazing how many people still want to have their portraits done. Or else want to commission me to paint someone else. Like a nearest or dearest.'

'Even if that's sometimes a pet?'

'I don't do animals,' Charlotte said firmly. 'Though I don't mind putting in a cat or something, if there's one around or the person specifically asks me to. But no horses. Definitely no horses.'

'Why not?'

'Because I hate them.'

'Any particular reason?'

'All my sisters are terribly keen horsewomen,' Charlotte said, as if that was reason enough.

'I see,' said Alex, though she didn't really. 'How many have you got?'

'Horses?' Charlotte frowned, her voice serious, heavy with disapproval of quadrupeds who leaped over fences or ran very fast round racetracks.

'Sisters,' said Alex, trying to bite back a smile.

'Four, actually,' Charlotte said fiercely. '*And* a mother.'

'Most of us have one of those.'

'Not one like mine. I was practically *born* on horseback. I don't suppose my mother took more than two minutes out of the saddle in order to produce me. I spent my entire childhood at gymkhanas. Wearing a hard hat and jodhpurs. Such a ridiculous garment, don't you think, jodhpurs?'

'There *is* something rather—'

'I kept falling off horses on to my head—'

'At least you had the hat . . .'

'– and every time I did, my father or my mother or my sisters would put me back on again.' Charlotte stared into her coffee cup, brooding.

'There are many different kinds of hell,' Alexandra said, trying not to laugh. Charlotte Hanover seemed so small and so intense, not at all David's usual type.

'David doesn't like horses,' Charlotte said. 'It was the first thing I asked him.'

'Was it?'

'Because if he did, I wouldn't have had anything to do with him.' Charlotte spoke with passion.

'Quite right.'

'Why I came up,' Charlotte said. 'I was wondering whether you would like to come to dinner one evening soon.' She blushed yet again. 'David will be there, of course. And a few other people. If you'd like to bring someone . . .'

'That's very kind,' Alexandra said. She envisaged the flat – on the top floor, had David said? – untidy, covered in tins with brushes sticking out, no chairs, some kind of pasta eaten off paper plates. 'I'll really look forward to that.'

'Good.' Charlotte got up.

'Can I bring anything? A bottle of wine, for instance?'

'Please don't bother,' Charlotte said coolly. 'I'm very fussy about wine.'

'Oh.' Not much you could say to that, was there?

'But thanks very much all the same.'

Alexandra closed the door behind her and smiled. An unusual young woman. She wondered how David handled her. If, indeed, he did.

# 5

'Wonderful,' Annie sighed. She sipped her coffee and glowed at Matthew across the table.

'Thank you,' he said.

'Everything's wonderful,' she said. 'Not just the coffee, but the steak, and your flat, and the wine—'

'You brought that.'

'– and,' she smiled at him – 'and you.'

'Thank you again.'

He leaned towards her and took her hand in his. She was a great girl, no question about that. And a nice one, too. The sort his mother would approve of. The sort who would make a terrific wife and a superb mother. Brains, too. And beautiful. That cloud of dark hair framing her face. That cute figure, barely up to his shoulder. Those amazing blue eyes.

So why did he keep remembering the dark eyes of the woman from downstairs? Was it the way she used them to speak for her, to tell him things he knew he wanted to hear, to convey messages? Of which there seemed to have been plenty.

He reddened slightly, remembering the evening he had come home to find the lift stuck, how he had leaned over the banister and said 'Short shrift' – or tried to. How he had wagged his finger at the woman in the most ridiculous fashion.

And her voice . . . Why did he keep hearing it again, just as he was about to fall asleep, or when he was trying to work? He had repeated their conversation a thousand times to himself since she had rung his doorbell at the weekend. Although they had barely exchanged half a dozen sentences, in memory it seemed more like a three-act play, one he could have watched over and over again.

He wanted to know more about her. He wanted to ask if she realized she had the sexiest voice he had heard in years. He wanted to ask if she knew that the earrings she was wearing had been designed by his sister Emma. Above all, he wanted to ask – to *demand* – whether the guy who'd been helping her move in was her husband, her lover, her fiancé, and if not, who, if anyone, was.

'You're thinking about something else,' Annie said. Part of her charm was that she said it without any negative undertone. Other women he knew would have started pouting or getting annoyed. She just seemed to accept that people did sometimes get troubling thoughts about their coffee-borrowing neighbours when they were in the middle of kissing the fingers of their dinner companions – or were just about to.

He bent his head towards Annie's hand.

The doorbell rang.

'Excuse me,' he said, and as he pushed back his chair, hoped he had managed to hide the relief in his voice. He needed to think. He could not, in all sincerity, embark on a programme of Annie-seduction, though that had definitely been in his mind all evening – as, indeed, it had been in hers, he could tell – unless he saw some kind of longer-term relationship developing between them. He might not be keen on commitment, but he had never been the kind of man who went in for one-night stands.

He had spent too much time around women – though hardly from choice, thanks very much – not to be aware that underneath whatever exterior they chose to present to the world, women were vulnerable creatures, and chronically insecure. How many times had he been through the mill along with his sisters, in the days before Victoria and Emma had finally married the men of their choice?

All that tearstained uncertainty. All that nail-biting self-doubt. All that 'Why hasn't he rung me?' and 'Did I make myself cheap by letting him kiss me?' and 'Do you think he's *dead*?'

Victoria had actually woken him once at four o'clock in the morning to ask him that.

'No, I bloody well *don't* think he's dead,' he had said, 'though right this moment I wish he *was*.'

'Then why hasn't he phoned me?'

'How the hell should I know?'

'Do you think he's gone off me, Matt?'

'That depends on whether he was ever *on* you, Victoria.'

More tears. More doubts.

'Ring him up yourself, if you're so worried about him,' he would say sometimes, and they would wail: 'But I *can't*. Girls *don't*.'

And all this angst over some sod of a man who just didn't realize how lucky he was to have Victoria or Emma even *speaking* to him, let alone involved. Nor how intense women were about relationships. How serious they were about the men they favoured with their love.

Standing in the hall of his flat, collecting himself before he opened the door, he smiled, remembering.

'Ma-att,' his sisters would wheedle.

'What is it?'

'*You're* a man, Matt—'

'I shan't be a man for much longer if you keep on waking me up at three o'clock in the middle of the blasted night.'

'– and if *you* promised to give a girl a ring in a couple of days to fix up another date and then a whole *week* went by, what would it mean?'

'It would probably mean I'd found someone I liked better,' he'd say, with the cruelty of a brother who has just been roused from some much-needed sleep.

'Oh, Matt. Would it really? Wouldn't you even have the kindness to ring up and say it was all over? Wouldn't you realize she was waiting at home for you to ring, not going out in case she missed your call, hardly daring to even go for a *pee* so as to be there when you telephoned? Wouldn't you, Matt? Wouldn't you?'

As he grew older and less self-centred, he began to hate the men who caused this needless suffering to his beautiful sisters. He grew protective of them. He altered the way he himself behaved towards women. He began to see what a rough deal women got, on the whole, the way they were hemmed about by the idiotic rules society laid down for them. Girls *can't* . . . there was something infinitely sad in that phrase. However emancipated and independent they might be – and no-one could call Victoria and Emma anything but one hundred per cent both of those things – they were still emotionally vulnerable, still hogtied . . .

All of which added up to the fact that he was not about to increase whatever uncertainties Annie Carter might carry about with her. Not until he was sure, not so much of her as of himself.

He opened the door.

*She* was out there again. Carrying a brown paper sack of shopping. Looking, if anything, even more gorgeous than last time he'd seen her, her amazing hair swept up into a French pleat at the back of her head, her huge eyes melting.

'You saved my life the other night,' she said, and he felt quite literally as though someone was playing a violin inside his chest. His mouth opened but he couldn't think of anything to say.

'The dinner party,' he managed to quaver. She was wearing what his sisters called a power suit, with a shirt whose collar emphasized the slenderness and elegance of her neck. What a ludicrous remark – *the dinner party*, when he hadn't even been there.

'The *coffee*,' she said, obviously taking him for some kind of moron. 'Very successful.'

And then he blew it. 'How can you ever thank me?' he said.

It was the kind of cheap come-on remark you heard in pubs on Saturday nights when the lads started chatting up the girls. Oh God, and that stupid leer he'd accompanied it with. He felt sweat along his spine.

She stepped back, putting on that cool expression he was already familiar with. 'I'll try and think of something,' she said coldly. 'In the meantime, at least I can return your coffee.' She took a jar out of the bag of groceries and handed it to him.

Still staring at her, he took it, thinking how easy – how *natural* – it would have been to invite her in, offer a drink, some coffee, anything. But Annie was sitting there at the table, waiting for him, and he had to let the moment go.

'Look, I'm in the middle of something right now,' he said, and wanted to kick something hard, especially himself for being so inept. 'But perhaps . . .'

She took it as a rebuff. Or something worse. Remembering his sisters, remembering the insecurities women suffered, he knew she'd be thinking: he thinks I'm coming on to him, and he's telling me he's not interested.

She turned away from him. Gave a small smile. 'Perhaps . . .' she agreed, and he knew the word had taken on a new meaning, that it no longer implied possibilities but had all the finality of a prison gate clanging shut, or a hatch being battened.

Meanwhile, there was Annie.

'Just a neighbour,' he said, returning to the dining table, and saw her face change. They exchanged some further pleasantries but she knew the mood had been destroyed, that something had occurred to prevent whatever might have happened between them. When she looked at her watch shortly afterwards and said she had to go, he could hardly bring himself to insist that she stay.

'I'll drive you, of course,' he said.

'No.' Annie smiled at him, and he tried not to see the desolation in her eyes. 'I'd rather get a taxi.'

They went downstairs together. When a cab arrived, she stood next to him, touched his face, reached up to kiss his cheek. 'I hope it all works out, Matthew,' she said.

As the cab drove away, he knew he would never see her again.

'You won't forget,' Emma said bossily on the phone. 'Thursday week. Eight o'clock. And don't be *late*.'

'Am I ever?'

'You were the last time. *And* the time before that.'

'I won't be on Thursday. Do you want me to bring someone?'

'It's all right,' she said. Defensively.

'Listen, Em.' It was time to put his foot down.

'Yes?'

'I am definitely not in the mood for one of your ghastly Miss - Completely - Wrong - For - Everyone - Else - In - The - Entire - World - So - Let's - Try - Her - On - Matthews,' he said.

'What?'

'You heard.'

'The woman I've invited to make up the numbers – *not* to meet you – is an extremely nice person.'

'A nice person, eh?' he said derisively. 'That means she's got an untreatable skin condition, at the very least.'

'Does it?' Emma spoke with nonchalance. 'You'll have to wait and see, won't you? Actually, she's doing a piece on me and my jewellery in her magazine.'

'That reminds me,' he said, desperately non-chalant. 'I met someone the other day who was wearing a pair of your earrings.'

Emma grabbed hold of the nonchalance like a Rottweiler. 'Really? What someone? Who is she? Are you going to see her again?'

'Just a neighbour.'

'Is that all?' Emma was disappointed. 'Anyway, you needn't worry,' she said. 'This woman who's coming is not the slightest bit interested in you or any other man.'

'You mean you expect me to spend the evening sitting next to some butch dyke in dungarees?'

'Don't be ridiculous, Matthew. She's *got* someone, that's all I meant. She told me all about it.' Emma's voice faded into uncertainty. 'An American journalist, I think she said. Or is that the one she's just finished with?'

'Don't ask me.'

'I'm trying to remember if she said she'd just met someone she rather fancied but that he was involved with another woman, or whether that was someone else entirely.'

'Em, you're beginning to sound like Mother on one of her off days.'

'Anyway, you'll like her. And even if you don't, it's only for one evening. I don't know why you're so belligerent when all I'm trying to do is have you round for dinner.' Emma heaved a put-upon sigh.

'I'm belligerent because I've learned through bitter experience that attack is the best form of defence,' Matthew said. 'I had dinner at Victoria's recently—'

'She told me about it.'

'– and I can't remember when I've had a worse time.'

'She said you were frightfully rude.'

'So would you have been, forced to listen to some woman banging on about her dog's operation all evening. I don't even *like* dogs.'

'Victoria says she's an exceptionally nice person and an extremely talented gynaecologist.'

'That was the other thing,' Matthew said.

He loved talking to his sisters. The cut and thrust was immensely invigorating. How marvellous if you could establish the same fond teasing relationship with someone who *wasn't* your sister. 'When this woman wasn't boring on about her dog, she was telling me about breech births and placentas and cracked nipples and stuff. All sorts of things I really did not want to hear about over the salmon mousse.'

'Victoria says women come from all over England to have their babies delivered by her.'

'She was practically drawing diagrams,' Matthew said, enjoying himself fully. 'I mean, I've got nothing against babies, as such, but I am definitely not interested in hearing about them before they've been tidied up and talcumed and stuck into nappies.'

'You just wait.'

'What for?'

'The day you get pregnant.'

'Never happen,' Matthew said. 'If there's one thing I can say with absolute confidence, it's—'

'Your wife, then. You know perfectly well what I mean.'

'What about it? Not that I've got a wife.'

'You'll bore us all rigid with it,' Emma said. 'Antenatal classes, and the Husband's Role and home-versus-hospital delivery. Gawd, I can hear it all now.'

'Poppycock.'

'Want to bet?'

'I wouldn't demean myself,' Matthew said with dignity, knowing she was probably right. 'Anyway, you'll be down at the weekend for Mother's birthday, won't you?'

'Can't wait.'

'See you then.'

It was a perfect English day. A lazy afternoon in rural Somerset, full of sunshine and his mother's flowers, and his sisters' voices, just as it had been when they were growing up. They all sat out on the lawn, drinking champagne, celebrating his mother's birthday. Behind them, the Queen Anne house glowed in the sunshine. Red brick, white paint, handsome doors and windows. Matthew loved it. He often thought that it was because of the house that he had ended up taking an art and architecture degree at university, and so been led into his present career.

Red brick, white paint, doors, windows – the same basic ingredients as Tony Cashman's place. But how vastly different.

He lay back with his eyes closed, enjoying the sun on his face. Birds chittered in the ancient trees; he could hear the laughter of Victoria's and Emma's children as they played on the big swing at the end of the garden, just as he and his sisters once had. Just as his own children would – if he ever had any.

His mother was rustling paper, untying bows, reading greetings cards aloud. '*You'd be surprised if you only knew how much and how often I think of you. Happy Birthday, Gran,*' she said. 'Timmy, what a sweet card.'

'It's a Valentine card, really,' Timmy, aged eleven, explained. 'That's all they had in the local shop, left over from February.'

'And a green frog made out of soap,' murmured Matthew's mother. 'How marvellous.'

'He saved up his pocket money,' Victoria said.

'Thank you, Timmy.'

More rustling. More exclamations. A scarf from Victoria. A double ticket to the opera from Emma and her husband. More soap. Matthew was half asleep when his mother said loudly, 'Oh Matt. How beautiful. Thank you, darling.'

'Let's see.' Emma and Victoria grabbed at the silver-topped scent bottle Matthew had found in an antique shop on the way back from seeing a client. 'It's lovely. Lucky Ma.'

'I'm so glad it isn't what I thought it was going to be,' his mother said.

'What was that?' Victoria asked.

'A hat,' his mother said. 'A purple hat.'

'A *what*?'

Matthew groaned. Both his sisters were on the alert now, ears pricked, tongues hanging out, tails wagging.

'Yes,' his mother said. 'He rang up in the middle of last week and said something about buying me a wide-brimmed hat and a pink Cadillac.'

'What in the world for?' Victoria said.

'I'm not sure, dear.'

Matthew opened his eyes and gave her a steely glance. 'Mother,' he said. 'You're stirring.'

She looked at him mischievously, her eyes bright, and he thought with affection how vivacious she was, how much his father had loved her, how he hoped he himself would find someone like her to love . . .

'Why did you want to buy Granny a purple hat?' Timmy said. 'Only pimps in New York wear hats like that.'

Matthew groaned again, while Victoria said sharply, 'Don't use words you don't understand, Timmy.'

'But I *do* understand. A pimp's a man who—'

'Thank you very much, Timothy,' his father said. 'Go and play with the others, will you?'

'I still don't quite understand why Matt was going to buy you this hat in the first place,' Emma said, in her best headmistress manner. 'You've got your Town Hat, and the one you wear to church on Sundays. And your Cricket Hat, of course.'

'Which one's that?' said Timmy, who had ignored his father's instructions.

'You know. The little straw number with the pink scarf tied round it.'

'Oh, yes. You look really super in that, Gran.'

'Thank you, darling.'

'So why Matthew thinks you need another one . . .'

'Mystifying, isn't it?' said Matt's mother. She glanced across at her son again, and he could see she was on the verge of laughter. 'I expect he was just trying to be kind.'

Negotiating the leafy roads back to the motorway and London, Matthew laughed himself. She really was too much. On the seat beside him lay a bundle of estate agent's particulars which he intended to go through when he got back that evening. If he ever found his dream cottage, he would be able to see more of her than he did at present, she could organize the garden for him, she'd like that . . .

Since they were operating on summer time, it was still not dark. But dusk was falling, the sunshine giving way to the tricky indeterminate light between daytime and night, requiring extra vigilance from the competent motorist which Matthew considered himself to be. He stared ahead, concentrating on the traffic in front.

In his mirror he saw a car come sweeping up behind him, headlights full on, going much too fast, so that when it braked it practically finished up in his boot. He shook his head in an exaggerated way, hoping the driver behind would see him. The driver behind couldn't have cared less. The driver behind suddenly pulled out into the fast lane and zoomed past Matthew at what seemed like a hundred miles an hour, only to squeeze into the space immediately in front of him in order to avoid a lorry approaching from the other direction. Matthew was forced to brake sharply to avoid coming too close.

'Road hog!' he shouted. He flashed his lights a

couple of times. Honestly, the way some people behaved once they got behind the wheel of a car. He couldn't see much of the driver but, judging by the ludicrous black trilby thing the guy was wearing, assumed he was young rather than old, some kind of Hooray Henry who fancied himself just because he was driving a Mercedes. Nice cars, admittedly, but anyone crass enough to wear a hat in a car was going to be a wally, for starters, before you even got on to the way he handled his vehicle . . .

Having reached the motorway, Matthew was able to put his foot down. For once the traffic was light, and driving conditions good. He switched on the car radio and listened to a concerned female voice rabbiting on about the ethics of surrogate parenthood. Two minutes of that was more than enough. He switched stations, heard a Labour backbencher sneering about the Government's education policies, heard a patronizing Conservative minister sneer back, switched stations again. Eventually he scrabbled among his cassettes and put one in. After some preliminary whirring, a couple of voices began screeching something in Italian.

Opera, for God's sake, he thought disgustedly. Where could that have come from? He *loathed* opera.

He opened the window, let the music float, too lazy to change the tape. Mozart, it sounded like. *The Marriage of Figaro*. It came back to him now, Victoria giving him the tape last Christmas, saying what a philistine he was, how he ought to listen occasionally to something that wasn't jazz.

'I do,' he had protested, staring down at the periwigged couple gazing into each other's eyes on the front of the cassette and knowing already that he was going to hate it.

'Victoria doesn't mean your seduction tapes,' Emma had chimed in. 'She means proper classical music.'

'Seduction tapes? What do you—'

'Oh yeah,' Emma jeered. 'We know all about the stuff you play when you've got *women* in for coffee.'

'If only coffee was where it stopped,' Victoria sighed.

'Popular classics,' Emma said, 'designed to make her drop her guard.'

'Not just her *guard*,' said Victoria.

'Which is the very moment at which he pounces,' Emma said.

'Girls, puh-lease,' Matthew said. 'This suggestive banter may be titillating you, but I personally find it absolutely disgusting.'

The two of them shook their heads. 'We're very disappointed in you, Matt,' they choroused.

Humph. Seduction tapes, indeed. If they only knew. Since Annie had left, he had scarcely spoken to a woman. They all seemed insipid, somehow. They all seemed too dark, suddenly, when he'd developed a kind of passion for – well, *tawny* hair. They all had grey eyes, when the only kind he really wanted to gaze into was brown ones.

And what about their shoulder blades?

None of the women he met had the right shoulder blades. Not that he got to look at them, but he just had this gut feeling that were he to strip off their blouses or their silk shirts or their body stockings or their dresses, not one of them would have a shoulder blade to compare with the woman who'd come up to borrow coffee from him.

Until now, he would have called himself very much a leg-and-bum man: he'd been converted in a moment of revelation which rivalled that of Paul on the road to Damascus. One second, he was into rounded posteriors, smooth thighs, slim ankles. The next, the woman from downstairs was walking past him in her little backless number and he was staring at what must surely be Olympic-class shoulder blades, realizing what he had been missing all these years.

It was just beyond the turn-off to Basingstoke that a white car came up behind him at a speed somewhere in the region of 390 miles per hour, its horn blaring, its lights flashing.

'This isn't bloody Brands Hatch,' he shouted, shaking his fist. OK: so maybe he'd swerved a fraction towards the central barrier. There was no need to make such a song and dance about it. He eased back into the middle lane and watched the car rocket past, the sound of its horn trailing on the wind-slip it left behind.

A white Mercedes. He recognized it instantly as belonging to the same trilby-wearing lunatic who'd cut him up earlier. For a moment he contemplated putting his foot down on the accelerator and showing the wally what a *real* car could do. But motorway competitiveness was strictly for joy-riders and idiots. He was far too mature for that kind of childish behaviour.

Half an hour later he passed a service station and saw the same Mercedes standing in the forecourt, the driver, hidden by the car, talking to one of the attendants. Childish or not, he was unable to resist a long derisive blast on his own horn as he sped past.

'That's all right then, innit,' Tony Cashman said. 'You tootle off to New York next month and see what you can pick up. One of these prunes or whatever . . . .'

106

'Prunes?'

'The sculpture bloke you were on about.'

'Koons,' Matthew said. 'Jeff Koons.'

'Yer. Whatever. One of his and whatever else you got in mind. And I'll sign the cheques, all right?'

'Sounds like a fair division of labour to me,' Matthew said, gathering his papers together. He seized the opportunity to sneak a look at his watch. Dammit, it was already five forty-five, and if he was to get back to London, shower, change and arrive at Emma's dinner party on time, he should have left twenty minutes ago at the very least.

'Before you go,' Cashman said. 'Something I want to show you.'

'I really ought to—'

'Won't take a minute.' Cashman heaved himself up from his seat – a pseudo-Tudor construction which looked like a cross between a camel stool and a director's chair – and walked to the door of his office. 'Come on.'

'Couldn't it wait until next ti—'

'Over here, Prescott.' Cashman took Matthew's arm and propelled him bodily out into the hall, down a passageway lined in mosaic depicting the Kingdom 'Neath the Sea (according to some wavy mosaic lettering along the bottom), and out through a doorway into an enclosed yard.

'Just had it delivered yesterday,' Cashman said. 'Wanted to know what you thought of it.' He pushed open a door leading into an outbuilding and said, 'There.'

He was pointing at a large oil painting which leaned against a trestle, surrounded by the debris of packing materials. It showed a maternal figure leaning with outspread arms over a motley brood of naked infants, all chubby arms, rounded bellies and huge spaniel eyes. It was the sort of thing which pubs with lavatories labelled GULLS and BUOYS hung in the saloon bar to add a bit of class.

What am I supposed to say? wondered Matthew, repressing a shudder. That the colours were execrable, the design a cliché, the execution incompetent? That this is pure kitsch, but *bad* kitsch? That I'm a horrible snob and wish I wasn't?

His first instinct was to fling himself to the ground and burst into tears. The second was to find the nearest tree and hang himself from it. He tried to think of something suitable to say. He had used 'striking' so often already in his acquaintanceship with Cashman that it was in danger of wearing out. Besides, Cashman was clearly expecting a paean of praise for his new acquisition.

He cleared his throat.

'So, what's your opinion, Prescott? Be honest,' said Cashman.

'Well,' Matthew said judiciously, when he could hold the silence no longer. 'I – I don't know what to say.' Which was no more than the simple truth.

'Knew you'd like it,' Cashman said.

'Is it . . .' Matthew swallowed. 'Is it called anything?'

'"Motherhood",' Cashman said.

'Just as a matter of interest, where did you find it?'

Cashman shook a knowing finger at him. 'Oh no you don't.'

'Don't what?'

'You can't kid me,' Cashman said jovially. 'If I told you, you'd be down there like a shot, buying up the bloke's entire output, wouldn't you?'

Matthew pulled at his tie which suddenly seemed

108

too tight around his neck. 'You saw right through me,' he said, and couldn't even manage a smile.

All he could think of, as he drove away, was the fact that he was commissioned to purchase works of genuine creative value for a man who could in all seriousness hang on his walls a painting like the one he had just seen. 'Motherhood' for God's sake. And although Cashman had expressed enthusiasm – admittedly of a guarded kind – for Matthew's choice of the works currently on offer, how would he react when they actually turned up at the Hampshire mansion?

Digging in turnips suddenly seemed a much more attractive way of life than flogging fine art.

There were roadworks on the motorway, necessitating single-lane traffic and long tailbacks. The more he glanced at his watch, the slower everything seemed to go. And then, as he was sliding cautiously through the streets towards his block of flats, already ten minutes late for the kick-off at Emma's, there was a flash of green and blue and a parrot landed on the bonnet of his car.

It was a familiar parrot. One he had come to know well over the four years he had owned his flat. It belonged to the old lady on the ground floor, from whose absent-minded care it constantly escaped.

He came slowly to a stop. Through the windscreen the parrot eyed him, its black eye wary but at the same time hinting at previous acquaintance. Matthew looked at his watch once more. He couldn't just leave it. The parrot had belonged to the old lady's sailor husband who had brought it home from Mauritius or somewhere – it varied each time the old girl told the tale – and had been her best friend ever since, more or less bringing up the old lady's children single-handed, according to her, *and* nursing her husband through his final illness. Not that Matthew believed any of that, but the general feeling of mutual dependence was clear.

Cautiously, he opened his door and got out. The parrot hopped to the far side of the bonnet and eyed him again. Matthew walked slowly round the front of his car and reached for the bird. At the very last moment, it evaded his outstretched hand and flew with deliberate impudence to the low wall of the nearest garden. Matthew opened the door on the passenger side of his car, walked back round to the driver's seat and closed that door. He made one more feint at the bird, which squawked loudly at him and flew sideways into a holly bush halfway down the path.

'OK,' Matthew said. 'If that's the way you want to play it.'

The bird put its head on one side, lifted a leg and scratched itself.

'I'll give you a count of ten,' Matthew said, looking at his watch again – Emma was going to have a *fit* – 'and then I'm going to drive away.'

The bird flew back to the wall and shuffled sideways towards him but when he reached for it, it reared away.

'. . . nine, TEN,' Matthew said loudly.

He got back into his car. After a while, there was a sheepish squawk and the parrot hopped on to the passenger seat.

'I knew you'd see it my way,' Matthew said. He leaned across, slammed the door shut and drove on.

'You're not going to believe this,' he said, walking into Emma's elegant flower-filled hall. He handed her the placatory bouquet he had brought and followed her towards the kitchen. He was still damp from the shower, and his suit needed pressing, something he had noted last time he wore it but had forgotten to organize.

'You're right, I'm not,' she said crossly.

It was obviously the wrong time to bring up either 'Motherhood' or parrots, or deaf old ladies watching *The Bill* and unable to hear the frantic peals of the doorbell. 'I'm really sorry I'm late,' he said.

'*Late?*' she hissed. 'We're on the coffee.'

He followed her into the dining room. Thank God he knew most of the people there, all of whom would forgive him, if they had even noticed he wasn't there. He waved at Leo, his brother-in-law, smiled at Susannah, the potter, at Bill and Bridget, at Susannah's husband who was in banking, at—

'Well now,' Emma said. 'I think you know everyone. Except – uh—'

It was *her*.

'We've – uh – already met,' he said, and heard, to his astonishment, his voice break with the emotion of the moment. How was it possible that she was sitting here in his sister's house, the girl with the hair, the eyes, the *shoulder blades*, who had haunted him for so many days?

He knew he was smiling idiotically as Emma turned and looked enquiringly at him. With the fine-tuned sensibilities of the sister anxious to see her brother settled, she had immediately cottoned on to something, some emotion, some frisson passing between him and the woman from the flat below his. He gave her a look of appeal. Tomorrow she would be on the phone, first to him, giving him the third degree, secondly to Victoria to pass on what she had

111

extracted from him, and thirdly to their mother.

He didn't care. He didn't care about anything except the fact that he was sitting down next to *her*, that she was alone, which must mean – mustn't it? – that she was unattached. He smelled her scent, took in the ringless fingers, felt her thigh warm for a moment against his.

'Are you always this late?' she said coolly, and her voice was as he remembered it, richer, smoother than any other voice he had ever heard in his life before.

The candles were reflected in her dark eyes as he said boldly, refusing to let the opportunity slip this time as he had been forced to before, 'I won't be tomorrow.'

'And what's happening tomorrow?' she said.

'I'm inviting you for dinner.'

A look of disbelief crossed her face. 'And what makes you think I'll accept?'

No reason really, he thought. Except that I want you to so badly. He made some facetious remark about the excellence of his coffee, and she smiled.

'By the way, I'm Alexandra Maitland,' she said.

'Matthew Prescott.' He wanted to add that names didn't matter, that he didn't care what she was called or what she did, where she came from. Past and future were of no consequence: it was enough to be sitting here with her, now.

Susannah asked him something and he answered, mechanically swallowed the food which Emma had saved for him, exchanged jokes with his brother-in-law, generally behaved like a dinner guest. But all the time he was intensely aware of the woman beside him, of the air she breathed, how her hair shone in the candlelight, the delicate way she held her head, the incredible line of her mouth.

112

From the end of the table he could feel Emma watching him, and some instinct of self-preservation finally roused him from the spell which seemed to have been cast over him.

He told them about the parrot, about the old lady, heard their shrieks of laughter. 'And that was *after* I'd finally got off the motorway,' he said. 'Which was horrendous enough in itself.'

'Motorways,' shuddered Alexandra. 'Don't talk about them. I had an absolutely nightmare drive up from the West Country last weekend.'

'Really?' He turned to her but she had already carried on.

'I got caught behind one of those ghastly BMW drivers who think they own the road,' she said. 'Veering about from side to side, slowing down and then speeding up when you try to overtake. It was awful.'

'Tell me about it,' Susannah said, raising her eyes to the ceiling. 'The roads are full of them.'

'And they're *always* men,' said Emma.

'There's something about a BMW,' Alexandra Maitland said, 'which seems to go to a man's head, turn them into traffic hazards.'

'Here, steady on,' protested Matthew. 'That's what I drive. And I'm one of the safest drivers around.' He drank some wine. 'And if you really want to know the worst drivers of the lot, it's the ones who drive Mercedes. White ones.' He looked solemnly round at them. 'And wear hats when they're driving. Don't you agree?'

They all groaned. 'It's a dead giveaway, isn't it?' his brother-in-law agreed. 'As soon as you see that gorblimey cap in front of you—'

'It was a rather flash black trilby in *my* case,' said Matt.

113

'– you know you're in for some of the worst driving on record.'

'*I* drive a Mercedes,' Alexandra said coolly.

'Do you?' Matt said. 'What colour?'

'As it happens, white.'

'I see.' He laughed. 'So perhaps it was you who came up behind me last weekend and practically ended up in my boot.'

'Very possibly.' Alexandra gave him a considering stare. 'And perhaps you were the idiot who kept swerving so dangerously between the lanes.'

'Almost certainly,' Matt said lightly. 'I *was* down in Somerset last weekend.'

'So was I.'

'Aha.' He lowered his voice. 'So what about it? Are you having dinner with me tomorrow?'

'I can't,' she said. 'I'm truly sorry.' She looked as if she meant it. 'But someone's flying in from New York – a former colleague – and I really have to keep myself available until I know what plans have been made.'

From the careful way she avoided mentioning this former colleague's sex, Matthew knew it had to be male. A kind of despair gripped him. He told himself not to be such an idiot: he couldn't be the only man who found her irresistible, after all. But until he had evidence that she was involved elsewhere, he was going to go for it.

'When's the first day you're free?' he asked urgently.

'Next Wednesday,' she said.

'You're no longer free,' he said.

She smiled at him. 'All right.'

# 6

Cameron was already half an hour later than Alexandra had budgeted for him to be. And that was including the very worst possible scenario of disasters she could devise. Even if there had been three fatal accidents on the Piccadilly line in from Heathrow plus two mechanical failures beyond London Transport's control, he should have been here by now.

He had said he would pick her up at the office, so that's where she was. The others had all gone home hours ago. Alone, with most of the lights out and the cleaning ladies dotting about in the corridors, she tidied the papers on her desk for the fiftieth time. In the weeks she had been here, she had managed to create an area of ordered calm which spoke of high efficiency and brisk management. Nina had already commented favourably on it, throwing pointed looks at both the Health and Beauty desk and the disordered alcove from which Fashion operated.

'And you always dress so well, too,' she said approvingly. 'That's *good*, Alex.'

'I'm glad you—'

'It gives the magazine the right image when people can see that its representatives *care*.'

'Quite.' Alexandra was not entirely sure that she chose her clothes with the magazine in mind. In fact, she knew darn well that she didn't. On the other hand, she did care about it. What surprised her was just how much. The others tended sometimes to laugh at Nina's dedication to *Athene*, the way she seemed to live and breathe the magazine, think of nothing else. It was a surprise to find that she was beginning to feel the same way about it herself.

There was an article on collagen injections lying in front of her. Collagen, she read, plumped out the flesh beneath the skin, thus eliminating those telltale wrinkles. Yes, well. Health and Beauty was a required factor in any woman's magazine, as was Fashion. But for her, the challenge in *Athene* lay in bringing to the attentions of the readers items which were not of specifically female concerns. There was *Vogue* to cater for the high-fashion interests; there was any number of weekly magazines which provided the usual mix of what society fondly regarded as feminine issues: child-rearing, beauty hints, recipes, light fiction, articles on celebrities and, of course, the obligatory occasional piece on the ghastly lives some of the 'ordinary' readers led.

As a formula, there was nothing wrong with it. As far as it went. But it didn't go far enough. It missed out on a small but significant slice of the market. So many women today were independent high achievers, controlling their own money and their own lives. They already knew what they looked good in, which make-up suited them, how to handle their bodies or their children. They were too busy forging their careers to want to spend much time in reading about ageing pop-stars marrying eighteen-year-old virgins, or the crisis in some show-biz liaison. They weren't particularly bothered by telltale wrinkles.

It was a question of how to give them what they wanted.

Thinking about it, Alexandra picked up the sample pack of a new hand cream and rubbed some into the backs of her hands. She looked through some copy which her assistant had left on her desk and crossed out a typing error. She read the first page of a review copy of the new novel by a Royal Shakespeare Company actor and put it down again when she realized she hadn't taken in a single word.

Where was Cameron?

Had he changed his mind about coming to England? Had he come to England and changed his mind about seeing *her*? Had his plane crashed?

Restlessly, she got up and went into Nina's office where a small black-and-white television sat on top of the filing cabinets. It was 9.57, three minutes to news time, an hour and fifty-seven minutes after the very latest she had thought he would arrive.

Waiting for the *Ten o'Clock News*, she wondered whether, if – no, *when* – he did arrive, she would melt into his arms. Whether he would even want her to.

She listened to the headlines and then switched off. The crisis in the Balkans, pollution on Mediterranean beaches, Sadam Hussein behaving like a cad, a Royal behaving even worse . . . Nothing about planes crashing, or delays in New York. Nothing like that.

She picked up the phone and dialled Heathrow, asked for Flight Information, was told that the flight from New York had arrived on time some three and a half hours ago.

So where was bloody Cameron?

She opened the top drawer of her desk. Lying there, together with a photograph, was a withered red rose tied with a piece of scarlet ribbon: the rose

117

Cameron had sent her before she left New York. It had been a sentimental gesture on her part to keep it; now she asked herself what was the point? She dropped it into her wastepaper basket. Then fished it out again. It was all she had left of him and of the days they had spent together. Yet she knew that if the scentless hothouse rose had symbolized something intangible about their relationship, the dead one surely signified something quite concrete: that it was finished, over and done with.

She picked up the photograph and studied it. She and Cameron, arms around each other, facing the camera and squinting into the sunlight. She had been so happy that day. They had driven up to Maine for the weekend to stay in the house on the coast owned by Cameron's aunt. It had been hot, humid almost to the point of unbearability. They had swum in the huge Atlantic breakers, diving from the tumbled rocks into cool green water, lithe as seals. And there had been seals, too, out on two offshore outcrops of stone, basking in the heat, barking sometimes at them. The crash of the waves, the drifting scent of pine from the woods on the shore above them, the salt on their skins . . . They'd barbecued lobsters, drunk wine, slept out all night in a hammock, wrapped in each other. She had wanted the night to stretch into infinity – but of course it had not. They had woken in the morning, stiff and damp, rushed into the house to warm themselves in the huge old-fashioned bathtub, cooked an enormous breakfast and driven back to the city so Cameron could interview some visiting fireman from Washington. And although he had promised they would return to the seaside house, somehow they never had.

'It was a day to remember for the rest of our lives,

wasn't it?' a voice said behind her, and she jumped, startled.

'Cameron!' she said.

'Sugar baby.' He held out his arms to her. He looked as he always had, with the same lopsided grin.

'Why are you so late? Where have you—'

'Don't start in with the questions,' he said. 'Kiss me.'

She stepped into his arms. He tasted of wine, of coffee. He smelled of cigars and, fleetingly, of herbs. Head against his chest, she frowned, thinking: herbs? More specifically, oregano. Has he already been out to dinner with someone before coming here?

If she asked, he would accuse her of nagging, of wanting to keep tabs on him. He would ask what the hell did it matter *where* he had been, now that he was here? He would say she always did ask too many questions and why didn't she stay cool, tell him she loved him?

That's what had happened before, in New York. That was why they had drifted apart. Against his shirt, she felt the old confusion again, the tangle of love and anger. How could you kiss someone properly when you knew they had let you sit there for hours waiting for them while they went off and had dinner with someone else? With some other *woman*, probably. How could you *melt*? Even though your knees trembled and your heart fluttered and you felt weak with longing, how could you *melt*, knowing that?

She pulled away from him. 'I'm starving,' she said lightly. 'Let's go and find somewhere to eat and you can fill me in on all the news.'

'OK,' he said. 'Let's do that. But I should warn you, I'm not all that hungry.'

119

'Aren't you?' she said.

He looked away from her and she knew she was right. She had seen that shifty look before. 'They fed us about five times on the plane,' he said. 'You know the way it is. They've got to keep the passengers occupied so they don't start worrying about how the plane manages to stay up in the air.'

'Yes,' she said. 'I know.'

They sat opposite each other in the little Covent Garden restaurant they used to patronize two years ago. Cameron had wanted to go somewhere else, but she had insisted. Francisco, the head waiter, seemed surprised when Cameron walked in. Quickly he led them to a table, produced menus and wine, but deep in her despairing heart Alex was convinced that it was the surprise of someone seeing a customer who had already been in once that evening. Definitely not the surprise and pleasure he would have shown at seeing Cameron again after so long.

Miserable, she broke a breadstick into pieces, let him fill her wine glass a second time. Was she being neurotic? She'd been waiting for this moment for so long, and all she could do, now that it had finally arrived, was think the worst of him, instead of simply being happy to see him again.

'How's the new job?' he said. 'Going well?'

'Terrifically,' she said.

'That's great, Alex.' His gaze wandered round the room as though he were looking for someone. Making an effort she could see quite clearly, he took both her hands in his. 'That's really wonderful, kid. I know you've got a great future ahead of you.'

'Do you?'

'Sure you have. With your looks and your talent, what's to stop you going right to the top?'

120

'Trouble is, I don't know exactly what the top is.'

'An editorship of your own, wouldn't you think?'

'Sometimes I wonder if that's really worth achieving.'

'Of course it is.' He pushed the candle stuck in a straw-covered bottle to one side and held her hands tighter, smiling at her. The long lines on either side of his face – starving dimples, she used to call them – deepened. 'Darling Alex, you're a career woman, after all. This is your chance to go for gold, you know. You work hard, you have a real flair, you're already a success at your job, and you know it fulfils you.'

'Does it?'

'Other women opt for husbands and babies,' he said. 'You want something more out of life than that.'

She looked at him steadily. 'I wonder.'

'Don't wonder. Just have faith in yourself.'

'And you, Cameron. What do you want?'

He looked away from her. 'What most guys want, I guess.'

'What's that, exactly?'

'Someone to love. A couple of kids. Somewhere to settle down.'

'That's not what you used to think,' she said and was horrified to hear the accusing tone of her voice, the almost-shrillness.

'No. But I was younger in those days. Maybe I've matured since then.'

Maybe you've met someone else, she wanted to say. Maybe you just had dinner with her, and wish you were with her now. She pushed away her plate, almost untouched.

'Are you coming home with me tonight?' she

121

asked, and knew the answer before he even started to speak.

'Well, honey, that could be kind of awkward. See, I've got to talk to this guy over a working breakfast at my hotel first thing in the morning.'

'I could stay with you,' she offered, despising herself.

'I'd have to get up real early,' he said. 'I'd hate to disturb your beauty sleep and all . . .'

'I don't mind,' she said, watching him squirm, feeling nothing at all except self-disgust at allowing herself to get into this situation. At still wanting him, even though she knew herself betrayed.

'But *I* do,' he said. He glanced at his watch. 'I can't have that. I've kept you up late enough as it is.'

She leaned forward. 'Cameron.'

'Yeah?'

'Just for once in your life be honest with me.'

'I'm always—'

'No. You're not, Cameron. But this time, please don't lie.'

He watched her warily. 'What's the question, Alex?'

'This person you've been with tonight, or you're going to . . . this *woman*—'

He opened his mouth to protest but she shook her head.

'Is she someone you just met, someone you went off with on the spur of the moment? Or is it a long-term thing, something which will lead to the things you just said you wanted: the wife, the kids, the home?'

Either way, she thought tiredly, it doesn't really matter. I love him but I value my good opinion of myself more. And if I carry on with this relationship

122

I shall just end up where I was in New York, miserable, unhappy, alone.

Cameron floundered, staring down at the checked tablecloth, drinking from his glass, checking hers. 'Beats me,' he said finally. 'I really couldn't say.'

'That means it's probably someone you met on the plane.'

'Yes, but . . . it's different, Alex. It really is. I've never felt like this before – not so suddenly.' He shrugged.

'I see.'

'It's different this time.'

Alex stood up. 'Cameron,' she said gently. 'Don't you realize that with you, it's *always* different? And probably always will be?'

Walking out, finding a cab, leaning back against its leather upholstery, she wished she felt something stronger than lethargy. Hatred, perhaps. Contempt. Even compassion for a man so much at the mercy of his physical urges. But she didn't. She felt nothing at all.

In the lobby of her building, waiting for the lift to come down, she found herself wondering whether she would bump into Matthew Prescott before next Wednesday. And later, falling finally into sleep with her heart as cold as a snowball in her chest, she thought: at least there *is* Wednesday.


'Any ideas, people,' Nina said, 'on this magnificent summer morning?' She surveyed her team, variously engaged in poking a pencil at an avocado (Helena, Health and Beauty), removing nail varnish (Felicity, Fashion), reading a raunchy letter from the author who was her lover (Lydia, Literary) and fiddling with the hinge of a pair of sunglasses (Petronella,

123

Problem Page). Carol, the Cookery Editor, was still down with chicken-pox, according to Barry, the husband they had thought she was divorcing, and with whose prowess on the orgasm front they were all far more familiar than they wished to be.

Only Alex seemed more than half awake.

'Ideas? What are those?' Felicity said, lobbing a disgusting cotton-wool ball at the wastepaper basket with the accuracy of a Harlem Globetrotter.

'How about something really radical on the dangers of sunbathing without blocker?' said Helena, who had just found a mole on her arm which had definitely not been there at the beginning of the summer.

'There's nothing really radical to say about it,' said Lydia, not looking up from her letter.

'And besides, we're talking about the November issue,' Nina said. '*If* you remember.'

She brushed at the folds of her silk Versace blouse and smoothed her short black skirt over her hips. Nina lived in the constant expectation that a horde of paparazzi was about to burst into her office and start firing off flashbulbs. Should this unlikely event take place, she did not want to be caught looking less than her usual immaculate self. She preened her elegant nose, turning her head slightly in order to give them all the benefit of her profile.

'November? Oh God,' said Petronella. 'I always go into a massive depression in November. Always. Every year. Never fails.'

'How about something on depression?' Felicity said. 'Why women suffer from it more than men do, why—'

'Do they?' asked Helena.

'*I* certainly do,' Petronella said.

'What about an Italian issue?' Alex suggested.

That roused them a little, apart from Nina who was in a permanent state of arousal.

'Italian – that's good,' Lydia mused. 'I was reading an awfully good crime novel the other day, set in Italy. Judging by the photograph on the back, the author's really dishy, too. I wouldn't mind doing an interview with him.'

'Italian fashions,' said Felicity, 'the ready-to-wear collections – one of us could go over to Milan . . .'

'And a whole feature on Italian food,' said Nina, 'presuming Carol's back in time. Otherwise we'll have to do it between us.'

'Italian restaurants,' said Lydia.

'Not just the food,' said Alex, 'but the wine, too.'

'Yes, please,' said Petronella.

'Italian shops in Soho.'

'Italian opera.'

'Films . . .'

'Shoes . . .'

'Art . . .'

'Politics . . .'

'And there's all those fabulous Italian princesses, ready to hand out their beauty tips and talk about their clothes and their parties,' Helena said.

'Good idea,' Nina said. 'Let's think about it some more – but it sounds like something we could go for.' She beamed approval. 'That's *good*, Alex.'

Wednesday arrived. At eight o'clock Alex was knocking on Matthew Prescott's door. She hoped he wouldn't be drunk. Although he had been late at Emma Chisholm's dinner party last week, he had seemed perfectly sober, but you could never tell with alcoholics. At least she wouldn't have far to go home

125

if the evening turned into an unmitigated disaster, with him weeping drunken tears and slobbering all over her shoes while he told her the sad story of his life.

She had taken a considerable amount of trouble over her appearance, she realized now, waiting for him to open the door. More so than was necessary. Or desirable. She didn't want him to think she had dressed up for him, or anything. It was just that after a weekend of weeping over Cameron, and two absolutely hectic days at the office with Helena now also down with chicken-pox, she felt like a bit of glamour. This was why she was wearing her Ralph Lauren silk crepe trousers and matching jacket with a white Armani shell underneath, and her favourite silver earrings.

Matthew Prescott seemed to be taking a heck of a time to open the door. Briefly she wondered whether he'd already drunk himself into oblivion and was lying in a paralytic stupor on the hearthrug while saucepans boiled dry on the stove and vegetables burned to a crisp. She lifted her hand to knock once again, and the door opened.

He didn't speak. Just stared at her. Was he sloshed? Shy? Or simply bewildered at seeing her there, having forgotten his invitation last week.

'You *were* expecting me?' she said.

'Of course. I've been waiting for this moment all week. Come in.'

She did so, leaning slightly towards him and giving a surreptitious sniff. Nothing but cologne, something discreet and lemony. No stale booze or anything.

'What can I give you to drink?' he said, leading the way into a sitting room which was the twin of hers.

'A glass of white wine, please.'

126

She sat down on a modern sofa in cream and chrome and surveyed the room. A fire leaped in the hearth under a marble mantelpiece identical to the one in her own flat. There was a lot of contemporary art on the walls, not exactly her taste but not overly crude and jarring. There were flowers, some handsome furniture, one or two pieces of sleek modern sculpture, good lighting. A pleasant room, she thought. A *warm* room.

'I'm going to have a whisky,' he said. 'My tongue's hanging out. It's been a horrendous day at work.'

'What exactly do you do?' she asked.

He told her. It sounded fascinating. She remembered one of the ideas chucked around at the brainstorming session a week ago: a series on Eligible Males.

'*Not* aristos,' Lydia had said. 'But ordinary good-looking chaps with decent careers and no ties – for the moment.'

They all knew she wanted to nominate her boyfriend as one of the Eligible Males. As an aspiring bestselling author, he could do with the publicity. Then Felicity had pointed out that *GQ* had run a feature along similar lines in their last issue, and they abandoned the idea.

Was Matthew Prescott an eligible male? It was a question she had not thought to ask until now, but there certainly didn't seem to be any obvious *Mrs* Prescott hanging about in the background. And he had turned up alone at Emma Chisholm's house . . .

'What about you?' he said, then checked himself. 'But you work for that women's magazine, don't you? *Athene.*'

'How did you know that?'

'Emma told me. Emma Chisholm.'

'She's terribly nice,' Alex said warmly. 'We got on really well.'

'I'm glad to hear it.'

'I'd only met her once before that evening, but I feel we'll be friends for life.' Alex sipped her wine, which was cool and fruity, with just the right degree of dryness. 'Do you know her well?'

Matthew looked at her quizzically. 'Extremely well.'

'Oh?'

'You obviously hadn't realized she was my sister.'

'No. As a matter of fact, I hadn't.'

Immediately Alex thought: so *that's* why she invited me to dinner, to try and match me up with her semi-alcoholic brother. And I thought it was because we seemed to be so much on the same wavelength.

'I've got two sisters,' Matthew said. 'And a mother. I love them dearly, but they're the bane of my existence.'

'Why's that?'

'They spend their entire lives trying to match me up with the most unsuitable women you could possibly hope to meet.'

'Really?' she said coldly.

He obviously realized how that sounded. 'Not that I meant to imply that that's why Emma – that *you* were—' He gestured helplessly, the sentence impossible to retrieve now. 'What about you? Have you got family?'

'A younger brother,' she said. 'David.'

'Is that the chap who was helping you move in the other day?'

'Yes. And I have a father, who lives down in Somerset.'

128

'Whereabouts?'

'In a place called Merry Beauchamp.'

'How extraordinary,' said Matthew.

'Is it?'

'It's just that my mother lives a few miles away from there, in Blindenhall.'

They stared at each other. Then Matthew said, 'I grew up there. Don't tell me you did too.'

She laughed. 'No. My father was in the Army. We moved around a lot, until we were old enough to go to boarding school. He retired there.'

'Does he like it?'

'Loves it. It's within reach of the cricket ground at Taunton. He likes watching cricket.'

'My father used to be a member of the County Cricket Club.'

'*My* father even used to play, until he broke his hip earlier this year.'

'Is he over it?'

'Not really. It's taking a long time to heal.'

'When you get older, these things take so much longer, don't they?'

'He's not that old,' Alex said. 'Sixty-one in a couple of months.'

'My mother's still only fifty-eight,' Matthew said, somewhat irrelevantly.

'His hip's not mending as quickly as it ought, which makes him very impatient. When he gets frustrated, he tends to shout a bit.'

'Don't we all?' murmured Matthew.

'Poor old Colonel – he does love his cricket and of course he can't drive a car at the moment. It's almost impossible for him to get to the decent matches.'

'Somerset's playing Kent next week.'

'I know. I was going to go down and take him, but

– well, something's come up and I can't. And my brother's in Hong Kong all that week.'

Matthew shook his head. 'It really is extraordinary, though, you have to admit. I mean, there was I, living in Blindenhall. And there were you—'

'Goodness,' she said. She opened her eyes wide at him, teasing. 'Maybe we even passed each other in the supermarket. Or got on the same bus. Or parked – wow! – in the *same car park*.'

'Come on,' he said, laughing. 'You can't deny it's a bit of a coincidence.'

She looked at the papers piled beside the arm of the sofa. 'And you're thinking of moving back?' She picked up a sheet of estate agent's particulars.

'Not really.'

'Then why these?'

He hesitated. 'It's just one of those dreams the urban yuppy like me goes in for,' he said. 'I'm not really into the whole bit of owning a second home, but I'd dearly love to have a cottage in the country.' He laughed self-mockingly and filled her glass again. 'I don't suppose it'll ever happen, but I can see it so clearly. Thatch and apple trees and lavender bushes by the door – you know the kind of thing.'

'Inglenooks,' she said.

'Absolutely. Masses of those.'

'Blackened beams.'

He smiled at her. 'How did you guess?'

'I've had the same dream,' she said. 'Sometimes London just gets a bit too much.'

'The man who is tired of London is tired of life,' he quoted.

'I know all that. But the noise and the traffic and the petrol fumes and the stress of getting around – occasionally I feel like just selling up, giving my designer clothes to Oxfam, and starting again in a simple dress of dimity—'

'Dimity?'

'– weaving my own bed linen and keeping bees and putting up preserves.'

'With me it's digging in turnips,' he said.

She wrinkled her forehead. 'You're obviously deeper into this dream than I am. I *loathe* turnips.'

'So do I,' he said. They both burst out laughing.

Over the excellent dinner he produced, they talked more about themselves. Although they discovered they had hardly a single taste in common, he was nonetheless a witty and amusing host and she found herself laughing in a way she had not done for a considerable time. It felt good.

As he began to take the cork out of a second bottle of wine, she said, 'Look . . .'

'What at? You?' he said. 'I'm more than happy to oblige.'

'I wanted to ask you something . . .'

'I read the *Independent*, I'm gainfully employed and all my teeth are my own,' he said.

'No. I'm serious.'

'What is it?' He came back to the table and sat down. His eyes were an amazing blue-grey colour, she could not help noticing. Almost aquamarine.

'I just have to know: have you got a drink problem?' she blurted out.

'A what? A *drink* pro—' He looked at her and flushed slightly. 'Look. I'm not going to pretend I'm a teetotaller. But I don't drink very much – it slows up the reflexes and I play squash and tennis two or three times a week.'

'But that night I moved in, you were—'

'Very definitely the worse for wear,' he agreed. 'I'd

131

been out with a client, and one thing led to another.'

'That's a relief,' she said.

'My sobriety is a byword among the members of the English judiciary system. Judges comment on it.'

'I'm delighted to hear it.'

'I'm almost afraid to offer you another glass,' he said, 'in case you get the wrong idea.'

'You've laid my fears to rest,' she said. 'So why not?'

He talked a little about Anthony Cashman. Nothing that could be labelled as a breach of client-confidentiality, but enough to engage her attention.

'Could be something of interest there for you, too,' he said.

'Why?'

'He's married to Cindy Hill.'

The name was, of course, familiar. 'But we don't go in for top models,' she said. 'For one thing, our readers don't expect it from us. For another, even if they did, we couldn't afford her fees.'

'She didn't strike me as awfully thrilled with things,' he said, staring into the fire, remembering the look on Cindy's face as she recognized him.

'Is that marriage problems, do you think?'

'I don't know. I haven't seen enough of her. I think not, though.'

'Why do you say that?'

'They seemed happy together. Lovey-dovey and so on. He was talking about having her portrait painted: you don't do that if your marriage is heading for the rocks.'

'Unless he hasn't noticed.' Alex frowned thoughtfully. 'I wonder if there's a feature to be written on the downside of fashion modelling. You always hear about the glamour – plus, of course, the obligatory remarks about hard work and the horror of it all. Maybe I should try and get in touch with her, see if she's got anything interesting to say.'

'Good idea.'

'Except, if I remember rightly, she never gives interviews.'

'Really?'

'I think I've got that right,' Alex said. She was feeling pleasantly buzzed. She smiled at Matt across the bowl of fruit he had put on the table, her perceptions heightened by the relaxed atmosphere of the evening, very much aware of the bloom on the grapes, the green of the apples, the soft fuzz on the peaches. The fragrance of woodsmoke from the fire hung in the air, mingling with the scent of wine, the warmth of lighted candles.

Reluctantly she put down her glass. 'If this was a restaurant, they'd be putting chairs on tables about now,' she said.

'And I'd be asking you back to my place for coffee.'

She smiled. 'But of course I wouldn't accept.'

He raised his eyebrows, murmuring something about it depending, surely, on the choice of coffee. 'Come and sit down on something more comfortable,' he said. 'I'll bring it in and you can decide then whether you'd accept or not.'

Alexandra leaned back against the sofa cushions. Matthew Prescott was a nice man, even though she could not imagine ever feeling about him the way she did – *had* – about Cameron. Not that burn-in-the-gut feeling, that melt-of-the-heart feeling.

'What do you think?' he said. 'Would you accept my invitation back to my place for coffee?'

'Mmm,' she said, sipping from her cup. 'Deserves to be savoured . . .'

She let her eyes linger on him suggestively and watched him react, watched him wonder what exactly she meant. He thought she was giving him an unmistakable message of availability. She remembered the time she had returned the coffee she had borrowed from him, and how she had instinctively known there was a woman waiting for him in this very room.

The memory chilled the warmth she could feel gathering inside her, the warmth which might have proved treacherous if she lingered here with this – yes – definitely attractive man.

She stood up. 'Pity I have to leave.'

He choked on his coffee. 'Leave? but we've—'

'I'm on the first flight to Milan in the morning.'

'But that's terrible,' he said. He put down his cup and got up to come and stand very close to her.

'Yes.' She raised her face to his. If he kisses me, she thought, I won't stop him. It might be quite nice – might be *very* nice. She knew she had drunk more wine than was wise.

And then he said something facetious, and she stepped away from him. She turned to look at him over her shoulder, then walked towards the front door. 'It was a wonderful evening,' she said.

'But now it's over?'

She smiled her enigmatic smile. 'For the moment.'

Milan was one of the big cities where she felt very much at home. She had spent a year here once, working as an au pair for the family of one of the big industrialists. For years she had holidayed in Italy and her command of the language was good enough for all but the most difficult of situations. And there was the opera house . . .

Kicking her shoes off in her hotel bedroom, hanging up her Chanel suit, removing her earrings, she couldn't help feeling glad – sorry though she undoubtedly was, of *course* – that poor Felicity had been laid low with the chicken-pox. The trip to Milan would otherwise have undoubtedly fallen to her, as the nominal fashion editor. Instead, Nina had said, 'It was your idea, Alex, this Italian issue. I think you should go and do the fashion bit in Milan.'

'Fantastic,' Alex had said.

'My assistant's prepared a list of people to see and places you should visit.'

'I've got some ideas on—'

Nina produced her terrifying crocodilic grin. 'But of course if you have any ideas of your own about who else you should talk to, go ahead.'

'Right.'

'We've called up the PR firm we normally liaise with and given them the name of the hotel you're booked into. Someone from there will be in touch. Do you want to be met at the airport?'

'No thanks.' She much preferred to take a cab in to the centre of town when she was on these assignments. It gave her a chance to put everything on hold for a brief while, recharge the batteries after a flight. She did not like flying and the mental energy involved in getting through the ordeal without flinging herself down in the aisle and drumming her heels was considerable.

'And remember, Alex, the whole magazine's behind you on this one.'

What did she mean, exactly? 'That's great,' Alex said.

135

'Win this one for *Athene*,' Nina said.

'Right.'

Win *what* one? Sometimes, Alex thought, eating a grape from the bowl provided by the management and then walking barefooted across to open the windows and step out on to the balcony, sometimes Nina seemed to be living on her own private planet.

Would she herself end up like that, if she achieved her ambition of becoming the managing editor of a magazine? Was that how *she* would talk to her staff, in that faintly surrealist way?

Behind her, the telephone shrilled. It was the hotel receptionist. 'Signorita Maitland?'

'Yes?'

'Signor San Lorenzo is here for you.'

'Signor who?' Alex had never heard the name before. Was he the man from the PR agency?

'San Lorenzo?'

'Uh – I'll be down in about half an hour,' she said. She hoped he wasn't somebody hugely important. She wanted to shower, to change, to relax for a few minutes. She had only just arrived, after all. 'Does he mind waiting?'

There was a murmur of conversation, then the receptionist said, 'He will wait for you in the bar. OK?'

'OK,' she said.

Carlo San Lorenzo was extraordinarily good-looking. He stood up when Alexandra came into the bar, held out his hand, smiled, showing beautiful teeth. He handed her something, murmuring, 'Welcome to Italy.'

She looked down at the two pink roses, the green spray of fern. 'Thank you so much,' she said. She

136

lifted the flowers and smelled their cool scent.

'Roses for an English rose,' he said. 'Though I am bound to say, Signorita Maitland, that you are more beautiful than any flower.'

Normally Alexandra was not susceptible to that kind of come-on rubbish. But there was no mistaking the admiration in his eyes, the way they lingered on her. And after the smarting ache left by Cameron's faithlessness, it was pleasant to bask in the kind of warmth – spurious though it might be – which such admiration provided.

They discussed business for a while, over the bottle of champagne he ordered. He planned to take care of her himself over the next five days, he told her. He had drawn up a long list of people she ought to talk to during the day: fashion houses, designers, a couple of artists' studios, a gallery specializing in contemporary prints. 'And on two evenings I have tickets for La Scala,' he said.

'You *have*?'

'Yes. We shall see *La Traviata* tomorrow, and *Ernani* the following evening. I hope this will not be too much Verdi for you.'

'Who can have too much Verdi?' asked Alex.

His eyes rested on her appreciatively. 'What an excellent response,' he said. 'And how – if I may say so – unEnglish.'

'What do you mean?'

'So often your fellow countrymen appear to despise the Italians.'

'The loss is theirs,' said Alexandra robustly. 'How could anyone despise a country which gave us the Renaissance, Venice, Michelangelo?'

'Leonardo.'

'The Sistine Chapel.'

137

'The Colosseum.'

'Benetton.'

They smiled at each other. I'm going to enjoy this week, Alexandra thought.

Carlo proved to be an informed and cultured man. He took his assignment seriously, accompanying Alexandra to the various meetings he had fixed up for her, talking knowledgeably about everything from architecture to fashion, from music to ice-cream.

She wore her Bill Blass cocktail dress to the opera, and was glad she had done so, finding herself by no means overdressed. When Rodolfo poured out his love for Violetta, Carlo sighed and put his hand on her arm. Turning her head, she saw tears in his eyes.

'So beautiful,' he murmured. 'So sad.'

She thought: and so Italian. How many Englishmen gave in to their emotions like that? She wondered whether Matthew Prescott would weep at the beauty of Verdi's music and remembered, with a little jolt of her heart, that he hated opera.

Carlo walked her back to her hotel, after they had eaten baked swordfish and a tender salad at a small restaurant he knew. She was afraid she might have a problem getting rid of him – not altogether sure she wanted to – but in the lobby he merely took her hand and raised it to his lips.

'*A domani*,' he said, and stared deep, deep into her eyes, leaving her feeling just a trifle breathless.

The two of them were sitting at a table in the open air. Lamps swung above their heads, red and green and white in the warm darkness. They were drinking wine, waiting for the *abbacchio* they had ordered. They had started with *fichi con prosciutto*, green figs with Parma ham, washed down with a light wine which Carlo had promised she would enjoy. And she had. She felt remarkably at ease with this man who only three nights before had been a total stranger. Was it their shared interests? Or the romance of Italy on a summer's night? Was it just the wine, or the heart-warming sense of being seen as a beautiful woman? Carlo projected approbation effortlessly, making no secret of his liking and admiration for her.

'I shall be visiting London very soon,' Carlo said.

'Then it will be my turn to look after *you*,' Alex said. The thought was curiously pleasant. After Cameron, it was wonderful to be so esteemed, so cosseted. Carlo brought her flowers each day when he picked her up from her hotel, often adding other gifts: a silk scarf, chocolate truffles, a pair of sunglasses after she had mislaid her own. Always small things, nothing she could have a qualm about accepting, which made them all the more delightful.

'I shall be looking forward to seeing you again from the moment we have to say goodbye,' Carlo said.

Alexandra smiled. With Carlo it was sometimes difficult to judge where his somewhat flamboyant courtesy ended and true feeling took over.

He held both her hands in his and brought them to his lips. 'Tell me, Alexandra . . .' He paused.

'Tell you what?'

'You wear no rings – is there, then, no man in your life?'

'Not at the moment.'

'How is this possible? Are you not inundated with men wishing to become your lover?'

'Not particularly.'

'Then Englishmen must be even more brutish than I have long suspected,' he cried theatrically.

'I have some say in the matter, too,' Alexandra said.

There was always this line to be walked, she mused. On the one hand, you wanted to play down the sleaze factor, not let it be thought that you'd been involved with hundreds of men, that you slept with just anyone. On the other hand, you didn't want to give the impression that no-one was interested, thereby making him wonder just what exactly was wrong with you.

'Ah yes,' he said. 'A woman of taste, like yourself, does not give herself to just anyone, isn't that right?'

You bet it is, thought Alexandra. 'That's exactly right.' She raised cool eyebrows over the rim of her glass. Make what you like of *that*.

'And the man who eventually wins you will be the luckiest man in the world, I think,' said Carlo.

'Mmm,' she said. There was no response to a remark like that which did not sound either conceited or simpering, or both.

He kissed her bunched fingers again, then quickly dropped them as an elegant woman paused by their table. '*Ciao*, Carlo,' she said in freezing tones, giving Alexandra a frosty look.

'Gina! *Caro*!' Carlo got to his feet. 'It has been such a long time! Where have you been?'

'Living in the same apartment as always,' Gina said. She seemed rather angry about something.

'But I have lost your telephone number—'

'– and I still have the same name in the telephone directory,' snarled Gina. 'Or have you lost your glasses too?'

'Gina,' said Carlo reproachfully, 'how can you speak in such a way?'

'Are you going to introduce me to your . . .

companion?' Gina said, giving the words shades of meaning which were new to Alexandra.

'This is Alexandra Maitland, one of my – uh – clients from England,' said Carlo uneasily.

'A client. I see.' Gina didn't need to express her opinion of so-called clients who allowed their fingers to be kissed – her look said it all. She was a stick-thin blonde, dressed in skintight black with a large amount of Etruscan-style silver jewellery hanging from various parts of her emaciated frame. She was carrying more weight on her face than on her body, her make-up being so thick, so perfect, that her cheeks looked as though they had been carved out of porcelain. Perhaps that was why she had such a hard expression. Unless she was simply a prize bitch, Alexandra thought. She held out her hand.

'How do you do?' she said. Very British. Very cool. Gina ignored the hand.

'Gina owns a chain of beauty salons,' Carlo said. 'Very successful ones, too.'

'Thanks, of course, to Carlo's – uh – *services*,' said Gina, flicking a finger at one of her earrings which began to swing back and forth. She left Alexandra in no doubt that whatever services Carlo might have performed on Gina's behalf, they had not been confined to public relations but had included private ones as well.

Not that Alex minded. A man with a past was always going to be more worth knowing that a man without one. Much better to get involved with someone who had plunged fully into the sea of life than with someone who had stood wimpishly on the edge, afraid to dip in so much as a toe. Not that she was planning to *get* involved with Carlo San Lorenzo, but the possibility was there . . .

141

'I must go,' Gina said, giving Alexandra a final inimical glance. 'We have to attend a reception at the Ambassador's.' She lifted her hand to her immaculate hair, causing the many bracelets along her wasted arm to clank and clatter like old dustbin lids. '*Ciao*, Carlo.'

'I will call you, Gina. Next week,' Carlo promised.

'I shan't be at home,' said Gina icily.

'The following week?'

'No. Nor the following year,' Gina snapped.

When she had gone, Carlo gave Alex a rueful look. 'This poor woman thinks she is in love with me,' he said.

'Does she?'

'Every time we meet, it is the same thing. "Why have you not rung me, Carlo?" "Here is my phone number, Carlo." What does she expect?' He spread his hands in a gesture of exaggerated bewilderment, lifting his shoulders to the level of his ears. 'Just because I do a good job for her business does not mean that I wish to sleep with her.'

Alexandra drooped her eyes a little. 'Oh, yes?'

'But certainly, Alexandra. What do you think I am? A man who tells every woman that he meets that he is in love with her?'

'I really don't—'

'No, no,' cried Carlo, his voice rising. 'I say this only to the very special women, of which there are few, and of which, my dear Alexandra, you are one. I do not say this to just anyone, it would not be correct to do so. Can I help it if this foolish woman – and others like her – have misunderstood the courtesy with which I treat them?'

'Carlo, really, there is no need to explain,' Alexandra said.

'But that's just it: there is nothing *to* explain,' said Carlo passionately.

Alexandra was enjoying herself. She knew he was lying. He knew she knew. Nonetheless, he continued to try and persuade that he was telling the truth. That he was no more than a simple well-bred Roman, going about his daily business, kind to animals and women, his motives constantly misconstrued . . .

And all about something completely trivial. So Latin, thought Alex. It really did not matter to her whether Carlo had slept with the entire population of Rome. Well, not much. She could make up her own mind about him without any help from hard-faced blondes, thank you.

'How about another bottle of wine?' she said. Gazing with deliberate dreaminess at him across the table, she watched him respond, smoothing back his hair, raising an eyebrow.

'An excellent idea,' he said.

# 7

In two days' time Matthew was off to New York. He
had not seen Alexandra Maitland since the evening
she had spent in his flat and, stupidly, he had not
asked when she would be back from Milan. He
himself would be away for nearly a month: already
his appointment diary for his time in the States was
crammed. Quite apart from specific commissions
from various clients – Anthony Cashman was by no
means the only one he would be representing – he
had auctions to attend and galleries to visit. There
were a number of contacts to make, both in New
York and on the West Coast; Cadogan's was thinking
of expanding to San Francisco to take advantage of
the considerable artistic activity out there, and he
had been asked to spend a week in reconnoitring and
reviewing possible sites.

In addition, he had been put in sole charge of
handling negotiations between Cadogan's and one
of the major American corporations. It was standard
procedure for such conglomerates to collect contemporary art, now that it had been recognized that such
art was plentiful, reasonably affordable, and able to
yield substantial returns. It was one of the big break-
through fields for houses such as Cadogan's but they
needed a good front man, since the collecting of
corporate art was an activity which needed to satisfy
shareholders and customers alike.

'We trust you, Matthew,' James Cadogan, the seventy-two-year-old chairman, said, having called Matt into his office the day before he was due to fly out.

'I'm aware of that.'

'I don't wish to embarrass you, but the board is very impressed by your ability to spot future trends.'

'Thank you.'

'Not only that, you're also extraordinarily astute at a purely commercial level.'

Anxious not to sound servile, and unable to think of a response which was not, Matt smiled but said nothing.

'It's all good for us here at Cadogan's, of course . . .' The chairman sighed. 'But I can't help thinking that this business of mixing aesthetics and commerce is a strange one. Don't you agree?'

'Come on, James. You know as well as I do that art and commerce have walked hand in hand since at least the Renaissance.'

'Maybe so . . .' James Cadogan looked gloomy. 'But these days, art collecting seems to have moved right away from any idea of personal passion or desire for beauty.'

'*Beauty*?' Matthew raised derisive eyebrows. 'Is beauty what we're in the game for?'

'It's certainly a major reason why I am.'

Quite apart from the little matter of inheriting the business founded by his grandfather over a hundred and fifty years ago, Matt thought.

'Anyway,' he said. 'Since when have either passion or beauty been the only rationale behind collecting works of art? Look at the wealthy English aristocrats of the seventeenth and eighteenth century. You don't think they collected paintings and sculpture simply for their aesthetic qualities, do you?'

'But what else?' James Cadogan spread his hands wide. He hated discussions of this nature.

'Art by the square foot was more like it. Just the way the nouveau riche of today buy leather-covered volumes by the metre, in order to fill the shelves of their libraries. Ever been to Woburn, for instance?'

'Took the grandchildren to the safari park only the other—'

'There's a room in there which has twenty-four Canalettos in it. Not because the current Duke of Bedford was obsessed with Canaletto's work, not even because they're very *good* Canalettos, but simply to cover the walls, and to be able to tell his friends he had them.'

'You seem to have adopted a very cynical viewpoint, Matthew.'

'And look at the Medici,' Matt said. 'They didn't collect art simply for art's sake, but also to demonstrate to those around them just how much power they possessed, that they could afford to hire the greatest names of the day. I don't suppose old Pope Leo the Tenth sat around gazing at the latest thing he'd just commissioned from Michelangelo, for instance. Much more likely he boasted about the fact that he had the top man working for him.'

'You're right, of course. But I still don't really like it. My poor father would turn in his grave.'

'I don't see why,' Matthew said robustly. 'What matters is that art – however you choose to define it – is still considered something worth bothering about.'

'Even if the business manager increasingly seems to be as important a factor these days in the acquisition of art as the dealer such as ourselves?'

'That's *good*,' Matthew said.

Privately he wondered if poor old James wasn't getting a bit past it. You couldn't go back to the time when the great art critics like Bernard Berenson and Herbert Read reigned supreme, even if you wanted to. And while to a certain extent the chairman was right that the aesthetic of art was being eroded, nonetheless a whole infrastructure of artists and those who dealt with them was being maintained and subsidized, thus providing creative freedom.

The chairman, looking subdued, said, 'We'll see you later on, shall we?'

'Wouldn't miss it for anything,' said Matthew.

'M'wife asked me to – er – remind you that you're welcome to bring someone if you wish.'

'That's awfully good of you, James, but—'

'Oh quite, quite,' the chairman said, clearly embarrassed. 'Absolutely.'

Later, changing into his dinner jacket in the executive cloakroom, Matthew wished he *had* thought to ask someone to accompany him to the chairman's party. The occasion was ostensibly to mark the birthday of his wife, Barbara, and was an excuse to mix business with pleasure, since invitations were issued not only to personal friends of the chairman's but also to various luminaries of the art world, and a few favoured clients.

The large ballroom at the back of the Cadogan building had been opened for the occasion. Normally used as a storeroom-cum-gallery, it had been cleared of extraneous clutter. The handsome parquet flooring had been rewaxed, the girandoles around the walls had been set with pure wax candles purchased from an ecclesiastical suppliers in Hounslow, elaborate arrangements of flowers graced gilded stands

147

all around the walls. The room was an elegant eighteenth-century fantasy, all gilt and white, with rococo plaster moulding and mirrorwork. Barbara insisted that in keeping with the period the only light was to come from the candles, which flickered romantically from the walls and the three Bohemian crystal chandeliers on the ceiling.

'You've done it again,' Matthew murmured, taking Barbara's hand and bowing over it.

'Done what?' She was James Cadogan's second wife, thirty years younger than her husband, and Matthew had sometimes wondered whether she roamed and if so, whether she would consider roaming with him. It was not a question he would ever have put to her. For one thing, he did not mess with the wives of other men. For another, it would definitely not be a smart career move.

'Managed to make us products of the late twentieth century somehow feel like eighteenth-century fops. Any minute now I shall produce a quizzing glass and start saying, 'Oh la, ma'am.'

'What a kind thing to say,' Barbara said. She glowed at him, her thick silvery hair piled elaborately round her head. 'And how very much what I had hoped people would feel.'

'Look at them,' Matthew said. Together they surveyed the room. 'Men I work with every day. Men who normally wear Armani suits or washed-silk shirts tucked into Joseph trousers: tonight they're all behaving like heroes in a historical novel.'

'Kissing hands,' said Barbara.

'Making a leg.'

'Too Jane Austen for words.'

'And they're only wearing DJs.'

'Perhaps I should make it a costume party next year.'

148

'Masks?'

'Doublet, I think. And hose. Definitely hose.'

'Actually,' Matthew said, 'I've always wondered how those girls managed to wear muslin to the crushes at Bath and not end up with pneumonia. But these candles generate a lot of heat, don't they?'

'Enormous.' Barbara took another glass of champagne from the tray which passed in front of them. 'Rather like yourself.'

'What?'

She smiled, showing dimples. Her eyes were huge and blue; she had beautiful skin. 'You heard.'

'My dear Barbara,' Matthew said lightly. 'Around you, even a snowman would generate heat.'

'So sweet.' She touched his cheek. 'You're a dangerous man, Matthew.'

'Am I?'

'It's time you took yourself off the market,' she said. 'Us older women sometimes have dangerous fantasies.'

At the far end of the room a musical quartet struck up some kind of tinkling dance music. It was difficult to know how serious Barbara was being; nonetheless Matthew was aware that things change, that boundaries could be moved, that the wives of chairmen might not always be sacrosanct. There was a burning sensation somewhere near the pit of his stomach. Barbara, snowy sheets, stolen weekends . . . it suddenly seemed important to remember that she was a tireless charity worker, a champion bridge player, an indefatigable rider to hounds. Above all, that she was the chairman's wife. He cleared his throat, casting about for something to say which would indicate that though he was game for anything, he nonetheless knew how to keep his hands to himself.

Before he could come up with a satisfactory formulation they were joined by Georgina, the chairman's daughter by his first marriage. 'You two look as if you're flirting in the most outrageous way,' she said.

'We were,' said Barbara. She was smiling, her eyes bright.

'We always do,' Matthew said. He hoped Barbara could read the sub-text here: that if she was offering him some kind of invitation – and he was not for a moment suggesting that he was worthy of such a thing if she were – then he was regretfully declining it, on the understanding that both of them knew why.

Very complicated. Sub-texts often were. Taking another glass of champagne, he wondered if he had really managed to convey all that. Or whether he just looked like a Cadogan employee who fancied his employer's wife.

'I'm jealous.' Georgina gave Matthew a sultry look. Sultry looks had been a speciality of hers for some years, so much so that Matthew sometimes wondered whether she practised them in front of a mirror for ten minutes each day.

'So you should be,' he said. 'Barbara is a fascinating woman.'

'So am I. Haven't you noticed?' Georgina was wearing a black Azzedine Alaïa and a choker of huge fake pearls. Her eyes were heavily outlined in kohl; her mouth was scarlet. Matthew, who had known her since she was a plump eight-year-old, smiled down at her.

'Of course. How could I help but notice?' he asked.

'Come and dance,' Georgina said.

'My quadrille footwork's a bit on the rusty side,' Matthew said. 'Or is this a gavotte?'

150

'It's an old Beatles number, actually,' Georgina said, looking at him scornfully.

'Silly me.' Matthew turned to Barbara. 'Will you excuse us?'

'But of course.' She had an imperturbable air. It was known at Cadogan's that she had once fallen from a horse while out hunting and had broken her collarbone, but continued to follow the hounds for the rest of the day until she collapsed as they ran the fox to earth.

'I fancy you, Matt,' Georgina said, leading him through the crowded room. 'You know that, don't you?'

'Yes. So does everyone else in the room,' Matt said.

'What? Fancy you?'

'Know that you fancy me.'

'Do you mind?'

'Not in the least. I'm extremely flattered.'

'I saw a picture of you in *GQ* the other day,' Georgina said. 'You looked stunning.'

'What's *GQ*?'

'It's a magazine,' Georgina said, making an obvious effort to keep the pity for someone Matthew's age out of her voice. 'You must have known you were in it.'

'Oh Gawd,' said Matt. 'I'd completely forgotten about it.'

'You can't have done.'

'But I did. They came months ago to take a picture. I don't know where they got my name, or why they thought I was suitable material for their article.'

'I do.' Georgina stood very close to him, swaying in time to the music. Looking down at the long fair hair flowing over her shoulders, at the skimpy dress, the unlived-in face, he felt immeasurably old for not wanting to sweep her off there and then and make passionate love to her. He wanted something more these days than mere bonking. He wanted—

'Matt!' It was his sister Victoria. 'I knew we'd see you here.' She looked approvingly at Georgina. 'Is this by any chance . . . ?'

He wanted to say, 'No, Victoria, this is not Miss Right.' Instead, he said merely, 'Georgina. This is my sister.'

As he introduced them, the two women nodded at each other. 'How nice to meet you,' said Victoria. Her eyes hoovered the younger girl, gathering up every detail of her dress, her make-up, her jewellery and shoes, in order to relay the information to Emma and his mother. He could see her give a mental thumbs-up: although she was a bit young, Georgina Would Do.

Inwardly he gave a world-weary smile. He supposed the women in his life would only stop this outrageous assessing of the women he went out with, when he finally stopped going out with any and settled at home with one. God knows what they would make of Georgina when Victoria passed on an estimate of her age.

She and Victoria were chatting animatedly. Georgina was in her last year as a law student at Cambridge and was joining the same set of chambers where Victoria herself had trained before her marriage. As so often when in the company of women, Matthew felt a little superfluous. Their lives always seemed to him to be more complete than those of men, more . . . *together*, somehow, less compartmentalized. And they did not seem to feel the same need to compete that men did, the urge to scatter

152

names, achievements, possessions about, like so much status-defining dandruff.

The group was joined by Hugo Bathurst, the firm's immensely tall specialist in medieval artefacts. He smiled benignly at Matthew, his quiff of white hair and heavy black-framed glasses giving him the air of a learned cockatoo.

'What an asset you are to Cadogan's,' he said.

'Aren't we all?' Matthew replied. 'Otherwise we shouldn't be here.'

'My dear, I don't mean for your professional expertise.' Hugo was smoking a thin cigarette through a long cloisonné holder which he now began to wave about, causing highly aromatic ash to fall on to the sleeve of his green velvet jacket. If that was a Benson & Hedges, Matthew thought, then he himself was Frans Hals. 'Though that, too, adds to your many charms.'

'Thank you, Hugo.'

The other man heaved a deep sigh. 'Ah, me,' he said. 'How swiftly one falls into the sere and yellow. How little attention one pays to the passing of the seasons when one is young and heedless.'

'You're in one of your melancholy moods, I see.'

Hugo shook his head. 'If only one could recapture one's lost youth.' He drew deeply on the cigarette – hand-rolled, Matthew could not help noticing and hoped no-one else had – in his holder.

'Which particular youth was that?' Matt said.

'There were so many.' Hugo trickled smoke out through his aristocratic nostrils. 'So many beautiful boys.'

'Is now the time to be talking of them?' Matthew looked round. 'You might regret this line of conversation tomorrow morning.'

'The great thing, dear boy, is to regret nothing.'

'Unlike yourself, I have very little *to* regret.'

'Then you are not living life to the full.' Hugo stared round the room. 'What I meant when I said you were an asset, Matt, is that you provide the sexual fillip which Cadogan's would otherwise lack.'

'I'm moved by this tribute, Hugo,' Matthew said, laughing.

'As you should be. I don't pay tributes lightly.' Hugo's restless eyes targeted a handsome dowager who stood in front of the long gilt mirrors. 'Ah! The very woman I was looking for.'

'You mean you've been a closet hetero all these years?'

'I mean I'm hoping to sell her a gorgeous blanket chest I discovered two weeks ago in Shropshire.' Hugo started to move away and then turned back. 'You're looking at the ideal client over there, dear boy. She has the money to spend, the taste to choose correctly and, above all, the right setting for what she buys. Perfection.' He kissed his fingers in a flamboyant sort of way and swept off, his quiff bobbing above the heads of the other guests like a small ship on a turbulent sea.

One of the newer recruits to Cadogan's came up. 'Georgina!' he said.

'Bootsy!' cried Georgina.

'You'll never guess who's here.' If Bootsy had a chin, it was not much in evidence and Matthew could see two distinct pimples beside his nose. Was this to be his destiny? he wondered. Was he doomed to spend the rest of his working life watching babes in arms wheeling and dealing the way he used to? Would he eventually be ousted by one of them, a toothless lion left to die of starvation while the rest of

154

the herd loped off after game he could no longer compete for?

'Who?' Georgina was asking.

'Rory.'

'Rory King-Lewis?'

'Yeah!'

Georgina turned to Matt. 'Rory's a chap Bootsy and I were at school with,' she said. 'I haven't seen him for ages. You don't mind if I go, do you?'

'Not at all.' Quite a relief, actually, Matthew thought, feeling older than Methuselah as Georgina rushed off to see Rory King-Thing. There had been no girls at *his* school, though the sixth form often fantasized richly and in great detail about the possibility. It was a fancy which occupied their thoughts by day and their dreams by night. Georgina's generation were much luckier. He tried to remember which school she had been sent to: Haileybury, was it? Or Oundle? Somewhere like that.

'Nice girl,' Victoria said. 'Very intelligent.'

'And very young,' said Matthew.

Victoria raised her eyebrows. 'Is she the one you . . . ?'

'No,' he said. 'She isn't. We aren't. We haven't. We don't. We shan't.'

Victoria put a hand on his arm. 'Don't worry, darling. You'll find her one of these days, I promise. Miss Right, I mean.'

Matthew groaned.

Waking early the day before he was due to go, he remembered something he had intended to organize. He dialled his mother's number; when she finally answered, he said, 'I'm your only son, right?'

'I think I can more or less guarantee—'

155

'And you dote on me, right?'

'I did once, dear,' his mother agreed cautiously. 'But—'

'But you will admit that—'

'Besides, you're rather big to be doted on.' His mother sighed, her voice taking on a nostalgic tone. 'You were so sweet once. Round about the age of four. I remember the little romper suit I bought in Harrods—'

'Mother, do you mind?'

'To answer your question, I won't deny that I'm extremely fond of you.'

'Not to put too fine a point on it, you'd do anything for me, wouldn't you?'

'No,' she said promptly.

'You want me to be happy, don't you?'

'Yes.'

'Then will you do me a favour?'

'Depends what it is.'

'I want you to take someone to watch the Somerset v. Kent match next Wednesday.'

'Is this "someone" a special someone?'

'Very special.'

'Who is she? What's her name?'

'It's not a she. It's a man who lives in Merry Beauchamp.'

There was a long silence. Then his mother said quietly, 'What are you trying to tell me, Matthew?'

'I'm trying to tell you – well, ask you, to be accurate – to take someone to the cricket match next week.'

'This special man.'

'Yes. I can't see that it is so diffic—'

'Oh God,' his mother groaned.

'What on earth's the matter?'

'Matthew, I'm trying to be very understanding and modern about this, but I want you to realize that for women of my generation, it's difficult to accept the prevailing mores.'

'*Mores*? What mores?'

'If you're – uh – gay, as they insist on calling it these days, then I'll just have to accept it, but I shall always blame myself, always wonder where I went wrong with you, wonder whether it was that school I sent you to, I was never sure if it was a mistake or—'

'MOTHER!'

'What?'

'For God's sake,' Matthew shouted. 'I am *not* gay. I simply want you to take a friend's father to a cricket match.' He gave her the name and address, and added, 'I'd take him myself if I was free.'

'This is a *female* friend's father?'

'As a matter of fact, yes.'

'Oh, Matthew. How thrilling. What's she like?'

After a pause, Matthew said, 'If you really want to know, she's the most wonderful woman in the world.' And put down the receiver, instantly regretting his words. They were no more than the truth, but now his mother would ring Victoria and Emma and they would ring him and it would be one question after another until he went completely mad and started calling for humming-bird sandwiches or something. Thank God he was off to New York tomorrow.

That evening he went down to Alexandra's flat and knocked on the door. It was opened by a man he had not seen before. He hid his surprise. After all, just because she had been unaccompanied at Emma's house, just because she had accepted his invitation to dinner, did not mean that she was unattached.

157

Of course this might be the brother, but it wasn't a question he felt like asking.

'Good evening,' the other man said. He was wearing a tie Matt recognized. Suppose this chap was Alexandra's special friend, her Significant Other, as they called it in the States, wouldn't he get a bit peeved if some strange man appeared at the door asking for her? He knew *he* would, if the circumstances were reversed.

'Do you want the lady of the house?' the chap said.

Was it his imagination or was there a certain edge to the way he said that? 'Well . . .' said Matt, not wanting to commit either Alexandra or himself.

'She's in the bedroom, getting changed,' the chap said, making it very obvious that he had proprietorial interests in her. *In the bedroom*, indeed. Establishing his territory, in other words, Matthew thought angrily. Like some damn dog, lifting its leg, leaving its mark. And then he had the blasted cheek to offer him a coffee, emphasizing his familiarity with the flat, his rights of ownership.

'No thanks,' Matt said. And then, just to clarify his position, added, 'I'm . . . a neighbour. If she's busy it really doesn't matter.'

'She is rather,' the chap said, a self-satisfied smirk on his smug – in Matt's opinion – face, and looked at his watch. 'We're going out to dinner, as a matter of fact, and we're running late.'

In other words, shove off, matey, she's mine.

'I won't keep you then,' Matt murmured, backing away, feeling a total and utter prat.

Next time he saw Alexandra he would establish for once and for all just exactly how committed she was, and just exactly to whom.

★　　★　　★

In fact, he was unable to do so. The next time he saw her she was emerging from the very lift he was waiting for. A host of foolish remarks rose to his lips. He wanted to blurt out that she looked beautiful in blue, that he'd like to kill the man who'd been in her flat the previous evening, that he hoped her date with him had been a miserable failure, that he had hardly slept a wink all night, beside himself with jealousy.

He said none of these things. Partly because of the stranger standing in the lift behind her. Partly because he had to catch his flight, was indeed already behind schedule.

'Hi!' she said, stepping out, searching in her bag for something, wrenching his heart.

'Hi.' He made a bit of a thing of bending down to pick up his bags, anxious to hide his confusion. Whatever happened to Matthew Prescott, the King of No Commitments? Given the slightest encouragement, he'd be on his knees swearing eternal devotion.

She looked at his luggage. 'Was it something I said?' she asked lightly.

He laughed. 'No. Just business.'

'Long?' she said. It was impossible to judge whether she was asking because she was interested or merely for the sake of politeness.

'A month.'

'That's long,' she said.

'I called round last night but you had company,' he said, dumping his bags into the lift, stepping after them.

'You mean my brother?'

His jaw dropped. 'Brother?'

He would have said more, but it was too late. The lift doors closed across his exclamation of relief and frustration and he was carried down to the ground floor. It *was* her brother. Immediately the smug features reassembled themselves in his imagination and took on the friendly demeanour of an irrelevant sibling. Come to think of it, he'd seemed rather a decent chap, someone it might be worth getting to know. Same college tie as his own, too. They were bound to have things in common, even if the difference in age made it unlikely that they'd have overlapped at university.

He was lucky. He found a cab immediately and the traffic was light enough for him to get to Heathrow with plenty of time to spare, in spite of the stringent security control that the American airlines now insisted on.

As soon as he could, he found a phone booth. He called Directory Enquiries and gave her name. The mechanical voice intoned, 'The number you require is—' and he found he hadn't got a pen handy, nor anything to write on, and had to start all over again.

She picked up on the first ring, almost as though she had been expecting him to call. He found himself less flustered now, more in control.

'I forgot to say I shall be in New York,' he said.

'I – uh – I hope you remembered to take your favourite coffee with you,' she said. It had become a joke between them; he had said something similar when she told him she was off to Milan.

Hearing her voice, he laughed, feeling as though a hundred years had dropped from his shoulders. He understood now all those clichés about hearts singing, feeling ten feet high, walking on air, cloud nine. It was all happening to him, right there in a see-through plastic telephone nodule in the airport concourse with the crowds jostling and plaintive

160

announcements coming over the Tannoy system, and the orange-juice machines gurgling and travellers humping suitcases about with those peculiarly tense expressions people always adopt prior to a long-haul flight.

'So you might like to know,' he said, studiedly casual, 'that I'm staying at the Plaza.'

She didn't say anything. She didn't need to. He could hear her smiling. He could feel the expression on her face. Hardly daring to trust himself, he gently replaced the receiver.

He turned, picking up his briefcase. 'I do believe,' he said, addressing a startled Arab trailing six womenfolk in metal face-masks and flowing robes, 'I do believe she's as keen as I am.'

And for a moment he was afraid that the huge grin he could not control was going to stretch his face permanently out of shape.

'I heard you were in town,' the voice said.

Matthew had been at the Plaza for a week now, with scarcely a moment to call his own. Quite apart from the working breakfasts, the working lunches, the sock-it-to-'em suppers and the power parties, he still had two or three hours of paperwork to deal with each evening after he stumbled back to his hotel room.

He squinted at his watch. Seven thirty. He was still in bed and felt like staying there for the rest of the day. The accepted rate at which New York life moved was at least three factors faster than in London. Exhilarating, yes. But also bloody exhausting. He was beginning to wonder how much more he could take.

The voice was familiar but he couldn't place it. He stifled a groan. 'Who is this?'

161

'Oh, Matthew . . .' The voice was full of reproach.

'I'm sorry. I'm still half asleep.' He wished his mouth didn't feel so dry – the air conditioning was hellish at this time of year, but the temperature and humidity without it would be even worse.

The voice laughed. 'How quickly they forget.'

It was a female voice. At least he was on the ball enough to realize that. And it belonged to someone whom he had known once; that, too, he could deduce.

The voice began to sing softly in his ear, something about a kiss being just a kiss, a sigh being just a sigh.

'Laura!'

'Hi, Matt.'

'Laura, for God's sake. How are you?'

'Getting by. And you.'

He shook his head to clear it. 'Getting by? I thought you were going to live happy ever after with the man of your dreams.'

'Yeah, well,' she said. 'Dreams have a funny way of turning sour.'

'Oh dear.'

'Why don't we meet sometime, Matt? I'd really love to see you again.'

'When? I'm fearfully busy – and that's not just an excuse.'

'Tell me when you're free.'

He got out of bed and padded across the carpet to his briefcase. 'How about two days from now? That's the first window I can see.'

'I'll be there,' Laura said. 'Shall I come to your hotel?'

If she did it could be awkward . . . 'No, I'll pick you up somewhere,' he said quickly.

Once they had settled when and where, he climbed

162

back into bed, hoping to catch another hour of sleep. But memories kept him awake, particularly of that last night with Laura, and all the pain and anguish she had subsequently caused him. In the end he got up and made himself some coffee, then watched the early morning skies above Manhattan as he recalled the past.

He had been working in San Francisco at the time, still learning his trade, revelling in the whole carefree Californian ethos, the sense of shackles dropping, of new horizons glimmering. He was beginning to see that his concept of Art with a capital A was European, based on a classical tradition that was never going to expand to meet the challenge of the new generations of painters because it was defined by its time.

He embraced the new dogmas, or lack of them, with enthusiasm. He wallowed in the shock of the new, absorbing, listening, learning.

And then he met Laura.

She was English, a little older than he was, working as a buyer for Gump's, the big department store on Union Square. She had lived in the States for several years but she still retained her British accent, though she often maintained that she loathed England and would never return to it. Her black hair seemed to gush from her scalp and her blue eyes were never still, constantly on the lookout for the next opportunity, the next adventure.

He had never before met a woman so entirely free of the constraints which he had come to associate with being female. Nor a woman with such a passion for living. 'Gather ye rosebuds while ye may,' she used to say. 'We might be dead tomorrow, Matt, so let's do it *now*.'

And 'it' might be a frantic drive down the coast for

163

a weekend over the border into Mexico, or a trip into the wine-growing country beyond the Berkeley hills, or trying a new recipe involving chocolate sauce and lobster claws or something equally revolting. It was with Laura that he had first tried hang-gliding, drunk tequila, fished in Alaska, eaten salt-water taffy, read Proust, watched a blue movie.

'Come on, Matt,' she would say, calling him at two or three in the morning, her voice hoarse with the cigarettes she chain-smoked. 'It's rosebud-gathering time . . .'

And off they would go on another frenzied dash to see, to feel, to *experience*, before it was too late. Long afterwards, when it was over, when he could finally bear to think of it all, he understood that, deep down, Laura had not expected to live beyond thirty and that, without realizing it, he had picked up on this and joined in the relentless, exhausting determination to sample life to the fullest.

Afterwards, of course, he told himself he should have been able to predict what would happen. How could Laura, eternally seeking new sensations, ever be satisfied with one man? At the time it had seemed that they shared so much that they must have some mystic chain binding them together.

Indeed Laura often said so: 'Twin souls, Matt,' she would drawl, as she lolled back on the velvet cushions which covered the floor of her apartment. 'We're twin souls, joined at the cosmic hip.'

Matt would sometimes try to develop this image but found it impossible. Did souls have hips, to start with? And if they did, how would a pair of Siamese souls work, exactly? Being one half of a cosmic Chang and Eng did not, somehow, appeal.

And then came the day when he came home to find

her standing by the door with her bags packed.

'I couldn't leave without saying goodbye,' she said.

'Who to?'

'You, dumbo,' she said affectionately.

'Why goodbye?'

'It's been really great, Matt. Some of the best times of my life. Truly. But when you gotta go, you gotta go.'

'Go *where*?'

'I'm going to Nepal,' she said.

'But why?'

'Why not?'

'Without me?'

'You're not free, Matt. You know that as well as I do. You're into career structures, office hours, pension schemes, all that kind of crap. You did a good job, you know,' and she had leaned forward and patted his cheek as though he were a well-behaved little boy. 'But you know and I know that deep down I'm about as alien to your concept of life as a creature from outer space.'

'But I *love* you,' he said, and even today the memory could make him wince with remembered pain and passion.

'So you got something positive out of this whole scene,' she said. 'That's good, Matthew. Hold on to it.'

'And I thought you loved me.'

'I do, Matt. You gotta go on believing that.'

'Then how can you leave me?' Back then it all seemed so simple. You loved someone; you wanted to spend the rest of your life with them. He had been too young to understand the complications which human beings establish for themselves, or the complex meaning of love.

165

'Would you believe, like this?' She hoisted her carpet-weave bag higher on her shoulder, about to pick up her bags and walk.

He stopped her. 'Who are you going to Nepal with?' he said. He was shaking now, taking in the fact that she meant it, feeling his heart begin to twist and crinkle like the burning books in *Fahrenheit 451*.

'Does it matter?' she said.

'To me it does.'

'What does "with" mean, anyway?' she said airily.

'You know damn well what it means.'

'If you really feel it's relevant, I'm sharing my personal space with Steve Lavalle.'

'And where is your soul joined to Steve Lavalle's?' he asked bitterly. 'At the cosmic crotch?'

'Ours is a spiritual relationship,' she said.

'Oh sure it is,' Matt said.

'It *is*. Not that I expect someone like you to—'

'Steve Lavalle is about as spiritual as a traffic bollard, and four times less intelligent – and you know it.'

She gave him her infuriating Wise Woman smile, picked up her bags and went.

He had postcards from her after that: from Amsterdam, from Athens, from Istanbul and Baghdad and Delhi. And finally, a card from Kathmandu. He had left San Francisco by then, and returned to London. The card followed him, its corners bent and the stamps half torn-off by the time it reached him. By then some of the hurt had lessened and he was able to look down at her scrawly handwriting and think: so she made it.

And four or five years later another card arrived, from San Diego, saying she was married and blissfully happy, that she had found her Prince Charming and life was great.

166

Standing in his hotel bedroom, Matt hoped he hadn't made a mistake in agreeing to see her. At best it was pointless; at worst it could be really awkward. By now the buds she used to gather so assiduously must be full-blown roses. And as for cosmic hips . . .

A cup of coffee in his hand, he looked out at the New York skyline and started to laugh.

'You look really great, Matthew,' Laura said.

'So do you,' Matt murmured, though in actual fact it was not entirely true. Californian sunshine was not particularly kind to the English complexion, and circumstances had evidently not treated Laura well. The lines of experience were marked on her face and although she still had all the exuberant charm which had drawn him to her in the first place, he thought she looked older than he knew her to be. Not that he would dream of telling her so. Not if he wanted to get out of the restaurant alive.

'So,' Laura drank her wine as though it was water, then refilled her glass. 'How's it going?'

'Very well indeed,' said Matthew. Looking at her across the table, it was hard to imagine that once he had thought her the most exotic extraordinary thing in the entire world. 'And you?'

'I get by, I guess.' She gazed into the middle distance. 'I'm on my third divorce, did I tell you that?'

'Not until now.'

*Three* divorces? When even one was not to be contemplated. Thank goodness he had never rushed into anything – though that was partly because he had never found the woman he wanted to rush into anything with. At least, not until now. The tawny hair of Alexandra Maitland brushed briefly across his mind.

He had been brought up to believe that marriage was for ever. And if not for ever, then for as long as possible. He thought of his own parents, blissfully happy together until seven years ago when his father had died suddenly of an unsuspected heart condition, just before their silver wedding anniversary. 'Any children?' he said.

'Two,' Laura said. 'Both by my first husband. They're staying with him now.'

'And what do you do? Apart from looking after them, I mean?' Matthew stumbled a bit on this question, trying to remember what the prevailing feminist attitudes were towards such things as parenting and families. Was it insulting to assume that mothers still raised their children? Were women expected to *do* things still, or was it all earth-motherhood and fulfilment-through-family these days?

'I work at Saks,' Laura said. 'Buying for the glass and china departments.'

'That's what you were doing when we—'

'When we met.' Her eyes glowed with the remembrance of things past. 'God, I was wild in those days. I wanted to have it all, see it all. I didn't realize that you can't.'

'You had a darn good try, Laura,' he said.

'I did, didn't I?'

'Tell me, whatever happened to Steve?' Matt asked.

'Steve? Which one? There are so many Steves. My first two husbands were both called Steve.'

'So you married him in the end, did you?'

'Married who?'

168

'Steve Lavalle.'

She frowned. 'Never heard of him.'

'You went off to Nepal with him, if memory serves.'

'Heavens above. So I did.'

'Where is he now?'

'I haven't a clue. He got lost in Istanbul and I couldn't wait so I went on without him.'

'That was a bit cool, wasn't it? He could have been murdered by a carpet-seller or something.'

'More likely run off with a belly dancer,' Laura said bitterly. 'It's the story of my life.'

'But didn't you check with the police?'

''Course I did. They couldn't find him.'

'And you just abandoned him?'

'He rang up from some baths or some place like that, said he'd be back soon. I waited two days and then I left. The hell with him,' Laura said. She reached across the table and stroked Matthew's face. 'It's really good to see you again, Matthew. Terrifically good.'

'Yeah.' Matt looked at his watch. She was getting amorous, and he wasn't. He needed all his skill and tact if he was going to extricate himself from this situation and spend the night sleeping in his hotel bed, alone. 'Listen, I hate to break this up and it's been wonderful to see you, but I have to get back to the hotel.'

'I'll come with you.'

'No!'

She looked at him in surprise as he almost shouted the word. 'What's wrong, Matt?'

'I've got this – this ferocious headache,' he said, massaging his temples in what he hoped was a realistic way. 'Migraine coming on, I should think.'

'Poor thing.' She gave him her bedroom look. 'Do you want me to come back and give you one of my special back rubs? Help you get rid of the tensions?'

'The only way to deal with it is lie in the dark and stay absolutely quiet,' he said firmly. 'No voices, no distractions. Otherwise it'll hang about – and I've got these really vital meetings in the morning.'

'I understand,' she said. 'Can we meet again before you go back?'

'Absolutely,' he said, nodding away. 'Call me.'

'I will. If I miss you, I'll be in England soon, looking at glass and porcelain. Maybe we could get together then.'

'Fantastic,' he lied. 'I can't wait.' He stood up, pushing his chair over to give the impression of a man going mad with pain. He staggered slightly, tried to make his eyes look wild. 'Ooh. My head.'

He felt really mean, sitting back in the cab, watching Manhattan by night. But Laura was a piranha; she'd have chewed him down to the bone if he had let her. Although he did not hold with lies, there were occasions when they were the best option. Like tonight. Much better to be untruthful and leave Laura thinking that but for a migraine, they might have spent the night together. Recovered their lost love. Their lost youth. Whatever it was she had so plainly hoped to recapture.

# 8

'There was a dwarf in here just now, looking for you,' Felicity said, as Alexandra came back from lunch. Her chicken-pox had turned out not to be chicken-pox but an over-violent reaction to a take-away pizza.

'What kind of dwarf?'

'How many kinds are there?' Felicity spoke without moving her lips since her face was covered in something hard and green, like the shell of an exotic beetle. As she spoke, she surveyed the result in the mirror.

'But I don't know any dwarfs,' Alex said. 'Are you sure he wanted me?'

'That's who he asked for. I think he left his card on your desk.'

A peach-coloured business card lay on top of Alexandra's papers. She picked it up and saw the name *Jarrett Keach* flowing across it in brown mock handwriting which was presumably a facsimile of Jarret's own signature. On the reverse Jarrett had written: *I'll call back in a couple of hours. How about dinner tonight?*

'I hope you were nice to him,' Alex said.

'Wha'?' Felicity was lying with her head resting on the back of her chair, gazing up at the ceiling, her long legs stretched across her desk. Even as Alex watched, the green stuff on her face was turning blue.

'I hope you were nice to the dwarf. He's Jarrett Keach.'

Felicity leaped up from her seat, her face contorted. Chunks of blue-green stuff flaked off and scattered over the floor. Other bits stayed where they were, making her look like something Special Effects was trying out for the next *Dr Who* series. 'The *designer*?' she shrieked.

'Yes.'

'Why didn't you *say*?'

'I wasn't here, was I?'

'Jarrett Keach,' moaned Felicity. 'Oh God. I've been trying to get through to him in New York for *weeks*, and when he finally shows up in the office I'm covered in green face-mask. He must have thought I was bonkers.'

'I don't suppose he thought you always look like that.'

'And on top of that . . . Oh *God* . . .'

'What else?'

'I told him to be sure not to fall into the wastepaper basket on his way out,' said Felicity, attempting to bury her parti-coloured face in her hands.

'What a strange thing to—'

'He ate my lunch,' Felicity said. 'Just picked up my yoghurt and cucumber sandwich and ate it before I could stop him. I told him to get lost.'

Straightening the accumulation of paperwork on her desk with rather more success than she was managing to straighten her face, Alex remarked, 'Well, at least he owes you one.'

'I suppose so . . .' Felicity sounded doubtful.

'Anyway, he's coming back.'

'He *is*? When?'

'In a couple of hours.'

Felicity grabbed her make-up case from the bottom drawer of her desk. 'That just about gives me time to make myself look presentable.'

'He wants to take me out to dinner tonight,' Alexandra could not resist adding.

Felicity paused between the desks and looked suspicious. 'Why? You're Features, not Fashion.'

'I'm also reasonably sane,' Alexandra said. 'For instance, I don't cover myself in gunge during working hours.'

'Nor do I, normally.' Felicity pulled at a loose bit of the stuff on her face, which detached itself from her skin with a small popping noise. 'But with Helena away, someone's got to try out the samples.'

'I see.'

'What's Jarrett Keach like?'

'Short,' Alex said.

'What else?'

'Talented.'

'You can say that again. His spring collection was absolutely beautiful. Bit beyond most people's prices, which is a shame. I wonder if he's thought of a ready-to-wear collection . . .'

'Why don't you ask him?'

'I will. If you don't mind, that is. I don't want to butt in—'

'You won't,' Alexandra said. 'Anyway, as you pointed out, you're the Fashion Editor. Tell him what you just told me about his spring collection and you'll have him eating out of your hand.'

'He'd have to stand on tiptoe,' Felicity said with a rare flash of humour.

'Better prepare some questions for him,' Alex said.

'Show him you're really interested in what he's done in the past and what he's planning to do in the future.'

'Good idea.' Felicity tugged another shard of blue-green shell from her face.

'It might be quite fun to hear his views on the whole phenomenon of fashion,' Alex said, thinking aloud. 'Why women follow it, why they tolerate it, the whole psychology behind it, the dichotomies it invokes.'

'The what?'

'Dichotomies.' Alexandra looked over and saw Felicity listening with attention. She was embarrassed, realizing that she had been sounding exactly like Nina. 'Come on, Fliss. You know as well as I do the sort of thing to ask him. You've done it a hundred times before.'

'But not to a midget who's just eaten my lunch and whom I've subsequently insulted, who then turns out to be one of the world's top dress designers. Oh *God* . . .'

'Never mind.'

'You're right.' Felicity shrugged it off, looking down at her notepad. 'Could be good, Alex.'

'Tempt him with the possibility of a spread on his designs.'

'I could ask him,' Felicity said thoughtfully, 'whether he felt fashion could be viewed as one means of pasting the fragments of self into the semblance of a unified identity.'

'You certainly could.'

'And if he thought fashion was one of the more potent means whereby women can achieve self-expression.'

'I'm sure he's got lots to say on that one . . .'

174

'And fashion victims: that'll get a dialogue going.'
Satisfied, Felicity loped off towards the loo.

Jarrett Keach reappeared two hours later, as promised. He looked like some kind of rare orchid, dressed in a Crocodile Dundee hat of soft green suede and miniature matching trousers under a jerkin of pink washed silk lined with purple. His T-shirt was pale blue. Had there been any butterflies around they'd have been stacked above his head three layers high, all waiting for a chance to land . . .

'Jarrett!' Alex exclaimed. 'How nice to see you again.'

'You too, baby.'

Alexandra bit back the unpleasant retort which rose to her lips. *Baby*, for heaven's sake. That was really rich, coming from an update of Little Lord Fauntleroy. She led him over to the Fashion desk, where Felicity was sitting, a vision of crystalline beauty and sparkling efficiency.

'Mr Keach,' Felicity said, rising from her seat with one fluid movement and holding out her hand. Her eyelashes swept slowly up and down like bellows, causing a small breeze to ruffle Jarrett's hair. 'How truly exciting to meet you.'

'Why, thank you.'

'I don't know if Alexandra has told you, but we've been hoping very much to feature your next collection in our spring bumper issue,' Felicity said.

'You'd have to talk to my agent about that,' Keach said.

'Oh, but a word from *you* couldn't go amiss, could it?' The dimples she kept for emergencies suddenly appeared in Felicity's cheeks.

Keach leaned his little forearms on her desk. 'Say, were you round here during the lunch-break?'

'No,' lied Felicity, 'I had an appointment in Bond Street.'

'If you want my advice, you should revise your security arrangements,' Keach said earnestly. 'I was able to walk right in here, you know.'

'We've never seen any need to—'

'And you oughta check if anything's gone missing. There was this real weirdo in here, rifling about the desks, wearing some kinda disguise.' He turned to Alexandra. 'Did you know that in New York a significant number of burglaries are now perpetrated by women?'

Alex shook her head. 'I didn't.'

'And the number's on the increase?'

'When you say disguised,' Alex said, looking over at Felicity, who was violently shaking her head, 'what exactly do you—'

'She had this sorta Hallowe'en mask on,' said Keach. 'Kind of a Monster-From-The-Blue-Lagoon type thing.'

'Would you recognize her again?' Felicity asked.

'How could I? Couldn't see anything of her face at all.' He looked around. 'Hey. Any chance of a coffee?'

'I'll make you one,' Alex said. 'Stay and talk to Felicity.'

She brought back three cups made from her favourite blend, gave one to Felicity and set the other two on her desk. 'So, Jarrett,' she said. 'How's things?'

'Just dandy,' he said. His tiny feet dangled above the carpeting as he reached for his cup. 'Look, honey. Are you free to have dinner with me tonight?'

She didn't like to say that she would sooner lick a toad. 'Actually, Jarrett,' she said, 'I've already got a prior engagement. So I can't—'

176

'Great, great,' he said. 'So you won't mind if I take Felicity instead?'

'Not in the slightest. The two of you can—'

'Great,' he said again, hardly listening. 'Is she shacked up with anyone?'

'I'm not sure.'

'So I'm in with a chance?'

Alex picked a bloom from the large bouquet of mixed carnations which stood to one side of her desk and held it to her nose, savouring the cinnamon scent. They had arrived two days ago, courtesy of Interflora and Carlo San Lorenzo. 'I wouldn't go that far,' she said coolly.

'Would *she*?' Keach winked at her. 'That's what I really want to know.'

'You'll have to ask her.'

Ghastly little unreconstructed midget, Alexandra thought. She already knew the answer to his question, which was a decided negative. Felicity was Saving Herself for her Wedding Night.

Although it was August, the flat seemed cold. She built a small fire in the grate, just for the comfort, then went into the kitchen. She made a chicken salad and poured herself a glass of chilled white wine, then put them on a tray and took them into her sitting room. She had lied to Keach. Instead of going out she was planning to spend a quiet evening at home, the first, it seemed, for weeks. She slipped a CD of *La Traviata* into the player and closed her eyes. Bliss. With two of the office down with chicken-pox, she hardly had time to think these days, let alone relax.

As Joan Sutherland soared through Violetta's anguished aria of love renounced, she thought of Carlo San Lorenzo. He would be over in England soon. She wondered how she would feel when she saw him again. And there was Matthew Prescott, too: she was by no means averse to him. After Cameron's laid-back attitude to any form of commitment, it was a boost to the morale to know that there were other men around.

When the telephone rang, she picked it up and heard the Colonel's voice. 'It's your father here,' he said.

'Hello, Pa. How're—'

'Colonel Maitland,' added her father, in case there was any doubt in her mind as to his identity.

'Oh, *that* father,' said Alex. 'How's the hip?'

A series of clicks and sounds like a heavy breather with asthma began. A high-pitched whistle screeched along the line. He was using the cordless phone she and David had bought him last Christmas.

'Pa,' Alex said patiently, 'leave it alone.'

'Dratted thing,' roared her father, his voice fading in and out of static. 'Blasted . . . modern . . . not like the old days . . . built to last . . .'

'Pull the aerial out.'

'. . . idiotic . . . no idea . . . call it progress.' He suddenly swam into vocal range again. 'Alexandra?'

'I'm still here.'

'What were you saying?'

'I was asking about your hip. And for heaven's sake stop fidgeting with the aerial.'

'My hip's much better, thanks.'

'It's a shame you had to miss the Somerset v. Kent match. I'm really sorry David and I both had to be away. Did you catch any of it on the local telly?'

'No.'

'Why not? Wasn't Mrs Hope—'

'Because I was there, wasn't I?'

'Were you?'

'Yes,' said the Colonel. 'Sitting right there in the Members' Stand.'

'How did you manage that? Did Freddy come for you?'

'It was that woman you sent.'

A piece of smokeless fuel fell out of the grate and on to the hearth. Alexandra watched it, wondering whether she ought to get up and put it back before it started to spit flame and muck on to the carpet. 'Which woman?'

'Knocked on the door, said she'd come to drive me up to the county ground, had a picnic in the car and she hoped I was ready.'

'Were you?'

''Course not. Still in my dressing gown, wasn't I? Damned embarrassing. Had to ask her in. She said she'd like to walk round the garden while Mrs Hope helped me to get some clothes on.'

'What was she, some lonely widow who'd heard about your hip?'

'She was a widow all right, but not exactly what I'd call lonely. Seemed to be on kissing terms with half the chaps in the cricket ground, when we got there. Said her husband had been a member for years.'

'This is rather weird, Pa. You don't usually go off with strange women like that.'

Her father chuckled. 'Don't often get strange women *asking* me to, m'dear.'

'So who was she?' Alex poured herself another glass of wine and sipped it slowly, saving up the details of her father's assignation in order to tell David when he got back.

'Trouble is, I can't remember her damned name,'

the Colonel said. 'Idiotic of me, really, but I just didn't have time to ask.'

'You can't have spent the day with some total stranger and not even found out what she was called.'

'First name was Erica, that much I do remember. Dashed rude about my roses, I may say. Said I obviously hadn't a clue about pruning.'

'What was her other name?'

'For the life of me—'

'Was she nice?'

'Damned nice. Pretty little thing. Could see why everyone was queuing up to kiss her. And the picnic she put up for us was first-rate. Only one thing wrong with her, as a matter of fact.'

Alexandra hadn't heard the Colonel sound this cheerful since he'd been confined to the wheelchair. Or even before that. Long before. She had been nineteen when her mother died, old enough to notice how poor old Pa seemed to shrink inside himself at the time. What she hadn't noticed until now, being much too busy getting on with her own life, was that he had never really come back out. A pale imitation had emerged, yes, but not the rambunctious roaring man she had loved. 'So what was wrong with this paragon?' she asked.

'She would keep banging on about her son. The way she told it, the fellow's a cross between the Pope and Einstein, with a hefty dash of film star thrown in. Put a stop to it in the end, though.'

'How?'

'I said, "Forgive me, madam, but I've got a blasted son myself, and I know what they're like. Sons, I mean. They just aren't that damned perfect," I said. "Wouldn't want them if they were."'

'You didn't!'

'Think I was a bit brutal, eh?' For once, the Colonel sounded unsure of himself.

'Real Attila the Hun stuff, Pa.'

'Had to stop her somehow,' the Colonel said uneasily. 'Hope I didn't overdo it.'

'How did she take it?' asked Alexandra, trying not to laugh, wondering who the intrepid widow could possibly have been. The whole story sounded very odd. Perhaps David knew some girl with a mother who'd been persuaded to co-operate. It was extremely charitable, whoever was responsible.

'Pretty well, considering,' answered the Colonel. 'Said she was anxious to see the lad settled and she was sorry if she was being a bore.'

'After driving you all that way, I should think she was entitled to be a bit boring.'

'No, no,' the Colonel said firmly. 'Start as you mean to go on.'

'You mean to go on, do you?'

'Good Lord, yes. She's coming over tomorrow, as a matter of fact. For lunch. Have a look at the roses, give me a tip or two about pruning.'

'Tips? *You*? You've gone on for years about being the only person in the West Country with the faintest notion how to prune roses.'

'You're never too old to learn.'

'You certainly didn't waste any time, did you?'

'That's one thing they taught you in the army,' said the Colonel, with more than a touch of complacency. 'If a job needs doing, get on with it.'

'The job in this case being the mysterious Erica.'

'Absolutely. Told Mrs Hope to pull all the stops out for lunch tomorrow. Smoked salmon and so forth. She was wearing a hat, you know.'

'Mrs Hope? What for?'

'Not Mrs Hope,' roared the Colonel. 'Erica . . . uh
. . . Thing. Fetching little number, made of straw,
with a pink sort of thingy round it. Haven't seen a
woman in a hat for years. Except in church, of
course. And not always then.'

'I wonder who she was.'

'I've already told you, Alex. I wish you'd learn to
pay attention. She'd come because of you.'

'Me?'

'That's what she said.'

'You must have got it wrong. I don't know anyone
called Erica. And if I did, why would I send her all
the way down to Somerset to take you to a cricket
match?'

Her father took some persuading but eventually
accepted that Alexandra had nothing to do with
organizing his trip. 'Hmm,' he said eventually. 'Bit
of a puzzler, really, isn't it?'

'Isn't it, though?'

Alex was in early the following morning. With two of
*Athene*'s editorial staff off sick, a heavier load was
falling on the shoulders of those remaining. She sat
down at her desk and sorted through her mail. At
least the postbag was relatively light at the moment:
so many people were away because of the holiday
season that the normal deluge of correspondence had
dried to a trickle.

She saw the thick envelope immediately. US
stamps. New York postmark. Familiar handwriting.

Why did her mouth go dry and her treacherous
heart start pounding away inside her chest like war
drums in the jungle? Deliberately she pushed the
letter to the bottom of the pile, to save it for later
while she got on with the work which awaited.

Halfway through the morning the telephone on her desk rang. When she picked it up, a feeble voice said, 'Alex?'

'Yes. Is that you, Nina?'

'Sort of.'

'What's wrong?'

'Seems ridiculous, really, but I think I've got chicken-pox. My husband's sent for the doctor but he hasn't arrived yet to confirm it.'

'Are you sure?'

'What else can it be when you're covered from head to toe in foul little pustules?' Nina said peevishly. 'And when I think that I paid the earth three days ago to have a facial at that new salon in Sloane Street . . .'

'Poor you.'

'I expect you'll be next,' Nina said gloomily.

'I've already had it.'

'I thought I had too, when I was a child. Obviously you can get it more than once. Anyway, the point is, can you cope?'

'We have so far. Felicity's here, and Petronella, and Lucy. All the editorial assistants except Hannah, who's on holiday, and all the production staff. I'm sure we'll manage. Just relax, Nina, enjoy a few days off.'

'How can I relax when I look like a blancmange covered in maraschino cherries?'

'Try.'

'I feel absolutely *awful*. Sore throat, runny nose, head like a cottage loaf. Alex . . .' A note crept into Nina's voice which Alexandra recognized with surprise as pleading.

'What?'

'Don't tell anyone about this, will you?'

'Not if you don't want—'

'*Private Eye* would love it. I've already had a couple of spats with them and they wouldn't pass up an opportunity like this to poke fun. I mean, chicken-pox is such a *stupid* thing to have at my age.'

'I won't breathe a word,' promised Alex. 'And Nina . . .'

'Yes?'

'Whatever you do, don't scratch.'

'Oh God.'

Together with Nina's secretary, Alex rescheduled most of the Editor's appointments for the next couple of weeks. The ones which could not be changed, or were too important to be missed, she shared out with the others and put a schedule on their desks. She hoped a fortnight was enough: she knew it was supposed to take about that length of time to get over chicken-pox, but perhaps it was more serious for adults.

She checked with all the contributing editors to ensure that the copy still needed for the forthcoming issue of *Athene* was in hand. She glanced through Nina's notes for her Editor's piece at the front of the magazine and since it was by no means complete, jotted down some further ideas.

Felicity staggered in late, looking tired. 'Hi,' she said hollowly.

'How was your evening?' asked Alex.

'Dreadful.'

'And Jarrett?'

'Frightful.'

'Why?'

'He took me to his hotel for dinner then spent the first half of the evening trying to get me drunk and the second half trying to get me upstairs.' Felicity yawned hugely.

'Cunning little devil,' said Alex. 'Did he succeed in either aim?'

'In the first one, yes,' said Felicity. 'I'm not sure about the second.'

'Fliss! You didn't!'

'I don't think so,' said Felicity, reaching for her hand mirror and examining the skin under her eyes. 'I'd look different, wouldn't I?'

'You'd *feel* different,' said Alex.

'Well, I don't.'

'That's all right then.'

'God, I hate men.' Felicity struck out her tongue and had a good look at that too. 'But at least I got a terrific interview. And all sorts of snippets and gossip. Plus a whole batch of original drawings previewing his next collection. You should see them, they're sensational.'

'Does he know you've got them?' Alex asked suspiciously.

'I'm not awfully sure,' Felicity said airily.

'Won't he kick up a fuss when he discovers they've gone?'

'Not as big as the fuss I'll kick up if he says anything. He wouldn't want to end up sharing a cell with Mike Tyson, would he?' Felicity's jaw jutted in a way Alex had not seen before.

Alex raised her eyebrows. 'May I have a look?'

The sketches *were* sensational, no doubt about that. They would make a splendid focal point in a forthcoming issue; the various editors could produce copy related in various ways to new trends in the States . . .

Alex sat down at her desk and took several very deep breaths. She pretended to be busy dealing with her correspondence but she did not see the letters she

185

appeared to be looking at. Instead, she was savouring the mix of power and excitement which surged through her. It was that *42nd Street* feeling – 'Hey gang! Let's do the show right *here*, whaddya say?' The overwhelmed sensation any understudy had when picked out of the chorus line to take over the leading role, the star having suddenly collapsed.

No-one else knew that Nina was sick. Nor how long she would be away. With Nina out of the office, however, someone was going to have to take nominal charge.

Why not her?

The notion exhilarated her. She thought ahead to the December issue and the one after that. They should both be in preparation now. Even the current one, though more or less wrapped up, still needed further work. And she, Alexandra Maitland, had a chance to put some of her own ideas into practice and see whether they worked or not.

If they did . . .

All she had to do was imply, without ever actually saying so, that the reins had been temporarily handed over to her. She knew none of the others possessed the ambition which fired her. If she told them what she was doing they would probably support her, probably do as good a job for her as they did for Nina. But if she told them Nina had given her the go-ahead, and Nina discovered the lie, she would be out. And unless they thought Nina had put her in charge, she would not be able to get things done the way she wanted.

So she had to tread carefully.

She stood up and clapped her hands loudly until everyone was looking up from their work.

'Nina's not well,' she said briskly. 'She's going to be out of the office for a while.'

'Heavens,' cried Felicity. 'Not chicken-pox, is it?'

Since her fiancé was a close friend of one of the *Private Eye* writers, Alex shook her head. 'Something gastric, I believe. Meanwhile, obviously she wants us to get on with completing the next issue.'

'It's just about ready,' the production manager said. 'Still one or two things needed. I'll come and have a word around lunchtime, if that's OK.'

'That's fine,' Alex said. Her heart thudded. He seemed to take it for granted that she was the one to talk to. And no-one else had raised any objection.

'I did want to ask about the photographs for the item on Herbal Remedies,' one of the part-time editors said. 'Can I speak to you about it this afternoon?'

'Of course.' Alex couldn't believe it was that easy. Although she was the most recent arrival on the team, nobody seemed to question her authority. 'And since we're already developing the Christmas issue,' she added, 'let's see if we can surprise Nina when she gets back.'

'How?' asked Petronella.

'We could start by taking an entirely new look at Christmas. Any ideas?'

Alex stayed behind when the others were gone. She made herself a cup of coffee and sat slowly drinking it, savouring the rich smooth brew. On the desk in front of her was the envelope which had arrived that morning. She put down her cup and took a paper-knife out of her desk. It was ridiculous to feel slightly breathless, but she did.

Inside the envelope was an airline ticket, an open ticket on Concorde. And with it, a note.

187

*Join me. I can't live without you, Alex. You know it, I know it. I guess we were meant to be, however much we try to fight it. The ticket is open-ended. Just telephone me and I'll be at the airport to meet you.*
*I love you.*

She sat back in her chair and closed her eyes. She was an idiot, a fool. She should have learned her lesson by now. And yet the longing to break out, to do the sudden impetuous thing, to drop everything and go running off to New York was suddenly irresistible. All her life she had played it safe, done what others expected of her, hidden her emotions behind the stiff upper lip the Colonel was so fond of, played the straight bat he always wanted her to. And now, sitting on her desk, was an invitation to change.

It was not the ticket alone – she could have bought one herself any day she wished. What mattered was what it represented. She looked at the stiff carnations from Carlo San Lorenzo. She looked at the layout she had been working on. If she went home and packed a bag, she could be in New York tomorrow.

But . . .

There were always buts. If she went, she would have made an irreversible decision. She remembered Cameron's voice: *This is your chance to go for gold . . .* If she went to New York, she would be saying, in effect, I choose love over gold, love over my career. I accept that my development as myself is less important than the chance to become part of a couple.

She thought of husbands and children and Volvo estates. Nappies. Dirty underpants. Measles. The school run.

She picked up the ticket, opened it, looked at the destination. She got up, made herself another coffee, sat down and picked up the note again.

There was a movement at the door of the office and she stiffened for a moment, remembering Jarrett Keach's warning about security. Suppose an intruder had got into the building? The cleaners weren't here yet: she was alone on this floor, even if there were still people working in the offices above and below.

Then she saw Matthew Prescott.

For a blank moment she stared at him. Then she said, 'You're supposed to be in New York.'

'I didn't like the coffee,' he said with a wry grin. Silently she handed him her cup and watched him sip it appreciatively, his eyes on hers the entire time. She had forgotten how good-looking he was, the intriguing way he managed to appear cool on the surface, nonetheless conveying an impression of passion ready to be ignited at a moment's notice.

He came over and stood by her desk. 'I thought you might have joined me in New York,' he said softly.

'Whatever gave you that idea?' she said flirtatiously.

His face was very close to hers as he bent and picked up the airline ticket from her desk.

'This,' he said.

He was so near her that she could smell his cool lemony cologne. Instead of pulling away she stayed looking up into his eyes, then slowly closed her own, waiting for his kiss. His mouth brushed hers. He came closer, and she felt herself begin to melt, anticipating the tenderness of his lips, the way they would harden as excitement took hold of them both, the way she would step into his arms and surrender to his embrace.

Behind them, on one of the editorial desks, a telephone began to shrill.

'Leave it,' Matthew whispered, as she stood up. 'Alexandra. Leave it.'

'I can't,' she said, and was surprised at the unsteadiness with which she walked across the room, lifted the receiver, handled the mundane enquiry. By the time she had dealt with it she had recovered her usual self-possession. When she reached her own desk, she perched on the edge and raised her eyebrows at Matt. 'Well?' she said.

'I think we should have dinner together and talk,' he said.

'What about?'

'Us.'

'You think there's something to talk about?'

'I *know* there is.'

She picked up the airline ticket and tucked it into her bag. She needed to think. And the decision she would almost certainly come to would be a hard one to take. Meanwhile, there was Matthew.

Following him out of the office and down into the street, sitting beside him in the cab which took them to Covent Garden, sitting opposite him in the warm restaurant full of good smells, candlelight, fresh flowers, her predominant feeling was one of surprise.

She knew she liked him. She knew he was fun to be with, someone whose company she enjoyed. She remembered the distinct thud of disappointment verging on alarm she had experienced when she had stepped out of the lift to find him surrounded by luggage, obviously leaving. But what really astonished her was the way she had responded to him just now in her office.

I haven't felt that melt of the heart since Cameron,

she thought. I never thought I would again, and certainly not so soon. I hardly know him, yet I wanted to fling myself at him, I wanted him to kiss me, make love to me.

She knew from bitter experience how treacherous such feelings could be, and the blind alleyways down which they led. She thought of the Concorde ticket in her handbag and Cameron's note:

*I guess we were meant to be, however much we try to fight it.*

Was it true? How could it be if she was able to think about another man in such physical terms? She forced herself to concentrate on the here and now. They drank wine, consulted the menu, ordered, but she took little notice of what she was eating, trying to calm the turmoil within her.

'Did your father enjoy his cricket match?' Matthew asked as they lingered over coffee.

'Yes.' She forced herself to concentrate. 'The most extraordinary thing. Some woman turned up on his doorstep and simply swept him off to the county cricket ground in Taunton in her car.'

'Really?'

'He had a fantastic time. Said she was a fetching little thing.' Alex laughed. 'I can't remember when I last heard him so animated.'

'Did he say who she was?'

'That's the extraordinary thing. He hadn't the faintest idea – and being the Colonel, didn't bother to find out.'

'Mmm.' Matthew was smiling at her over the edge of his glass.

'All he knows is that her name is Erica. He didn't even know her surname. But she was coming round the next day to have lunch with him.'

'Good.'

'I told him the first thing he has to do is establish who she is and where she comes from.'

'Absolutely,' Matthew said. 'A man of his age can't have strange females dotting in and out at any time of the day or night. What *will* the neighbours think?'

'Right.' Alexandra giggled. 'She's going to get him right on his roses. Apparently she thinks his pruning technique leaves a lot to be desired.'

'Mother's a bit bossy when it comes to gardening, I'm afraid.'

Alex stared at him. 'Mother?'

'That's right.'

'This Erica person is your *mother*?'

'Yes.' He looked away, as though embarrassed.

'But . . . how did she know about the poor old Colonel's hip?'

'I told her.'

'And how did she know he was dying to go to the match?'

Matthew didn't answer.

'Matthew . . .' Alex said insistently.

He opened his eyes very wide and leaned towards her. 'I told her, all right? It's no big deal. I asked her if she'd take him.'

'Oh, Matt.' Sudden tears pricked Alexandra's eyes. 'What an incredibly sweet thing to do.'

'Not really.' He tried to pass it off. 'She's quite a cricketing fan herself, so I knew she wouldn't mind.'

'But for you to remember about my father . . .'

Wordlessly, she leaned across the table and put her hand on his. She tried to imagine Cameron doing something so thoughtful. Or even Carlo San Lorenzo. It was impossible. She sensed that the man

192

opposite her had spent his lifetime in such small acts of kindness.

'By the way,' she said. 'I've been asked to dinner by one of the neighbours.'

'Which one?'

'Charlotte Hanover, she's called.'

'Isn't she a portrait painter?'

'That's right.'

'Rather a good one, I believe. She won the BP Portrait Award a couple of years ago – and something at one of the recent Royal Academy summer shows, if I remember correctly.'

'She said she'd won one or two things. But not in a boastful sort of way, only because I asked her.' Alexandra wondered if there was a feature in it: successful younger women, the varied careers it was possible for them to take up these days, the chances they had to rise to the top in their chosen professions, whether or not those professions were less orthodox than the ones chosen by their male counterparts. It could be interesting . . .

'I didn't know she lived in our block,' Matthew said.

'I think she's seeing something of my brother,' said Alexandra. 'Anyway, she came to my door and invited me to dinner.'

'Prospective sister-in-law vetting, do you think?'

'I don't know if it's got that far . . . anyway, she suggested I might like to bring someone.'

'And?'

'Would you like to be that someone?'

'Love to. When is it?'

'Next Saturday.'

He checked his diary. 'I'm free. Shall I bring a bottle?'

'Bring something, but *not* a bottle. Lady Charlotte

193

Hanover is *very* fussy about the wine she drinks.' Alex recounted her meeting with the young painter and they laughed together.

'She looks about sixteen,' Alex said. 'When I was that age, I slunk about in an agony of embarrassment in case anybody looked at me.'

'I worried about spots.'

'God, yes. Remember how they used to feel as though they were the size of grapefruit?'

'Neon-lit . . .'

'Throbbing like jukeboxes . . .'

'I don't believe you ever had a spot in your life,' Matthew said. He smiled warmly at her, reached across the table and gently touched her face. 'It's a contradiction in terms.'

'I'm glad I'm not a teenager any more, aren't you?'

'Yes. On the other hand, they're far more self-possessed these days, aren't they?' Matt said.

'Or seem to be.'

'Though this Charlotte Hanover can't be all *that* young, when you think about it.'

They drove home in silence. When they stopped outside her door, Alex knew he wanted her to invite him in. Standing close to him in the hallway, she looked up at him and bit her lip.

'I need to think about this some more,' she said.

He nodded. 'That's all right.' His voice was gentle. 'We needn't rush into anything. I'm not going anywhere.'

*But I might be* . . . 'No.' Alexandra reached up and kissed his cheek. 'Thanks, Matt. I enjoyed the evening.'

Closing the door of her flat behind her, she thought: something rather important has passed between the two of us.

# 9

It was a hell of a day. For a start, Matthew had not slept well, lying awake in his bed with what seemed like every pulse in his body hammering away with the insistence of a drumbeat. Leaving Alexandra at her door, unkissed, untouched, was one of the hardest things he had ever done, especially when what he had really wanted to do was to carry her into her bedroom – or his – and make love to her. Lightheaded from a combination of wine, jet lag and lack of sleep, even thinking about it made him breathless. Several times during the night he was forced to get up and go into the kitchen for a glass of water. The thing which kept him in such a feverish state was the unmistakable message her brown eyes had sent him as they stood so close together outside her door. She might not have kissed him, but for the moment he knew he was willing to settle for that message: I love you – I think.

Or had he read it wrongly? Was he merely indulging in wishful thinking? He had naively assumed that the Concorde ticket he had seen on her desk had been one she had gone out and bought in order to join him in New York. But when he thought back, there was no logical reason whatsoever why she should do such a thing. It might not even have been hers. And if it was, perhaps she was supposed to fly to New York sometime soon, on business. Or perhaps it had been a present from a – he swallowed, feeling sweaty with embarrassment – from a lover or something. Given the brief span of their acquaintance, the even briefer time they had actually spent together, how could he have been so presumptuous as to imagine that she would wish to fly out and join him at the Plaza? He had never even kissed her.

And yet, those eyes of hers, those messages . . .

He remembered all the nights when his sisters had sat at the end of his bed and sobbed their hearts out over some man. How he had soothed and advised – most of the time, that is. He wondered whether he dared ring Victoria or Emma, but when he saw what the time was, he knew he could not. All three of them were adults now, supposedly able to cope with the crises life flung at them. For the hundredth time he turned over, rearranged his pillows, tried to put his brain into neutral, think of nothing. It was hopeless. All he could see was Alex, her mouth, the way her head tilted. And beyond that, some fairytale kind of Hansel and Gretel cottage full of apple trees and roses and Alex herself stooping under a low lintel in a summery dress . . .

In the end, he got up, unable to sleep any further. He stood under the shower for a long time, trying to relax, feeling the alcohol of the night before still burning through his veins. He twisted the nozzle of the shower-head and turned off the hot tap, revelling in the icy needle-sharp spray stinging his body. A game of squash or a hard workout was what he really needed, but the gym wouldn't be open for another three hours, nor did he know anyone he could call at such short notice to partner him . . .

He got into Cadogan's early, and found himself with two empty hours in which to get on with his work before anyone else showed up. There was a huge amount of correspondence waiting in his In tray; a start had to be made on completing the business he had transacted in the States, clients had to be notified, shippers contacted, import permits sorted out. There was a heap of sales catalogues from all over the world to be sifted through, magazines to be trawled for items of interest . . . By concentrating hard on the papers in front of him, he gradually found himself calming down, normality taking over.

And then the phone rang and it was Alexandra.

'I don't think this is going to work,' she said. She sounded frightened, a little distraught. There was a note in her voice which reminded him of his sisters, and he smiled to himself. Though neither of them mentioned it, she was obviously feeling much the same as he was and he was overcome by a longing to rush to her side, hold her, comfort her, whisper that everything would be fine.

'You may be right,' he said soothingly, though frankly he thought it would work wonderfully well.

'We – we don't seem to have much in common,' she said.

'I know.' There was mock resignation in his voice. 'I hate opera, you hate jazz.'

'And I loathe modern art—' she began.

'It's my job,' he said firmly.

'So, about the only thing we do have in common is . . .' she said, and hesitated as though she could think of nothing they shared.

What did things in common matter, when it came to love? he wanted to ask. It's the big things which matter, not the details, and those we surely have in common. Besides, if it's understood from the outset that you have entirely different tastes, perhaps you're

197

less likely to disagree. '. . . Our taste in coffee,' he said lightly.

'Yes.'

She needed reassurance of some kind, he could tell. 'Have faith, Alexandra,' he said. 'In both yourself and in me.'

'Yes.' But she did not sound convinced.

He could see Ruth at the door of his office, frowning, shaking her head, looking back over her shoulder. He raised enquiring eyebrows at her, and she mouthed, 'Trouble!' at the same time jerking her thumb over her shoulder at the reception area.

He said into the telephone, 'We'll talk about it later, all right?'

'Yes.'

'And, Alexandra—'

'Yes?'

'I l—'

But before he could complete the sentence, he saw Tony Cashman, solid as a double-decker bus, loom into view behind Ruth, who was gesticulating and trying to explain the reason for the interruption. The lines of his short-cropped ruthless hair were disturbed, as though he had forgotten to comb it that morning or else, having combed, had continually run his fingers through it since then.

Matthew stared, nonplussed. Cashman had not come into Cadogan's before, preferring Matthew to go down and see him in Hampshire. So why was he here now? In his ear he heard Alexandra's voice saying, 'You what?'

'I'll tell you some other time,' he said, putting down the receiver. Standing up, he advanced towards Cashman with his hand outstretched. 'Tony!' he said warmly. 'Good to see—'

It was at that point the day started to spin badly out of control.

'Where is she?' Cashman shouted, ignoring Matt's hand, walking across the room to lean on the desk as though he was finding it difficult to remain upright without support. He looked terrible, his face blotched and patchy, his eyes red, as though he had been up all night.

'Where is who?' Matthew said. 'Tony, I—'

'Cindy!' Cashman exploded. 'My wife. Where's she gone?'

'I really don't know,' said Matthew. He wondered what was wrong, wishing he had had a chance to talk to Ruth – though from the expression on her face as she hovered behind Cashman she didn't know either. 'Has something happened to her?'

'I wouldn't be here otherwise, would I?' Cashman said loudly. He pounded the desk with a large fist, shaking the vase of freesias so that a single crimson flower detached itself and dropped to the shiny mahogany surface. 'Fact is, she's disappeared.'

'Sit down, Tony,' Matthew said. He came round the corner of his desk. 'Sit down and tell me about it.' He looked over at Ruth. 'Two coffees, I think. All right?'

She nodded, her face concerned. 'I'll get them right away.'

Cashman lowered himself heavily into a chair and sat with his face buried in his hands. 'She's gone,' he said in a muffled voice.

'And obviously you don't know where,' said Matt.

'Stands to reason, dunnit? Otherwise I'd go and get her, wouldn't I?'

Imagining the scene, poor Cindy hustled out to some waiting car with one of Cashman's beefy paws

199

grasping her arm like a manacle, Matthew tried to repress the thought that it might have been exactly to escape such strong-arm tactics that the beautiful Cindy had vanished, Matthew said, 'Why do you think she might have come here?'

'Because she fancies you, doesn't she?'

'She *what*?'

'Fancies you. I knew it when she met you that first time you came to my place.'

'Tony, I can assure you you—'

Cashman held up one of his bulldozer hands. 'No worry about it, old son. I don't blame you – though if I thought you was messing around with her, anything like that, you'd be in dead trouble, believe you me.'

'I haven't spoken more than half a dozen words to your wife in the whole time you and I have been working together,' protested Matt. The last thing he needed at the moment was an outraged husband on the warpath. 'If your wife fancies me – as you put it – she's been keeping it very much to herself.'

'Yer, well,' Cashman said. 'I know Cind. And I'm telling you, she's dead keen on you.'

Though he hoped he remained outwardly calm, Matthew was conscious that his spirits had taken an ominous dip. There had obviously been something wrong with the Cashman ménage for some time – why else would Cindy Hill have lied about her whereabouts, telling her husband she had been in Wales when she had really been in a London nightclub? Though he had no idea what lay behind it, he knew that by virtue of having witnessed Cindy in the execution of a lie, he himself was – whether he wanted to be or not – somehow involved.

'Have you called her mother in Wales?' he said patiently.

200

''Course. First place I tried. Drove straight down to Ebbw Vale, didn't I? She wasn't there. Not unless she was hiding in the loft or something.'

'You searched the place, did you?'

'Wouldn't say searched, exactly. Had a good sniff round, though. I didn't trust the old girl to be telling the truth – though I think she is. She's as worried as I am. Nuts about Cindy she is, always has been.'

Matthew settled into his own chair on the other side of the desk. He leaned back and stared at the window. 'It's one of the perks of being a parent, isn't it?'

'What is?'

'Being nuts about their children.'

'Wouldn't know, would I?' Cashman said, easing his shoulders as though they hurt him. 'Never had any.'

'Do you want any?' Matthew said. 'Do you and Cindy plan—' but Ruth was coming into the room with a tray, setting it down on his desk, handing one of the white bone china cups with the delicate gold rim to Cashman, watching him take his first appreciative sip.

Matthew's unruffled manner had evidently soothed the businessman a little. He looked up and managed a somewhat wavering smile. 'Sorry, Matt,' he said. 'Shouldn't have come barging in here. I know it's nothing to do with you really, but honest, I'm at my wits' end.'

'Has she ever done this before?' Matthew asked. 'Gone off without telling you, I mean?'

'No,' Cashman said. He shook his head. 'Never.'

'Have you tried asking around her friends?'

'Rung them all, haven't I? Been on the dog for hours. Unless they're covering up for her, none of them have seen her.'

'Have you contacted the police?'

'The police?' Cashman stared at Matthew as though he had suddenly levitated. 'The *police*?'

'You know,' Matthew said lightly. 'The guardians of law and order. Those chaps in helmets who're always willing to tell you what the time is.'

'Not round where I grew up, they're not,' Cashman said. 'I wouldn't ask the fuzz the time if it would save me old granny's life.'

Matthew felt a certain embarrassment. He had been brought up to believe that policemen were havens of security, to whom you turned in times of trouble. He knew, from reading the newspapers, that there was a wide stratum of society for whom this did not hold true.

On the other hand, if Cindy Hill was genuinely missing, who better to find out where she had gone – or been taken – than the police? 'Don't you think it might be a good idea to get in touch with them?' he said quietly. 'The longer you leave it, the colder the trail will be.'

'Yes.' Cashman twisted in his seat, the first time Matthew had seen him in anything but complete control of any situation in which he found himself. 'Well, that's why I come to you, really. Thought you might be able to help.'

'I honestly don't see how. I'm an art dealer, not a private detective.'

'Yes.' Cashman stared down at his big hands, his shoulders bowed. Familiar with his usual belligerent stance, Matthew found it strange to see the brash, self-confident businessman reduced to the kind of helplessness he was now displaying.

'Tony,' he said, 'I don't think I can be of much help to you. But you might find it helpful to talk about it, don't you think?'

'Talk? I'm not much of a one for talking,' Cashman said. 'What d'you want to talk *about*, exactly?'

'Well, had you and Cindy had any – uh – sort of, you know, *marital* difficulties?' Matthew found it difficult to suggest such a thing to a man like Cashman, but, surprisingly, the businessman did not seem to take the question amiss.

'Marital?' he said. 'You mean, like, was we quarrelling a lot?'

'That sort of—'

'No sex life any more – that what you mean?'

'I wasn't exactly—'

Cashman leaned forward and narrowed his eyes at Matt. 'Was our marriage on the rocks? Straight up, that's what you want to know, isn't it?'

'I wouldn't go so—'

'Nah,' Cashman said. 'I don't think so. I love Cindy and as far as I know, she loves me. Never seen any signs that she doesn't, anyway.'

'Any – uh – areas of dispute?' Matthew asked, thinking that at least he'd be able to get a job with a marriage guidance bureau if Cadogan's suddenly folded.

'Areas of dispute,' Cashman repeated, slowly nodding his head. He gave the matter a certain amount of consideration. 'Not really. Nothing more than you'd get with any married couple. You know the kind of thing: do we have steak or salmon for dinner? Should we go to Corfu for the summer or to the house on Mustique? Annabel's or Tramp? – that sort of thing.'

'Ah.' Matthew did his best to look sophisticated.

Annabel's or Tramp, indeed, he thought. Night after night, all over the country, ordinary married couples must be wrestling with exactly this sort of knotty problem. No wonder the divorce rate was soaring.

'Or Regine's,' Cashman added thoughtfully.

'But you didn't argue about anything serious?' Though, as he had already noted, Matthew was aware that to one stratum of society the choice between Annabel's or Regine's could be *seriously* serious.

Cashman avoided his eye as he said, 'Like I told you, nothing. Not what you'd call important.'

Behind his back, Ruth appeared in the doorway. Soundlessly she mimed picking up a phone and speaking into it. Her expression indicated that the call was urgent.

Matthew got up. 'Just a minute, Tony,' he said. 'Something I must do. I'll be back in a moment.'

'What is it?' he said quietly, closing the door of his office behind him.

'It's her,' Ruth whispered. 'On the phone.'

'Which *her*?' Matthew's thoughts immediately flew to Alexandra.

'Cindy Hill,' hissed Ruth. 'She's asking to speak to you, and she sounds as if she's crying.'

Matthew went into Ruth's office and picked up the receiver. 'Hello?'

'Mr Prescott?' a choked voice asked.

'Yes.'

'It's Cindy Hill here.' There was a gulping sound as though the model was choking back a sob.

'How can I help you?' Matthew said.

'It's the most tremendous imposition, I know, and I have absolutely no right to call you up like this or anything, but I just – I just . . .' Cindy's voice began to wobble out of control in a way which was familiar

204

to Matt from many late-night sessions with his sisters.

'Anything I can do, I'll be glad to,' he said soothingly.

'Mr Prescott, would you do me a favour?'

'Of course. And please call me Matthew.'

'Would you – could you possibly meet me?' There was some further snuffling. Then Cindy said, 'I really *really* need to talk to someone.'

Matthew did not need to ask why. Although he hardly knew the super-model, he was aware that there were times when a semi-stranger was a better confidant than a close friend. And a lot more likely to offer advice that could be trusted to be impartial. Which was what he was prepared to bet Cindy wanted.

'Where and when?' he asked.

'Uh – oh God, I don't know. Um . . .'

'I'll be at the Ritz at one o'clock,' Matthew said. 'I'll see you there.'

'Oh . . .' Cindy Hill breathed out a long sigh of relief. 'Thank you so much.'

'But before I do that, there's something I'd like you to do for me,' Matthew said firmly.

'What's that?'

'Tony's in a fine old state. Don't you think it would be kind to give him a call on his portable telephone and—'

'I can't, I can't, he'll start shouting and—'

'– tell him you're all right?' said Matthew.

Cindy gave a laugh which was half a sob. 'I'm not sure that I am.'

'At least let him know you're alive.'

'Yes. It's not fair not to, is it?'

'Not a bit fair.'

'I'll do that. And I'll see you at the Ritz at one. You don't know how much better I feel.'

'I don't suppose there's much I can do,' said Matthew cautiously. 'Except provide an ear.'

'That's practically all I want,' said Cindy, and put down the receiver.

*Practically all* . . . Oh Lord, thought Matthew. The words implied at least one something else, if not more. He had a premonition that providing an ear would be a piece of cake; it was the something else which was likely to prove complicated.

Ruth raised questioning eyebrows at him. 'Everything OK?'

Matthew shrugged, rolling his eyes. 'I don't know. I can't work out what's going on.'

'Why's she ringing you?'

'Would you believe, because she knows a soft touch when she sees one?'

'And what does she want the soft touch to do?'

'I won't know that until I meet her at lunchtime. Perhaps I'll be able to find out what this is all about.'

Back in his own office, he found Cashman talking on the cellular phone he carried wherever he went.

'Where the hell *are* you?' he was saying loudly. 'Cind, for God's sake, why don't you just—'

He fell silent while the voice at the other end said something. Then he spoke again. Matthew could see that anxiety was making him sound angry and bullying, qualities which Cindy Hill, in her current distressed state, was bound to find threatening. How did you tell a man like Tony Cashman to lighten up, to ease off?

'But I *love* you!' Cashman shouted. 'You know I'm crazy about— Cind? Cindy?' For a moment he stared in disbelief at the instrument in his hand. Then he said, 'She's only gone and cut me off, hasn't she?'

'You were shouting rather.'

Cashman continued to gaze at his phone. 'Cut me off,' he said again. 'Do you believe that?'

'Mmm,' Matthew said, very noncommittal. He'd have done the same in Cindy's place. 'At least you know she's not in any danger, don't you?'

'Yer.' Cashman sighed and shook his head. 'I dunno. You work and scrape your way into the big time, you achieve most of the things you want – houses, cars, gorgeous wife, foreign travel, all the things you dreamed of when you were a grubby kid – and then, when you settle back to enjoy them, it all goes wrong.'

'Life's a bitch,' Matthew said.

'You can say that again, mate.'

'I expect it'll come right in the end.'

'Gawd. I bloody hope so,' Cashman said, with feeling.

She looked beautiful but fragile, tucked into one of the big armchairs in the central hall of the Ritz. She had ordered nothing. Without consulting her, Matthew asked for a bottle of white wine to be brought. When they both had a glass in their hands, and Matthew had watched her drink at least half of hers, he said, 'Right. What's this all about?'

She was wearing huge aviator glasses, designed to hide but only drawing attention to the palely perfect face, the unlipsticked mouth, the silvery blonde hair fine as maize silk, which was drawn back into the nape of her neck. She was wearing a Ralph Lauren silk shirt tucked into tight leather jeans and a Hermès belt; she caught the attention, whether she wished to or not.

At first he thought she was going to ignore his question. Then, leaning forward, she picked an olive out of the glass dish in front of them and held it between thumb and forefinger. Not for sustenance, but so that she had something on which to focus her attention while she thought about her response to him.

After a while, he said, 'Look, Mrs Cash—'

'Cindy.'

'– Cindy, I can't help you unless I know what's wrong.'

'I need somewhere to stay,' she said flatly.

'How do you mean?'

'Not a hotel, not with any of my friends, not with my mother. I need somewhere where he can't find me. Somewhere he doesn't know about.'

Matthew frowned. 'Are you in some kind of trouble? In danger? Has he threatened you or something?' He certainly wouldn't put a spot of wife-beating past Anthony Cashman. Yet the man had seemed sincere when he said he loved Cindy.

She shook her head. 'Nothing like that.'

'Then why do you want to hide from him?' Neither of them needed to spell out the fact that the 'he' they were talking about was Cashman.

'I need some time to think. And he won't let me. Wherever I am, he rings up or follows me or wants to be with me.'

'Is that so awful?'

Cindy gave him a long look through her sunglasses. 'It is when it becomes an obsession,' she said. 'I can't go anywhere without him tagging along. Which is rather sweet, I suppose, of course it is. But he's a busy man, with a lot of interests. What it means is that I have to be with him, except when I'm

208

working, since he can't always take time to be with me.'

'And is that why you've run off?'

'Basically, yes. I want some space. I need to get my act together, work out exactly what I want, and then keep on telling him until he hears what I'm saying.'

She took off her glasses and stared at Matt. Her eyes were the clearest of blues; her skin was flawless, without the faintest line to mar its perfection. Matthew wondered whether it was simply a lucky draw from the gene pool that she had ended up with such spectacular looks, or was it the result of years of careful nurturing? And would his sisters envy her superlative looks? Or Alexandra? He rather thought not.

It was not something he had considered much before now, but he could see that outstanding looks could be more of a curse than a blessing. They raised expectations; they got in the way of the person behind them.

'You know what he's like,' she said, and drank a little of her wine.

'How exactly do you think I can help?' he asked gently. He took an olive himself. 'And why me, anyway?'

'You, because I already know that you're kind, and discreet,' Cindy said. She looked away from him, a faint blush beginning at her jawline, and he knew she was referring to the fact that he had not betrayed her, even though he knew she had lied about being with her mother in Wales.

'And what about the first half of my question?' he asked.

'It seems odd, I know,' she said. 'I look like I've got it made, don't I?'

'Frankly, yes.'

'Looks, money, career, handsome husband, several homes . . .' Cindy ticked them off on her fingers.

'The girl with everything is how it looks.'

'In actual fact, I haven't got anything,' Cindy said, and a desolate expression crossed her perfect face. 'I could pay for a hotel, of course, but he'd find me.'

'How?'

'He'd track me down through the credit cards I use,' she said.

'It could be weeks before he—'

'Not for Tony,' she said. 'And if he didn't do that, he'd get one of his men to ring round every hotel in England. In the entire universe, if necessary.'

'Couldn't you use a different name?'

'Of course. But I can't use a different face,' she said. 'And whether I like it or not, it's a face everyone knows. Anyway, Tony's people would ask if there was a model staying, or someone who looked like a model. Even if people don't know my name, they know I'm someone.'

She said it without conceit, simply as a fact. Again, the realization of the downside of being beautiful hit Matt. You could not hide extreme good looks any more than you could disguise extreme ugliness. Most people were average, neither particularly hideous nor outstandingly lovely, and departures from the average were always noticed.

'I see.'

'Mr Prescott, all—'

'Matthew, please,' he said.

'All I want is a bed for a few days.'

Matthew thought of his flat. The second bedroom had long ago been turned into an office. Besides, he could just imagine Cashman's fury if he discovered that Cindy had been staying unchaperoned with Matthew. He was the sort of man who would come to the worst possible conclusion. Even thinking about his reaction made Matt's mouth go dry.

He thought suddenly of Emma and her huge Hampstead house. 'A bed?' he repeated.

'That's all. And time to think. I love my husband very much, but he just won't give me room to be me. And right now, that's what I need.'

Matthew realized he still didn't know what this was all about. Never mind. If anyone could get it out of her, Emma could. He stood up. 'Don't go away,' he said. 'I've just thought of something.'

'I knew you would,' Cindy said simply.

He could see that she was a gentle uncomplicated creature, whose life ran on clearly defined tracks. For Cindy Hill, things either were or were not. There were no in betweens, no grey areas. She was not a woman who would see both sides of a question, or want to analyse a given situation.

He went away and found a pay phone. He called Emma. 'It's Matt,' he said.

'Hi!' she said. 'How was the States?'

'Terrific, thanks. I got a lot of—'

'Tell me about this new girl,' Emma said. 'Fantastic. Ma says you made her take her father to a cricket match.'

'Whose father?'

'Hers. This girl's. Wasn't it . . . ?' Emma trailed off uncertainly.

'What are you talking about?'

'This girl of yours.'

'I didn't take a girl to a cricket match,' Matt said, deliberately obtuse. 'You must be thinking of

211

someone else. Look, Emma, how's your bump of philanthropy these days?'

'But I'm sure Ma said— My *what?*'

'Are you feeling charitable, in other words?'

'I gave twenty quid to Oxfam only the other day,' said Emma. 'And stood outside the Tube station rattling a tin for the RNLI a couple of weekends ago. What more do you want?'

'The loan of a guest bedroom.'

Emma said cautiously, 'Who for? Not another of your lame dogs, is it?'

'I don't know what you mean.'

'Yes you do. That Bulgarian.'

'Bul*gari*—'

'The artist Cadogan's was sponsoring to attend a symposium or something. The one who drank a whole bottle of vodka before making off with *all* Leo's boxer shorts.'

'Emma, hasn't anyone told you it's wrong to harbour grudges?'

'Leo actually had to go to work in a pair of my knickers,' Emma said.

'You can't surely hold me responsible for that.'

'I most certainly can. He spent the entire morning with his legs crossed, not daring to go to the loo in case one of his colleagues was in there at the same time and came to the wrong conclusion.'

'Emma, would you please shut—'

'So who is it this time? Some Latin-American gigolo like the one you took down to Ma?'

'He was *not* a gigolo. He's a highly respected artist.'

'With a nice sideline in bottom-pinching. Poor old Ma was black and blue for weeks afterwards.'

'Once,' Matthew said. 'He pinched her once.

Where he comes from, it's probably considered insulting *not* to.'

Emma drew a sharp breath. 'This isn't a Norwegian, is it?'

'No. It's a—'

'Because I absolutely refuse to have any more Norwegians, not after the last one tried to cut his throat in the drawing room.'

'It's Cindy Hill,' Matthew said quietly.

'What?' Emma sounded incredulous. 'The model?'

'Yes.'

'You want me to put Cindy *Hill* up for a night?'

'Or two. Maybe even three or four.'

'Matthew! Is this the girl Ma was talking about? Is it Cindy Hill you're so keen on that you even force our poor Aged P out into the snow to take her father to a county match?'

'Emma, why you ever took up silversmithing instead of romantic fiction, I'll never know.'

'I can't spell.'

Matthew sighed gustily. 'Just to put you in the picture. Cindy Hill is married to someone else with whom I rather think she's madly in love. And for your meteorological information, it rarely snows in Somerset in the summer. Nor have I ever been able to force Ma to do anything she didn't want to.'

'But why do you want me to have Cindy Hill to stay?'

'It's too complicated to explain this minute. But say yes, and I'll tell you all about it later.'

'Yes,' Emma said.

'You will? That's great.'

'When will she arrive?'

'This afternoon. I should think.'

213

'There's one condition.'

'I *knew* there would be.'

'That you swear to tell me all about this woman you told Ma was the most wonderful girl in the world.'

'I swear, Emma.'

'And I don't mean next year,' Emma said, wise in the ways of brothers. 'I mean like, before the end of the week.'

'Um . . .'

'The end of the month?'

'Yes. Before the end of the month.'

'Matt . . .'

'What?'

'You did say Cindy Hill, the *model*, didn't you?'

'Yes.'

'That's what I thought.'

Putting down the receiver Matthew returned to his table. Cindy Hill was nibbling an olive. She looked up at him. 'All right?' she asked.

He nodded.

'That's wonderful.' She smiled trustingly at him and his heart melted the way it did when his small nieces slipped their hands into his when he took them out. Complete faith, he thought. An absolute certainty that no-one wishes you harm.

He cleared his throat. 'I asked my sister,' he said.

'Oh, thank you, Mr Pres— Matthew. Thank you so much.'

'Here's the address.' Matthew wrote it down. 'She's expecting you. You can go up there whenever you want.'

Cindy was looking at the piece of paper in her hand. 'Emma Chisholm? Isn't she a jewellery designer?'

214

'Among other things.'

'I've got some of her pieces,' Cindy said. 'The most gorgeous silver breastplate sort of thing.'

'She's good on armour.' And even better at finding chinks in other people's.

'It'll be great to meet her. Perhaps I could commission something special from her while I'm there.' Cindy suddenly seemed more animated.

'I should think she'd be really pleased,' Matthew said.

Although he had had no such thoughts in mind, he realized that Cindy might well be in a position to do Emma some good, just as Emma was undoubtedly doing Cindy some. He felt decidedly pleased with himself.

After seeing Cindy into a taxi, he went back to the office. A pile of queries was waiting to be answered. There was an awkward problem to sort out concerning a shipment which had been damaged in transit from Rio de Janeiro to the Cadogan warehouses. He had several phone calls from Japan to deal with, and a request from a Bombay-based Hindu businessman that he fly out in the next few weeks to – as Mr Kapoor put it – 'spring clean' his collection of modern primitives. Which meant sorting out wheat from chaff, and living like a rajah while he did so. Yes please, Matthew thought.

He left the office late and dropped into a nearby wine bar to have a glass of the house Chardonnay and unwind from the day's traumas, his thoughts drifting haphazardly from Cindy to Alexandra to Emma and back to Alexandra. Undoing his Sulka tie, he rolled it up and put it in his pocket. Women, he thought, smiling a little. What *would* we do without them?

A friend he had not seen for ages came into the bar

215

with his wife, and, in the end, the three of them went on somewhere for dinner. It was exceedingly late by the time he got back to the mansion block. Leaving the lift at the third floor, instead of the fourth, he stood outside Alexandra's front door, listening. He could hear nothing. For a moment he wondered whether to knock, but decided against it. There was definitely some unfinished business between the two of them, but he was extremely tired.

He remembered what he had said to Alexandra the night before: *'We needn't rush into anything.'*

Opening his own door, he thought how great, how truly fantastic it was that there should be something into which they need not yet rush.

# 10

Alexandra woke late, feeling tired and sluggish. After her evening with Matthew Prescott she had slept badly, lost in feverish waking dreams, in memories which whirled kaleidoscopically through her brain, hurling fragmented images of Italy and crashing seas, roses and carnations, the aroma of coffee and the taste of wine, Carlo, Cameron, Matthew, the sound of bat on ball, thatched roofs and dusk falling across an English lawn.

She lay in a hot bath for a long time, thinking of nothing, letting her mind float free of the here and now. There was no need for life to be complicated, yet it invariably turned out to be so. The only way to handle it was to ignore it and hope that at least some of the complications would sort themselves out on their own. Go with the flow. She remembered Donna Fratelli's raucous laugh, the number of times the two of them had sat together over a glass of wine or a plate of pasta, discussing the things which really matter: men, or life, or the latest movie.

'In the end,' Donna used to say, 'that's what it all comes down to. You gotta go with the flow.'

The trouble was, Alexandra thought, walking into her kitchen wrapped in a bath sheet, the trouble was that you couldn't really go with the flow until you'd had time to work out which way it was going. Pointless trying to swim against it, but sometimes it just wasn't that easy to see which way the current went.

On impulse, she picked up the phone and began to dial Donna's number. It would be great to talk to her again, to get a blast of her reassuringly down-to-earth Stateside common sense. But she caught sight of her watch and realized that it would be half-past three in the morning in New York. Not exactly the hour for making social calls. She put down the receiver again.

The Concorde ticket to New York was where she had left it the night before. She picked it up and stared blearily at it. Today its message seemed less equivocal, and the accompanying note no more than one of Cameron's spur-of-the-moment enthusiasms. Nice gesture, Cameron, she thought. He probably hadn't even paid for it, just put it on his credit card.

She rang the *Athene* office and got Prunella. 'I'll be in a little late this morning,' she said. 'Is everything all right?'

'A bit of a blip in that special offer on silk scarves we're running in the next issue,' Petronella said.

'How big a blip?'

'The importers just rang to say their shipments have been held up in Delhi. Some question of whether they're liable for import taxes or not.'

'There's not a lot we can do about it at the moment, is there?'

'It can certainly wait until you get in,' Petronella said. 'It might even have cleared itself by then.'

She seemed to accept without question that Alexandra was the one who would handle the crisis, if it was still a crisis by the time she got into the office.

When she was dressed and ready to head for work, Alex sat down with a cup of coffee and thought once more about Matthew Prescott. The kiss – the nearly-kiss – last night had changed things. No question about that. She felt like someone who suffered from vertigo and suddenly found themselves standing on the edge of a deep abyss. Either she took a step back, or she stayed where she was, aware that sooner or later she would plunge into that unknowable chasm. Before she could stop herself, she had pulled the phone towards her again and was dialling Cadogan's.

'Matthew Prescott, please,' she said.

She was put through to his office. 'Matthew Prescott's secretary. Can I help you?' someone said. It was a pleasant voice, with an undertone of humour, and Alexandra was immediately jealous, envisaging Matthew and his secretary in his office, laughing together, sharing jokes about his work, perhaps going out for a quick meal before they both went home. Perhaps *not* going home but booking into a hotel and—

'I'd like to speak to Matt – to Mr Prescott,' she said, and could feel her voice trembling.

'Who may I say is calling?'

'Just tell him it's a – it's a personal call.'

'One moment.'

Then he was on the line. She closed her eyes. 'I don't think this is going to work,' she said, not announcing herself, confident that he would recognize her voice and the thoughts which filled her mind.

He seemed to grasp immediately what she was talking about. 'You may be right,' he said calmly.

'We – uh – we don't seem to have much in common.'

'I know,' he said. She thought how steady his voice sounded, how soothing. She could not imagine him chasing after other women once he had committed himself, could not imagine him being so insensitive as to leave a woman – *his* woman – wondering why he was so late arriving home, or whether he was coming home at all. He went on, 'I hate opera, you hate jazz.'

'And I loathe modern art,' she said.

He paused. Then he said firmly, 'It's my job.'

She found that reassuring. No passionate declarations about changing for her sake, about chucking it all in and finding something else to do. This was a man secure in himself and what he did.

'So,' she said flippantly, 'about the only thing we do have in common—'

'– is our taste in coffee?' he said, and she could almost hear him smiling.

'Yes,' she said in a tiny voice.

'Have faith, Alexandra,' he said. 'In both yourself and in me.'

'Yes.'

'We'll talk about it later, all right?'

'Yes.'

'And, Alexandra—'

'Yes?'

'I lo—'

'You what?'

She heard someone in the background, a voice saying that Mr Cashman was insisting on seeing him.

'I'll tell you some other time,' he said.

The office was seething like a beehive when she got in. Two of the production team were absent, down with suspected chicken-pox. Lydia had rung in to say she was chasing a story in the Lake District, though everyone knew that what she was really chasing was the ravaged-looking thriller writer she had met at the launch of his last book and slept with the *very same night*. Felicity had come out in a severe facial rash and spent the time either screaming or staring fixedly at the paperknife on her desk.

'It's probably that face pack you put on,' Alexandra said. 'Write it up.'

'I can't do that unless I know for sure, can I?' shrieked Felicity. 'They could sue.'

'Ring round some of the other magazines and see if the same thing's happened to them,' suggested Alex. 'The manufacturers are bound to have sent samples to other people, not just us.'

'That's an idea.'

'And for heaven's sake give me that paperknife.'

'But supposing it hasn't happened to anyone else,' Felicity said. 'Supposing I'm the only one?'

'Then it could be something you ate, couldn't it?'

'Like what?'

'I don't know. What do you eat?'

'Pure things,' said Felicity. 'Grapefruit and yoghurt. Stuff like that.'

'Could be an allergy,' said Helena, peering closely at Felicity's skin. She looked up at Alex. 'As a matter of fact, I think it's time we did another piece on allergies.'

Felicity picked up her mirror and began studying her face again. 'Look at me! I look like the title role in *Night of the Iguana*.'

Helena reached out and stroked Felicity's cheek. 'Allergy,' she said wisely. 'Definitely.'

'Yes, but what *to*?' Felicity shouted. 'And how long before it clears up? I'm going to a party on Friday and I can't turn up looking like this.'

'Perhaps you've been overdoing the yoghurt and grapefruit,' said Alex.

'Incidentally,' said Helena. 'Did you know that Marilyn Monroe was a size sixteen?'

Felicity let out a high-pitched shriek. 'What are you trying to tell me?' she demanded. 'Not only have I got skin even the Elephant Man would have rejected, but I'm *fat* as well?'

'I was talking to Alex,' Helena said defensively, stepping back a couple of paces. 'She was saying the other day about the way the media make women afraid to enjoy their own bodies. I thought we could hang something on the fact that one of the most enduring sexual icons of the age was in fact what today would be called – uh – big.'

'I read somewhere that more than 47 per cent of British women are size sixteen or over,' Alex said.

'I'm not,' said Felicity.

'Big, Bold and Beautiful,' Alex said, ignoring this piece of egomania and looking at Helena.

'Love to be Large,' said Helena. 'I could ring round, find some of the women who've come out as Frankly Fat.'

'That one who was in that movie about that writer,' said Felicity, tearing herself away from herself and her rash. 'You know, where she keeps him prisoner.'

'Dawn French,' said Alex.

'Or Roseanne Barr,' said Helena.

'I'd still rather be thin,' said Felicity.

'Oprah Winfrey,' said Helena. 'Or Liz Taylor, if you get right down to it.'

Felicity stared. 'You don't seriously imagine Liz Taylor's going to give an interview about how fat she is, do you?'

'Not really, but—'

'I mean, didn't the last husband say something about "Lose the fat or lose me"? And we all know which she chose.'

222

'Wouldn't you?' said Helena. 'All those blond-streaked curls?'

'Liz Taylor's gone *blonde*?' said Felicity.

'Not her, *him*,' said Helena.

'People, could we get serious here,' said Alex, and heard again the authentic Nina-note in her voice. 'Helena, put something down on paper. See what you can make of it and we'll discuss it later. Felicity, see whether you're alone in this reaction to the face pack or not, and then we'll take it from there.'

One thing about having a job, she thought, sitting down at her desk and leafing through the messages which had been left for her, it certainly takes your mind off your worries. One of the pink slips was a Returning-Your-Call message from a recently-elected female politician she had been trying to contact for days. Ringing the woman's number again, she found her in, and more than ready to offer her somewhat trenchant views on the House of Commons and the way that seminal institution seemed to cling to the outmoded notion that women were an inferior breed.

'Which,' said the lady politician, in her famous gravelly voice, 'they are not, as you and I both know.'

'Quite the opposite,' said Alexandra.

'Superwoman,' the lady politician said. 'That's what they want us to be. And you know why?'

'Why?'

'So they can laugh at us when we fall flat on our noses. They set it up deliberately so that we force ourselves to do more than any *three* men could do, and naturally quite a lot of the time we can't manage it.'

'But you believe in the innate superiority of women?'

'I do, as it happens. But try suggesting that down

223

here in the Royal Palace of Westminster,' said the lady politician robustly, 'and they'd all spontaneously combust. They pay lip service to equality but they don't want to have to do anything committed about it. I mean, look at the hours we're supposed to keep – Parliament is all about being a gentleman amateur, and absolutely nothing to do with working mothers or the demands of a family. And as for the loos . . .'

Having set up an interview, Alex sat back, making notes, trying to think of other entrenched bastions of male privilege, circles from which women were excluded. The Garrick. The Athenaeum. The MCC. This reminded her of the Colonel and his visit to the Somerset County Cricket ground, courtesy of Matthew Prescott and his mother. Perhaps she could go down next time there was a one-day match and drive him to Taunton herself, interview some of the club's officers, work something up.

She spent the rest of the day going through copy, dealing with the Customs and Excise men in an effort to sort out the red-tape tangle about the silk scarves, fielding telephone calls for Nina, running down elusive editorial, discussing layout.

The others had been gone for an hour by the time she was ready to leave. She stood up, stretched, packed her briefcase. There were still things she wanted to go through, if she was not too tired by the time she got home. She was meeting friends for dinner that evening, but she might be able to snatch an hour later that night.

As she was about to walk out of the office, the telephone rang. For a moment she stood at the door, watching it, wondering whether to answer it or not. Whoever it was could ring again in the morning if they wished to. Then, unable to resist the telephonic siren song, she picked it up.

A transatlantic voice said, 'I'd like to speak with Alexandra Maitland, please.'

'Donna!' exclaimed Alex.

'Hey, is that you, honey?'

'Yes.'

'Well, aren't I the clever one, getting you first time?' Donna said.

'You're not going to believe this,' said Alex, 'but I actually picked up the phone to call you this morning, except I realized it would have been the middle of the night your end so I put it down again.'

'Smart move,' said Donna. 'I'm not at my best at two in the morning.'

'Just for the record,' Alexandra said innocently, 'do you actually have a best? If so, I can't quite remember when it is.'

'Is that what they call dry English wit?'

'No, schoolboy humour.'

'Smart ass.'

'Did you ring for any particular reason?' asked Alex. 'Or just to insult me?'

'That too,' said Donna. 'But mainly – guess what!'

'What?'

'I'm coming over to stay with you.'

'That's *great*,' said Alex. 'How long for?'

'Why? You gotta problem with that?'

'Only that I thought I might move house in a couple of years. But you're welcome to stay until then.'

'Alex, it'll be just terrific to see you again.'

'And you, Donna. Absolutely wonderful.'

'How're things?'

'Terrific.'

225

'Any men?'

'Men? What're those?'

'You remember: they wear pants and take us out to dinner if we're very lucky and kick us in the teeth every chance they get.'

'Oh, *those*.'

'So?'

'Any of them around?'

'I'm a career girl, Donna, you know that.'

'Aren't we all, baby? But not so much so that we'd junk a permanent commitment to a *man* in order to keep on our job. And talking of junk, how's Cameron?'

'Steady on,' said Alex, laughing, slipping back easily into the comradely banter she'd always enjoyed. She hadn't realized how much she had missed Donna. 'I know you don't like him—'

'In spades—'

'– but he's all right.'

'He's all wrong for *you*, Alexandra Maitland. Juvenile, selfish, conceited, immature. If you really want to foul up your entire life, take my advice and go for him, white dress, veil, the whole shtick.'

'Well, thank you, Aunt Donna.'

'How to live unhappy ever after . . .'

'Some things never change,' sighed Alexandra.

'How do you mean?'

'The sun comes up each morning, the Pope's a Catholic, and Donna Fratelli's still sticking her nose into other people's business.'

'I care about you, Alex.'

'I know. So, when are you arriving?'

They discussed arrangements for a while. By the time she had replaced the receiver, Alexandra's mood was definitely up. She looked at her watch, cursed, ran for a taxi. She was late arriving at the restaurant where she had arranged to meet her friends, but they were women she had known since university days and were busy catching up on everyone else's news. Most of them were married, with children: they seemed to be set fair on the roads they would be travelling now for the rest of their lives. She alone was unmarried, though one had recently divorced.

Alex listened to them with a smile on her face but an increasing chill in her mind. Had she opted for the wrong values? Was her career that important? Her friends plainly felt sorry for her, a little embarrassed at the fact that she did not have a husband to contribute to the conversation, nor children, nor any of the little ups and downs of family life. They asked her questions about her job, professed to be envious, but she knew that they were not. Yet these were all women who, ten years ago, would have called themselves liberated, independent, ambitious. All of them had pursued careers and then, thankfully, relinquished them.

The euphoria of Donna's phone call slowly evaporated as the evening went on. She felt solitary and isolated, as though she were missing out on something very necessary, while the others discussed their families, raising their eyes to heaven, complaining about the circumstances of their lives in that particular way women do when they don't really want to change a thing.

Back at her block of flats, Alexandra stepped into the lift, then, about to press the button, hesitated. Instead of getting out at her own floor she went on up to the fourth floor, and stood in front of Matthew Prescott's front door. She listened but heard no sound. She put her finger to the bell, and then dropped it quickly.

In her own flat, although she normally drank very little, she took one of her best cut-glass tumblers and poured herself a stiff whisky – Laphroaig, bought on her last trip abroad. Sometimes it was important to spoil oneself – Helena had written a piece on it for the last issue of *Athene*, explaining that when women felt the need for a little luxury they should give in to it, that pampering oneself created an inner glow which proclaimed that this was a Special Woman. As a matter of fact, the whole issue had been built round a concept which Nina had labelled Special Women.

Curled up in a corner of the sofa, Alex took the Concorde ticket out of her bag once again, and set it on the cushions beside her. She had a choice: she could go or she could stay. If she went, much as her emotions screamed at her to do so, she knew deep in her heart that eventually it would just be more of the same, more of Cameron's evasion, his neglect, his unexplained absences. More of the gradual deterioration of the relationship into nagging on her part and lying on his. More of the helplessness of simply not being on the same wavelength as the person you were supposed to be closest to.

There would also be more of that marvellous exhilaration that comes with being in love. More of the excitement Cameron always generated, more of that sense of being swept up into something wonderful and outside her control. There was nothing circumspect about Cameron, nothing held-back. The unpredictability of the man was more than made up for by the heady feeling of surrendering to life at its sweetest and most bright.

On the other hand . . .

She got up and poured herself another slug of whisky.

Donna Fratelli was absolutely right. Cameron *was* immature. Cameron *was* selfish. And she knew that nothing would change, that she herself, a Special Woman on her second glass of neat spirits, deserved something better than Cameron could – or would – offer.

And then there was Matthew Prescott. With him, she felt none of the seething intoxication of love or lust or whatever it was which called her to Cameron. Yet, if she stopped to examine it, wasn't there something better than intoxication being built between them, as delicately as a spider's web, line by gossamer line? If they went on seeing each other, would they not eventually produce the same complicatedly beautiful pattern of commitment as her friends had? Wasn't that implicit in whatever it was which was going on between the two of them?

And wasn't the sexual element there too? Hadn't she felt stirred, moved, breathless when his mouth had trembled on hers, before the telephone rang and broke the spell?

The answer to all those questions was an emphatic yes.

She poured herself one last mouthful of whisky and tossed it back. Then, before she could have second thoughts, she picked up the telephone and dialled his number. When he answered, she said quickly:

'I want to see you. Now.'

# 11

Matthew's phone was ringing as he put his key into the lock of his door. Racing into his flat, he picked it up and heard his mother's voice.

'You're up very late,' she said reprovingly.

It was the kind of flanking attack which always left Matthew speechless with admiration. 'What about you?' he said. 'Old ladies shouldn't be up at—' he squinted at his watch – 'at eleven fifteen at night.'

'I can't think why not. And anyway, who says I'm old?'

'Not me. I wouldn't dare.'

'You're as young as you feel,' his mother said.

'Erica, the Cliché Queen,' Matthew said with affection. Carrying the telephone with him, he walked into the kitchen and poured himself a small whisky. 'Did you ring to say something important or just because you wanted to check up how late your son got home?'

'I rather like your Colonel Maitland,' his mother said.

'I'm delighted to hear it.'

'I don't know why you should have led me to believe he was some kind of old buffer.'

'Isn't he?' Matthew went back into his living room, sat down on the sofa and began to take off his shoes. Sitting down, he realized just how tired he was. He swung his feet up and leaned back with his head on a cushion.

'Not at all,' his mother said. 'Quite the opposite. Rather dashing, actually.'

'Isn't he confined to a wheelchair at the moment?'

'Yes, but—'

'Can one actually dash when one is in a wheelchair?'

'Believe me, Matthew, Richard can.'

'Richard?'

'Colonel Maitland. I don't know when I've enjoyed myself more.'

'Really?'

'After the match, he took me out to dinner.'

Matthew thought his mother sounded very young, her voice bright with some emotion he could not quite define but which made him feel instantly – pa*tern*ally – protective. 'Quite right too,' he said.

'He even got out of his chair. He said it was the first time he'd done so but he was damned if he was going to be wheeled into a restaurant like a blasted mental patient out with his nurse.'

'A wheelchair doesn't imply lunacy, does it?'

'Not really.'

'But I can see his point,' Matthew said. As he talked, he glanced with pleasure round his flat. It always looked immaculate after his cleaning lady had been in. He took in the carefully chosen objects, the discreet lighting, the gleam and shine of it. On the table in front of the sofa was a vase holding four pink roses, the blooms in various stages of uncurled perfection. He reached forward to brush one of them with his finger, and thought suddenly of Alexandra.

'Yes,' said his mother. 'So in he stumped with his leg in plaster, sort of roaring. He's got this roar he does.' She giggled, the way Emma and Victoria used to when they were young.

'Mother, are you giggling?' he said, rather touched.

'Why shouldn't I?'

'No reason at all.'

'Actually, there's only one thing wrong with him, really.'

'What's that?'

'He goes on about his daughter rather a lot.'

'Does he?' Matthew was not going to rise to the bait his mother dangled so expertly in front of him.

'Yes. He said most girls, no-one would drink champagne out of their slippers if you paid them to, but a girl like Alexandra – that's her name, Alexandra . . .'

'Is it really?'

'. . . he wouldn't mind betting they'd queue up to drink plain tap water out of her Wellington boots and count themselves blasted lucky to have the chance. Isn't that sweet?'

'Adorable,' Matthew said, thinking, just pass me Alexandra's wellie and I'd do the same.

'At least the two of you agree,' his mother said.

'On what?'

'On the fact that she's the most wonderful girl in the world. I can't wait to meet her. Richard said he'd invite me over next time she came down for the weekend.'

'Did he, indeed.' The thought of his mother meeting Alexandra under other auspices than his own was vaguely alarming. 'I gather you've been fairly stern about the way he prunes his roses.'

'Someone had to be,' his mother said. 'What a mess they were in! Anyway, I've sorted them out now. I went over and had lunch with him. Took my own secateurs, of course. You can never rely on anyone else's.'

'Mother, I asked you to take him to a cricket match, not to start hacking the poor chap's rosebushes to pieces.'

'He loved it,' said Matthew's mother. Thoughtfully, she added, 'So did I.'

'Just watch it,' Matthew said. 'These retired military men can get a bit frisky if you don't keep an eye on them.'

'I don't know why you should think I'd object to a frisky man, military or otherwise. I may be getting on a bit but I still know a thing or two.'

'Mother, *please*. You're making me blush.'

'How old-fashioned you are, Matthew,' said his mother. 'You sound like a throwback to the days of Queen Victoria.'

'Absolute rubbish. I'm—'

'You'll be wanting us to stand round the piano singing hymns next,' said his mother unfairly, and forestalled his indignant riposte by replacing the receiver.

He lay where he was, the whisky glass balanced on his chest. Heavens, he was tired. In a minute he would go and run a hot bath, luxuriate in it for ten minutes or so, and then get his head down. For the moment, it was enough to lie back and do absolutely nothing.

He was fast asleep when the telephone rang beside his bed. He scrabbled for the light switch, saw the time – my *God*! – picked up the receiver. It couldn't be Emma, could it, with some ghastly news about Cindy Hill slitting her wrists or something? Or Cashman, drunk and abusive in the lobby, looking for somewhere to lay his head? Or—

'Hello?' he said.

233

It was Alexandra. 'I want to see you,' she said, in a breathy little voice. 'Now.'

Before he could respond, she had put down the telephone.

Unfinished business, he thought. He remembered her phone call at the office that morning, and the declaration he had been about to make when Cashman appeared. Was he really going to commit himself to that extent? Had he really made up his mind that firmly? For a moment, throwing back the duvet, he paused. Ahead of him stretched the future, and this time, instead of a summer landscape full of lush green fields, it suddenly took on a closed and wintry air. Instead of Alexandra with her tawny hair loose about her shoulders, he saw a muscle-bound Fury wielding a rolling-pin, like something out of a Christmas pantomime.

It occurred to him, as indeed it had occurred many times before, that commitment to one woman had as its inevitable corollary a lack of commitment to all the others. Was he ready to retire from the fray – the rather delicious and exhilarating fray – just yet?

On the other hand, it could be argued that Alexandra Maitland was a woman for whom it was more than worth abandoning the rest of the female sex. And she had sounded fairly unequivocal about what she wanted from him, too. Yawning, he got out of bed and, unhooking his dressing gown from the back of the bedroom door, shrugged himself into it. Unequivocal or not, it wouldn't do to open the door in the altogether – though with any luck, that would be the next step . . .

The doorbell rang. Walking towards it, he yawned again, and hoped he wasn't too exhausted to cope with whatever might follow Alexandra's arrival in his flat. At the same time, he found to his astonishment that his feelings about this late-night call – this unequivocal late-night call – were mixed. On the one hand, the promise, the expectation, warmed the pit of his stomach and flooded him with a sense of delicious possibilities; on the other, something in him wondered whether this wasn't all too easy, especially since the reins seemed to have been removed from his hands and were being expertly manipulated by someone else. He wasn't used to it. In any relationship, there was one who led and another who followed. Maybe only a pace behind, maybe almost shoulder to shoulder, but definitely there was an alpha person and a secondary one. He wasn't all that sure he wanted to be Mr Beta. Or rather, since he indubitably wanted a relationship with Alexandra, perhaps what he hoped for was to dictate the terms, rather than have them dictated to him.

This made him what, exactly? Some kind of sexist beast? As impenitently chauvinist as – as Anthony Cashman, for instance? Surely not. Yet, if he was honest, he found that when it came right down to it, he wanted to call the shots, not have them called.

He reached the door. Opened it.

Did a double take.

'Hi,' the woman outside said.

'Laura!' he said. Of all the damned inconvenient times . . .

'You always did stay up late,' she said, moving towards him, standing provocatively close, before walking past him into the hall.

'Uh – how long have you been back?' he said. Though back was hardly the word since she had dropped her English origins, as so many other things, along the littered roadway of her life.

'About a day and a half.' She shrugged, looking flirtatiously at him. 'I was just – uh – passing by.'

'At this time of night?'

'Are you – uh – alone?' She waggled suggestive eyebrows, stared at him from under her eyelashes.

'Ye— I mean, no. Look, I'm expecting someone. A neighbour.'

She gave a half-laugh, enjoying his obvious confusion. 'At *this* time of night?' she countered. 'Do we at least have time for a . . . coffee?' Her tone made it clear that if he wished, coffee was only the beginning of what they might have time for.

The situation was one he found it difficult to handle. He could hardly order her out of the flat. On the other hand, Alexandra would surely be here any second. What did women mean when they said 'Now'? Usually they meant in about fifteen minutes, didn't they? Nose-powderings and so forth. He plugged in the kettle and reached down the jar of coffee.

'Just a quick cup,' he said. 'And then you'll have to go. It's been a real stinker of a day.'

'And on top of that, there's this neighbour dropping by,' Laura said archly. He could see mischief in her eyes.

He spooned coffee into a cup, poured boiling water on to it, handed it to her. 'Laura,' he said warningly. 'Just drink up your coffee and go. We'll talk another time, when I'm less exhausted, when I've got my diary in front of me. We'll have dinner, OK?'

'Heavens to Betsy!' she said in a teasing manner. 'Must be one hell of a neighbour for you to be acting so twitchy about her.'

He opened his mouth to speak and she put her

hand over it. 'And don't tell me it's not a her,' she said. 'I recognize the signs.'

'I wish you'd go, Laura,' he said coldly. It was extraordinary to think that once he had loved this woman to distraction, and now all he wanted was never to see her again. 'Drink your coffee, all right?'

'It's hot,' she murmured, peeping suggestively up at him over the rim of her cup.

The doorbell rang again. He had a premonition of imminent disaster. 'Just stay here!' he said.

This time, when he opened the door, it was Alexandra. She stepped up to him, put her arm round his neck and leaned in towards him, waiting for his kiss, while he wondered how he was going to explain Laura's presence in the kitchen. 'I hope I didn't get you out of bed,' she murmured.

Then she stiffened. He saw her eyes grow huge, saw their softness replaced with bewilderment and something which wrenched at his heart. Behind him he heard Laura's voice, shiny with malice. 'This coffee tastes good,' she said.

He turned. She had taken off her coat, somehow contrived to make herself seem a little dishevelled, as though the two of them had just been snogging on the sofa or something.

'Hello,' she said brightly, head on one side, as though she belonged in the flat, making it obvious that Alexandra didn't.

In Alexandra's expression as she drew away from him, stepped back, turned to leave, in her brown eyes, Matthew read a hundred messages.

And knew, with a sinking heart, that there wasn't a single one he wanted to hear.

The next morning, after another sleepless night – this

237

really had to stop or he was going to start dozing off at his desk – he got up, made himself a coffee and, wincing already in anticipation of her reaction, called Alexandra's flat.

As soon as the first ring sounded he knew she was not there, that the sound of the telephone was reverberating through empty rooms, as lost and desolate as wind crying across a salt marsh, as hopeless as he felt his own heart to be. Nonetheless he let it ring, feeling closer to her even through this tenuous connection, because *his* phone was ringing in *her* flat. In the end, he had no choice but to replace the receiver. He picked up his briefcase and found his way to the car park, where slots were reserved specifically for residents of the block of flats.

As he drove out of his allotted space, to his astonishment he saw Alexandra about to get into her white saloon. She looked wonderful, in a short skirt which showed off her long legs and a hip-length jacket which emphasized her shape.

Quickly he rolled down his window. 'Good morning,' he said, pretending a nonchalance he did not feel. He gave her a wide toothy grin, and immediately realized it was exactly the wrong approach. She would inevitably interpret it as some kind of macho statement about the fact that even as he entertained one woman in his flat, another was on her way upstairs with . . . *what* on her mind? Whichever way you looked at it, something fairly explicitly sexy.

She glanced down at him as though he were something she'd found smeared on the sole of her shoe after visiting an abattoir.

'Good morning,' she said. Her tone was dismissive, her voice icy.

'Look,' he said, braking and getting out – at least

they would be on the same level then, instead of *her* being ten frigid feet tall and *him* crouching six inches high in the driving seat of his car – 'about last night . . .'

She appeared to be astonished. She raised cold eyebrows. 'You don't have to explain,' she said, the way a school matron might have spoken on finding a member of the Fifth Remove engaged in some filthy practice in the school dorm. Without looking at him again she riffled through her leather handbag, found her car keys and opened the door of her Mercedes.

'Laura's just an old friend,' he said, knowing it was hopeless, that he had blown it or rather that Laura had blown it for him, and found he was speaking to the back of her neck. Perhaps if he seized the moment, lifted her long mane of hair, kissed the tender little place where the fragile bones disappeared into the collar of her jacket . . .

'I understand,' she said, as though she didn't give a damn. She got into the driving seat and began revving her car unnecessarily loudly. Maybe she was hoping to asphyxiate him with carbon monoxide fumes.

He bent down, still trying to keep them both at the same height. Over her shoulder, lying on the black leather upholstery of the back seat, he could see a black velour trilby which was vaguely familiar, though for the moment he did not have time to sort out exactly why or how. Alexandra was backing out of her parking space, much too fast. To get away from him, probably. Her expression was steely.

'I'll call you,' he said quickly, before she could disappear.

She looked at him with a derisive little smile – the sort of smile a lamb might bestow on a wolf promising that being eaten alive won't hurt.

'Sure,' she said, and she was gone, in a cloud of exhaust.

He stood looking after her. What was the next step? What kind of a lecher did she think he was? His mind went back to their brief conversation of the night before: 'I want to see you,' she had said, 'now.' And had put down the receiver before he could say anything at all.

She had given him no opportunity to indicate that there was an old friend with him – not that there *was*, at that point, but there *might* have been, and if there *had* been, it was hardly his fault if Alexandra had chosen to come knocking on the door without giving him a chance to explain – and then getting stroppy when she found someone had got there before her.

All the way to Cadogan's he worked on this scenario. By the time he reached the office Matthew was feeling distinctly indignant. Alexandra was clearly in the wrong but, in a typically female way, she refused to acknowledge it, blaming the whole fiasco on him. Her attitude that morning was unreasonable. If anyone deserved an apology, it was Matthew, not her. And was he going to get one? Was he, hell!

Handing his keys to the parking valet, he decided that he would take a firm stand. Until an apology was forthcoming, he was damned if he was going to get in touch with her. She could stew in her own juice.

In the lift to his floor he thought how odd it was that taking a firm stand should make him feel so bad-tempered.

He walked into his office.

'Good morning,' Ruth called.

'Mmm,' he said crossly, not looking at her.

'Coffee?'

Flinging open the door of his office so that it

hurtled back against the wall, he didn't even bother to answer.

'Nothing urgent so far this morning,' Ruth said.

He grunted.

'I've put your letters on your desk.'

'Good.' He banged his briefcase down, causing the tiny Giacometti bronze he kept on his desk to topple over.

'Anything else I can do for the moment?'

'No.'

'Aspirin?' murmured Ruth. 'Arsenic?'

He pulled himself together. 'Do I look that bad?'

'Well, let's say if I was choosing someone to share my fortnight for two in Majorca, you wouldn't be my first choice of companion.'

'Mmm.'

'In fact, you wouldn't be my *tenth* choice. Not in the mood you're in. In fact, given the choice of you or a bear with a sore wotsit, I'd take the bear every time.'

'Très droll.'

'What happened? Cleaning lady move the bed and you got out the wrong side or what?'

'Ruth, if you *don't* mind—'

'OK. All right. I'll get the coffee. Perhaps it'll cheer you up.'

As soon as she was out of the room he pulled the nearest phone across his desk and punched out the number of the *Athene* office.

So much for firm stands.

'*Athene* magazine. Can I help you?' a female voice enquired.

He asked to be put through to Alexandra's desk and was disconcerted when the voice wanted to know who was calling.

241

'Uh – Matthew Prescott, Cadogan's, Art Dealers,' he said, too flustered to give a false name. He hoped he at least sounded businesslike, as though it were not a private call, and realized immediately that Alexandra would refuse to take the call if she knew it was him.

There was a pause.

Then, two seconds later, just as he thought: 'I'm afraid Miss Maitland is not available right now,' whined the voice. 'Can I take a message?'

Yes, he thought. You could tell her it's *her* fault, not mine and next time she's feeling like a bit of fun – *if* that was what she had been feeling like – maybe she'd give a chap a chance to explain that there's already a woman in his flat, a woman he will kick out with the utmost speed if she'd just hang on, a woman he never even invited into it in the first place.

'No,' he said. 'Do you know when she'll be available?'

'I couldn't say, I'm afraid,' the girl said.

Was he being paranoid to imagine that she was looking at her fellow switchboard operators, rolling her eyes, one hand over the receiver, saying, 'It's him! Matthew Prescott! The one Alex told us not to put through!'

He could see them all sitting there, earphones on their heads, giggling themselves silly at his expense. He clenched his fists.

After a moment, he stood up and went over to the window. Below him traffic crawled down Bond Street. Among the press of cars he saw a taxicab painted like a page from a newspaper and another advertising a brand of beer. He pressed the redial button and was connected to *Athene* again.

'*Athene* magazine, can I help you?' a singsong female voice – a different one – replied.

'I'd like to speak to Alexandra Maitland,' he said, deepening his voice, adding a hearty note which was alien to him.

'Who can I say is calling?' the voice asked.

'Uh – Michael Watney,' he said. 'Of – of Cartier.' Across the road, a taxi drew up in front of the august jewellers and a man in pinstripe trousers and black jacket got out, then helped a woman with magnificent grey hair to alight. Either an eminent barrister, Matthew decided, about to buy his wife – not his mistress, not with that hair – some expensive bauble, or else he worked in Fortnum's, down in Piccadilly, where all the salesmen dressed like that, and was just showing off to his mother.

'One moment, please.'

The voice came back, seconds later. 'I'm afraid Miss Maitland is not available right now. Can I take a message?'

'That's all right,' Matthew said, and put down the phone. Did he feel better or worse that neither the genuine Matthew Prescott nor the spurious Michael Watney was able to get through to Alexandra? He burned with embarrassment.

For the rest of the morning he had no time to think about her. The hours passed quickly. At eleven thirty he was called into James Cadogan's office to talk about the best way to handle their latest commission. An Australian who had acquired millions through the construction industry now also wished to acquire respectability.

'Extraordinary people, the Aussies,' James said. He lit one of the cigars which he smoked nonstop and blew rich smoke upwards. The habit had given his

243

room – it was hardly an office, packed as it was with artefacts from all over the world – a curious olfactory patina, as though the whole place had been dipped in aromatic tobacco and then hung out to dry. The ceiling had the creamy colour of a pub and everything in the place smelled; it was always a simple matter to discover which files had passed through James's hands, just by sniffing them.

'I agree, but in what sense, exactly?' asked Matt.

'This chap, for instance.' James tapped the folder in front of him. 'He says he's interested in building up a representative collection of primitive and tribal art, but when we tell him the best place to look is in his own back yard, as it were, he tells us he doesn't want Abo art,' James said, trying unsuccessfully to pronounce the last two words of his sentence with what he imagined was an Australian accent.

'He's not the only one,' said Matthew.

'Seems so shortsighted, though. Some of the work the Aborigines have produced is quite beautiful, especially where it hasn't been corrupted by commercial interests.'

'I know.'

'So how can this chap ignore it?'

'If you despise the race, then you're not going to rate its art works, are you?' murmured Matthew.

'Perhaps not. But then aren't you taking a political stance, rather than an aesthetic one?'

'How long have you got, James?' Matthew said, looking at his watch. 'Because that's one of those questions we could debate for some considerable time.'

'Well, are you prepared to take this man on?'

'Absolutely. The first thing I'd do would be to point out, in the gentlest possible way, of course . . .'

244

'Of *course*.'

'. . . that it would look much better if he was seen to be supporting indigenous native art as well as looking to Africa or Latin America. There's a big surge of Australian nationalism at the moment.'

'Trying to ditch the Queen, aren't they?'

'Among other things.'

'Wouldn't blame you, Matt, if you refused.'

'Why should I?'

'It'll almost certainly mean a trip or two out there. You won't mind?'

'Not in the least.'

'No-one who – er – might object?' The chairman picked up a small Graeco-Roman bronze from his desk and turned it between his fingers, while a faint flush crept up the flesh above his stiff collar.

'No.' Matthew allowed a small uncomprehending frown to appear, though he knew exactly what the chairman was getting at.

'No-one who might miss you . . .' The chairman gave an audible gulp. '. . . if you were away for as long as – say – a month?'

'My sisters might, I suppose,' Matthew said innocently. 'And my mother, of course. Otherwise . . .' He shrugged, feeling more cheerful. He guessed that the chairman's embarrassment stemmed from the fact that these personal questions had been instigated by Barbara, or even Georgina, rather than from any curiosity on his own part. 'Otherwise, I don't really know what you mean.'

'You know. Some kind of a . . .' James waved a hand that strove to be nonchalant, encompassing the various paintings and sculptures which surrounded him and which, as it happened, featured an extraordinary number of nubile and semi-naked ladies in a recumbent posture. Realizing what they represented, he added quickly, 'Not that I think for a moment that *you* . . . though, of course,' he floundered ever deeper, 'naturally, a man like, you, presentable and so forth, you probably have several . . .' He stopped, looking Matthew severely in the eye. 'I don't know what you're laughing at,' he said plaintively.

'James, you really are priceless.' Matthew grinned. 'And, for your information, at the moment there isn't anyone who would mind if I flew out to Sydney for a month or two. Or even six. So don't worry about it.'

'At the moment?' James said keenly, scenting a titbit to take home to Barbara and Georgina. 'But there might be soon?'

'Honestly, you're worse than my mother and sisters,' said Matthew.

'It is a truth universally acknowledged that a single man in possession of a good fortune must be in want of a wife,' said James.

'I'm not going to argue with Jane Austen on that one,' Matthew said. 'Only trouble is, I haven't got a fortune. And on the miserable pittance you pay me, I'm unlikely to amass one.'

To his surprise, although he had been joking, James took him seriously. 'Perhaps that's something we could discuss when you get back from Australia,' he said. 'Can you wait until then?'

'Just about,' said Matthew.

He called Emma. 'All right if I drop in for a drink this evening?' he said.

'Absolutely fine.'

'How's the patient?'

'What swine you men are,' Emma said, and banged down the receiver.

It occurred to Matt that this was the third time in about twelve hours that a woman had done that. A stop must be put to it. And where did Emma get off, calling her only brother a swine?

Perhaps it meant that Cindy Hill had revealed at least some of whatever it was that bothered her, which was a good thing, really. He dialled the *Athene* office again, and was told once more that Alexandra Maitland was not available.

Later that day he parked his car outside Emma's house and knocked at the door. Leo, his brother-in-law, let him in.

'I just want to say that you've made an old man very happy,' he said, leading the way into the high-ceilinged drawing room and pouring Matthew a drink.

'What do you mean?'

'It's not every day that a man gets up and finds one of the most gorgeous creatures in the western hemisphere spooning in the cornflakes at the breakfast table,' said Leo.

'You mean Emma, of course.'

'Of course, old boy. Who else? You can't imagine I meant that hideous model you sent round to stay with us, can you?'

'Not for a moment.'

'Seriously, both Emma and I are thunderstruck,' Leo said. 'I mean, Emma's no slouch in the looks department, as you know, but this Cindy of yours is like – well, like something turned out by a machine. Absolutely perfect.'

'I'm sure she wouldn't enjoy hearing that very much.'

Through the open French window leading out into the garden, Matt could see Cindy sitting on a swinging bench with Emma's children on either side of her. She seemed to be reading to them, while they listened with close attention.

'Exactly,' Leo said. 'Which seems to be part of the poor girl's trouble. A lifetime of being treated as an object rather than as a human being must be very debilitating.' Leo's voice took on a lecturing note. 'The cult of the beautiful, it seems to me, has its roots in the ancient fetishistic worship at the shrines of such earth mothers as Dea—'

'For God's sake, Leo, save it for your students,' said Matthew.

'What? Oh sorry, was I beginning to bang on a bit?' Leo grinned good-naturedly. 'Don't mind me.'

'Has she . . .' Matthew indicated Cindy '. . . talked to Emma at all?'

'Yes.'

'Any hint as to what it's all about?' Matthew raised his eyebrows.

'Difficult to say, old boy. However, the two of them stayed up late last night, drinking my best booze, and this morning Em's been slamming doors quite a bit, and giving me dirty looks. From which I deduce that it's the same old scenario, don't you?'

'What scenario's that, exactly?'

'The one where all the male characters are foul-mouthed and lecherous with only one thing on their minds, and the females are all patient, suffering, submissive angels with hearts of gold.'

'Oh, that one.'

'Sometimes, old boy – and I speak as one who has changed a good many nappies in his time and is not a total stranger to either the washing-up bowl or the kitchen stove – sometimes I wish we were still living in the good old bad old days.' Leo looked owlish and

248

splashed more whisky into their heavy cut-glass tumblers.

'I know what you mean.'

'No-one in his right mind would want to revert to the horrible inequality of the Victorian era or anything like that,' Leo said earnestly.

'Good God, no . . .'

'Those benighted days when men slogged their guts out oop at t'mill, or died of dysentery out in India, while their poor wives led lives of cruel hardship, bringing up the children with the help of a couple of nursemaids and a skivvy or four.'

'Terrible, terrible,' murmured Matthew.

'Not for a single *moment* would one want those days to return. On the other hand . . .' Leo stared out into the garden and drew a deep regretful breath. 'They had a certain something, don't you think?'

'Definitely,' said Matthew.

'A certitude,' said Leo, gesturing with his glass and sloshing whisky over the carpet. 'A – how shall I put it? – sense of everything knowing its place, and keeping to it.'

'By everything, you mean women?'

'What else, old boy?'

'Don't let Emma hear you.'

'I know my place, and I keep to it.'

'I've noticed.'

'Actually, that poor girl's a bit cut up about something,' Leo said, putting an affectionate arm around the younger man's shoulders as they watched Cindy in the garden. She was looking down at the two children, her face animated as she turned the page of the book on her lap. 'Good idea of yours to send her here. Can't imagine anyone better than Emma for sorting things out, really.'

249

'Good.'

'Oh, there you are.' Emma herself appeared, looking a mite unfriendly.

'Yes. Here I am,' said Matt.

'Humph,' Emma said.

'I see we're in militant mood,' said Matt.

'You could say.' Emma was carrying a glass of white wine, which she proceeded to sip aggressively.

'So before we go any further, could I just state that I am not personally responsible for burning any witches at the stake.'

'And I,' said Leo quickly, 'have never sexually harassed any female employee in the workplace by word or deed, though I confess to the occasional lewd thought.'

'I've never recommended an induced birth to a pregnant woman merely in order to fit in with my golfing schedule,' Matt said.

'And I have never turned down any woman for a job on the grounds that she might go and get married, or have a baby, thus necessitating six months' paid maternity leave.'

'Nor have I ever suggested to any working woman that she'd be better off at home where she belongs. And it's not *my* fault that women have periods,' finished Matt.

'May I also put it on record that I love you for your *mind*?' said Leo earnestly.

'What do you men think you are: NW3's answer to the two Ronnies?' Emma asked.

'Gosh – are we that good?' Leo said.

'You gave me that line about my mind ten years ago,' Emma said.

'It worked, didn't it?'

'I wasn't fooled then,' said Emma, smiling at him. 'And I'm not fooled now.'

'Darling,' said Leo.

'Sweetheart . . .'

'I hate to interrupt this love-fest,' said Matthew. 'But, Emma, I wonder if you'd mind having a quick business discussion with me before things get out of hand?'

'OK.'

'Come and sit down over here.' He indicated one of the big Chesterfields which stood on either side of the fireplace.

'I'll go and fix something for the kids' supper,' Leo offered. 'Give you two a chance to have a natter.'

Emma allowed herself to be led over to the sofa. She sighed. 'Sorry,' she said. 'It's not really you or Leo I'm against. But sometimes men can be so . . . so ob*tuse*.'

'Tell me what it's all about,' Matt said.

'I don't know if it's confidential or not . . .' Emma glanced out into the garden.

'She *did* come to me in the first place.'

'I know. But . . .'

'She obviously wants some help. But unless we know what it's about, we can't do much.'

'She had an abortion,' Emma blurted out.

'What?'

'Cindy was pregnant, and she had an abortion.'

'That's dreadful.'

'And she can't forgive her husband for it.'

'Did he know about it?'

'No.'

'Then how is it his fault?'

'Because,' said Emma patiently, 'he wants her to continue her career as a model. He wants her to be the top model in the world. He says she's got plenty of time to have babies, but for now she's got to focus on her career.'

'What's wrong with that?'

'She doesn't *want* to. She doesn't particularly want to be a top model. She doesn't need the money. She's one of those women who wants to stay home and be a sweetheart-wife, as she puts it. And he keeps shooing her out into the cold hard world.'

'Does he know how she feels?'

'She's told him, hundreds of times. But he doesn't really know, because he doesn't really listen.'

'I see.' Matthew looked down into his glass.

'And having an abortion—'

'Is that what she was doing in London when she told him she was in Wales with her sick mother?'

'Yes. She told me about seeing you at that nightclub.'

'Odd place to be, if you'd just got rid of a baby.'

'It was an act of defiance, she told me. If he wanted her to be a top model, she'd behave like one. But she wants to be at home, with her husband, and lots of children, and dogs everywhere.'

'Really?'

'She's got it all worked out. Two girls and two boys. Piano lessons. Ballet classes. Brownies. No boarding schools or anything like that. No nannies.'

'It's not a hugely ambitious desire, is it?' Matthew said sadly. 'You'd think she ought to be allowed to get on with it.'

'It actually,' said Emma, raising a hand to her face and brushing it across her eyes, 'made me rather weep, listening to her. As it's doing again, thinking about it.'

'Do you think I ought to tell her husband?'

'I don't know. She's slightly terrified of him, but she seems to adore him.'

'Has she said what she wants to do about any of this?'

'I don't think she knows.' Emma put her hand on Matthew's arm. 'Bit bloody ironic, isn't it?'

'What is?'

'Most women moan about the problems they have trying to get out of the house to pursue their careers. And here's one who's desperate to throw up her career and stay home, only she's not allowed to.'

'Can you bear to have her for longer?'

'As long as she wants. She's absolutely wonderful with the children. And she's been sitting with me down in my studio while I work. She's given me a couple of great ideas. Moving in the kind of world she does, she has a real eye for what looks good.'

'I'd better go and have a word,' Matthew said.

'There's one other thing, Matt,' said Emma.

'What?'

'I'm not sure how well she is. She's hardly eaten a thing since she got here, and last night I went into the kitchen and found her looking terrible.'

'How do you mean?'

'All sweaty and pinched-looking. She said it was nothing, but I'm sure she was in pain.'

'Do you think something's gone wrong?'

'I don't know. She was crying a lot yesterday.'

'I can imagine.' Matthew frowned. 'Cashman's not exactly the most sensitive chap I've ever met, but I'm sure he'd be appalled to hear about all this.' He got up as Leo walked across the lawn outside and smiled down at the trio in the swing-seat. 'Once the children have gone I'll talk to her.'

But Cindy, when he joined her in the garden,

seemed withdrawn and cold. She sat, not meeting his eye, her fingers restlessly turning the pages of the book on her lap.

'Shouldn't you tell Tony?' Matthew asked gently.

'He won't listen.'

'But he'll have to, eventually.'

'No.'

'It was his child too,' Matthew said.

'He's forced me to be a murderer,' Cindy said, and burst into tears.

Matthew put his arm round her and she burrowed her head into his shoulder. 'If only he would *listen* to me,' she said.

'Can I ask you something?' Matthew said.

'What?'

'Do you love him? Do you want to stay with him?'

'Yes,' Cindy said. '*Yes*. But unless he stops forcing me to be something I don't want to be, I shall have to go.' She sat up and stared at Matthew, her eyes red with tears. 'I think it's the thought of leaving him as much as anything else which is worrying me. I don't want to. But sometimes I feel he doesn't give me any choice.'

'Shall I talk to him?'

'I think it would just make him angry. He'd see it as some kind of betrayal, that I'd allowed someone from outside to see that things aren't as perfect as they ought to be.'

'Well, think about it some more,' Matthew said. 'If it would help, I'll go down and see him.' He took her hand in his and stroked it gently, as he might an unhappy child's. 'Meanwhile, why don't I pick you up and take you out to dinner one evening?'

'That would be lovely.'

'I'll ring you in the morning to fix it.'

'Thank you all for being so kind.' Cindy began to cry again and for a while the two of them sat in silence, gently swinging to and fro.

Standing in the foyer of his mansion block later that evening, waiting for the lift to descend, Matthew was joined by a small blonde girl of about twelve or fourteen. He assumed she was the younger daughter of the couple who lived on the second floor, until she spoke.

'You work at Cadogan's, don't you?' she said.

He turned, surprised, his head full of Cindy, of Alexandra. Looking at her more closely, he realized she was much older than he had at first thought. There were lines around her mouth and eyes, and a kind of earnestness which he did not associate with prepubertal girls. 'How did you know that?' he said.

'I saw you at Sir James Cadogan's party recently.'

'Oh.' He smiled. 'And you are?'

'Charlotte Hanover.' She put out her hand and he shook it.

'Ah. The portrait painter.'

'Yes.'

'I've heard of your work, of course,' he said.

He was about to add that he was supposed to be coming to dinner at her flat very soon, then wondered if that was still on, since he had been invited by Alexandra who presumably would now rather eat maggots than go anywhere with him.

'Look,' Charlotte said. 'It's fearfully short notice, but if you're available next Saturday, I'd be awfully pleased if you could come to dinner.'

'Gosh,' he said, pretending to think. Obviously Alexandra had not mentioned the possibility of him coming as her . . . what? Escort? Companion?

'That's nice of you,' he said. 'As a matter of fact, I *am* free. Something just fell through today. So thank you – I'd love to come.'

'Good. See you about eight then,' Charlotte said.

Shutting the door of his own flat behind him, Matthew wondered if Alexandra would still be planning to attend. Almost certainly, he decided. For a start, she was the original invitee. And then it wouldn't occur to her that after what had happened, he would have the nerve to go under his own steam. But since he had been invited in his own right, he *would* go. It would be a chance to see her on neutral ground, maybe even a chance to explain that it wasn't *his* bloody fault that Laura had shown up at the door only seconds before she herself had. He wished he felt more positive about it than he did.

Remembering his own thoughts as he walked towards the door last night, not knowing it was Laura, thinking it was Alexandra and feeling his freewheeling lifestyle threatened, his macho image slightly dented, he realized he must be mad. How could he have been so shortsighted, so absolutely *thick* as to worry about commitment when the girl he was worried about committing to was Alexandra?

The fact that it turned out to be Laura on the doormat, instead of Alexandra, made no difference whatsoever to his sheer idiotic lunacy.

# 12

Donna came out into the arrivals concourse at Heathrow wearing Day-Glo cycling shorts, a shiny purple baseball cap and a big T-shirt emblazoned with the words KEYCUTTERS DO IT WHILE YOU WAIT.

Wow! Alexandra blinked. No chance of missing *that*. Confronted with Donna's exuberant wardrobe, she realized there were only two courses open to her: either she took it on the chin (*'straight spine, old girl,'*), or she slunk away and refused to answer the phone when Donna called to see why she hadn't been met. And obviously she couldn't do *that*. She squared her shoulders and, facing up to the challenge of those uninhibited Spandex-covered thighs, waved vigorously. Catching sight of her, Donna opened her arms wide and started screaming.

'Alex! Honey!' she shrieked. Heads turned as, oblivious, she surged towards Alexandra like an excitable goose. 'How *are* you?'

'I'm just fine.' Alex gave her a big hug. 'And you?'

'Never better, kid. You better believe it.' She planted a boisterous kiss on Alex's cheek. 'You look fantastic.'

'Wish I could say the same about you.' Alex held her friend at arm's length. 'Is this dress-to-impress couture or *what*?'

Donna looked down at herself and shrugged. 'I

read somewhere you gotta wear loose comfortable clothes on a long-haul flight.'

'Otherwise what happens?'

'I don't know – I didn't read any further.'

'Well, you certainly look comfortable,' said Alex.

'I am.'

'Not to mention loose.'

'Loose? I sure hope you're not going to give me a hard time after I just travelled three thousand miles to see you,' Donna said, her eyes crinkling as she gave Alex another bear hug.

'Did you really come just to see me?'

'Not quite.' Donna picked up her bags and followed Alex towards the exit. 'I got myself a few commissions – did I tell you I was thinking of going freelance?'

'Think you can make a go of it?'

'I hope so. Otherwise, I starve. Which wouldn't be a bad thing, I guess.' She twirled, big as a bus. 'I put on twenty-three pounds in the past two months. Look at me.'

'Difficult to look anywhere else,' Alex said.

'Thing is, I just got sick and tired of nine-to-fiving. Is this all there is to life, I asked myself.'

'And?'

'And what?'

'What did you answer yourself?'

'Yeah, I said. Or do I mean no? Anyways, I decided to go for it. So though I'm officially on vacation, I'm actually *working*. Got people to see, places to go, the whole bit.'

'Great. I'll introduce you around. Maybe you could do a piece for *Athene* – a Yank's-eye view or something.'

'I want to go to Paris, Madrid, Prague, Vienna,

places like that.' In the passenger seat of Alex's Mercedes, Donna stretched luxuriously. 'It's years since I was in Europe.'

'The place has changed,' Alex said.

'I can see that already.' Donna turned and stared intently at her friend. 'OK, Alex. Let's hear all about this new man of yours.'

'New man?' Alex wished she had not immediately thought of Matthew Prescott, who was not only emphatically *not* her new man, but unlikely to be any kind of man at all, as far as she was concerned.

'I know you have one, otherwise you wouldn't be looking so great.'

'I always look great, thank you, Ms Fratelli.'

'Uh-oh,' said Donna. 'Is this where she goes all English and uptight on me?'

'Not at all.'

'Not at all,' mimicked Donna.

'Hey,' said Alex. 'Don't call us, OK? We'll call you.'

'Don't like my English accent, huh?'

'Is *that* what it was?'

'So what's he like?'

'Who?'

'This guy you're obviously so mad at you don't want to tell me about him.'

'There's nothing to tell.'

'But there *is* a guy?'

'There was,' Alex said.

'So what happened?'

Alex told her. It felt good to talk about it, to describe her sense of total humiliation at having, as it were, bared herself to Matthew only to find him in a dressing gown, with some . . . *strumpet* drinking coffee with her dress half-unbuttoned.

259

'Some *what?*' Donna said.

'Strumpet,' said Alex.

'Where the heck did you find a word like that?'

'That's what she was. And the awful thing, Donna, was that it was my own fault really. I just assumed that he'd be alone. I didn't give him a chance to say anything, just said I was coming to his place right that minute, and then I put the phone down.'

'Sure it wasn't his sister or something?'

'Absolutely certain. Sisters don't have that Things-Were-Just-Getting-Interesting look.'

'What look's that?'

'You know – sort of bedroom eyes.'

'Bee-stung lips?'

'Lots of those. And sort of moving about inside her dress as though her bra was suddenly too tight.'

'She could have been putting it on.'

'Or taking it off,' Alexandra said.

'Perhaps the poor baby was just feeling a bit hot.'

'Oh, *sure.*'

'Come on, Alex. If he'd got her to that state, why was she drinking coffee? I mean, you don't get down to things and then break off for refreshments, do you?'

'I suppose not.'

'And you said he was wearing a bathrobe, and she was still in her dress?'

'Ye-es,' Alex said uncertainly. By now they were part of the endless stream of traffic speeding towards west London.

'I bet what happened was, just after you called him, this witch turns up out of the blue.'

'Two women showing up late at night within five minutes of each other? Bit of a coincidence, wasn't it?' Alex dodged a pizza delivery van with a poor sense of timing.

'They happen, honey, believe me. Remind me to tell you some time about my Uncle Morton's wife and his mistress both turning up to his funeral in the self-same dress . . . Anyhow, there's the witch outside your guy's door and he tells her to bug off, she can't come in, he's expecting someone and *she* says, oh please, baby, sweetie, honey pie, can't I have just a teensy weensy little coffee after I've come all this way to see you, and *he* says – because he's a proper English gentleman, right?'

'Right.'

'*He* says: well, OK, but get your skates on, sister, because I'm real keen on this someone I'm expecting, so being this really obnoxious kind of a female, she decides to kill his chances.'

'It *could* have happened like that.'

'I'll just bet she was some broad he used to be in love with or something, and he's been giving her the brush-off while she's trying to fan the embers, get back to the way it used to be.'

'Hmmm.'

'*Bet* you.'

Alexandra was beginning to feel a lot more cheerful. Donna always had that effect on her. At the same time, she felt a creeping guilt about Matthew. Perhaps it *had* happened the way Donna said. Perhaps it *was* by pure chance that the other woman had been there, and Matthew was entirely innocent. Innocent of what? She hadn't really given him time to explain, just looked at that horrible creature prancing about in the hall all sexed up, and assumed the worst.

She decided that as soon as she got back to the flat, she'd call him and apologize.

* * *

'Hey, I love it!' Donna cried. She turned slowly in the middle of the living room, like a gyrating parakeet. A parakeet with, Alexandra had to admit, extremely large thighs.

'Love what?' Alex had forgotten Donna's wonderful exuberance, the zest with which she approached life.

'This apartment. All the amazing stuff you've got. That *gorgeous* bureau thing. Where did you get it, for heaven's sake?'

'It belonged to my grandmother.'

'Looks like it ought to be in a museum,' Donna said with awe, fingering the inlaid panel on the top. 'And those dishes – what are they? Limoges, or something?'

'Coalport, actually. My mother gave them to me when I left university.'

'They're just beautiful,' breathed Donna. 'I know it's a terribly Yank thing to do but while I'm here, perhaps we could go and do some antique shops, yes?'

'London's awfully expensive for that kind of thing. Maybe you'd like to come down to visit my father and we could look around there, too.'

'Love to.'

'Make yourself at home while I fix you a coffee,' Alex said, 'then what would you like to do? Take a shower, have a nap? We'll go out somewhere to eat, if you want, or stay in, whatever. I've got some complimentary tickets for the theatre tonight, nothing too heavy, a murder mystery, which you might like. You say.'

'I'm not that jet-lagged right this minute,' said Donna. 'A soak in the tub first, maybe, and then let's hit the town, OK?'

'OK.'

'I'll be really spaced-out tomorrow morning, so we might as well not waste tonight.'

'We're invited out to dinner tomorrow evening,' said Alexandra.

'Anywhere nice?'

'I don't really know. It's this friend of my brother's who lives in the same block. She looks about eight years old but has to be more than that.'

'Why'd she invite you – checking you out?'

'For what?'

'Sister-in-law material?'

'Could be. Anyway, she told me to bring someone so I phoned and asked if I could bring you.'

As she said this, Alex felt her face begin to flush, aware that she had originally invited Matthew Prescott. She had not had a chance to mention it to Charlotte Hanover before their . . . their *contretemps* of the other night, and assumed that he would have the decency to realize that she would not, in any case, want him to accompany her now.

Going into the kitchen, filling the kettle, finding cups and saucers, she wondered if Donna's version of the events of that night could be anywhere near correct. *Two* women showing up at nearly midnight? It was possible, of course. But was it likely? On balance, she had to admit that it could have happened that way. And if so, then the least she owed Matthew was an apology.

While Donna lay in the bathtub, inaccurately bawling the bits she could remember of *My Fair Lady*, Alex dialled Matthew's number, only to find that he had switched on his answering machine. She listened to his calm voice explaining that he was not available and if she would like to leave a message . . .

but the message she would like to have left was far too complicated, so she rang off without saying anything.

Waiting for the kettle to boil, she thought about the other night, and the more she thought about it, the more obvious it became that Donna had got it wrong. After all, if things had really been the way she said, wouldn't Matthew have rung up and tried to explain?

She remembered her own off-putting attitude the day after it had happened. She remembered coming back into the office after spending the morning talking to a woman who had started her own cosmetics business in her kitchen, and the pink message slip on her desk, saying that Matthew Prescott had called her. She had scrumpled it up and tossed it into the wastepaper basket with an insouciant laugh . . . well, more of a furious scowl, actually, and then had had to put up with Helena asking whether Matthew Prescott was that rather super chap who had been featured in *GQ* a short while ago.

'Was he?' Alex had said, feigning indifference.

'Yes. Wearing Armani. Rather dishy, I thought,' Helena said. She reached into Alex's wastepaper basket and fished out the message slip. 'Matthew Prescott, from Cadogan's,' she read. 'Yeah. That was him. "Unmarried but still hoping", the magazine said. There were some other guys featured but I definitely picked him out as the best.'

'Really?'

'Aren't you going to call him back?'

'No,' Alex said curtly.

'I'll do it if you like,' offered Helena.

'That's all right. I know what it was about.'

264

'But you—'

'And I've already dealt with it,' said Alex firmly.

And there had been that other message . . . she had rung Cartier to speak to someone called Michael Watney, only to be told that there was no-one called Michael Watney working there, and did she mean Michael Courteny, and if so, would she hold on?

This she had done, only to find herself talking to a horribly languid sort of character who obviously fancied himself rotten and who, she was prepared to swear, was wearing brown suede shoes and a shirt featuring tattersall checks, accompanied by a green knit tie. He kept asking her to get to the point as he was in a meeting, while she was waiting for *him* to get to the point, since, as far as she was aware, *he'd* made the call to her in the first place. Very embarrassing.

Could it possibly have been Matthew?

And had she given him a chance to explain?

She dialled his number again. Again she got the answering machine. Perhaps he was away for the weekend. Perhaps he'd gone down to Somerset to see his mother. His mother, called Erica, who wore a straw hat to cricket matches, and who was obviously as kind as he was, since she'd taken the trouble to drive the Colonel – a complete stranger – all the way to Taunton in order to watch the one-day county match and – and . . .

Alexandra suddenly found she was crying, great gulping sobs, tears splashing down on to the kitchen counter, an aching sense of something very precious which she had discarded without even a second glance. It was like the time she had thrown a cheque for one hundred and twenty pounds into the fire one Christmas, thinking the envelope was empty, though luckily it had been a present from her godfather, and he had good-naturedly written her another.

Would it be as easy to make things up with Matthew? She went on sobbing and gulping, imagining him down in Somerset. Maybe his sisters would be there, with their husbands and children. Maybe his mother would have organized a dinner party, invited the girl next door to make up the numbers. Maybe Matthew would look at her with fresh eyes, realize that the innocent freckled little creature he used to take swimming (or riding, or bicycling or something) had suddenly grown into a beautiful woman. Maybe, even as Alexandra Maitland wiped her eyes on a tissue and sniffed unalluringly in the kitchen of her London flat, Matthew Prescott was facing his destiny across a Somerset dinner table, and liking what he saw.

In the bathroom, Donna had segued clumsily from 'I could have danced all night' to 'I'm getting married in the morning', her attempts at a Cockney accent so ludicrous that normally Alex would have been falling about. All she wanted to do today, however, was get into bed, pull the covers over her head and hope the world would go away.

Instead she blew her nose, splashed her face with cold water, carried a cup of coffee to the bathroom door and knocked.

'Who is it?' Donna said.

'My name's Peeping Tom and I want to eyeball your luscious body,' Alex said.

'In that case, come right on in.'

'Honestly, Donna, who did you think it was?' Alex said, pushing open the door.

'Could have been anyone,' said Donna. She lay wallowing like a rosy dolphin in clouds of foam, with her exuberant hair pinned up on the top of her head.

'I mean, how was I to know you weren't a sex-mad pervert who'd broken in and hideously raped you before coming after me?'

'Do you think I'd have bothered to knock first, if I were?'

'You could have been a well-brought-up sex-mad pervert.'

'Yeah.'

Donna twisted about in the bath, sending water sloshing over the edge and on to the cork-tiled floor. 'Have you been crying?' she demanded.

'No.'

'Funny.'

'What is?'

'The way your eyes are all puffed-up and red and your face is all blotched and hideous and your—'

'Thanks, Donna. You know how to make a girl feel really good.'

'What's up?'

Alexandra bit her lip. Then she said, 'If you were a good-looking chap who wore Armani suits and washed-silk shirts and things, and you found yourself sitting across from a girl with freckles and a ponytail – or at least, a girl who *used* to have freckles and a ponytail – and you realized she'd grown up to be gorgeous, would you go for her?'

'That depends.'

'On what?'

'Where are these two – the Armani guy and the ex-ponytail?'

'Um . . . in the country.'

'And what're they sitting across: a fence? A ravine? A chessboard?'

'A dinner table,' said Alex. 'Or maybe a picnic table, having lunch.'

267

'Are there other folk around or are they alone, in shimmering sunlight, with violins in the background, making a commercial for shampoo or coffee or something?'

'They're with other people.'

'No,' Donna said decidedly, holding one leg straight up in the air and looking at it critically. 'If I was him, I definitely would not make a play for her. Especially not when I'd left my heart with this fantastic woman up in London.'

'This fantastic *career* woman?'

'This amazing brown-eyed, gorgeous, strong yet – let's face it – *vulnerable* career woman,' said Donna. 'Hey, if I have to go on with this much longer, I'm going to start fancying you myself.'

The two of them laughed. Alex could not help thinking how much easier and less complicated it was to enjoy the company of women, how much less fraught with the possibility of misunderstanding.

Much later that night, coming back from dinner and the theatre, followed by a stroll round Trafalgar Square and Whitehall so Donna could glimpse some of the sights, Alexandra looked up at Matthew's windows. In the dark it was impossible to see whether the curtains were drawn, but certainly no chink of light showed and she could not tell whether he was there, asleep, or whether his flat was empty.

'Am I supposed to wear a tiara to this kindergarten kid's place tonight, or what?' Donna asked.

'Difficult to tell,' said Alex, her head on one side as she appeared to give the matter some consideration. 'Charlotte's an artist, so she might be bohemian. And she's young, ditto. On the other hand, she's titled

'. . . yes, on balance, I think the tiara would strike just the right note of gracious elegance.'

'Boy,' said Donna. She smoothed the black cycling shorts she was wearing and shimmied a little inside her baggy grey workout top. 'You want gracious elegance, you came to the right place.'

'I think we'll have to ask David what we ought to wear. He'll be here any minute and he ought to know what's best.' Alexandra was still in her dressing gown, trying to decide on the appropriate garments for dinner at a portrait painter's flat. Not just any portrait painter, either, but one who might possibly end up as part of the family and on whom it was therefore important to make a good impression.

'I'm looking forward to seeing your brother again,' Donna said, sipping the dry martini Alex had given her a few minutes earlier. 'I really enjoyed his visit to New York, and talking of New York . . .' She gave her friend a significant glance and then clamped her lips together, in a parody of someone who was not going to say whatever it was that had just crossed her mind.

'What?' Alex said.

Donna shook her head.

'*What?*' demanded Alex.

'Did I say anything?'

'Not yet.'

'Not ever.'

'That I *don't* believe.'

'Not about this, anyway,' said Donna.

'About what?'

'This thing I'm not going to say anything about.'

'Cameron' said Alex. 'That's who you're not going to say anything about.'

'Right.'

269

'You mean, where is he? Do we still speak? Are we still an item?'

'Something like that.'

'Last I heard, he was all set to get married and live happily after,' Alex said.

'Oh, *sure*,' said Donna, with heavy sarcasm.

'Except a few days ago, he sent me a ticket to New York. Open-ended. Via Concorde.'

'What'd he do – rob a bank?'

'Plus he included a note about the two of us knowing we couldn't live without each other.'

'Which I hope you promptly tore up and flushed down the nearest john.'

'I've still got it.' Alex went over to the mantelpiece and picked up the Concorde ticket. 'Here.'

Donna made a lunge for it. 'Give it to me and *I'll* flush it down the john,' she said.

'I can't.'

'Come on, Alex. You know this guy is seriously bad news.'

'What about love?'

'Love? Get outta here.'

The doorbell rang. 'That'll be David,' said Alex.

When she opened the door, David said, 'I hope you're not going dressed like that?'

'I was, actually. I often wear a towelling dressing gown when I'm invited out to dinner,' said Alex.

'Do you take it off before or after they've wheeled in the birthday cake?'

'I hear there are some great openings for stand-up comics in Mongolia,' said Alex.

'I applied but they turned me down.' David leaned forward and kissed his sister.

'Come and say hello to Donna,' she said.

She walked behind him down the passage to the living room and watched, smiling, as her brother and her friend hugged each other.

Donna asked, 'So what do we wear to meet your child bride?'

'We haven't quite got that far,' said David.

'I'm glad to hear it. There are laws against that sort of thing, aren't there? Alex says she's only seven years old.'

'I'm sure I said eight,' Alex said.

'You know my sister,' said David. 'Never been able to get to grips with the difference between illusion and reality.'

'Is that right?'

'You mean Charlotte *is* actually over the age of consent?' asked Alex, wide-eyed.

'Illusion and reality,' said Donna. 'You hit the nail on the head there, David.'

'I so often do . . .'

'I've been saying the exact same thing with regard to this Mr Wrong she's so darned keen on.'

'Cameron, do you mean?'

'Yes.'

'I don't quite know how to handle it,' said David, lowering his voice and putting on a mock-serious face. 'But I've been wondering whether I ought to consult someone professionally about it.'

'I would. Can't go on like this.'

'Frankly, I'm worried about her.'

'Me too.' They both stared over at Alex with expressions straight out of some medical soap opera on their faces.

'Thank you both for your concern,' said Alex. 'Could you tell us what we're supposed to wear, so I can drag Miss Loudmouth here off to her boudoir?'

271

'That little black dress thing you wore to Pa's last birthday party would be perfect,' David said.

'You don't think it's too dressy?' Alex was astonished.

'Absolutely not,' David said positively.

'I don't have a little black dress thing,' complained Donna. 'Only a ginormous coral jacket and pants thing.'

'Sounds great.'

'Looks it, too,' Alex said. 'I've seen her in it.'

'Best thing about it is, it hides my thighs,' said Donna.

Charlotte Hanover's flat was a surprise. Built diagonally on the corner of the top floor of the mansion block, it had windows on three sides and an extra reception room. Apart from a pleasant faint odour of oil paint there was no indication that this was a working studio, though the walls of her hall were hung with examples of her work.

'This is fantastic,' Alex said, stopping to admire, while Charlotte gave David a decorous kiss. There were various elongated portraits, all painted on canvases of an idiosyncratic size, roughly six foot by two. The result was a curiously concentrated view of the subject.

'Thank you,' Charlotte said in her self-contained way.

'I love the way the length of the canvases forces the viewer's eye up towards the face.'

'Which is what portrait-painting's mostly about, isn't it?' David said.

Charlotte smiled. She had pinned her long hair up in an elegant knot on top of her head, and was wearing a chic little number which Alexandra recognized

272

immediately as a Thierry Mugler. Obviously the portrait business was doing very nicely.

'Part of it,' she said. 'Do come on in.'

She led the way to her living room. For a moment it was as though they had stepped through the doorway and into a Mediterranean resort. All round the walls, above the old-fashioned dado, was a mural of a beach scene, blue skies, brilliant sea, sunshine, swimmers, sunbathers. Concealed lighting made it seem so naturalistic that Alexandra almost expected to smell the salt and hear the cry of the seagulls which dipped and swooped at intervals around the walls. The theme was continued in the furnishings, which consisted of thick carpeting and a number of low sofas covered in sand-coloured linen, offset with candy-striped cushions placed here and there. Everything was light and airy and immensely inviting.

'Gee. I wish I hadn't left my swimsuit downstairs,' Donna said. She was looking magnificent, the long loose jacket hiding her hips and thighs, the silky trousers adding height. Once again, Alex was struck by the absurdity – no, the *cruelty* – of the self-image that society tries to impose on women. When you looked like Donna, why did you have to fret about not looking like the average social X-ray you saw in New York? Or Paris, or Milan, or London?

'It's great, isn't it?' said David, smiling at Charlotte.

'Did you do it yourself?' Alex said. She went closer to the walls, marvelling at the detail: the starfish flung up on the painted sand, the panting dog, the discarded bucket and spade, the bottle of sun oil.

'It was done by a friend,' said Charlotte. 'I think he's going to be really big one of these days.'

'It's a marvellous piece of work,' said Alex.

She thought of Tony Cashman, the man Matthew

273

had mentioned. Perhaps he could be persuaded to commission the muralist to cover some of the acres of bare wall which Matthew had described.

The doorbell rang again and a couple came in, followed at intervals by two more separate people. Introductions were made and conversation became general as Charlotte poured drinks and David passed round nuts and olives.

It was nearly half an hour later that the doorbell sounded again. David bounded up from his seat and went towards the door. 'I'll get it,' he said to Charlotte who was supervising something last-minute in the kitchen.

When he returned, he was followed by Matthew Prescott.

At the sight of him, Alexandra grew hot. She knew her face had gone red. She raised a hand and fingered her heavy silver earrings, trying to compose herself. How dare he? she thought, after more or less flaunting that – that woman in front of me. Admittedly she had never got around to telling him that the invitation was off. But wouldn't a man of any sensitivity have attempted to check with her, wouldn't he have assumed that, without needing to be told?

And yet, perhaps he had tried, and, not hearing from her, had decided to come anyway.

Charlotte appeared. 'This is a neighbour of mine,' she said, introducing him to the others. 'Matthew Prescott. He works for Cadogan's, the art dealers.'

There was a murmur of recognition for the name. Alexandra grew even crosser as it became obvious that Matthew had been invited in his own right. She watched covertly as he sat down with a drink on the opposite side of the room from her and then proceeded carefully to avoid her eye, by turning to talk to the person seated on the sofa beside him. He looked tanned, fit, his hair recently cut; he looked *good*, she thought fondly, then frowned, annoyed with herself.

What the hell did it have to do with her whether he looked good, bad or indifferent? It was ridiculous. Why should she care whether he was tanned, or when he had last been to the barber?

Much more to the point, why hadn't he said he knew Charlotte Hanover when she'd asked him to accompany her here this evening? Though, thinking back, surely he *hadn't* known her at that stage, had hardly known who she was. So when did he suddenly become so buddy-buddy with her? And how? Above all, how could he have the nerve to come here after what had happened the other night?

Beside her, Donna said quietly, 'If I had freckles and a ponytail, do you think that guy would make a play for me?'

'Which guy?' Alex said repressively, knowing quite well whom Donna referred to.

'The hunk over there in the Armani suit.'

'I really couldn't say.'

'Or do you think he's got the hots for this fabulous brown-eyed career woman he's acquainted with in London?'

'I wouldn't know.' Alexandra stared up at the piece of mural nearest her, which showed a rocky little headland, some twisted pines, a stretch of white sand lapped by azure waves. Still hot with embarrassment and irritation, she could feel a sheen of sweat on her forehead.

'You're either lying or having your first hot flush,' said Donna.

275

'You don't miss a trick, do you?'

'Never have, never will,' Donna said complacently.

'Have an olive.'

'You make it sound like a hand grenade with the pin pulled out.'

'I wish I thought it would have the same effect.'

'Did you learn to talk so nice in charm school, or does it just come naturally?' Donna said, grinning. 'Actually, I have to say he's damn dishy.'

'I think we could sit down now,' Charlotte said in her clear voice, smiling at them from the door, and they followed her into the dining room. She had placed Donna next to Matthew Prescott, while Alex was seated beside one of the other men.

As Matthew drew out the chair and waited for her to sit down, Donna said suddenly, 'My God! That plant!' Her voice was bloodcurdling. Everyone stopped where they were and stared as she pointed dramatically at a dark green house plant which stood on some kind of plinth behind the seat she'd been allocated.

'What's wrong with it?' A delicate frown creased the smooth skin between Charlotte's brows. This was clearly a departure from her script for the evening.

'I'm most terribly sorry,' Donna said. 'But I'm afraid I have this real phobia about plants.'

'Phobia?' said Alex coldly. 'First I've heard of it.' She knew Donna was up to something.

'Would you mind too much if I sat . . . um . . . over there?' Donna said, pointing to Alexandra's chair.

'If that's what you really—'

Donna flashed a wide and, to Alexandra's mind, extremely phoney grin. 'I guess I just saw too many of those sci-fi movies when I was a kid. You know, the ones where the killer cauliflower or the deadly

276

cucumber or whatever comes down from Venus in a spaceship and proceeds to devour everybody in sight.'

'Killer cauliflower?' said David disbelievingly. 'I must have missed that one.'

'I can easily move the—' Charlotte began, looking at the house plant.

'No, no. If Alexandra doesn't mind changing places, I'll just sit over there, if it's not too inconvenient.'

'Alexandra?' murmured Charlotte.

'That's fine,' said Alex, trying not to look furious.

Donna threw another big smile around the table. 'I guess you polite English people would have suffered in silence, wouldn't you?'

Everyone murmured awkward disclaimers except Alexandra, who, seething with embarrassment, now found herself seated next to Matthew. Curse Donna.

She turned pointedly to the man on her other side, who had been introduced to her as Harry. 'What a lovely room this is,' she said. She looked round the deep red walls of the dining room, set off with black paintwork. Heavy gold-framed paintings of Hanover ancestors hung from a picture rail; in each corner of the room were columns of shiny black marble topped by big dark green plants which drooped out of white marble urns. A black upright piano stood against one wall, the candles in its sconces burning brightly. 'It's perfect for evening occasions.'

'Isn't it?' he said. 'Charlotte's fearfully clever about that sort of thing, always was, even when we were all kids.'

'You're old friends, then?'

'Her sisters and mine went to the same school.'

'I believe her sisters are keen on horses,' Alex said.

277

'So are mine,' said Harry, shuddering. 'Much too keen. Always trying to get me up early for gallops through the morning mist. Never seemed to cotton on to the fact that I don't like morning mists. Nor gallops, for that matter.'

'I see.'

'Charlotte and I used to try and hide together, so as to avoid all that ghastly heartiness our families went in for. Stirrup cups and so forth.' He tasted the delicate fennel-flavoured soup which sat in a shallow bowl in front of him. 'Do you hunt?'

'No.'

'Glad to hear it. I always think the world divides into those who do and those who don't, and I know which half I belong to.'

'Me too.'

'Loathe horses,' Harry said broodingly. He picked at a home-made roll and popped a piece of it into his mouth. 'Great brutes, liable to trample all over you at the drop of a hat.'

'Quite.' On her other side, Alex could hear Matthew talking to Charlotte about painting and some man he knew – was it Anthony Cashman? – who was interested in commissioning a portrait of his wife.

'And dashed ungrateful, too,' said Harry. 'You wouldn't believe the number of times I've offered the beastly things a sugar lump and been nipped like billyo in return.'

'Biting the hand that feeds you.'

'Absolutely.'

As the soup plates were removed by a white-overalled woman who appeared from the kitchen, the person on Harry's other side stirred and turned her head towards him. Some signal had obviously been

278

given, though Alexandra had not seen it, and now it was plainly time for everyone to turn and talk to their other neighbour. For, far from being the paper-plates-and-pasta evening which Alex had imagined, this dinner party had turned out to be solid English upper-middle-class stuff of the most formal kind.

She felt a sinking of the heart. Etiquette clearly demanded that she now speak pleasantly to Matthew Prescott for the required length of time, something she did not wish to do. She stared down at her plate, determined not to look at him. But, beside her, he said under his breath in a comical Bertie Woosterish voice, 'I say, old thing, do you hunt?'

'You shouldn't have come,' she said.

'Why on earth not?'

'Because you knew I'd be here.'

'That's precisely why I accepted the invitation that Miss Hanover was good enough to extend to me,' Matthew said. 'So I could see you.'

Alexandra didn't say anything.

'You've been avoiding my eye all evening.'

'I know,' she said.

'If you don't turn your head and look at me,' he continued, still in a voice inaudible to anyone but Alexandra, 'I shall be forced to make you.'

'And how would you do that?'

'By grabbing hold of your chin and pulling your beautiful face round towards me,' Matthew said softly.

'Who was that woman in your flat the other night?'

'I told you – an old friend.'

'Why didn't you explain?'

'I tried to. But you were off like a startled gazelle, and since then you've refused all my calls.'

'All which calls?'

279

'The ones from me. And the one from—'

'Michael Watney?'

'Yes.'

'I *knew* that must be you.' Alexandra did at last turn to look at him. 'Do you know I got landed talking to some chinless wonder at Cartier for nearly eight minutes under the mistaken impression that he'd called *me*?'

'You mean that there *is* a Michael Watney at Cartier?'

'No, there isn't. That's my whole point.'

'And it took you eight whole minutes to discover that he *wasn't* Michael Watney and *hadn't* called you?'

'Not exactly. I—'

'Goodness,' Matthew said. 'And here I'd been thinking you were one of the brightest women I'd ever met.'

'Is that right?'

'When I say brightest you have to understand that, for me, the word encompasses much more than mere brains.'

'Does it? Such as?' Alexandra asked coolly.

Had they made up their quarrel, if quarrel it could be called? Were they back on their former footing? His gaze, she couldn't help noticing, had rested rather frequently on the extremely attractive woman opposite, a blazingly red-headed creature with a figure that would have made Helen of Troy spit. Alex was glad to note that she felt nothing at all, no emotion such as jealousy or possessive rage, no urge to pull the other woman's ginger hair out by the roots, if it wasn't, in fact, a wig, which it might well have been, judging by its artificial shade and lifeless appearance. Not to mention the way the woman's

280

chin sagged under her jawline, and the frightful nose which—

'Such as fantastic,' Matthew was saying. 'Such as wonderful. Gorgeous. Strong.'

'Strong yet – don't tell me – vulnerable?' She turned for the first time and found his face very close to hers.

'The very word I was searching for,' he murmured.

Despite herself, Alex found herself laughing.

'I love to see you laugh,' he said, his voice very low.

'Not a lot I can say to that.'

'You could laugh again.'

Across the long stretch of polished mahogany set with gleaming candelabra and heavy glasses, flowers of a red which matched the wallpaper, silver which obviously came from Charlotte's family, Donna was watching her, bright little Fratelli eyes picking up every last detail.

More to put her off the scent than for any other reason, Alexandra laughed again, throwing back her head a little, hoping no trace showed of the churning emotion she felt.

'I think he's *fabulous*,' Donna said, the minute they had said their thank-yous and Charlotte had shut the door of her flat behind them.

'Who?' said Alex.

'Who? Who the hell do you think?' said Donna.

'My brother?'

'Your boyfriend, that's who.'

'I don't remember seeing him there this evening,' Alexandra said, wrinkling her brow as though trying to recall a face.

'I mean Mr Matthew Prescott, as well you know,' said Donna, sailing, like a ship with all coral-coloured sails set, down the curved stone stairs to the third floor, her heels clicking with each step.

'Liked him, did you?'

'Sure did.' Donna looked up at Alex, lingering on the floor above. 'But not as much as you did.'

'What's this – womanly intuition or something?'

'No, honey. Simple observation. The way your eyes lit up when you talked to him.'

'They did *not*.'

'They did so. And your mouth got all soft and tremulous.'

'Rubbish.'

'I never saw you look like that with Cameron. Not once.'

'That's because we tried, whenever possible, to be together, rather than part of a threesome. Didn't your mother ever explain about two being company?'

'Not as often as she explained how you can tell about two being in love.'

'I am *not*,' Alexandra shouted down the stairs, 'in love.'

'Sure,' said Donna, now two floors below. She looked up the oval stairwell to where Alex hung over the banisters. 'Or, as you would say, quite.'

There was a huge bunch of red roses on Alex's desk when she came into the *Athene* office the following Monday morning. Her assistant had put them in a vase of water and, seeing the dark tightly-furled petals, the perfection of each bud, for a moment her heart lifted. Who were they from? She picked up the white envelope and took out the card it contained. In florist handwriting, she read: *Always yours. I shall be in England on Thursday and long to see you.* It was signed with the name Carlo.

She tried to hide her let-down feeling. Why on earth should Matthew Prescott send her flowers, for heaven's sake? And why, in any case, should she want him to? Because she didn't. Whatever Donna had hinted, whatever she went on hinting as they visited the National Gallery, sat in the Festival Hall, walked round St Paul's, she was not and never had been in love with the wretched man. Never would be, either. If there had ever been anything between them – and she was far from sure that there had – it was now over.

Nonetheless, she felt a sudden reluctance to see Carlo again. They had talked occasionally on the telephone; he sent flowers. But did they have that much in common? Was the time she had spent with him in Milan special in some way simply because it had been in Italy, somewhere romantic and foreign, somewhere very different from England? How would she feel when she saw him again?

The thought of him reminded her that very soon they ought to be putting together the Italian issue of the magazine. For the rest of the morning she busied herself with the material she had garnered during her Milan trip, thinking that Carlo might enjoy looking at it when he arrived at the end of the week. Her brain locked into the magazine: she started work on a presentation which she hoped would show various well-known facets of Italy and Italian life in a new and exciting way.

Carol was back at her desk this morning, looking wan but happy. 'Derek and I have decided to stay together,' she said.

'That's great!' exclaimed Alex. 'I'm really happy for you.'

'Well, you know,' said Carol, bobbing her head in an embarrassed way. 'What with the recession and everything . . .'

'Recession?'

'Seems easier all round,' mumbled Carol, and Alex guessed she was regretting the candid way in which she had thrown Derek's inadequacies – or were they her own? – around the office prior to catching chicken-pox.

Nina telephoned. 'I might be back next week,' she said.

'That's wonderful,' said Alex, not meaning it. No-one wanted to ill-wish anyone else, she told herself, but it would be nice if Nina caught some further non-threatening but nonetheless infectious disease which would keep her at home for longer, thus giving Alex more time to establish herself. 'We'll be so gl—'

'Or I might not,' said Nina mysteriously.

'What do you mean?' asked Alex.

'I'll let you know definitely by the end of the week,' said Nina. 'See how I feel.'

'Great.' Alex sighed. 'About the Italian issue, I've sorted out the—'

'You're doing a fantastic job,' Nina said. 'Really fantastic.'

'The thing is, I—'

'Got to go,' Nina said hurriedly. 'Sorry.'

'I'll give you a ring la—'

'Great.' The telephone receiver was slammed down.

Alex was still frowning at it when Felicity appeared. She was wearing black leggings and a big Versace printed silk shirt. As she moved, she clanked.

'Don't do that,' Felicity ordered.

'Do what?'

'Frown in that forbidding way.' Felicity adopted a huge unnatural smile and dumped a brown paper bag on her desk. 'It's fearfully bad for you. You should smile more. Like me.'

'If you go on grinning in that idiotic fashion,' said Petronella, who was standing at the copier, 'they'll take out committal papers.'

'Besides, I'm long past worrying about lines and wrinkles,' said Alex.

'Me too,' Carol said. 'Derek says they lend character to a woman's face.'

'Derek would,' said Petronella. She was wearing shorts this morning, an error of judgement in Alex's view, since the sunshine outside the window merely pointed up the blackness and thickness of the hairs which covered her legs.

'What's that supposed to mean?' bristled Carol.

'The man's obviously a wimp,' Petronella said carelessly. 'I mean, everything you've ever told us about him makes that *per*fectly clear.'

'He's not.'

'Come on, Carol. You've been telling us for years that he is. So what's different?'

'Nothing.' Carol had gone very pink. 'He's just not a wimp.'

'I say, girls.' Petronella loudly addressed the room at large. 'I do believe old Del-boy's finally managed it.'

'Managed what?' asked Felicity, peering vaguely into the bottom of her brown paper bag.

'You know – to make the earth move and all that,' said Petronella, grinning in a predatory way which Alexandra hated.

285

'Shut up, Petronella,' she said.

'I bet I'm right,' said Petronella, and turned back to the copying machine which was belching out sheets of paper with careless abundance.

'Look at this,' Felicity said. She waved a square black box at them. Her wide artificial smile made her resemble a kewpie doll.

'What is it?'

'A revolutionary new break-through,' said Felicity.

'But what does it *do*?' Alexandra said patiently. She knew that behind Felicity's butterfly façade, behind the big tortoiseshell-rimmed specs with the plain glass lenses, there lurked a brain as ferocious as any tiger's.

'It removes the top layer of your facial epidermis,' Felicity explained, still inanely smiling.

'And what do you do with it when you've removed it?' Petronella asked nastily. 'Leave it lying about, I suppose, for the rest of us to fall over, or breathe in, or something.'

'That's disgusting,' said Carol.

'Doesn't it make your face sore?' Alexandra said.

'No. Feel . . .' Felicity shoved her smile-bunched cheeks in Alex's direction. Dutifully, Alex stroked them.

'Real baby's bottom stuff,' she said admiringly. 'But you look a bit red, Fliss.'

'She would, wouldn't she?' Petronella said. 'I mean, quite apart from that ludicrous grin on her face, she's basically flaying herself, isn't she?'

'Like they used to do to first-century Christian martyrs?' asked Carol.

'You aren't overdoing it, are you?' Alex said.

'Not down to the second or third layer of epidermis, I hope,' said Petronella. 'I hope you

286

realize it takes seven years to replenish lost skin. I'm sure I read that somewhere.'

'I'm sure you didn't,' said Alex firmly. 'Now could we stop gossiping and get on with things? Nina's hoping to be back next week and it would be great if we could show her how well we all got on without her.'

'She'd probably much rather we'd got into a hopeless muddle,' Carol said.

'Quite,' said Petronella. 'Not much fun to realize you've been away from your indispensable position, only to find that no-one's even noticed you weren't there. Someone's retroussé little nose is going to be badly out of joint.'

'Someone's going to get their retroussé little wrists slapped if they don't start behaving like a human being instead of the Fiend from Hell,' said Alexandra, as lightly as she could. Petronella was in a bad mood, and when Petronella wasn't feeling kindly disposed towards her colleagues she was as bitchy and hurtful as any high-school gossip could possibly be.

The morning ran smoothly, so Alex was able to go out at lunchtime with a clear conscience. She had arranged to meet Donna, who was spending the morning sightseeing, at a restaurant in Covent Garden. It was only as she went in and was greeted by the waiter that she realized it was the same one she had last been in with Matthew Prescott. But so what? As long as she didn't let Donna know . . .

'You can't sit there,' she said, as Donna prepared to slide into a seat against the wall.

'Why not?' Donna stared at the padded bench. 'I don't see anyone else there.'

'Look!' Alex pointed to a palm-like plant which

acted as a divider from the next table. 'What about your phobia?'

'What are you talking— oh,' said Donna, remembering. 'My *phobia*. Don't you worry about that – I took my pills this morning.'

'I see.'

Donna was noisily chomping her way through a radicchio salad when Alex saw her suddenly falter, the fork halfway to her lips.

'What's the matter?'

'Uh – nothing,' Donna said. She continued eating. 'Say, Alex, did you say we were going down to visit your pop some time?'

'Would you like that?'

'Adore it,' Donna said. 'He lives down in the country, doesn't he?'

'Somerset.'

'All rural, is it?' Donna was clearly having a problem not staring at something behind Alex.

'Very much so. Perhaps you'd also like to take part in the greatest British tradition of them all . . .'

'What's that, honey?' Donna asked absent-mindedly, jaws slowly chewing her food.

'A cricket match,' Alexandra said.

'Is that right?'

'Yes. In Somerset, we play a different version . . .'

'Uh-huh,' said a preoccupied Donna.

'. . . using kiwi fruit instead of balls and teaspoons instead of bats— Donna, what the *hell* are you staring at like that?'

Alex turned round.

Across the room, she saw Matthew Prescott. He was sitting opposite one of the most beautiful girls she had ever seen – a girl whose face was familiar though she couldn't exactly place it at the moment –

and gazing into her eyes with every appearance of rapture. Even as Alex watched, he reached across the table and took the beautiful girl's hand in his own.

She turned back.

'Gee, I'm sorry,' Donna said. 'I shouldn't have stared like that. But she was such a gorgeous girl. I didn't even realize who she was with at first.'

'Donna,' Alex said, with a pretty good imitation of patient friendliness, 'I keep explaining that Matthew Prescott means absolutely nothing to me.'

This was why her heart was now pounding with rage and grief, and why she had the idiotic desire to burst into a screaming frenzy, start pounding the table and chucking glasses all over the place. She had never in her life indulged in such undisciplined behaviour; she wondered if it would help release the huge tension which she could sense building up inside her chest. Quickly she drank from her glass, took a bite of food, felt it pass down her throat without giving the faintest hint as to what it was or how it tasted.

'Do you want to go?'

'Go?' said Alex, and just about managed to produce a trilling laugh. 'What in the world for?'

'I'm sure I've seen that girl somewhere before,' Donna said. 'Isn't she a model?'

Of course: Alex realized why the face was familiar. And remembered, too, Matthew talking about Cindy Hill and her possible marital problem. He had seemed a disinterested party at the time, but perhaps since then he had fallen madly in love with the delectable Cindy. Or perhaps he had merely brought her into the conversation in the way lovers do, because they long to talk about the beloved object.

'She's called Cindy Hill,' Alex said. 'One of our top models.'

'She looks very – um – friendly with Matthew,' said Donna.

'Does she?' Alex was glad she had her back to the room. She knew one thing for absolutely certain: she would never – *ever* – speak to Matthew Prescott again.

# 13

'Cindy, you simply must talk to Tony,' Matthew said. Around them was the bustle of the restaurant, the sea-murmur of other people's conversations, the clatter of knives and forks. He tried very hard not to remember that the last time he had been in here was with Alexandra . . .

Cindy shook her head. 'No.'

Matthew was beginning to learn that the beautiful model was not as frail as she looked. 'I had him on the phone yesterday,' he said. 'He seems absolutely distraught.'

'I ring him every couple of days,' Cindy said. She took a breadstick from the packet in front of her and nibbled at it. 'He knows I'm alive and well.'

'*How* well?' Matthew asked. 'Emma says you eat hardly anything and you seem to be in some pain.'

'I'm fine.'

'Don't you want to see Tony again?'

'Of course I do. But not until I've sorted things out for myself. It's too soon. Besides . . .'

'What?'

'That woman called me up the other day. The portrait painter you spoke to about me.'

'Charlotte Hanover?'

'That's right. I went to see her yesterday and we fixed up some sittings.' Cindy looked away from him. 'Maybe it sounds childish and stupid to you . . .'

291

'Nothing you say ever sounds even remotely either of those things,' Matthew said encouragingly. He was pained by the girl's lack of self-confidence and wondered who could have been responsible for it. From things she had let drop, he guessed there was a bullying father somewhere in the background. It was ironic – or was it perfectly logical? – that she should have chosen another bully to marry. Though, to be fair, Tony Cashman's bullying was not so much unkind as merely insensitive.

'. . . but I've got this kind of feeling that by the time the portrait's finished, I'll be ready to talk to Tony again.'

'How long is that likely to be?'

'She told me she works fairly fast. She thought maybe a week or ten days, if I've got time to fit in all the sittings she wants.'

'And meanwhile, have you spoken to Tony about any of the things you've discussed with me?'

'Not yet.'

A waiter appeared and laid a plate of lasagne in front of Matt, a green salad before Cindy.

'It's been over two weeks since you left home, Cindy.' Matthew leaned forward and took the girl's cold hand in his. 'Don't you owe him some kind of explanation?'

'Doesn't he owe me the courtesy of at least listening to me when I try to talk to him?' Cindy said. Her eyes were very bright, as though full of unshed tears. She did not look well. Although nothing could really touch her bone-deep beauty, there were greyish shadows under her eyes and she looked much too thin.

Almost gaunt, Matt thought, forking pasta into his mouth and feeling guilty about it as Cindy pushed

292

a lettuce leaf around her plate. Her jawbone was much too sharply delineated; the muscles of her neck stood out.

Worried about her, Matthew said, 'I'm going down to visit my mother next weekend. Would you like to come? It would get you out of London – and Somerset's very peaceful at this time of year.'

'I'd like that very much,' Cindy said shyly.

'We could drive down on Friday, immediately after lunch.'

'Thank you, Matt.'

'I'll give you a ring later in the week, then.'

'Will your mother mind?'

'She'll be delighted,' Matthew said. 'I already asked her if it was all right.' He grinned. 'Naturally she wanted to know if you were some kind of romantic attachment and was very disappointed when I said you weren't.'

Cindy smiled rather sadly. 'I wish I were, sometimes. You're such a kind man. But it's Tony I want.'

'I know.' A sort of pang cut across the area where Matthew's heart was located; a vision of a brown-eyed woman with long tawny hair flitted briefly through his mind. Alexandra . . . But that was over. Over before it had ever really begun. What made him mad about the whole fruitless episode was that he'd never even managed properly to kiss Alexandra's beautiful mouth, let alone feel her in his arms for more than a fleeting second. Something always seemed to intervene: telephones or Lauras or brothers or misunderstandings.

But perhaps they could never have got it together anyway. He told himself that the fact that he still quite fancied her – still, if the truth be told, longed quite desperately for her – could be put down to the circumstances which had ensured that he never had the chance to get really close to her.

'What about you, Matthew?' Cindy asked. She had managed to consume three tiny bites of her bread-stick and sip the top quarter-inch of a glass of mineral water; now she speared a slice of cucumber and lifted it to her mouth.

'What *about* me?'

'Isn't there someone you fancy? I've been so selfish, so self-absorbed recently – I've never even bothered to ask if you were – were in love or anything.'

'In love?' Matthew strove to produce a heartyish laugh. 'Don't you read the magazines? I'm officially an Eligible Bachelor.'

'So?' Cindy did not laugh back.

'So I have far too much fun wining, dining, womanizing, being a man about town, thanks.'

'Do you?' Cindy said quietly, and he knew she didn't believe a word he said.

Neither, unfortunately, did he.

It was difficult to talk to Cashman these days. Though still continuing to control his business empire with his usual efficiency, he was inwardly raging. Part grief, part fury at being thwarted, Matthew decided. It was probably the first time in Cashman's adult life that he had been bested by a weaker creature than himself.

Knowing why, Matt was not comfortable with the Judas role which he found himself playing. He very much wanted to talk to the tycoon about his wife, to explain some of the things which were bothering her.

But if he did so, would he be betraying Cindy's

confidence? There was no denying that he was already betraying Cashman, to a certain extent. It was difficult to know where his loyalties, if any, ought to lie, but in the end he had opted for Cindy, considering her to be less capable than Cashman of dealing with the blows life handed out with such regularity.

'Have you thought about collecting modern furniture, as well as art?' he said to Cashman now, as the two of them sat in one of the conservatories which bulged from the walls of the Cashman mansion like so many blisters.

'Furniture?' Cashman looked at him with less than his usual attention. 'I leave all that sort of thing to my wife.' An expression of pain crossed his solid features which he tried to conceal with a ferocious frown.

'I'm not talking about soft furnishings or sofas from Heal's,' Matthew said, trying to hide his impatience. 'Some of the things being produced by Italian or German designers are going to be considered art forms in the future – where they aren't already.'

'Like what?'

'Ever heard of Ruhlmann? Or Lalanne?'

'Can't say I have.'

'This house would be a fantastic showcase for some of their work. And the Americans, too. They're producing some really exciting things.'

'Oh, yeah?'

'You're not listening to me, Tony,' Matthew said without rancour.

'I'm sorry.' Cashman turned to look directly at him and Matthew could see the misery in his eyes. 'It's just . . . my wife. I wish she'd come home.'

'And if she did, Tony, what would you do?'

'Same as I did before. Give her anything she wants, anything in the world she chooses. She knows that. What's it all about, working and scraping, if you can't give things to the people you care about?'

'Do you ever give her time?' Matthew asked. He hoped the question wasn't too intrusive.

'Time for what?'

'Not for anything. Just to be together?'

'When I can, I do,' Cashman said truculently. 'I'm a busy man, Cindy knows that. But I do my best.'

'Perhaps your best isn't good enough,' said Matthew.

'What're you on about?'

'Maybe you should drop some of your business responsibilities. Maybe Cindy's more important than money.'

''Course she is. But while she's still working at her career, I'm—'

'Which career's that?'

Cashman stared. 'Have you gone off your bleeding rocker?' he demanded. 'You know as well as I do what career – her modelling, of course.'

'I see.'

'She's right at the top,' Cashman said proudly. 'Got at least another ten years, if she plays her cards right. And after that there could be all sorts of other openings. I got my eyes on cosmetics, perfumes, even a line of sportswear. It's all there, waiting for her, soon as she's ready to move into it.'

'Tony,' Matthew said. He paused. There was a tremor in the pit of his stomach. He looked at the man, at the anger seething beneath the hard exterior, and knew Cashman was only a wind's breath away from explosion. And there was no getting away from the fact that a single blow from one of the tycoon's

296

gigantic fists could land him in hospital without any trouble whatsoever.

'What?'

Wincing inwardly, Matt said, 'Has it ever occurred to you that perhaps Cindy doesn't actually *want* to be working as a model for another ten years? Let alone branching out into all these subsidiary things?'

'No.' Cashman's tone was blunt.

'Are you sure?'

'Well, every now and then she says things about chucking it all in. But it's only when she's tired. She doesn't really mean it.'

'How do you know?'

Again Cashman stared at Matthew. 'I'm her bleeding husband, aren't I?'

'Yes, but—'

'But what?' Cashman said dangerously. Was it Matthew's imagination or had he swollen to about five times his normal size?

'– do you really listen when she talks to you about it?' Matthew said bravely. The table between them was made of glass and chrome; he had a sudden image of Cashman bringing a huge fist crashing down on it, seizing a lethal shard, slashing Matthew to ribbons before—

''Course I listen to her. I love her, don't I?'

'Look,' Matthew said. 'You said she fancied me.'

'Yer,' Cashman said warily.

'And perhaps you're right about that, though it's only in a sisterly sort of way. But maybe that's why she felt free to say to me once that what she really wanted was not to be a career woman but to have a—' Matthew gulped slightly – 'a baby.'

'A *baby*?' Cashman said, as though the word referred to some exotic endangered species.

'Yes.' Matthew prayed that Cashman wouldn't ask when this conversation was supposed to have taken place. On the few occasions when he and Cindy had spoken during his visits down here in Hampshire, Cashman had always been present and would know perfectly well that babies had never formed part of any discussion. 'Or even several.'

'She's got plenty of time for that,' said Cashman indulgently, and Matthew could see why Cindy despaired of getting her husband to listen to her. He had taken on board what Matthew said, digested it and spat it out, all in a matter of microseconds. The actual meaning of the words, the resonances behind them, had completely passed him by.

All it needed was a white horse, Matthew told himself. He tilted at Cashman once again, a modern-day knight in slightly rusting armour, fighting on behalf of a damsel in distress.

'But perhaps she doesn't want to wait. Some women like to have children while they're still young,' he said. 'I mean, not everyone's into this modern trend of putting it off until they're over thirty.'

'Not everyone's got the chance to be a world-famous model, either,' Cashman said triumphantly, as though that was a clinching argument.

'But suppose you have that chance and don't want to take it?'

'What?'

'Suppose you're married to a man you love and you have a – a beautiful home and no financial worries and all you want in the entire world is to settle down to producing a family?'

'What's that got to do with Cindy?'

Matthew sighed. It was absolutely hopeless. Cashman's mind ran along well-worn grooves and seemed incapable of taking in any new information. Cindy had an uphill struggle ahead of her, he could see that. For the moment, it seemed easier to drop the subject of babies and Cindy and unwanted careers.

'About this Balthus painting I mentioned earlier,' he said quietly. 'I think it would look magnificent in your main hall above that stone fireplace. It'll cost you something, but I don't think you'll regret it.'

And how much would Cashman regret it if Cindy gave up trying to communicate with him, looked to another man who was more ready to listen, was willing to give her what she wanted?

It was not a question Matthew was prepared to ask.

He lay back in his deckchair and listened as his mother led Cindy round the garden. The two of them had got on from the first moment Erica had come out to greet them as they pulled up in front of the house a couple of hours ago.

'Just in time for tea,' she had said. 'I've made some scones,' and, at his side, Cindy had let out a little sigh as though she had been waiting all her life for someone to step out from a wisteria-covered porch and announce that there were freshly-made scones for tea.

Possibly, Matt thought, she has. After his own bruising encounter with Cashman he felt he understood Cindy a great deal better than he had, and was much more able to sympathize with her dilemmas.

He opened his eyes and looked across the sweep of lawn to where the two big chestnuts stood. Already their leaves were turning bronze and orange: autumn was in the air. In a few minutes he would get up and bring out a tray of glasses, since Colonel

Richard Maitland would be joining them for dinner.

He found the thought of meeting Alexandra's father here on his own home ground was curiously disturbing. He wondered what she would think, if she knew. Or perhaps she did, and didn't care.

He closed his eyes again. The heat beat down on his eyelids and once more he reflected that all too soon summer would be over and the slanting yellow sunshine of autumn would lengthen across the grass. Vividly he remembered the feel of heavy September dews under his bare feet, in those waiting days before it was time to go back to school after the long summer holidays. Soon Emma's children, and Victoria's, would hunt for conkers among the fallen chestnut leaves, pick blackberries from the hedges in the fields behind the house, try to catch the drifting leaves.

'Each one you catch means a day of good luck,' his mother used to tell him when he himself was a child, and of course he had believed her, as children do. He had never caught more than forty-seven . . .

He could feel a melancholy mood coming on. He stood up and walked towards the house. Whisky for the Colonel, dry sherry for Erica, gin and tonic for himself. Cindy, he already knew, would drink only mineral water. He found himself looking forward to meeting the redoubtable Richard Maitland, and particularly to hearing him roar.

He heard feet crunching on the gravel path which ran around the house and stopped, shading his eyes to see who was arriving.

What he found completely unexpected – though afterwards he told himself he should have seen it coming – was the way his mother relinquished, somehow, her role as a mother the minute the

Colonel appeared. He was limping slightly, raising a walking stick in greeting, putting a soldierly and – in Matt's opinion – much too familiar arm around her shoulders. This was not the Erica he knew and loved but an unexpected teenager, a kind of elderly facsimile of her daughters when they were bringing young men home for inspection.

'This is Richard,' she said, as though she was afraid Matthew had taken leave of his senses and assumed the visitor was the milkman or the new curate or something. There was a possessive note in her voice which made him frown.

'How do you do,' he said and added, without quite knowing why, 'sir?'

'Great pleasure,' the Colonel rumbled. 'Heard a great deal about you, good to meet you at last.'

'And this is Matthew's friend, Cindy Hill.'

'I say!' said the Colonel. 'How do you do?' He shook Cindy's hand energetically.

'She's a famous model,' Erica said.

'Quite right too,' said the Colonel. 'I can see that. However . . .' He looked down at Erica, the top of whose head came more or less to the level of his heart, and murmured something which had his mother, to Matthew's intense shame, in a fit of girlish giggles.

She put a hand on the Colonel's chest and said, 'Richard, honestly!'

Matthew looked at Cindy. Cindy was watching the two of them with a benign smile on her face. He had a sudden sense of foreboding.

Did the girls – Victoria and Emma – know about this – this *dalliance*, he wondered? Probably not. Almost certainly not. Otherwise they'd have been on the phone at all hours, bending his ear, demanding that he go down and suss this Colonel out.

Well, he was down here now, and he didn't like what he saw. The whole thing – if thing there was – was entirely unsuitable. Suppose the two of them were to – well, *get together*, so to speak. Visions of future family celebrations – Christmases, for instance – came to him: Alexandra swam before his eyes. There would be the hideous embarrassment – would there not? – of shared yuletides, communal turkeys, joint cracker-pulling. Shuddering, he imagined the shrill voices of his nephew and nieces: *'Go on, Uncle Matt – kiss her!'* and, urged on by family enthusiasm, himself forced to embrace Alexandra – who by then would be his step-sister, wouldn't she? – under some horrible bit of mistletoe.

'No!' he said aloud, and turned it into a cough as the Colonel tore his eyes from Erica and swivelled them enquiringly at Matthew. It was not on. It was simply not on. As soon as he decently could, Matthew told himself, he would seize the opportunity to tell his mother so.

'No reason why the two of you shouldn't watch cricket together, and stuff like that,' he would say, in an understanding sort of voice. 'But anything more than that wouldn't really be suitable. I'm sure you can see that.'

The trouble was, he could hear his mother's response all too clearly. 'What on earth are you talking about?' she would say, gathering her forces, as she always did. 'I most certainly don't see anything of the sort.'

'You know perfectly well what I'm talking about,' he would say. 'You and this – this Colonel chap. It's simply not – well – *on*.'

302

'What isn't on?' she'd say. 'What are you trying to say, Matthew?'

And he'd be left with the embarrassing task of pointing out that a woman of her age should behave more discreetly. Or something. The thought of actually having to talk about – well, *sex*, for heaven's sake – to his mother was more than he could stomach. He gave a low groan, wishing his sisters were there. It wasn't fair the way they left everything to him to deal with, just because he was the man of the family.

'Are you all right?' his mother asked. 'You're making some very peculiar noises.'

'One noise,' Matthew said. 'And not a very peculiar one. A simple groan, that's all.'

'Why are you groaning, dear?'

That was when he should have come out with it. Forbidden it, said it was not suitable for people of their age to be so blatantly in love. Especially when people *his* age were having such a hard time actually falling in love, let alone being blatant about it. But he couldn't find the words.

'Something I suddenly remembered I forgot to do at the office,' he said, and cursed himself for wimping out.

'M'daughter's coming down tomorrow,' the Colonel said.

'Is she?'

'Bringing some Yankee friend down. Why don't you all come over to lunch on Sunday? She'd be delighted to see you, I'm sure.'

Matthew was quite sure she wouldn't. Another vision of Alexandra appeared on the screen which someone seemed to have set up inside his head. This time she was presiding graciously over a luncheon table, passing vegetables in a covered dish, being charming to his mother, glaring at him whenever she caught his eye.

'That's awfully nice of you,' he said hastily. 'But I've already arranged to take Cindy up to Taunton.'

His mother frowned. 'What for?'

'There's one of those forty-over bashes on at the cricket ground,' Matt said. 'Somerset v. Glamorgan. I thought Cindy would enjoy just sitting in the sun for a few hours.'

'She can do that in m'garden,' said the Colonel.

'Yes but—'

'You can watch cricket any time,' said his mother.

'Yes, but I've also arranged to – to meet some friends from – from Yeovil.'

'Which friends are those?' Erica demanded.

'You don't know them,' he mumbled.

'I've never heard you speak of friends in *Yeo*vil,' Erica said, as though it was some village perched on a high peak in Mexico or somewhere. The trouble with his mother, Matthew thought, was that she had never really understood that her offspring lived independent lives of their own and were no longer necessarily answerable to her for anything beyond a spot of filial duty now and then.

It was useless trying to explain this concept to her, especially with the Colonel present. He was just the sort to start harrumphing and muttering things about it being no way to speak to your mother, m'boy. Funny how little resemblance there was between him and Alexandra.

'He's a chap I knew at university. He's just got married and wants me to meet his new wife.' Matthew felt quite ill after delivering this lie. He foresaw years of inquisitions about the friend in

304

Yeovil, the new wife, the eventual offspring, the kind of house they lived in, what their parents did . . . A plane crash, Matthew decided. As soon as there was a suitable plane crash his nonexistent friends would sadly perish – their children, too, and their parents . . .

'Couldn't you go on to Taunton after lunch?' asked the Colonel.

'Not really. We've already made arrangements,' said Matt. 'And anyway, we don't want to miss the start of play.' He hated telling lies, but anything was better than the possibility of having to make polite conversation with Alexandra over a leg of lamb and mint sauce.

'Shame not to meet m'daughter,' the Colonel said. 'Lovely girl, even if I am her father. Don't know about the Yank, mind you. Funny lot, Yanks, when you get right down to it.'

'But I thought Matt and Alexandra had already met,' his mother said, wrinkling her forehead in a perplexed sort of *stirring* way.

'Have they?' The Colonel suddenly stiffened. 'Do believe there's a fox at the end of the garden, m'dear.'

'Is there?' Erica too stared towards the boundary hedge. 'So there is. They often pass through here. I think it's some kind of short cut.'

'A fox – how marvellous!' Cindy said. 'We've got a lake at home, with all sorts of birds on it – herons and crested grebes and teal and things – but I've never seen a fox.'

'Get a lot of badgers, too,' the Colonel said. 'Ever seen one of those?'

'No. But I'd love to.'

'Next time you come,' said the Colonel. 'There's a

305

sett up behind the house. Bit of a nuisance at times, aren't they, Erica? Overturning the dustbins and that sort of thing.'

'I've always had a soft spot for them because of all the stories one used to read to the children,' said Matthew's mother. '*The Wind in the Willows*, and so on.'

'Used to take the children out at dusk, sometimes,' said the Colonel. 'Sit there in the bracken and wait for the badgers to come out to play.' He coughed. 'Some of my happiest memories, as a matter of fact, squatting there quiet as mice, with the ferns up to our ears, hardly daring to breathe. Alexandra could sit without moving for hours. Like a little statue.' He coughed again. 'They like jam sandwiches, you know.'

'Your children? With Matthew and the girls it was always banana and cream cheese, unless they—'

'The badgers, m'dear. Jam sandwiches'll always bring them out in the end.'

Matthew glanced at Cindy, who was biting her lip. He hoped she wouldn't start to cry. He did not want to think about Alexandra sitting in the bracken like a little statue: all too clearly he could imagine the rapt expression on her face, those huge brown eyes of hers watching the ungainly black and white creatures as they rolled under the trees and munched jam sandwiches . . .

Sharply, surprisingly, he wished he was with her now.

'One of the nice things about the county ground,' Matthew said, as he settled Cindy down in the Stragglers Pavilion, 'is the number of women who come. Cricket's always thought of as a man's game, but you'd never guess it from looking round here.'

'I haven't watched much, I have to admit,' Cindy said shyly. 'Not any, really. Except sometimes on the box. Tony's more of a football man.'

'You'll have to watch out,' Matthew warned her. 'With only forty overs to play, they do tend to lash out a bit. Sixes landing among the spectators, and whatnot – I don't want to take you back to London suffering from concussion.'

'It's beautiful here.' Cindy glanced round the field at the tents, the two church towers rising behind the pavilions, the host of small excited boys, the cider drinkers, the sun beating down on the smooth green wicket and, beyond, the soft blue outline of the Quantocks.

'And this is definitely the best corner. You don't get the sun in your eyes, for a start.' Matthew looked down at her. Even after such a short time she seemed more rested, though the shadows under her eyes were deeper today, and there was a bluish tinge to her mouth which he had not noticed before. 'I'm going to get you a glass of cider.'

'No.' She raised a hand and he could not help seeing the effort it cost her. 'Thank you, but I don't drink.'

'Then you'll have to have a sip of mine. No-one's allowed to watch Somerset play cricket on their home ground without tasting the local brew.'

When he returned she seemed to be asleep. Looking down at the pale, almost bloodless face, he felt a spurt of alarm. She *was* all right, wasn't she?

'Cindy?' he said, overloudly, and she woke with a frightened start, staring at him as he stood over her, black against the bright sky, as though he were some kind of demon.

'I . . . must have dozed off . . .' she said weakly, and the sentence trailed away as though she did not have the strength to finish it.

'Jeffrey Archer's over there,' Matthew said. 'The author?'

'Mmm.'

'He often watches matches here. And I think I saw John Cleese, too.' He touched Cindy's arm. 'Ever heard of Viv Richards?'

She nodded.

'He'll be playing today, for Glamorgan. Ironic, really, when this used to be his home team. There was a bit of a bust-up a few years ago, I don't suppose you read about it in the papers . . . Botham, Richards, Joel Garner . . .' he babbled on softly, aware that his companion was almost too exhausted – or dispirited – to speak.

To one side of them, he heard a brash American voice. '. . . Just *love* those white pants they wear . . .' and a murmured female response.

The umpires would be walking on to the pitch any moment now, and the game would start. He was pleased with the way he had so skilfully managed to avoid seeing anything of Alexandra Maitland. She was fun to be with, no doubt about that; he had certainly enjoyed sitting beside her at Charlotte Hanover's dinner party, watching the way her face crumpled so beguilingly when she laughed, and the brown eyes lit up. Her American friend had pulled that ludicrous stunt about a pot-plant phobia. He smiled to himself. Killer cauliflowers, for goodness sake – then jerked upright.

That American voice, that murmured reply . . . he twisted in his seat, trying to locate the direction from which it had come. Wasn't that . . . ? Yes, it most certainly was. He had caught sight of them now, Alexandra, and her friend Donna, the latter in some woeful combination of cycling shorts and T-shirt with half a novel written on it, the former looking, as she always did, coolly elegant, in an apple-green linen dress and sunglasses.

He scrunched down low in his seat. Surely they were supposed to be at her father's place, having lunch with the Colonel and his mother? That was the whole *point*. That was why he had dragged all the way up here, precisely so he would miss seeing Alexandra Maitland. So what was she doing here?

Before he could begin to come up with any kind of an answer to this question, a shadow fell across his face. He opened his eyes.

'I just *knew* it was you!' Donna said triumphantly. She turned to Alexandra who had come up behind her and stopped abruptly at the sight of him. 'Look!'

Alexandra did so. The cold contempt on her face as she turned away made Matthew feel pretty annoyed. So did the anger which replaced it as she looked down and saw Cindy. Where exactly did she get off, looking at him – or Cindy – like that? He struggled to his feet.

'I – er – I thought my mother was having lunch with you today,' he said.

'She is,' Donna said. 'Except we aren't there.'

'Any particular reason?' he asked lightly.

'Miss Temperamental here said she'd already made other arrangements,' Donna explained. 'Soon as her father mentioned about your mother coming, she said she wanted me to see a cricket match while I was in England. Swept us off so fast you couldn't see us for dust.'

'I see.'

'I don't believe you do.' Donna took Matthew's arm and led him a few steps away from Alexandra, who appeared to be studying her card with the utmost concentration.

'Why's that?'

'Because as soon as the Colonel – isn't *he* a sweetie? –said this Miz Prescott was coming to Sunday lunch, having previously mentioned that her son and his friend *Cindy* were staying, Alex was going, like: 'Sorry, Pa, but we shan't be here.' So when he went on to say that unfortunately the said son and the said Cindy couldn't make it for lunch, it was too late. We were committed.' Donna laughed, a horribly raucous sound which had the nearby spectators staring from under their panamas.

'What's so funny?' demanded Matt.

'I just don't see why you two can't get it together.'

'We don't want to, that's why.'

'That's bull and you know it.'

'Not at all.' The information that Alex was as loath to see him as he to see her did not strike an answering chord of fellowship in his breast. Rather, it made him want to grind his teeth and use appalling language.

'What's with your friend?' Donna said suddenly.

Matthew turned. Ten yards away from them, Cindy had slid from her seat to the ground, white as a sheet, her dress rucked halfway up her thighs. Her eyes were closed. She lay so still that for a long dreadful moment he was afraid she was dead. 'My God,' he said.

'What's wrong with her?'

'Get the ambulance men, quickly,' Matthew said, running towards Cindy.

'Where are they?'

'Over there.' He pointed towards the black and

white uniforms of the St John Ambulance people and looked back at Cindy. 'Tell them she's recently had an abortion, and I think it's gone horribly wrong.'

It took him over two hours to locate Tony Cashman. When he finally ran the business tycoon down, he was feeling savage enough not to pussyfoot around.

'It's Matthew Prescott,' he said, when Cashman was on the end of the line.

'Prescott? What the hell's going on? You've called me out of—'

'If you want to see your wife alive again,' Matthew said brusquely, 'you'd better get down here immediately.'

'My wife? Alive? – Down where?'

'Taunton.'

'Taunton? What on earth is she—'

'She's haemorrhaging badly,' said Matthew. Then added, without expression, 'From an abortion.'

'An abortion? Oh my God.'

'Don't hang about, Tony. She's in a bad way.'

'Is it – was it . . . ?'

'It was yours, you damned fool,' Matthew shouted. To his annoyance, his voice was not quite steady. The sight of Cindy's white face in the ambulance, the skin almost transparent, the eyelids fluttering, had filled him with such a sense of loss and pain that he felt as if he himself was responsible for what had happened. And perhaps, to a certain extent, he was. Perhaps he should have told Cashman days ago exactly what was going on. He told himself he had tried, as the ambulance hurtled towards Musgrove Park Hospital through light Sunday traffic. He had tried, and Cashman had not wanted to know. Had he tried hard enough?

311

Well, he had no choice now.

'I'll be at the hospital until you come,' he said, more quietly. '*I* won't leave her alone.' And he put down the receiver.

If Cashman wanted to hear reproach or blame in the words, that was all to the good. Even on a Sunday the wretched man was conducting those interminable meetings of his. Maybe it took something as drastic as this to make a man like Cashman rethink his attitude to his wife.

Matthew knew he ought to feel guilty for implying that Cindy was fighting for her life. In fact, she was not in any mortal danger. But it wouldn't hurt Cashman to think for a while that she was. He could not help wondering what Cashman's thoughts would be as he travelled towards Taunton.

Meanwhile, there was Cindy to consider. He had arranged for her to be transferred to a private room, had called his mother and asked her to drive over, had asked if she would bring flowers so that when Cindy woke up, that was what she would see. He had also, with the help of a friendly operator and the interlocking network of rural communications, located her mother in Ebbw Vale and informed her of her daughter's condition; even now Mrs Hill was being driven down from Wales by a neighbour.

All that was left to do was to wait.

It was nearly seven o'clock when the door of Cindy's room was pushed open and a nurse came in, followed by Cashman. There was a defeated expression on his face which Matthew had never seen before, and his eyes were red and curiously desperate. He tiptoed to the foot of the bed and gazed at his wife, her face pale against the heaped pillows, her

312

arm lying on the white hospital counterpane attached to various tubes and drips.

'Will she be all right?' he said hoarsely, and cleared his throat. He was carrying sheaves of hothouse flowers, exactly the sort Matthew hated – and suspected Cindy did too: gladioli, tight little dahlias, overgrown carnations and stiff white lilies. They looked very formal against the tall delphiniums, white and blue and palest lavender, which his mother had brought up with her from Blindenhall, and the armfuls of cottage-garden blooms Cindy's mother had arrived with, which had been set in vases about the room.

'She's lost a lot of blood but she's out of danger now,' the nurse said briskly.

'Can I . . . ?' Cashman looked at the nurse. 'You know . . . would it be all right if I kissed her?'

'Of course.'

Awkwardly, Cashman moved to the side of the high bed and leaned down to brush his lips against his wife's unresponsive cheek. When he stood up there were tears in his eyes.

'What happened?' he said.

The nurse looked at Matthew. 'She'll be asleep for at least two more hours,' she said. 'Why don't you take Mr Cashman along to the canteen and give him a cup of tea? You could have a talk there without disturbing our patient.'

'Good idea.' Matthew took Cashman's arm. 'Come along, Tony.'

Once out in the passage, he stopped. 'Look. Cindy's mother is in the canteen—'

'Why?' Cashman seemed completely lost. 'How did she know?'

'Because I told her. And my mother's there too—'

'Why? I mean . . . *why*?'

'Because she's very fond of Cindy.'

'I didn't even know she knew her, for Gawd's sake.'

'I think there are rather a lot of things you don't know about Cindy,' Matthew said firmly. 'And I also think you'd better learn some of them damn fast or you're going to find yourself minus one wife.'

'What?'

'You heard. Now come along. There's a pub just outside the hospital gates. I'm going to give you a treble whisky and a good talking-to – though God knows it didn't help much last time I tried – and let's see if you can come to your senses before Cindy wakes up.'

He felt powerful and strong, ordering Cashman about. A real Master of the Universe. He just wished it were possible to deal with Alexandra in the same high-handed manner. Put it to her straight. Tell her what was what. Explain what he had come to realize with sudden blinding clarity during the frantic drive to the hospital, the dreadful wait while Cindy was prepared for the operating theatre and wheeled in, the awful moment as the surgeon came towards him to announce her condition.

He loved Alex. He wanted to marry her. He was not prepared to hear any more excuses or put up with any more misunderstandings.

Would she listen? That was the big question. And as soon as he got back to London, he intended to find out the answer.

# 14

*'Abortion?'*

'That's what he told me,' said Donna.

'But . . .' Alexandra was torn between bewilderment and anger. 'Was it . . . *his* child?' It all seemed so unlike everything she had come to expect from Matthew. What made matters so much worse was the fact that she was filled with the bleakest misery she had ever known in her life.

'He didn't say.'

'Whether it was or not, the whole thing is just – just horrible.' Alex looked around the cricket ground. 'That poor girl . . .'

The green of the grass seemed to have dimmed now; the whites of the cricketers were somehow dingy. In her ears she could still hear the wail of the ambulance's siren as it whirled Cindy Hill away towards the hospital. 'Donna, would you mind awfully if we just went?'

'Whatever you want, honey.'

'I really wanted you to see some cricket – it's so English – but after all this . . .'

Donna put a hand on her friend's arm. 'Look, don't take it so hard, Alex. These things happen.'

'But—' Alex cut herself off.

'I know how you're feeling,' Donna said, as they made their way to where the car was parked.

'Do you?' How could she? Alex thought. How

315

could she possibly begin to understand the churn of mixed emotions she was experiencing? She was going to have to sit down somewhere and work out exactly what her feelings for Matthew Prescott *were*. She had an idea that seeing him with Cindy Hill, the pang of ugly jealousy which pierced her, had finally made her realize just how she felt about him. But seeing his anxious face as he climbed into the ambulance behind the stretcher bearing Cindy, she had understood that it was far too late. He was obviously deeply involved with the beautiful model – and who would want ordinary Alexandra Maitland after her, even if she was married to someone else?

'Alex,' Donna said, breaking into her painful thoughts. 'Things are often quite different from what they seem.'

'Are they?'

'Just because we saw him the other day with her, and now we discover she's trying to recover from an abortion, doesn't mean that it's anything to do with Matthew. Nothing serious, I mean.'

Alex didn't want to talk about it. She said wearily, 'I don't really care, either way.'

'And Mickey Mouse doesn't wear shorts. Come on, Alex. You care, all right.'

'Even if I did – which I'm not saying I do – but suppose I did, *he* obviously doesn't.'

'What's with you two?' demanded Donna. 'You're both adult independent people. You've both seen enough of the world to know when you've found something worth grabbing hold of. And you both seem to spend your entire time misunderstanding each other.'

'Something worth grabbing hold of? What, exactly?'

'To put it as plainly as I know how,' Donna said – 'hey, watch out! You nearly killed that yokel or bumpkin or whatever he was.'

Alexandra slowed down. She knew she was going much too fast, that she was overwrought and ought not to be driving. 'Sorry.'

'As I was saying, it's as plain as daylight to me that the two of you are in love with each other,' Donna said.

'That's rubbish.'

'No it isn't.'

'We could have been, maybe,' Alexandra conceded. 'But things got in the way.'

'What's all this maybe and this could have been? You *are*, OK?'

'Anyway, it's far too late for either of us to do anything about it.'

'Says who? Or do I mean whom?'

'This girl, for instance – Cindy Hill.'

'What about her?'

'He's obviously heavily mixed up with her.'

'From what I've seen of him, I'll just bet it's not in the way you think,' Donna said. 'Anyway, why don't you ask him, give the poor guy a chance to explain?'

'I suppose you're right,' Alex said. She wished she didn't feel so exhausted.

'You don't sound too convinced.'

'Maybe I'm not.'


That evening, Donna was going out with some friends from New York who were also visiting Europe. When she had finally blown out of the flat, Alex fixed herself a salad, poured a glass of white wine and lay full length on the sofa, listening to *The Marriage of Figaro* and wishing she didn't feel so

317

depressed. Tonight even Mozart's delicious musical froth was failing to work its usual magic spell.

The phone rang. When she picked it up, a deep voice said, 'Alexandra! *Cara mia!*'

'Carlo. You're here, in London?' Alexandra swung her legs down from the sofa.

'That's right. And hoping I can see you as soon as possible.'

'Where are you staying?'

'I'm at the Grantchester Hotel.'

'But that's only just round the corner from me.'

'Is it?' asked Carlo, in the kind of voice which made it clear he was well aware of the fact.

'If you're not too exhausted, why don't you come round and have a coffee?'

'Too exhausted to see the beautiful Alexandra? Never.'

'Give me half an hour to straighten things up,' Alex said. 'I've got a rather untidy house guest staying, though she's out this evening with friends from home and won't be in until later.'

Just so Carlo got the picture . . . As an Italian, he might think that by asking him to visit her in the privacy of her own apartment, she was implying that she was ready to receive whatever advances he might feel like making. With a returning house guest in prospect, he would know that she wasn't.

Half an hour later the doorbell rang and she let him in. He was carrying flowers and a small white-wrapped gold-tied package, which he handed to her with a little bow. He looked round appreciatively.

'You have a lovely place here,' he said. 'But no more than I would have expected. And you are playing Mozart – how perfect.'

'Coffee? Or something stronger?' she asked.

318

'Coffee would be wonderful.'

While the kettle boiled, she opened the white box. Inside was a scarf by Schiaparelli, made of heavy aquamarine silk with a batiked border of lighter blues and greens. 'It's absolutely gorgeous,' she said appreciatively. 'Thank you so much, Carlo.'

In the kitchen, she laughed quietly to herself. There was no way she could possibly tell him that he had given her the identical scarf while she was in Milan. What did he do: order them by the gross? she wondered irreverently. And if so, how often did he make a mistake and give the same scarf more than once to the same woman?

She carried in a tray, and poured coffee for him. As he sipped it, they chatted companionably, catching up on each other's news. She told him about the Italian issue of *Athene*, now nearing completion. 'Why don't you drop into the office tomorrow and have a look?' she suggested.

'An excellent idea. If I came towards the end of the day, would that be all right?'

'Of course.'

'And how have you been, Alexandra? You seem a little, how shall I say, subdued?'

'Do I?'

'Not as happy, perhaps, as when I last saw you.'

'Really?'

'Is this a matter of the . . .' delicately Carlo touched his fingers to his breast pocket '. . . *heart*?'

'I can't imagine why you should think that,' Alex said, attempting one of the insouciant laughs she seemed to have lost the knack of these days. 'I'm much too busy to be involved with such things.'

'Ah, yes. The complete career woman,' said Carlo, leaning back and watching her over his coffee cup.

319

'And tomorrow, you shall show me your work, yes?'

'Yes.' Alexandra smiled at him. 'And you, Carlo? How are your affairs going?'

'In business, very well. But within the family . . .' He shook his head. 'Terrible. Terrible.'

'Why's that?'

'I have an uncle,' said Carlo. 'A rich uncle who lives in Venice. For many years he has been collecting pictures. He has always talked about turning his *palazzo* into a museum to house these wonderful works of art and now . . .'

'Now what?'

'He has a mistress. A terrible woman, formidable, with a nose like the beak of an eagle . . .' Carlo shaped the nose in the air for her, drawing in his mouth and giving an imperious glance, so that he did indeed look like some vast bird of prey.

'And what does this mistress want him to do?'

'She is trying to make him change his will and give the art collection to her son – that, at least, is what she calls him, though the whole of Society – both Venetian and Roman – suspects that he is, in fact, her lover.'

'Good heavens.'

'And it falls on me, as the rightful heir, to see that this does not happen.'

'What would you do with all these pictures if you had them?'

'But I do not want them, Alexandra. They are modern works, in which I have no interest. I have already said that, in the event of my poor uncle's death, they are to go to the City of Venice. I have seen them from time to time and, frankly, I do not like them at all.'

320

'I don't really like modern art, either,' Alexandra said.

'Then that is one more thing we have in common.' Carlo crinkled his eyes becomingly. 'But equally, I do not wish this . . . this *toy boy* to have them, as you can imagine.'

'Of course not,' said Alexandra, laughing.

'Why do you laugh?' Carlo asked reproachfully. 'This is a matter of the utmost seriousness. Tomorrow I must go and see the firm of art dealers who has been most instrumental in advising my uncle. I want them to make absolutely sure that these ugly – but expensive – pictures are not free to be given away to some – some motorcycle mechanic.' An expression of pain crossed Carlo's face. 'This is what I am given to understand the young man is.'

'Which art dealers are these?'

'Cadogan's. In Bond Street. They have a man there who spent some time in Italy, you understand. It was he who organized my uncle's affairs, and now I wish him to make absolutely sure that the will is watertight.'

'Who will you be talking to?' Alex said. But she knew the answer already: surely Cadogan's could not have *two* men newly back in London from the Rome branch.

'He is called Prescott. Matthew Prescott.'

'I see.' Alexandra bent over the table and picked up the two coffee cups, in order to hide her sudden confusion. Sometimes it seemed that wherever she went, Matthew dogged her footsteps. 'More coffee, Carlo? Or some whisky? Some brandy?'

'A glass of brandy would be very good,' he said.

There was a sudden irruption in the hall, and the sound of a slamming door.

'What a goddamned awful piece of absolute sh—' Donna said, bouncing into the sitting room and stopping short at the sight of Carlo on the sofa. 'Oh, hey – I'm sorry. Am I interrupting something?'

'Absolutely not.' Carlo was on his feet and bowing smoothly over Donna's hand as Alex came to the doorway of the kitchen. 'And you are?'

'Donna Fratelli. From New York.'

'Fratelli: this is an Italian name, is it not?'

'Italian name, Italian mother, Italian father and four Italian brothers,' Donna said vigorously. 'If it's Italian you want, then look no further because believe me, Donna Lucia Fratelli is the genuine article.'

'Please.' Carlo indicated the sofa and, when Donna had seated herself, sat down beside her. 'So tell me more about this Italian family of yours, Donna.'

In the doorway, Alex coughed, clearing her throat with unnecessary emphasis. 'Did I mishear you earlier, Donna,' she said, 'or were you supposed to be going to a concert at the Festival Hall with your friends who're staying out in Putney?'

'You didn't, and I was.' Donna clicked her tongue angrily. 'I stood there for hours, waiting for them to show, and they never did, and finally there was this message over the intercom, saying would Miss Donna Fratelli please make her own arrangements for the evening since her friends couldn't make it, so the *whole* audience, sitting there knocking back the gin while they waited for the concert to start, knew I'd been stood up. Boy, was I mortified. And all dressed up like this, too.'

She was wearing her coral outfit; anger had flushed her cheeks and the damp weather outside had turned her exuberant hair even curlier. She was wearing a pair of elaborate silver earrings designed by Emma Chisholm, which Alex had last seen in her own jewellery box and had no recollection whatsoever of lending to Donna.

Carlo was giving the American girl a lot of eye contact. 'This is terrible,' he said. 'I very much hope, Miss Fratelli, that you will allow me to compensate for the dreadful disappointment you have suffered.'

'How do you propose to do that?' Donna said. From where Alex was standing, the only way to describe the way she said it was flirtatious.

'Might I be permitted to take you out to dinner, for instance?'

'You bet. How long are you in London?'

'For a week,' Carlo replied, though Alex could have sworn he had said five days when discussing it earlier.

'Well.' Donna looked down at her hands. 'I'd really enjoy that.'

'Tomorrow?'

'Tomorrow I can't.'

'But lunchtime? You are free tomorrow at lunchtime, perhaps?'

'Uh – yes.' Donna glanced over at Alex.

'Then I meet you tomorrow, and we make arrangements for the following day, yes?'

'Yes, *sir*,' said Donna. As far as Alex could see, she and Carlo seemed to be having some problem actually taking their eyes off each other.

'Your brandy, Carlo,' Alex said, coming in and setting the balloon glass down in front of his seat. He had managed to tear himself away from Donna and was examining Alex's collection of CDs. 'And Donna, *dear*,' she added with sweet sarcasm, 'what can I fetch *you*?'

'How about a cold shower?' Donna murmured, not moving her lips and opening her eyes wide at Alex. 'My God – who *is* this guy?'

'I told you about him,' Alex said, sotto voce.

'But not *all* about him. Not that he's spectacularly *gorgeous*.'

'That must have slipped my mind. I'll get you a long cool drink, shall I? And a wet towel to wrap round your head, bring down the fever?'

'That would be wonderful,' Donna said loudly.

When Alexandra came back, the other two were deep in conversation, talking in rapid Italian, eyes and hands flying as they discussed Italian politics, the best way to make spaghetti, the state of Italian football. They clearly didn't need a third party; after a bit, she gave a few unconvincing yawns and went to bed. Neither of them even noticed.

'You *can't*.' Alex said.

'But I am.'

'Not for *lunch*.' Alex looked without appreciation at Donna's Spandex cycling shorts – at least they were the black ones, not the Day-Glo ones – and the T-shirt with the first page of the *Iliad* inscribed on it in ancient Greek.

'Why not?'

'That T-shirt . . .'

'He'll think I'm cultured,' Donna said.

'He'll think you're a *slob*, is what he'll think.'

'Which I am.'

'Anyway, it's the wrong culture,' Alex said. 'He's an Italian, not a Greek. And those shorts . . .'

'What's wrong with them?'

'Nothing at all, if you're taking part in the Tour de France,' said Alex. 'But if you're planning to have lunch in the West End with a man who, by anyone's standards, especially his own, is one of the suavest in Europe, I don't think they're all that suitable.'

'My coral thing's too dressy,' said Donna. 'And there's nothing of yours that would fit me.' For a moment she gazed at her reflection despondently.

'Even if I was prepared to lend it to you.'

'Which, of course, you would be, in the interests of feminine solidarity.' Donna tutted at herself. 'I guess I'll just have to go and do some clothes shopping, which I absolutely hate.'

'Meanwhile, lunch today,' Alex said.

Donna shook her head, running her hands down her hips. 'He's gotta see it like it is. If it turns him off, then what the heck? He's not worth bothering about in the first place.'

'Possibly.'

'Listen . . .'

'Yes?'

'Has he – does he have . . . do you know if he's ever been married?'

'Not as far as I know. Why do you ask?'

'Because my mom would *kill* me if she thought I'd fallen for a married man.'

'Fallen for? Isn't this a bit sudden?'

'Isn't that the best way?' Donna clutched at Alex. 'What about lady friends waiting back home in Rome?'

'I'd be lying if I didn't say I thought there were probably several hundred of *those*,' said Alex.

'Darn it.'

'But whether any of them mean anything to him, I don't know. Perhaps he's been looking all this time and not found the right one.'

The possibility that lovely, warm but undeniably

slobby Donna Fratelli was that one seemed remote. Look at all the chic Roman women Carlo had taken out. Remember his remarks about the importance of fashion, his cultured approach to music, his deep knowledge of food, art, history. Although Carlo had undeniably seemed attracted to Donna, was he going to be able to withstand the onslaught of the shorts or the thighs inside them? Especially when taken in conjunction with Homer?

'It was fantastic,' Donna said, breathing heavily into the telephone. 'It was absolutely wonderful and amazing.'

Alex sat in Nina's office, leaning back in Nina's chair. 'Are we talking a simple lunch, here?' she said. 'Or more?'

'I don't know what *you're* talking,' said Donna. 'I'm talking Carlo.'

'I see.'

'He said – get this, Alex – he said I reminded him of – gulp – his mother.'

'Oh!' breathed Alex. 'Wow-*ee*!'

'You may mock, but when an Italian man says that to a girl, it's the biggest compliment he can pay.'

Alexandra tried not to laugh. 'Are you saying – and I'm really anxious to get this right, Donna – that Carlo's mother wears Lycra cycling shorts?'

'I don't know. Not yet. But when I go to Rome, I sure intend to find out.'

'You're going to Rome?'

'Of course. Didn't I say that when I arrived?'

'You said Paris. You said Madrid. I'm pretty sure you said Prague and Vienna. But not Rome.'

'Courses for horses,' said Donna breezily. 'Whatever blows your skirt up.'

'Mmm.'

'And then he can meet *my* momma when he comes to New York.'

'When's that?'

'Pretty soon,' Donna said. 'Alex . . .'

'Yes?'

'I really think I've fallen in love.' And Donna put the phone down before Alex could say anything more.

So have I, she thought. So have I.

'An intriguing presentation,' Carlo said. He was holding the folder which Alex had given him a little earlier; inside were the roughs for the Italian issue of *Athene.* He had been studying them in the little reception room while she finished dealing with the day's enquiries and problems.

It had been a busy one, with more than she could comfortably handle. Petronella had phoned in sick, Nina had proven unobtainable, Lydia was in Hay-on-Wye, tracking down a reclusive author, though they all knew the only author she was interested in tracking down was not only far from reclusive but also happened to be delivering a talk in the town that very afternoon.

'Thank you,' Alex said.

Carlo knitted his brow in a way which a thousand Roman matrons had probably told him made him look absolutely *cute.* 'Perhaps we might discuss it over dinner,' he said.

'I'd enjoy that.' Looking at her watch, she added, 'I know it's late but I still have a meeting to attend. Could you – would you mind . . . ?'

'I'll come back in an hour,' he said.

Hannah, one of the assistants, came up. 'Sorry to

butt in, but that chap from Cadogan's rang again – could you ring back?'

'Again?'

'He's already rung twice this afternoon – I did leave a note on your desk.'

'Cadogan's?' Carlo said.

'Yes. Some – uh – enquiry I was chasing up with them.' Alex smiled graciously, hoping she was managing to maintain her image of calm poise, although Carlo's knowing eye was fixed on her.

'What a coincidence – I have an appointment with them tomorrow morning.'

'Isn't it, though?'

When Alex said nothing more, Carlo said, 'I'll see you later,' and worked his eyebrows at her suggestively before his broad shoulders disappeared out of the office door.

What was *that* all about? Did he suspect that she had been less than honest when she denied any involvement in what he called 'matters of the heart'? Or had Donna been shooting her big mouth off?

For a moment she stood there, thinking of Matthew, imagining him in his office at Cadogan's, the telephone pressed to his cheek, his mouth close to the receiver, waiting to be connected to her. He'd rung her three times that afternoon – she was tempted to go and find a telephone, call him back. But the magazine had to come first.

Later, the meeting over, Alexandra emerged to find Carlo waiting for her in the reception area. Downstairs, in the marble foyer of the office building, she took his arm.

'Happy about the meeting?' he asked, as they strolled towards the big glass doors into the street.

She was about to reply when she heard feet

running behind her. Hannah appeared, looking flustered. 'I'm sorry,' she said. 'He rang again, for the fifth time.'

No need to ask who 'he' was. Alexandra could not help the smile which lit up her face. She walked ahead of Carlo, trying to subdue it, but not succeeding.

He caught her up. 'Problems?'

'No,' she said, shaking her head. 'Just an – uh – old friend.'

An old, dear friend, she thought. What she hadn't quite worked out was why he had kept ringing her. Nor why she had not responded. She hated to think she played those silly games that women went in for. But she could not deny that there was a certain sense of keeping Matthew waiting, of not playing into his hand, letting him see that it wasn't all going to go his way. That morning Donna had talked to her sternly about at least giving the man a chance to explain himself and she was definitely going to do so – but not quite yet.

Dinner with Carlo could come first. And she fully intended to enjoy herself that evening. This was why she had chosen the same restaurant where she had first gone with Matthew, the same restaurant where only a few days earlier she had seen him with Cindy Hill.

The day before she had telephoned Emma Chisholm, ostensibly to discuss jewellery designs. During the conversation she had managed somehow to turn the talk to Matthew, and had elicited the information that Cindy's husband had swept her back to their house in Hampshire, cancelled all her engagements, hired a live-in nurse and called Harrods to send down a specialist in nursery design.

'I went down to see her,' Emma said. 'She's like a different person. So is he, for that matter – or so Matt says.'

'I'm glad she's getting on all right.' Alex would not easily forget Cindy's pale face lying on the grass, nor the evil jealousy she felt at the sight of Matthew bending over her.

'Matt's been absolutely brilliant,' said Emma.

'Sounds as if you have too.'

'I only put her up for a few nights. He lived through this whole thing with the poor girl,' said Emma. 'He actually bearded that horren*d*ous husband all on his own. But he's like that. Really brave. Terribly caring. I know he's my brother, but I really admire him.' There was a pause which Alex had no problem recognizing as meaningful. 'I do wish . . .'

'Wish what?'

'That he'd find someone he could fall in love with and marry,' Emma said.

'Do you?'

'You don't know how much.'

'Does *he* wish it, though?'

'Yes. The awful thing is, I think there *is* someone, but he just doesn't seem to be able to get it together with her.'

'Do you know who she is?'

'Don't ask me. He told my mother she was the most wonderful girl in the world – but it's not much to go on, is it?'

'Isn't it? Sounds like quite a bit to me.'

'Yes, but he *would* say that, wouldn't he? If he's in love with her, I mean. What I don't understand is why none of us have met her yet.'

'Perhaps he hasn't told *her* that she's the most wonderful girl in the world,' said Alexandra.

'Then he's being terribly inept about it, frankly.'

'She doesn't sound much epter, if you ask me.' There was a big smile on Alexandra's face as she said this.

'I agree. Still,' Emma sighed. 'I can't live his life for him, much as I'd like to.'

Alex sat now across the table from Carlo, drinking coffee. They had had a pleasant meal together; she had answered as well as she could all the questions he asked about her time in America – a barely-disguised excuse, she realized, to talk about Donna. The idea of Miss Slob and Mr Suave making an item still seemed strange but, for all she knew, there beat the heart of a homebody under Carlo's smart exterior, and there was no doubt that Donna was excellent wife material.

While he wittered on about the ideal woman – who bore a strange resemblance to Donna Fratelli – Alexandra allowed herself to think of Matthew and her own conversation with Emma. There was a warm glow in her stomach. For some reason, she had no doubt at all that when he had spoken to his mother of wonderful girls, it was to Alexandra he referred. She knew that when she got home that night she would knock on Matthew's door – and take it from there.

Some kind of disturbance at the door of the restaurant distracted her from her train of thought, and she looked up to see Matthew Prescott himself marching straight for their table with a determined look on his face. Then suddenly he was bending over them, visibly shaking with emotion, and starting to speak rapidly. He was obviously highly agitated.

'Always the same restaurant. I thought we had this thing under control. Can we afford another scandal?'

331

'Wha—' Alex began, so angry she was almost lost for words. But Matthew was unstoppable.

'Well, even the children are starting to ask questions.'

Now Carlo, taking his cue from the astonishment on Alexandra's face, was beginning to rise from his seat. 'Excuse me? I'm sorry . . .'

But it was Carlo's turn to be cut off in mid-sentence. 'You wouldn't happen to be Italian?'

'Yes,' Carlo managed to stammer in reply.

'Opera lover? It's always Italians.' Matthew was shaking his head in a knowing way. 'Has she talked offshore investments yet?'

As Carlo was again struggling to answer, Matt leaned nearer Alexandra, who was now staring at him with a mixture of amusement and amazement, and drew her suddenly to her feet. 'I think we'd better leave before the paparazzi get here. Which way is the kitchen? Come on, darling,' he said tenderly. 'I'll take you home.'

'How terribly kind of you, *darling*,' Alexandra said. 'By the way, before we go, have you met Carlo San Lorenzo?'

'What?' Matthew's face changed rapidly.

'Carlo,' continued Alexandra remorselessly, 'this is Matthew Prescott.'

'*Who?*' demanded Carlo.

The two men were staring at each other.

'*You're* Carlo San Lorenzo?' Matthew's voice had a strangled quality which Alexandra found a more than sufficient reward for his outrageous behaviour.

'If you're Matthew Prescott, then I shall certainly have something to say to the chairman of Cadogan's,' Carlo said stiffly.

'What about?' Matthew had clearly opted to tough it out.

'The way you have interrupted a – a meeting with an old friend,' Carlo said.

'An old friend with whom I happen to be on intimate terms,' Matthew said, staring hard at Alex, daring her to contradict.

'Are you her husband?'

'Not yet,' Matthew said. 'But—'

'Because she has never mentioned you to me. Nor these children . . .' But already Carlo sounded uncertain of his ground. For all he knew, Alexandra *did* have children, *had* been involved in a scandal. Perhaps she *was*, as this Matthew Prescott was suggesting, a little crazy.

Alexandra could never be sure, afterwards, why she played along with Matthew. Whatever the reason, it was clearly more than time to leave.

'See you,' she said breezily, waving her hand in what she hoped was a sufficiently spaced-out off-the-wall sort of way as she moved rapidly towards the restaurant door. For Carlo's benefit she added a faint weaving stagger to her walk, like a woman disorientated by being deprived of medication. Behind her she felt Matthew take her elbow and, turning her head, caught a glimpse of his expression, a subtle blend of concern and courage. Anyone watching would have known that this was a man coping nobly with whatever life had chosen to fling at him – and life had flung plenty: those poor neglected children, a batty wife, the constant strain of watching over her . . .

'I don't know why I let you do that,' Alexandra said.

They were in Matthew's flat, facing each other on his sofa. There was Napoleon brandy in huge

333

balloons on the coffee table, and something sharp and sweet was playing softly somewhere in the background: a clarinet, Alexandra thought, its cadences as cool, as embracing as warm snow.

'Because I ser—'

'You serve better coffee,' Alexandra said, her mouth still curved with amusement. The two of them had clung together in the back of the taxi which brought them home, helpless with laughter.

He leaned towards her. 'Besides,' he said, very softly, 'I love you.'

# 15

October in Venice. A soft golden morning with one of those deep blue skies which made you realize all over again the wonder of being in love.

Lying against lace-edged pillows in the big wooden *matrimoniale*, a cup of cappuccino balanced on his chest, Matthew Prescott sighed contentedly. He could not remember when he had last felt this good. A year, six months ago, it would have seemed no more than a fantasy from some romantic novel that he should be here again, in arguably the most perfect city in the world, on a perfect autumn morning, yet here he undoubtedly was. Courtesy of Ricardo San Lorenzo, here he was in one of Italy's most perfect buildings, almost the last of the Venetian *palazzos* still in private hands. Above all, here he was with what, as far as he was concerned, was undeniably the most perfect woman in the world.

The tall windows were open, the white net curtains stirring slightly in a warm breeze. From where he lay he could hear the faint cries of gondoliers, the toot of the *vaporetto* as it neared the quayside, the shrieking of gulls. He could see a tranche of blue sky, a gilded dome, a length of elegantly fretted stonework. And, far more beautiful than any of these, he could also see Alexandra Maitland.

Although he was not entirely sure what the word 'diaphanous' meant, he knew it was the only way to describe the scandalously flimsy robe thing she was wearing as she stood on the balcony outside the windows and looked down at the Grand Canal. Ranging lazily across the vast collection of painted images which lay stored in his brain, he tried to think of a more beautiful, more sensuous picture than Alexandra, but could not.

'Alex,' he called, knowing he did so only for the pleasure of saying her name, of seeing her turn, look at him with soft eyes, smile.

'Matt,' she said, in that warm rich voice he had never really thought he would be lucky enough to find. It seemed incredible to him now that only a few weeks ago he had wondered if a woman with such a voice really existed. She did, and because he had promised himself that if he ever found her, he would bring her here, he had done so.

'Yes?' he said.

'You really ought to come out here. It's fantastic. Like a Canaletto come to life.'

'I will, as soon as I've finished my coffee.'

Alexandra looked at him over her shoulder. Her eyes were huge, her face soft with love.

'Coffee,' she said. 'What a marvellous idea. Shall I come back to bed and share it with you?' She smiled at Matt meaningfully.

She stood silhouetted against the brilliant day, and he could see the shape of her under her loose robe, the long lines of her body. He wanted to tell her that she was beautiful, more beautiful than anything he had ever seen. He wanted to say that every time he saw her, his heart lurched with love. But he had already learned that too many such protestations frightened her.

Looking at him, Alexandra felt a quiver of anxiety.

Words trembled on his lips, she could tell. She knew what those words would be if he spoke them, and part of her yearned to hear them. In the past few weeks they had scarcely been apart. Having acknowledged that she loved him, the rest had been easy. She knew that what she felt for Matthew was the strongest passion she had ever experienced in her life, she knew too that there had been a quality to their love, something, beneath the passion, that was delicate and precious, far better than anything she had ever experienced with Cameron.

And therein lay the seeds of doubt which still sprouted somewhere in the dark reserves of her hidden self.

For she was still not sure whether or not Matthew was the man she wanted. Was she safe in allowing him into her heart, or would he prove to be another Cameron? Would he wait until she had finally surrendered herself to him in every possible way, and then, like Cameron, proceed to tear her vulnerable self into tiny unmendable pieces?

However much she told herself that Matt wasn't like that, however often she reminded herself of his solid strength, his kindness, his gentleness, the doubts were still there.

It was impossible for her to forget the woman who had been waiting for him the very first time she had knocked on his door, or the dreadful harpy who had leaped out of his kitchen with a coffee cup in her hand that night she had screwed up her courage (all right: the night she had drunk more than she ought to have done) and told him she wanted to see him immediately – the woman he had kept on insisting was an old friend. Cameron had a lot of 'old friends', too. And what about Cindy Hill?

Despite all Matthew's protestations, she could not shake off her uncertainties about him.

'Don't be such a *nerd*,' Donna had said, with her usual forthrightness, when Alexandra tried to explain some of this. 'The guy's terrific, he clearly adores you, what the hell more do you want?'

'I don't know.'

'You want a kick up the butt is what you want,' said Donna. 'I mean, come *on*, Alex. He's even offered to make an honest woman of you—'

'Yes, but—'

'– and all you can do is kvetch and moan, worry about the future, wonder whether he's gonna dump on you like Cameron did.'

'I couldn't go through all that again.'

'You're not gonna have to. Not with Matt. We're talking Mr Nice Guy here. Mr Terrific and Sensational Guy, if you really want the truth.'

Yes, Alex thought, walking slowly towards the bed. He was all of those things, and more. And yet . . .

Stretching out a hand to her as she sat down on the bed and reached for his coffee cup, Matthew thought suddenly of his rose-wreathed, inglenooked cottage. In all the years of dreaming about it, he had never really envisaged anyone there except himself. Now, as he tried to conjure up an idyllic picture of himself and Alex declining gently together, old and creaky under the apple boughs, his imagination stubbornly refused to work. Himself, turning sods of earth with a spade, green-wellied and Barboured, yes. Very much so, especially after the generous pay rise the board of Cadogan's had recently offered him. A golden Labrador dreaming on the grass with its head on its paws. A trug of ripe fruit beneath a pear tree, lavender

338

bushes, a Land-Rover parked behind a hedge.

But no Alex.

Why not?

What did his imagination know that he didn't? He stifled a groan. Surely, at this late stage, he wasn't backing off again, was he? He wasn't shying at the thought of the final commitment, was he? Dammit, he *wanted* commitment. He longed to put his bachelor days behind him, to forsake all others and cleave only to this one, this Alex. He had even asked her to marry him, in as unemphatic a way as he dared, knowing how easily she was scared off. And her response had been unemphatic, too. She had laughed, kissed him, said what a great idea it was – and neither of them had referred to the matter again.

He refilled his cup from the pot which some pretty little Italian maid had brought in earlier. He deliberately willed himself back to the inglenooks and apple trees – in Devon, was this cottage? Or Somerset? Somwhere like that – and tried to conjure up a couple of kids.

This time his imagination came up trumps, producing one of each. There was a girl with big brown eyes and plump little plaits, a girl with Alex's smile. There was a boy with the same gangling sort of kneecaps as his father – as Matthew's – wielding a cricket bat and looking ready to try out for the county team in a matter of months. There was even, in some kind of basket thing lined with frills, what appeared to be a further bit of offspring, waving tiny little fists about and grinning toothlessly up at the sky. But where was Alex? And did it matter that he couldn't place her in this idyllic scenario?

'Darling,' he said.

'Sweetheart.'

'I love you.'

She looked solemn. 'And I love you.'

'Come to any conclusion about the job?'

Alexandra looked away. The job. Everything she had worked for all these years: at last it was there for the taking. A month ago, Nina had telephoned the *Athene* office and asked to speak to Alex.

'I'm not coming back,' she said.

'You're *not*?'

'No.'

'Because of the chicken-pox?' Alex asked. It seemed an unlikely reason for someone like Nina to stay home.

'It wasn't chicken-pox.'

'What was it, then?'

'I'm pregnant.'

'But that's . . .' Alex could not think exactly *what* it was '. . . that's wonderful, Nina.' How in the world did one confuse chicken-pox and pregnancy?

There was a creamy edge to Nina's voice. 'You don't know just how wonderful. We've been trying for simply ages. The doctor's been telling us to relax about it and I guess staying at home must have finally done the trick.'

'Congratulations, Nina. I'm really thrilled for you.' Alex cast a look at the rest of the open-plan office. 'And I know everyone else will be, too.'

'Which leaves the question of the future,' Nina said.

'It does rather, doesn—'

'Priorities, Alex,' Nina said in a deep voice, launching into her enigmatic mode.

'I know what you—'

'Is one looking for a personal or a professional fulfilment?'

340

'That rather dep—'

'I know which I'm going for. And I would advise you to think very carefully before you apply.'

'Apply?'

'Because you're the obvious choice, Alex.'

'Choice for wha—'

'Not that I'd want you to quote me on that, obviously. Not around the office, at least.'

'Absolutely no—'

'After all, you're the most recent recruit at editor level. But you're also the only one with the necessary – how shall I put this, Alex?'

'If I had the faintest idea what you're talk—'

'Pizazz!' Nina said, explosively.

'Piza—'

'Pep! Energy! Originality! That's what we want to see, Alex. Energy and originality. And you're the one to provide it. I can confidently say that. So don't worry, my dear. You'll have my wholehearted endorsement, I can assure you.'

'That's terrific, Nina. Um. Endorsement for what, exactly?'

There was a pause. Then Nina said frostily, 'You disappoint me, Alex. I thought we were in tune on this one.'

'We are, I'm sure. It's just, I'm not entirely sure which one we're—'

'I thought we spoke the same language.'

Now there, thought Alex, you are definitely out of whack. Because one thing you do not do, Nina, is speak the same language as anyone else I've ever come across.

'Yes,' she said. With Nina, short answers were usually the best answers. Mainly because they stood a chance of getting said.

341

'And naturally I assumed that you would put in for the post, now that it's fallen vacant.'

'Oh.' Comprehension dawned. '*Your* job, you mean?'

'Of *course*, Alex. What on earth else do you think I've been talking about for the past ten minutes?'

Hard to say, really. 'Um . . .' Alex said again.

She had sat there with her eyes closed, and wondered why she did not feel more elated. With Nina rooting for her, with proven work to her credit – the Italian issue of *Athene* was looking terrific – she would have no problem in being awarded the job she had set her heart on. So why had it all suddenly seemed so pointless?

And why had it gone on seeming pointless? All she had wanted, during the past month, was to be with Matthew. She had delayed filling in an application for Nina's job; she had mooched around with only half her mind on her work. When Matt had suggested she accompany him to Venice, she had jumped at the chance of spending a whole week with him, even though the Christmas issue was already beginning to need close attention.

'Any conclusion about the job?' she said slowly. 'No. Not yet.'

'You'll have to make a decision soon, won't you?'

'Yes. The magazine can't go on indefinitely without someone at the helm.'

'And who better than you, my love?'

Alex wanted to explain her doubts, ask him what he thought. She wanted his advice. She wanted to say that she was no longer sure about her priorities, that suddenly, staying at home, having babies, turning in her Mercedes for a Volvo estate, seemed like the most exciting career move in the world.

But if she did so, it might look as though she was asking him to offer an alternative, and she didn't want him to feel pressured. He had already suggested they get married, but only in a light-hearted way, not as though he really meant it. And she had dared not assume he *did* mean it, for fear of looking like an idiot when his face changed and he realized she thought he had actually been in earnest.

Meanwhile . . . From the glass beside the bed she took the red rose he had bought her the day before. The petals had been tight-furled then; now they were open, showing the crimson heart, releasing the rich scent. It seemed to her to be the scent of promise.

She took a deep breath. Why worry? Here they were, in romantic Venice, with four more days ahead of them. For the moment, that was all that mattered and she intended to enjoy them to the full. Removing Matt's coffee cup, putting down her own, she threw back the elaborate lace-fringed covers of the bed.

'Move over,' she said softly. She ran her hand over his chest, then bent and kissed the smooth skin above his heart. 'I love you, Matthew.'

'Darling.' As Matt drew her closer, feeling the warmth of her, pulling at the satin ribbon around her waist, he suddenly saw his cottage, illumined as though by a bright shaft of sunlight. And standing right in the very heart of it, with roses and lavender and the fecund shapes of pears at her feet, was Alexandra.


THE END